THE MIDNIGHT SERPENT

STAR CROSSED CROWN

BOOK TWO

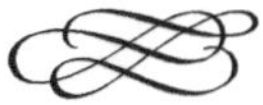

ALINA KRAMER

To my grandma, who would have pretended to be mortally offended by the amount of spice in this book, but would have read it anyway in private and been proud of me.

To Aunty M, who I'm raising a glass of Glenmorangie to.

CONTENTS

PROLOGUE

Ressa

The Godslayer is going to die.

This is the price of my freedom. And now, as the time grows near, anticipation curls its trembling fingers around my bones and holds me close. I can almost taste it, like iron on my tongue.

I've been so patient.

This putrid cell is no place for a lady of the Celestial Court. I'm rotting down here in the dark labyrinth beneath the palace, far from the comforts that a noble Demigod woman of my station deserves. The shapeless gray shift I wear chafes my delicate skin and the scars where Kartas' lightning left its mark. The plain bread and hard cheese the guards bring me taste only of betrayal. And I won't even speak of the chamber pot.

How is it that I'm imprisoned in this lightless, festering dungeon, yet the Godslayer remains free and unshackled in the world above?

She breathes clean air, eats the fine foods served by the palace kitchens, and walks the glowing halls of the Celestial Court as though she isn't just some lowborn Starless whore.

And soon, she will sit on the throne.

My throne.

I claw my fingers in the air at the injustice of it all.

From the chatter that spreads among the guards like a summer plague, I know that Syran takes her to his bed every night, but he has not yet wed her. She is not yet Queen.

There is still time.

Syran can still be mine.

And now the moment is upon me. I can feel it in the way the grimy walls of the cell shiver as my friend approaches, in how the shadows in the far corner creep and swirl into something that's barely just the outline of a man.

Two eyes blink from the darkness.

Yes.

Yes!

He's here.

I've waited for this day for so long. I spent countless hours imagining how my hands would feel as they tighten around the Godslayer's throat and how Syran's lips would mold to mine when we finally meet again.

And now it's time.

My savior has arrived.

"Good afternoon, Lady Ressa," the thing murmurs in a voice like wind rattling through the eaves of the palace cathedral.

While Syran and his wretched crossed star may have banished me down here with only common criminals and the dregs of the palace guards for company, they will not break my spirit. I am a highborn lady of the Celestial Court, a powerful Demigod in my own right, and I will act as such.

I stand from my cot and curtsy toward the corner. "Good afternoon," I say, as though I'm greeting another courtier instead of some creeping thing swathed in darkness.

It's hard to tell if this pleases my companion. Shadows, as deep as the heart of Syran's flame, coil around him to obscure everything but those glittering eyes. A strange light flickers within them, and, once again, I'm reminded that whatever this is, this is not Demigod magic.

This is something else.

Something older.

Something forgotten.

A shudder runs through me, but I tamp it down. Whatever this creature is, I have made a promise to him, one that I intend to keep.

He will grant me my freedom, and in return, I shall lead the Godslayer to her doom.

I wonder how he'll uphold his end of the bargain. The walls of the cell are far too thick for my powers to shift, and all of my many attempts to breach the grimy surface of the rock have produced little more than dust and loose mortar. Perhaps my friend is stronger, or maybe he has another avenue of escape in mind for me.

Before I can ponder this further, he asks, "Will you do as you agreed?"

"I will bring death to the Godslayer," I vow. The thought of watching her lowborn features slacken in the face of oblivion has me baring my teeth in something that festers between a grin and a snarl. When I make my promise, I feel as sure as the ground beneath my feet. "I swear it to you."

The thing in the darkness blinks. For a moment, I worry that this is all some cruel trick and that I'll be locked away in this place forever, but then my savior extends one shadowy hand toward me.

"Come, Lady Ressa," he offers. "Your freedom awaits."

I do not want to take his hand. The fine hairs on the back of my neck rise at the very thought of my skin brushing against this unnatural thing, but I cannot afford to be impolite, not when my deliverance is at stake.

Ignoring the way my fingers shake as I step toward him, I place my palm in his. Where I thought he would be solid or cold, he simply feels like nothing, no different from empty air. Mollified, I offer a demure smile and say, "Thank you, my friend."

While I can't feel the shape of his hand against mine, I do recognize the tugging sensation as he leads me forward to the door of the cell. His touch and guidance leave a strange impression on me, one that turns my stomach in a most unpleasant way. But I don't dare voice it as we stop at the threshold of my prison.

Excitement rises in my chest now, replacing my unease. Will he tear the door from its very hinges? Never has such a thing happened in the dungeons of the Celestial Court, and I find the mere thought of it oddly enticing.

"Close your eyes," he croons.

Once again, I am reminded of how unnatural my companion is. Everything within me screams to keep my gaze fixed on him, and I'm gripped with an awful surety that something *terrible* will happen if I look away.

And yet, is my own existence not equally aberrant?

I do not belong down here in the darkness with the rats and the crawling things. I am Lady Ressa of the Celestial Court, the rightful betrothed of Syran, who now sits on his father's throne. Would the other Demigod nobles shy away from me now if they were to see me in the light of day? Would they think me a wretch, or a traitor?

Yes. I believe they would.

Perhaps this dark, blinking creature is not so different from me after all.

And so I close my eyes.

The memory of Syran's poisoned flame dances in the empty space behind my lids. I recall how his fire leaped the night the stars crossed him to the Godslayer, as though it was reaching for the very heavens.

Will he ever reach for me again?

Or will it always be *her*?

I grind my teeth together so that I don't snap out at the air.

The Godslayer *must* die.

This resolution grips so tight that I almost forget that there's supposed to be a door here until it's too late. I flinch, expecting to bump into the cold, solid bars of the cell, but there's only empty air.

How is this possible? We take one more step and then another, but there's no resistance. Surely we must be past the threshold?

Unable to control myself any longer, I open my eyes and glance behind me.

The barred door of my cell, along with everything in it, stands closed at my back. And at my front…

"Freedom," I whisper.

The dismal corridor stretches on either side of me, unimpeded, both directions leading off into the murk. Barred doors line the walls, and behind them, I can just barely make out the shapes of prisoners lying in their cots. In the distance, low chatter and the telltale scrape of armor betray the presence of the guards.

Guards.

They will have to be dealt with. Perhaps my escort can assist me further. I turn to him, the question already forming on my lips, but no eyes glint from the darkness at my side.

He is gone.

I am alone.

"No matter," I mutter to myself. I have no blade, but this whole palace is built on a foundation of stone. The only weapons I require are in the very walls. All I need is to find the right piece.

Closing my eyes once again, I lift my hands and call on my powers. The moonstone and quartz, the very bedrock of the Celestial Court, whisper back. There's a crack at my feet, one that gouges several inches into the floor. There's something down there.

Something sharp.

I open my eyes and focus on the stone shard. My powers are weak, and it takes everything within me to draw the wicked sliver from the depths of the crevice. By the time the jagged stone shard falls into my hands, sweat crawls down the nape of my neck, and my body sags from the effort. I so desperately want to sink to the floor and rest, but there is still much to be done.

My friend may have helped me conquer one obstacle in my path, but there are others. By the laughter that erupts from somewhere around the corner, I'd guess at least a pair.

I confirm my suspicions by creeping to the end of the corridor and risking a quick glance around the corner, where two Celestial

Knights lounge in their pompous golden armor and gossip like Starless hags around a cooking fire.

As a lady of the Celestial Court, I prefer not to bloody my own hands. Still, I can't deny how wonderfully heavy the stone shard feels against my palms. What will it feel like to bring it down, to feel it tear through skin and muscle and bone?

But then I think of the Godslayer and how she cleaved through bodies with that monstrous greatsword like they were nothing. The last time I saw her, she had blood in her hair and all manner of viscera coating her armor.

No.

I will *not* be like her. These guards must die, but I will not debase myself in the process.

With my mind made up, I summon what little remains of my strength and urge the moonstone shard to rise from my palms. The jagged end glints in the gloom. With a flick of my wrist, I send it flying around the corner in a shining arc.

The first guard barely has time to cry out, and even then, his surprised shout is cut off by a heavy, wet thud. My breath hitches at the sound and, for a moment, my focus breaks. But the rattle of armor as the second Celestial Knight jumps to attention is enough for me to raise my hands once more.

This next strike is easier, even though it saps the very last of my strength. I barely cringe, even when the clatter of the guard's armor as his body falls to the ground echoes through the corridor.

Still, it takes me several seconds to compose myself before I'm ready to step around the corner. And when I do, I freeze when I catch sight of the sheer amount of blood that seeps into the moonstone at my feet.

At first, hot horror flickers through my bones, but then I imagine the Godslayer lying there instead of those golden-clad soldiers, and the tension in my chest eases.

Though I killed these guards, the Godslayer is the one responsible for their deaths. Did she really think she could snatch Syran and the throne so cruelly from me without consequence? Does she understand the price she will pay for how she's wronged me?

Not yet, but she will.

She will.

Laughter bubbles up in my throat, but I swallow it down. I have to be silent now, like a shadow, like a flame. My powers are spent, and I can't risk being caught after coming so far.

But the giddiness doesn't leave me as I creep ever upward through the dungeons until I eventually find myself in the lowest level of the main palace.

From here, I know how to weave unseen through the corridors and hidden places that even Syran isn't aware of. I know that the door leading to the rear gardens is always left unlocked and unattended, and I know how I crave the feeling of the sunlight hitting my skin for the first time in months when I step out onto the grass. I know that the woods are right there in the distance, and they'll keep me safe from the prying eyes and flashing swords of the Celestial Knights.

I know that I am free.

And I know that the Godslayer is going to die.

CHAPTER 1

Lyanndra

The air is cool and smells of steel.

I slide along the ground, the worn soles of my boots kicking up clouds of dust as I duck low beneath the falling blade of one of my opponents. A second later, his sword crashes down in the dirt where I was just standing, missing me entirely.

The failed swing gives me the opening I need. Ignoring the deep thrum of my heart as it pounds against my ribs, I dart in close to the soldier's back and swipe my own longsword out at the meat of his thighs. The dulled blade doesn't pierce his armor, but there's enough force behind the blow to send him reeling forward onto his hands and knees. His helmet tumbles off, revealing brown hair that hangs limply around his face. Blood drips from his nose down onto the dirt below.

One down.

Four to go.

Steel flashes at the edge of my vision, and I spin just in time to parry the horizontal strike designed to cut me off at the ribs. My blade squeals against this new knight's sword as I use the momentum of my weapon to push my attacker off balance. He stumbles to the side, clipping one of his compatriots in the shoulder as he goes.

That fumbling moment gives me the time to gain some much needed ground. But my relief is short lived as the other two soldiers close in to flank me.

I turn to face them.

If I had my greatsword, I could cut them both down in a single swing, but my favored weapon is currently stowed away in Syran's chambers, far from the reach of my gauntleted hands. Instead, I'm stuck with this scrawny little longsword, which feels more like a child's toy than an instrument of death as I heft it in my palms. Still, I've faced more enemies with worse tools at my disposal. This time will be no different.

Knowing that the element of surprise is my best strategy here, I stand my ground as my opponents prepare to strike. Let them make the first move. Let them show me their weaknesses.

Sure enough, they rush forward in tandem, aiming to converge upon me in a coordinated attack. Normally, I'd dance backward out of range, but I'm hotly aware of the other two soldiers I left behind, and so I instead fling myself forward in a quick roll.

I only just manage to squeeze between the tightening pincers of their combined blades. The move carries me past them and to their rear, and, before they can even process the nature of my evasion, I'm on my feet again.

Spinning on my heel, I bring the hilt of my sword down on the small of one knight's back. He hasn't even hit the ground before I do the same to the second. Both men collapse into the dirt, gasping in pain.

They don't get up again.

Two left.

When I turn to face my last remaining opponents, I find that both of them have recovered from the effects of my earlier parry. We circle one another now, sizing each other up.

What must they think of me?

I'm wearing my distinctive tarnished armor, and my dragonhide leathers underneath. Gleaming scales, each inlaid upon the blackened steel by Syran's careful hands after the death of the usurper, glint in the thinning evening light. My black cloak is draped at my shoulders, and the golden helm sits atop my head, a beacon and a threat.

I am the Godslayer.

I was carved out on the battlefield and baptized in ash.

I will not relent.

I will not fall.

Behind the visor of my helm, I bare my teeth in a silent growl. I killed a king. I felled a god. I am more than these two men who quake before me in the golden shells of their armor.

They seem to know it, too, because their hands tremble as they raise their swords. My own blade remains steady and sure in the face of this final battle.

This time, I move first. I feint forward and raise my longsword like I'm going to rush them, but as soon as they rally toward where they think I'll strike, I pivot to the side.

There's no time for them to change course. By the time they even realize what I'm doing, I manage to slap the flat of my blade against the side of the closest soldier's helmet. The impact rings out with a metallic thud, and the sword slips from his slackening grasp while the shockwaves shudder up my arms and into my shoulders.

One left.

I grab the last knight by the shoulder, spin him around, and plant my knee squarely in his crotch.

A high-pitched whine sounds from the depths of his helmet, and then he, too, crumples.

I step back and lower my sword.

My heart pounds from the adrenaline of the fight. Beneath the plates of my armor, my chest heaves as I struggle to catch my breath. Blood roars in my ears. The sides of my helm seem to close in on me, squeezing, suffocating my entire world down to a single rushing point.

A year ago, I would have suffered through this bout of madness at the cost of concealing the truth of me, but things are different now.

I am a knight, I am the Godslayer, and I am a woman.

There is nothing left of me to hide.

So it is without hesitation that I spear my sword into the hard ground before I fumble with the clasp beneath my chin and finally pull the golden helm from my head.

Cool air licks my skin, soothing the sweat that beads on my forehead and at the nape of my neck. I immediately feel less claustrophobic. Half of my hair, which I had braided tightly to my scalp before the fight, has escaped. Now, the wayward locks fall into my face in a golden tangle. I must look a mess, but at least I'm not rolling on the ground moaning and clutching my unmentionables.

Giving that particular soldier a little more time to regain his dignity, I leave my sword where it is and stroll over to the nearest Celestial Knight. This is the first one I struck, and now he sits on the ground, nursing a bloodied nose.

What was his name again? Wayre, I think. The cream-colored mantle he wears betrays his Demigod heritage and his skills as a healer.

I stop before him and offer him my hand. He stares at it, then me, for a long moment before he finally slaps his gauntlet into mine and allows me to haul him to his feet.

"Well met, Godslayer," he says, though his tone is somewhat sheepish.

I acknowledge him with a nod.

Wayre isn't the best fighter among Syran's prospective generals. This Celestial Knight was the first to yield to me in this latest trial, and he did so with little resistance. And while his style is competent, it's also predictable, which makes him a better fit for a well-organized battalion than a command role.

Still, he was also the first to get back to his feet, and I admire the respect he shows in the face of such a humiliating loss.

I can't say the same about the others.

Mallan, the one I hit over the head, is Starless, like me. He certainly proved his valor while fighting against Kartas' forces in the

Battle of Nexus, but he's hotheaded and brash, and he challenges me every chance he gets. I'm not sure if it's because I best him every time we spar or because I'm a woman. Seeing how he glares at me now, I think maybe it's both.

The three remaining soldiers are all Demigods. Noros has some control over temperature, but he can do little more than make an opponent sweat or shiver in their armor. Syran tells me that Irtas can manipulate water, but I have yet to see those powers for myself. And Orobos, the one moaning on the ground, glows ever so slightly in the dark, though I'm not sure what, exactly, that's supposed to achieve.

None of these men have the makings of a general. Other than Wayre, I know how they talk of me when they think I cannot hear. And while my armor is impervious to both steel and the crude remarks they make about my body, I have little tolerance for those who would so quickly speak ill of their own comrades.

Luckily, I don't have to deal with them for much longer. Just as Wayre wanders away to help Mallan to his feet, the evening bell tolls, signaling dinner for the soldiers. I wave them away in a formal dismissal, glad to be rid of them.

Once they're gone, I turn and survey the training grounds. In the twilight, the vast space beside the palace feels desolate. I think about how Syran spread Kartas' ashes here so many months ago. Am I standing on what's left of the usurper right now?

Perhaps that notion should make me uneasy, but it doesn't. Kartas betrayed my crossed star and my kingdom. I only brought him justice in the end.

I linger until the shadows begin to seep into darkness. Only then do I move to retrieve my sparring longsword, with its blunt and harmless edges, from where it rises from the ground like a grave marker. But as soon as I touch the hilt, a strange heat wells beneath my gauntlet, signaling that I'm no longer alone.

A grin creeps across my face.

The Lord of the Midnight Flame has arrived.

I pull the sword from the ground and turn to face my latest opponent.

Syran.

King of Alastria and the Celestial Court, Lord of the Midnight Flame, my crossed star—all of those versions of him belong to me.

Untamed desire floods every inch of me as I drink in the sight of him. He's a golden vision in his royal armor, a collapsing star against the backdrop of his matte black cloak. I know that the back boasts the emblem of our joint rule, stitched in gold. The flame of his red hair is tied back from his face with a strip of leather, and further tamed by the jagged black crest of his crown. Beneath, brilliant green eyes survey me with heat that contradicts the cool mask of his features.

I know what Syran wants.

I think I'll give it to him.

Tossing my golden helm aside, I brandish my blade in a silent challenge. He meets it by drawing his own sword in one hand. A coil of black flame, as beautiful as it is deadly, snakes around the other.

For a moment, we're still, just two celestial bodies orbiting one another in the darkness.

My crossed star is the first to move. He surges forward in a flash of steel and fire, but I dodge easily to the side and then dip under the midnight sparks that skitter in his wake.

It's my turn now. I jab to his left, forcing Syran to step in the opposite direction to avoid my blade. And when he does, I clip him in the shin with the toe of my boot, earning a hissed breath and a burning glance.

When he lunges again, I bring my blade up to parry his. Using his height to his advantage, he slides his sword up and locks his hilt with mine in an attempt to disarm me.

But I've been short all my life, and I know how to foil such simple tricks.

I simply let my knees buckle and drop all my weight into my sword arm.

The sudden burden on his weapon draws both of our blades down far enough that I'm able to slip mine free and use the hilt to butt him in the chest while he's off balance.

Surprise flashes across Syran's face as he loses his footing and falls flat on his back in the dirt. I'm on him in an instant, my legs straddling his hips as I press the blunt blade of my longsword against his neck.

"Do you yield?" I ask.

He smirks up at me. "For you? Always."

Then it's my turn to be surprised as he flips us over so that I'm pinned underneath him, though the blade of my weapon remains digging into his jugular. And there's something else, something very distinct, digging into my thigh as well.

"Do *you* yield?" Syran demands, punctuating the question with a roll of his hips.

My breath rushes out in a hot gasp as I stare up at him defiantly. "Only if you make me."

Never one to back down from a challenge, Syran growls and grabs my wrist, finally forcing my blade away from his throat. Then his lips are on mine, just in time to swallow up the moan that slides from my mouth as he thrusts his hips once more.

Far too soon, he breaks the kiss, only to bring his lips to the shell of my ear. "Will you let me take you right here?" he whispers.

I shiver, both from the feeling of his heated breath on my cheek and the request he's made of me. Part of me longs to say yes, to give in to his desire.

It's dark. Everybody is already at dinner, far from the training grounds.

But a vicious splinter of logic forces me to remember the vulgar things the Celestial Knights mutter about me when they think they're alone, how they speculate that I've only won Syran's admiration through my performance in his bed, and I shake my head.

"Take me to your chambers," I say. "I want you all to myself."

"*Our* chambers," Syran corrects. He presses a searing kiss to the crook of my neck, earning him a wholly undignified gasp, and I grin.

Ours.

Our chambers.

Our kingdom.

Our crown.

CHAPTER 2

SYRAN

Lyanndra is mine.

I knew it when I first took her in our dreams, and I am only more certain of it now as I capture her lips in a punishing kiss.

Her back is pressed flat against the marble wall of our chambers, and her legs, now bare, are hiked up around my hips. She's entirely naked against the golden planes of my armor, and I long to feel more of her, but my need to ravage her upon our arrival was far too strong for me to bother undressing. Even stripping her down to her small-clothes seemed to take an unbearable eternity, as did the process of unlacing my trousers.

Still, I accept this grueling punishment without complaint. It's enough to feel her slick heat around my cock as I thrust into her again and again. And when she struggles to find purchase against the cool stone of the wall as I fuck her, that only serves to excite me more, for I can think of no greater honor than for a woman as wild as the Godslayer to relinquish the control of her pleasure to me.

And when she tilts her head back and moans, "Syran," I know that as much as she is mine, I, in turn, belong only to her.

I want to show her that. I need her to understand that the ache I feel for her goes deeper than the mere will of the stars.

With great regret, I wrap my arms around her waist and ease out of her. She growls at the sudden loss, but I don't give her time to complain before I whisk her over to the waiting surface of our bed. Then I'm back inside of her, hissing with pleasure as her dull nails scrabble over the smooth surface of my armor at the sudden intrusion.

In this position, Lyanndra is able to meet me thrust for thrust. The grip of her powerful thighs around my waist is ferocious, but I wouldn't have it any other way.

I think about how I watched from the palace windows as she effortlessly obliterated five of my best Celestial Knights earlier today, and how the same arms responsible for those powerful swings of her longsword clutch me now, and I start to unravel.

This woman has killed for me.

She's lived for me, too.

And by the stars, the way her hazel eyes flashed with raw power when she pinned me down on the training grounds will never leave me for as long as my heart still beats.

The phantom edge of her remembered blade presses into my neck, and I groan as heat pools in my palms. My hands fist into the black silk sheets as I draw my cock out of her until only the tip teases her entrance. And just as Lyanndra opens her mouth to admonish me, I slam back into her, so that all that spills from her lips is a low whine.

I torment her as she's punished me, drawing out her pleasure until she's nothing but a shuddering mess beneath me.

Only then do I let her peak.

She shatters on my cock, which, in turn, drives me over the edge. A snarl rips from my throat as I empty everything I am into her. My black flame blazes in my very soul, and it's all I can do to channel it out and into my hands. Sparks singe the sheets where I clutch them between my desperate fingers.

I am consumed.

I am ash.

And then I collapse on top of her, thoroughly spent.

We lay there, panting, for a long moment. Finally, I gather enough strength to roll off her, and Lyanndra sighs as I settle in beside her and pull her close.

But then, as she curls into the hard surface of my armor, she wrinkles her nose. "What's that smell?" she asks. "Is something burning?"

I smirk and nod down at the sheets. Two perfect, smoking handprints are singed into the black silk on either side of where I fucked her soundly into the mattress.

"Again?" she teases.

"They're a casualty of our battle," I toss back. "Proof that you bested me once again."

She rolls her eyes, but her barely suppressed grin gives away how pleased she is that she managed to debase me so thoroughly. Then she melts back into my side and tucks her face into the crook of my neck.

Comfortable silence descends over us as we bask in the glow of our union. I trace one finger over the curve of her hip, and she shivers at the contact. She's so vulnerable like this. Naked and dozing, it's hard to picture her in the bulk of her armor or hacking away with her monstrous greatsword. To see her stripped down, and to know that I am the only one she trusts to view her in such a state, makes me want her all the more.

Something tender tugs in my chest, and I'm once again reminded that whatever this is that's growing between us is something far past lust or fate.

And I think that what I feel for her has a name, and when it rushes into me all at once, I cannot deny it.

I know what this is.

I *know*.

What I feel for her is *lo*…

Lyanndra sighs and pushes herself up on her elbows. The movement shakes me from my thoughts, and I turn my head to watch her as she sits up fully and stretches her arms high above her head until her shoulders pop. Between the excellent silhouette of her chest and the small, contented sound that hums from her lips, I can't hold back the second round of desire that sets my blood aflame.

But before I can act on it, my crossed star slips from the bed and strides in all her naked glory toward the washroom. I openly admire the curve of her ass as she goes. From there, my eyes can't help but slide down to where the evidence of our passion drips lewdly down her thighs.

Noticing where my heated gaze has landed, Lyanndra glances over her shoulder at me and smirks. A second later, she disappears across the threshold of the washroom, presumably to clean herself up.

Normally, I'd enthusiastically assist her with that particular task, but it's late and I'm hungry. Given that the Godslayer has never been one to turn down a meal, I ring for a servant and send the lad down to the kitchens to fetch enough food for a small army. By the time Lyanndra reemerges, still clad in absolutely nothing at all, I've got a variety of her favorite dishes laid out and waiting for her.

"Do we have a new general yet?" I inquire when she's once again settled down beside me, this time with a full plate balanced on her lap.

She shakes her head. "I wouldn't trust any of them to clean the latrines, let alone lead an army."

"You do realize that those five are, by far, the most talented soldiers in our ranks?" I point out. Yet, I have to concede that she has a point. None of these Celestial Knights could ever fill the void that Kartas left behind, in skill or in camaraderie.

"I'd hate to see our worst," she jests through a mouthful of roasted fish. She chews thoughtfully, swallows, and then nudges my leg with her bare foot. "Wayre," she states, her tone once again serious. "His skill is… adequate. But he shows some promise, I think."

I wonder how she reached that conclusion. In my mind, Wayre is the weakest candidate I've put before her so far. Wasn't he the first to fall to her dulled blade this evening? No, Mallan or Orobos would be my top choices. Both men have shown a rare combination of sense and fortitude on the battlefield, and I find Orobos in particular to be quite genial in times of peace.

Then again, I admit that perhaps my judgment is not as sound as the Godslayer's. After all, Kartas deceived me for many years, as did Ressa. What does my crossed star see in these knights that I do not?

But it seems I won't receive these answers tonight. Lyanndra practically inhales her food, which is understandable considering how many hours she spent training and sparring. And as soon as she pushes her plate aside, her eyelids start to droop.

I clear the remaining dishes away so she can rest, and then I finally begin the process of removing my armor. By the time I've changed into a loose pair of sleeping trousers, Lyanndra is already snoring lightly amid the singed silk sheets.

My heart thrills at the sight of her.

She really is the most stunning woman I've ever seen. She's short, but powerfully built, a far cry from the slim frame idealized by the ladies of the Celestial Court. Every inch of her is forged for combat, from the corded muscles of her arms and thighs to the wide spread of her shoulders. Her features, too, intrigue me. That aquiline nose, those hazel eyes that flicker back and forth beneath her closed lids, and the set of her mouth all draw me in, especially against the golden backdrop of her hair.

I crawl into bed beside her and turn on my side so I can watch the way her chest rises and falls as she breathes. How lucky am I that the stars crossed me to such a unique and untamed creature?

It seems unfathomable now that I once sought to make her smaller than she was, to fit her into the shape of what I thought a woman should be.

Now, I wouldn't want her any other way.

She is the Godslayer.

She is my crossed star.

And soon, she will be my queen.

My cock stirs as I imagine her riding me while wearing nothing but a golden crown, and I struggle to push the fantasy aside.

We have to wed first.

Torran has scheduled the ceremony for the Winter Solstice, in honor of the date we formed our alliance against the usurper. The old

Demigod doesn't need to know that it's also the same night we consummated our bond. At least he seems content to shoulder most of the burden of planning the celebration, which is a task that would have historically fallen on Kartas.

A pang of grief echoes through me at the memory of my cousin. At times like these, I wish he were still here by my side, with his quick tongue and steadfast nature. But I remind myself that the façade he showed me was just that. He hid his treachery well, but it was still festering just beneath the surface. Every thought of him is tainted now.

It's as if I mourn who he wasn't, rather than who he was.

I shake my head, as though that will dislodge my morbid thoughts, and then focus back on the woman sleeping soundly in my bed. Desire once again overpowers the darkness that wells within me as I drink in the sight of her.

I've long since memorized the curves and angles of her, from the swell of her breasts to the slope of her shoulders. My eyes linger on the scars that litter her body, proof of her many victories, and a handful of losses, in battle. Notably, she has none on her back, which is unusual in a warrior.

Is it because nobody has ever been able to sneak up on her?

Or is it a mark of honor, a sign that she never turns her back on an enemy?

Perhaps it's both, I decide as my eyes skim over the familiar patchwork of scars.

Several shiny patches of skin lick up her forearms, which are easily recognizable as well-healed burns. She's never told me where she got them, but I'd be a fool to assume that they didn't have something to do with the dragonhide leathers she wears.

Further down, there's a clean, clipped scar low on her belly. From the neatness of the wound, I surmise that it was made by a relatively small blade, probably a knife. But Lyanndra speaks little of this one, too, and has only ever acknowledged it by confirming that somebody stabbed her many years ago during a confrontation in a tavern.

The ragged starburst on one thigh, however, is less of a mystery.

According to Lyanndra, she received this particular wound in one of her first battles against my father's forces. She was so frightened of being found out as a woman that she limped away and pulled the arrow from her leg to avoid revealing her secret. It's a wonder that it healed as well as it did, though I'm glad for it.

And then, of course, there's the puckered scar I left on her ribs with my flaming sword.

Shame floods through me at the memory of how I nearly killed her. She glared at me with such hatred back then, such defiance. I recall the horror when I realized what I had done, how it rose in my throat like bile, like a scream.

I shake my head once more. There's no use in dwelling in the past. Lyanndra has forgiven me for what I did to her. Why can't I do the same?

As if sensing my troubled thoughts, my crossed star stirs in bed beside me, though she does not wake. Once again, I'm reminded that this woman has chosen to remain by my side in spite of everything, in spite of *me*.

I shift closer to her and drape one arm over her sleeping form, pulling her into my chest. I nuzzle my nose into her hair and breathe in the battlefield scent of her. She's here, she's real, and she's mine.

Reassured, I press a tender kiss to her forehead and then allow my eyes to close as sleep begins to dull my senses.

Lyanndra is here.

She's not going anywhere.

CHAPTER 3

Lyanndra

I wake to total darkness.

For a moment, I struggle to remember where I am.

My bedroll?

An inn?

Wherever this is, it's immediately obvious to me that I'm wearing absolutely nothing, which means that I'm vulnerable.

That I'm in danger.

But then the familiar scent of ash fills my nose, and I finally register the liquid silk of the sheets against my bare skin, and I realize that I'm in Syran's bed. His well-muscled arm is curled around my waist, holding me tight against his broad chest. The familiar warmth of his breath fans out over the shell of my ear.

I sag into the comfortable nest of his arms and sigh.

Safe.

I'm safe.

Still, my heartbeat doesn't slow. I draw in a shallow breath and listen to the wind as it rattles through the open balcony doors. I can't explain it, but I feel that something is off.

Something is *wrong*.

Tamping down the urge to panic, I scan the room, searching for anything strange or unfamiliar that could have woken me.

The darkness feels more oppressive now. The black flame that flickered in the fireplace when I dozed off is down to shadowy embers, and the many candles littered throughout the space have long since been snuffed out. On any other night, the marble walls of Syran's bedchamber would be awash in moonlight, but one glance toward the balcony doors and the bruise-colored clouds that blot out the sky beyond tells me everything I need to know.

A peal of thunder rumbles in the distance. Seconds later, the first drops of rain patter against the side of the palace.

It's only a storm.

The snarled knot of tension in my chest finally ebbs away.

I sigh again and burrow deeper into the comfort of my crossed star's arms. I feel like a fool. What would my people think of me if they knew that the great and terrible Godslayer panicked in the face of a little thunder?

At least Syran wouldn't think less of me.

Still, I'm glad that he isn't awake to witness my most recent flirtation with madness. He remains still and silent at my back, a solidly reassuring presence. I close my eyes and try to time my breathing to his as I will my heartbeat to slow.

But I cannot relax.

Lightning streaks outside, so bright that the flash is visible even behind my closed eyelids, and then another roll of thunder growls through the night. This time, it's close enough that I feel the vibrations in my very bones. At the same moment, the rain intensifies. The scent of it swirls on the cool wind that blusters in through the open doors of the balcony.

Once again, the surety that something is wrong grips me with creeping fingers.

I open my eyes and sit up.

At first glance, everything in the room appears normal. Nothing's moved since I fell asleep. Even the door to the washroom still stands open, exactly as I left it earlier.

So why do I feel like I'm being watched?

Over the cacophony of the storm, I know I won't be able to hear breathing or movement even if I try, so I focus on using my sight. Squinting in the low light, I struggle to discern what's shadow and what's not.

For a moment, I can't pick out anything suspicious, but then my eyes land on the far corner of the room where the darkness seems deeper somehow.

Alive.

A thrill of fear skitters up my spine. The air hitches in my chest as I stare into the shadows.

There's nothing there.

Is there?

And then the patch of darkness undulates in a wholly unnatural way that reminds me of breathing, and I know, *I know*, that there is something in the room with us.

Is it a person? Could an animal have come in through the balcony doors?

I don't think so. Whatever it is doesn't seem solid.

But then what *is* it?

Hopefully something that bleeds.

I keep my eyes trained on the dark thing in the corner as I reach slowly over the edge of the bed. Even when my hand brushes the worn leather of the sheathed dagger I have stashed away beneath the mattress, I don't dare blink. My fingers work blindly at the clasp, but this is not the first time I've done this in the dark, and I manage to draw the short, wicked blade with little trouble.

With the hilt of the dagger pressed squarely in my palm, I get ready to strike.

But before I can move, a fresh fork of lightning cuts through the night sky beyond the balcony doors, throwing the whole room into sharp relief for a single shard of a second.

Two gleaming eyes stare at me from the corner.

The thing blinks.

And then the darkness returns with a roar of thunder in its wake, and I howl with it as I throw the dagger into the shadows.

Everything happens all at once.

Alerted by my primal yell, Syran jumps up before my blade even reaches its mark, black flames ready and coiled in his hands while he snarls blearily into the night. Across the room, the dagger careens into the marble wall and clatters down to the floor, indicating that I missed. But I'm already out of bed and flying toward the corner with my fists raised.

"What?" Syran calls from behind me. His voice wells with the same panic that's pumping through my veins. "What is it?"

I throw my weight forward and swing at the thing in the corner. But the darkness simply dissolves to nothing beneath my knuckles, and then it's too late to change course. My fist glances off the cold stone wall, and I howl again, this time in pain.

"Lyanndra!" Syran closes the distance between us. His hand loops around my wrist, and he pulls me into him while a plume of black flame flickers to life in his free palm. The eerie glow illuminates his face and spills far enough outward that when I glance back into the corner, I can see clearly that there's nothing there.

Not anymore, at least.

"What in the fucking stars is happening?" he demands in a voice heavy with fear and alarm. His eyes dart around the bedchamber as though he expects to see a great beast lurching out of the shadows at any second.

"There was something here." The words rush out of me in an urgent stream. "It was watching us, Syran. *There was something here.*"

He doesn't doubt me for a second. Instead, his flame surges outward from his body in serpentine tendrils to curl around the wicks of every single candle in the room. Almost immediately, the bedchamber is alight with flickering shadow.

Clutching my throbbing hand to my chest, I spin around in a tight circle.

There's nothing here. From where I stand, I can even confirm that the washroom, too, is empty.

Where did it go?

How did it go?

I could swear on the stars that it was *right there* when I punched it, but my hand passed through it like it was nothing. Now, all I have to show for my efforts is the stinging pain that blooms forth from my knuckles to radiate up my wrist.

Still, Syran checks every single crack and crevice of the room. While he does that, I stoop down and retrieve my dagger from where it lies on the floor. The blade should have at least hit whatever the stars that thing was, but the steel is clean. Did the knife fly right through it like my fist did?

"Whatever you saw, it's gone now," Syran states as he returns to me. "What was it?"

"I don't know," I tell him. "But it blinked at me."

"Blinked?"

"I know how it sounds, but I *saw* it," I insist.

Syran glances down at my hands. In one, I hold the dagger, the same blade that I slid between his father's ribs that fateful day on the battlefield. The other is streaming blood from the knuckles and swelling rapidly at the wrist.

"I believe you," he says softly, and I can tell he means it.

Relief wells inside of me. The panic is starting to fade, and for the first time, I realize how cold it is in here with the rainy breeze whipping in from the balcony. A shiver runs through me, and Syran frowns. He strides to the washroom, where he retrieves his black velvet robe, and returns to wrap the heavy garment around my shoulders. Then he turns to the doors and pulls them shut, latching them securely against the weather.

"Let me see," he requests as he holds out his hands for my injured one.

I do as he asks. I wince as his fingers brush over my split knuckles. An apology flashes over his face before he gently examines my hand first, then my wrist. It hurts, but the telltale, jagged pain of a broken bone is blissfully absent.

"Just a sprain," he confirms.

I let him guide me back to the bed. While he fetches supplies from the washroom, I perch on the edge of the mattress and close my eyes as I try to recall everything I can about what I saw.

It was dark, and it had eyes. Now that I can focus, I think it had the vaguest outline of a man. It wasn't solid. And while I never saw it enter, I cannot fathom how it escaped so cleanly from Syran's locked bedchamber.

In all my years wandering Alastria, I've never come across anything quite like this.

My thoughts fragment when Syran joins me once again. He places a basin of water on the floor beside my bare feet, and then he makes a second trip to the washroom to retrieve a roll of bandages, a washcloth, and various ointments.

Finally, he kneels before me.

"May I?" he asks, holding his hand out for my injured one.

I oblige.

He takes the washcloth, dips it in the water, and then carefully begins to dab at my split knuckles. It's not lost on me that we've been in this position once before when he cleaned and bandaged my burned hands in his chambers so many months ago. I hated him then, or at least I thought I did.

And now?

I don't even know what to call the heat that sparks in my chest at the mere thought of him.

Does he feel it too?

Does he understand how lost to him I am?

I want to ask, but my crossed star speaks before I can.

"I saw it, too," Syran reveals. "Just before you ran over there. It was… dark."

My gaze flickers up to meet his.

"What do you think it was?" I ask.

He frowns. "I don't know. Did it do this to you?" he presses, nodding down to my split knuckles.

I shake my head. "I tried to hit it, but my hand went right through and into the wall. The dagger, too."

"And you saw it blink?"

"Yes."

Syran's expression only darkens further. "We should speak with Torran. If anybody will know what we saw, it's him."

"First thing in the morning," I agree. While I doubt either of us will be going back to bed tonight, there's no use in waking the old Demigod now. He's been rather fragile since Kartas put an arrow through his leg on the Winter Solstice. The least we can do is let him rest undisturbed.

But sleep doesn't seem to be in the stars for any of us tonight.

Just as Syran finishes splinting my wrist, a frantic knock sounds on the door of his bedchamber.

We share a disconcerted glance before he rises and crosses swiftly to the threshold. Who would dare disturb the King of Alastria at such a late hour? Or worse, the Godslayer?

When Syran pulls the door open, I'm shocked to see Torran standing in the corridor just beyond the portal. He looks as he always does, dressed in his purple robes with his silver hair pulled neatly back in an intricate braid. His eyes, as blue as ice, pass over my crossed star to find mine.

He nods, and then turns back to Syran.

"Get dressed. Your presence is required in the dungeons," he says urgently. He glances at me again and adds, "Both of you."

"Why?" I ask as I rise from the bed. Clutching Syran's robe shut with my uninjured hand, I cross to join him in the doorway. "What's happened?"

A troubled look passes over the old Demigod's face. "It's Ressa," he explains.

Syran frowns. "Ressa? What about her?"

"She's gone."

CHAPTER 4

SYRAN

Ressa's gone.

The words ring through my mind as I throw on the first tunic I can find.

What does Torran mean, *gone?*

Has she escaped?

Did she perish?

Combined with tonight's mysterious visitor, news of my former betrothed's apparent absence is most unwelcome. I feel unsteady and overwhelmed, like everything is crashing down around me. Desperate for some sense of stability, I glance over to Lyanndra.

My crossed star is already dressed in her dragonhide leathers and is in the process of buckling on her tarnished armor. She moves confidently, as though she's entirely unbothered by Torran's revelation, but I know her well enough to catch the tension in her shoulders and the way she grimaces when she pulls her gauntlet over her injured hand.

She had the chance to kill Ressa during the coup but chose not to. She never told me why. Does the Godslayer regret being merciful?

Do I?

The question plagues me as I take Lyanndra's lead and retrieve my golden armor. By the time I place the heavy weight of my crown atop my head, she's already got her sheathed greatsword strapped to her back over her cloak. Her golden helm rests in the crook of her arm. She looks every inch the fierce and formidable warrior I know her to be.

Beneath her grim expression, does she feel as rattled as I do?

When she reaches out with her uninjured hand and curls her fingers around mine, I know that she must, even if she doesn't show it.

We leave our chambers side by side, though Lyanndra's grip loosens as we step out into the corridor where Torran awaits.

"What happened?" I demand.

The old Demigod shakes his head. "It's better you see for yourself," he replies. He shuffles past us before I can question him further. His gnarled cane taps hollowly along the marble floor as he starts toward the sweeping staircase. Lyanndra and I share a troubled glance before following close behind.

Torran leads the way down to the dungeons. We whisk past the throne room and the library, and then the kitchens, until finally we find ourselves at a pair of reinforced iron doors tucked away at the very back of the palace. The guards stationed there look pale and on edge. They don't meet my eye as they step aside for us, and they both flinch as the Godslayer strides past them.

What in the stars is going on?

If Torran won't tell us, there's only one way to find out.

I push the iron doors open, revealing a jagged flight of stairs that descend like teeth into the bowels of the kingdom. Torches flicker on the walls. A foul smell wafts up from the passage, a noxious mixture of sweat, decay, and waste. It takes all of my decorum to keep my face schooled into a neutral mask, though Lyanndra seems to have no problem curling her lip in disgust.

Torran is the first to venture across the threshold. In spite of my reservations, I hurry after him, and Lyanndra promptly falls into step beside me. The two guards on the door trail a short distance behind us.

Our footsteps echo off the worn stone, which grows grimier with every step we take. Darkness closes in on us in spite of the flickering pools of light cast by the torches, and I find myself summoning my flame before we're even halfway down the treacherous flight of steps. The midnight glow, however, does little to quell my growing unease.

It's been a long while since I've ventured this far into the depths of the Celestial Court. It strikes me that Lyanndra has probably never been to this part of the palace at all.

A pang of guilt flashes through me as I recall how Kartas wanted to throw her into this dismal pit. I never agreed with him, but I did imprison my crossed star, even if it was within a gilded cage rather than a cramped cell. Was she ever afraid that I would toss her down here and forget her in the dark?

Like I did with Ressa, I admit ashamedly.

My conscience only sours further when I consider how I treated my former betrothed. I never loved her, and I should have had the courage to tell her sooner. Maybe I could have spared her some pain or from the many months she spent rotting away like the traitor she chose to become.

But I don't have time to dwell on the topic further, for, as we descend deeper into the underbelly of the palace, the sharp and unmistakable stench of blood assaults my nose.

At my side, Lyanndra seems to notice it too. She reaches over her shoulder and curls her good hand around the hilt of her greatsword, though she does not yet draw her weapon. I do the same and palm the grip of my blade. My eyes scan the semidarkness for any sign of an attack, but all is quiet and still.

And when we reach the bottom of the stairs, I understand why Torran wanted us to witness this scene for ourselves.

There's blood everywhere.

Arterial spray paints the walls. There's so much crimson pooled on the floor that some of the patches appear black in the low light.

Two bodies, both clad in the golden armor of Celestial Knights, lie heaped in the corridor. The smell is so strong that it's nearly unbearable, and I resist the urge to gag as I kneel next to the nearest corpse.

I turn the dead guard over, and it's immediately obvious what killed him. There's a gaping wound in his neck. My stomach turns at the sight, and I quickly look away.

The second soldier is in much the same condition. The only change is that the murder weapon remains lodged in this guard's throat.

"Stone?" Lyanndra asks as she crouches down beside me. She brushes the blunt end of the jagged shard with the tips of one gauntlet, sending a small plume of iridescent dust into the air.

"Ressa," I mutter. "It has to be."

My crossed star glances around, scanning the corridor for any signs of danger. "She might still be here," she warns.

Straightening up, I turn to guards who followed us down and command, "Sound the emergency bells. I want Celestial Knights searching every inch of Nexus. If Ressa's in the city, you *will* find her."

"Yes, Your Highness," they acquiesce in tandem before they scurry back into the darkness from whence we came.

When I'm sure they're far enough away that they won't be able to overhear us, I ask Torran, "How did this happen? *When* did this happen?"

The old Demigod stares down at the corpses with a pained look. His face appears sallow and ancient in the dark light of my midnight flame. "The guards arrived to relieve these wretched souls at their shift change, only to find them… like this." He waves his hands at the dead knights for emphasis. "They had the good sense to check the prisoners, and that's when they discovered that Ressa's cell was empty. I came to you as soon as I heard."

Lyanndra, who hasn't moved from her position on the floor, traces one finger through the nearest patch of blood. "It's been hours, at least," she observes. "It's all dry." She finally stands and, turning to Torran, requests, "Take me to her cell."

"As you wish, Godslayer," he concedes. "This way."

I linger behind as my crossed star follows our advisor further into the labyrinthine darkness of the dungeons. I trust Lyanndra to investigate thoroughly, and I will do the same. Surely, somebody saw something, even down here where the light doesn't reach?

The nearest cells all stand empty, but the first one around the next sharp twist of the corridor is occupied. A man, surprisingly clean for such a wretched place, peers out from the other side of the barred door. He meets my gaze with a scowl at first, but, when his eyes alight on the crown I wear atop my head, his expression loosens into hot fear.

"Your Highness," he mumbles as he drops his head in deference.

We are past such pretenses, I think, but I do not voice that opinion. Instead, I say, "There has been… an incident."

The prisoner nods down at the filthy floor of his cell. "Yes, Your Highness."

"Did you witness it?"

"Yes, Your Highness."

"Tell me," I prompt. "What did you see?"

The wretched creature shuffles his feet against the grimy stone and answers, "A woman, Your Highness. The Lady Ressa."

My eyes sharpen in the dark.

"She had a touch of madness about her," he continues. "She was talking to herself before she killed them."

That doesn't surprise me. I'm well aware from the guards' reports that Ressa's grip on reality has lessened over time, though I admit that I did not expect her to devolve into an outright murderess.

"And how did she slay the guards?" I ask. This question is purely a test. While I think this Demigod speaks the truth, he is still a criminal. He has nothing to gain from his honesty, but he does serve to benefit from telling me what he thinks I want to hear. What might he request in exchange for information? A pardon, perhaps? A lighter sentence for his transgressions?

But the prisoner only replies, "She used her powers, Your Highness."

Ah.

Perhaps integrity is not lost down here after all.

Now that I'm confident this Demigod isn't trying to deceive me, I decide it's time to pry deeper for the information I truly seek. "What else did you see?" I inquire. "Was she alone?"

"Alone, Your Highness. I only saw her walk past and kill the guards. Then she left." He points in the direction of the stairs leading up to the glittering palace above.

Disappointment creeps through me. I hoped for more information, but this Demigod isn't the only prisoner locked away down here. Maybe the others will be more helpful.

But alas, I'm horribly mistaken. The next few criminals I pass, two men and a woman, are all asleep on their cots, and the last occupant of the cell before I reach Ressa's is nothing more than a gibbering mess.

Ignoring the prisoner's mad ravings, I continue on to the small, cramped space that served as Ressa's quarters until earlier today. Torran stands against the far wall, his shocking blue eyes affixed to Lyanndra as she carefully inspects the interior of the cell.

"Any theories on how she escaped?" I ask my crossed star.

"She shouldn't have been able to," she replies. "The door was locked from the outside. There's no damage or sign of tampering."

Confusion rises in my gut as I inspect the lock. Sure enough, Lyanndra is right. The metal is sound. There aren't any scratches or dents, no indication that it had ever been opened at all.

"So you're saying that she, what? Walked through the wall?" I question.

"No," she answers grimly. "I'm saying that somebody let her out and locked the door again behind her."

Cold realization hits me in the chest as I register the implications of the Godslayer's words. Unbidden, the memory of Kartas admitting to sending the courtiers after Lyanndra in the infirmary surfaces to the forefront of my mind, and my shock quickly boils over to hot rage.

"You think one of the guards released her?" I utter.

She seems to pick up on my dangerous shift in mood, for her

expression darkens. "Perhaps. Did any courtiers have access to the dungeons? She may still have friends in the palace."

"All of the traitors are dead," I say in a tone more clipped than Lyanndra deserves. I want to believe that I wiped clean all insubordination in one fell blow after the failed coup. I want to believe that my kingdom is safe, and that my crossed star is, too.

"That we know of." Lyanndra's hazel eyes meet mine in the semidarkness. The challenge in them is clear. She thinks that a Demigod is behind this.

I agree.

Yet, I cannot bring myself to say it aloud, so I turn to Torran and ask, "Has anybody been down here other than the guards?"

The old Demigod shakes his head. "No visitors, as you ordered. The guards report that she barely spoke to them, either. I don't see any opportunity for her to, shall we say, *form alliances*."

Then how did she escape?

Various possibilities rush through my mind, but I dismiss them all quickly. She had help, of that I'm certain, but from *who*?

Lyanndra comes up beside me and places her uninjured hand on my forearm. Her gauntlet is heavy against my armor, as though weighted by her own dark thoughts.

"There's nothing more we can do down here," she says quietly. "If somebody did aid Ressa, they're long gone. We're better off overseeing the search."

"You're right," I affirm, though I feel defeated by the acknowledgement.

She squeezes my arm once more before slipping her hand down to the crook of my elbow. And while I'm always proud to escort her, her closeness is particularly comforting in this dreadful place.

Once again, Torran leads the way, this time out of the dungeons instead of into their depths. As we pass by the cell across from Ressa's, the ramblings of the Demigod inside reach a fever pitch. I tune them out and keep walking, but Lyanndra stops short.

For a moment, I don't understand why, but then I realize that she's listening to the piteous rantings with her head cocked attentively to the side.

"Darkness and shadow, alive, alive," the prisoner chants. "Alive, alive, alive...."

I open my mouth to speak, to explain to Lyanndra that it's just some poor wretch clenched between the rabid jaws of madness, but she holds up one hand to silence me before I can begin.

"Eyes in the dark, alive, alive, blinking, alive...."

Ice creeps through my veins as I remember what Lyanndra said earlier.

It blinked at me.

And I saw it, whatever the thing was. It was like a shadow, like a patch of darkness thicker than the rest. And it moved like it was sentient, like it was breathing.

Like it was *alive*.

The prisoner's voice rises to a piercing wail that echoes through the stone corridor in a shrieking tide. "She talked to the shadows, she did! And they blinked back, they watched, and they talked, and the dark was alive! Alive! Alive! Alive!"

Lyanndra's gaze rises to meet mine. I see my own fear reflected back at me there as she, too, comes to realize the scope of this.

Ressa's flight is far more sinister than one escaped prisoner.

Whatever was in our chambers tonight was down here, too.

And if this thing can disappear in an instant, if blades and fists pass right through it, then what else can it do?

I can't even begin to answer that question, but I know one thing for certain.

Whatever this creature is, it is no friend of ours.

CHAPTER 5

Lyanndra

The whole of Nexus seems to be holding its breath.

Weeks have passed since Ressa's bloody escape from the dungeons, and we're still no closer to finding her than we were the night she fled. The guards we sent out to scour the palace and the city beyond uncovered some signs of her in the woods surrounding the Celestial Court, but from there, the trail went colder than the northern mountains in winter.

Neither has the shadowy visitor to Syran's chambers left my mind.

For the first few nights after that initial encounter, my crossed star and I would sleep in shifts, watching over one another throughout the moonlit hours. But exhaustion won out over vigilance after the first week, and we quickly abandoned that plan with the assumption that, between the two of us, we would wake if the threat were ever to return. And while there has been no further sign of that dark, blinking thing, I have yet to rest soundly once the sun sets over the midlands.

As much as both phantoms plague me, Syran seems positively

haunted by the specter of his former betrothed. He spends his nights tossing and turning beside me, and his days are punctuated by frequent reports on any clues that might speak to Ressa's whereabouts.

This morning is no different. Orobos, who's been tasked with leading the search efforts, stands before us in the throne room, his helmet in his hands and his head lowered.

"There is still no sign of Lady Ressa, Your Highness," he states. "We've canvassed every town and village within a week's ride, and nobody claims to have seen her."

"Just because she wasn't seen doesn't mean she wasn't there," I observe from where I sit at Syran's right hand. Technically, the golden throne on which I perch is meant for the queen, but I will bear that title soon enough. What difference does the matter of a few months make?

Syran glances over at me, and I can tell from the way his brows knit together that he doesn't follow. Neither does Orobos, if the way he opens his mouth to argue is anything to go by. But he remembers his station just before he can say something he'll regret and manages to snap his jaw shut again while I suppress a scowl.

"Have there been reports of thievery in those villages?" I ask. "Missing rations? Stolen horses?"

Orobos blurts, "How did you know that?"

Resisting the urge to roll my eyes, I explain. "A desperate woman on the run wouldn't want to be seen. She would seek shelter or the next best things: clothes, food, and transportation."

The Demigod has the good sense to at least look embarrassed that he didn't think of that himself.

"Compile the reports," Syran commands. "If we can figure out where these incidents have occurred, perhaps we can focus our search to those areas."

"Yes, Your Highness," Orobos acquiesces.

"Dismissed," the King of Alastria commands.

The Celestial Knight follows the order without question.

Once the throne room doors slam shut behind the guard, Syran's royal posture breaks, and he slumps back in his throne. "I believe I'm starting to understand why you think Orobos is unfit to lead," he mutters. "Though to be fair, it didn't occur to me to ask about thievery, either. Kartas was always the one to notice such things."

His eyes trace over the marble room with a faraway gaze, and, in that moment, I feel his grief like it beats inside my chest. I reach out my hand, which is mostly healed from its brief affair with the wall of Syran's chamber, and lace my bare fingers through his.

"We're trying to replace a general," I tell him, "not your kin."

Syran squeezes his palm against mine but says nothing. We both know there are no words to fill the gaping hole within him.

After a few moments, he straightens up once again. "At least we might be able to track Ressa down," he sighs. "Her escape must have been premeditated. What more might she have planned?"

"Whatever her scheme, we should tread carefully," I warn. "Ressa is dangerous."

My crossed star shakes his head. "She's been locked away for months. The guards said she barely ate or slept. She's weaker than she's ever been. We just have to find her before she regains her strength."

"You saw what she did to those knights," I argue. "If that's Ressa at her weakest, what will she be capable of when she's at her peak? And what of this shadow? An ally such as that cannot bode well for us."

"I… I don't know," Syran admits. He looks exhausted as he says it, as though the mere act of voicing our collective ignorance has drained all the energy from him. I take stock of how pale he is, of how the shadow of stubble, a shade darker than his flaming red hair, swathes his jaw. I wish I could ease what troubles him, but I know that I, too, am just as spent.

We both need a good night's sleep.

I linger by Syran's side for a while longer, but restlessness takes hold of me eventually. I bid him goodbye with a kiss that promises more to come this evening and then head up to his chambers to change out of my dress and into trousers and a tunic.

Then, I make my way down to the stables.

It's my humble opinion that there is no better view of the world than through the ears of a mount, and the idea of running with Barra across the flat plains of the midlands breathes a spark into me that I haven't felt for weeks. When was the last time I took a ride just for the fun of it? I can't even remember.

By the time I stride across the cobbled yard and into the beckoning stable scent of straw, leather, and manure, I can practically feel the wind twisting through my hair and the easy burn of my muscles as I steer my trusted friend over the grassy landscape.

But the bubble of my daydream bursts as I step inside the long, dimly lit building to find somebody already standing at Barra's stall.

My first instinct is to shout out a threat and charge the stranger, but then I realize that the silhouette of the figure almost certainly belongs to a woman, and Barra, whose huge head hangs over the stall door, doesn't seem at all alarmed by her presence.

In fact, I can tell by the upright set of her ears that she's happy.

Thrilled, even.

I approach slowly, sizing up the woman who has so enamored my closest companion. She's tall and willowy, like many of the Demigods who inhabit the Celestial Court. Her jeweled dress is rather fine, but not quite so ostentatious as some of the highest-ranking members of the court. And, when I get closer, I recognize the delicate coil of her brown hair and the thin, sharp set of her nose as those belonging to a lady I've passed in the palace corridors once or twice.

She doesn't seem to notice me as I approach, though Barra's red eyes flicker over to mine. The kelpie curls her lip, revealing jagged, needle-like teeth housed within the crocodilian set of her jaw, and shakes her head in greeting.

But the Demigod quickly steals her attention away by dangling a piece of a meat pie in front of the monstrous steed's head.

"How about this?" the lady asks in a cooing voice that seems more suited to talking to a puppy or small child, rather than a beast like Barra. "Would you like to try it?"

Barra answers by snapping her jaws forward to cleanly snatch the pie out of the stranger's outstretched hand.

Well, *that* certainly explains the kelpie's good mood.

And to give the woman credit where it's due, she barely even flinched. I've watched grown men soil themselves in a most spectacular fashion at the mere sight of Barra.

"Did you like that?" the Demigod murmurs, seemingly unperturbed.

"Barra likes anything she can get her teeth on," I interject. "Including your fingers, if you're not careful."

The woman gasps and spins, her hands flying up to her mouth in shock. Recognition replaces surprise in her doe eyes, which quickly widen in fear. "My Lady... Your Highness," she stutters as she tries to figure out how to address me. Finally she settles on, "Godslayer," which suits me just fine. "My apologies—my sincerest apologies. I just... I only wanted to see it for myself. The kelpie, I mean. I heard the guards talking about it and I've seen you riding it and—"

"She," I say, cutting off her petrified ramblings. "Her name is Barra."

"Barra," the woman repeats.

I step up to the stall door and allow myself a small smile as my old friend bumps my cheek with the soft sealskin of her nose. I reach up and scratch the spot she likes at the base of her ear for a few seconds before I turn my attention back to the woman.

She's standing rigidly in the aisle, her eyes fixed upon me. Is she afraid of me? Does she think I'll punish her for her presumptive behavior? I watch her and wait to see what she will do.

After several tense seconds, she ducks down in an awkward curtsy and says, "Please pardon my insolence, Your High... Godslayer. It will not happen again."

"I wouldn't deprive Barra of a good meal," I reply. Horror flashes over the lady's face, and I realize that I may have just implied that I'd feed her to the kelpie, so I hurry to add, "She likes fish the best. If you ask the cooks nicely, they'll give you her favorites."

The woman nods, but she still looks a bit queasy.

And while I enjoy the respect I've earned as the Godslayer, I do not want to rule through fear. I want my people to trust me to defend them, to rely on me when they need help. Perhaps I've gotten so carried away with my new station that I've forgotten what it was like to have nothing, to be nobody, to be at the whims and commands of others.

So I ask, with great effort, "What is your name, my lady?"

The Demigod eyes me for a moment, as though she thinks I'm playing some sort of trick on her, but then she once again drops into a curtsy and answers, "Lady Carolissa, Godslayer."

I hold out my hand out between us in an offer of friendship. The action is automatic after so many years spent among my fellow Starless soldiers.

But when Carolissa stares down at my outstretched palm with equal parts surprise and confusion, I realize that I've never seen any Demigods share such a gesture. They curtsy and bow and kiss fingers, but they do not shake hands.

We stand there awkwardly, me with my hand out and the lady unsure of what to do, before I let my arm drop down to my side. I am once again reminded that I'm an outsider here, even after I killed the usurper and claimed one half of the throne for my own.

My eyes slide over to Barra. That's a safe topic, one that we may find common ground on.

So I ask, "What interest do you have in kelpies, my lady?"

The mortifying spell is broken as her eyes light up. "I've never seen one until now, but I read about them in books. Is it true that they'll devour men whole?"

I nod.

"The guards say you cast a spell on this one. Is that also accurate?" she continues eagerly. It's like a dam has broken and her excitement is flooding right over her well-bred manners. I can't say that I mind this new development.

To her latest question, I shake my head. Barra stays with me by choice. We've long since reached an accord. I keep her fed, and she cleans up my messes.

Carolissa stares at me now with open curiosity. All prior traces of fear are gone, replaced by bright interest. "I've heard all the stories about you," she says. "Did you really slay a dragon?"

I nod

"And the strix?"

I nod.

Admiration tempers her features. "You must have seen every creature on this continent."

To this, I shrug.

"I would love to observe some of them someday," she sighs. Yearning threads through her words, and I wonder if she, like Ressa, has never ventured outside the city limits. "It's my dream to study the fauna of Alastria, to create my own books like the ones in the library. But for now, I just copy the sketches I can find."

"That sounds like a noble goal," I say. While it's not a particular passion of mine, it's impossible to miss the way this Demigod's face transforms when talking about such creatures. She looks so young, really just on the cusp of becoming a woman, and I find myself hoping that she does make her way out into the kingdom to see her monsters and draw her pictures.

"Alas, it's not one fit for a lady of the Celestial Court," she laments. And with that, the light in her eyes fades, replaced once again with the flat dullness of a courtier. "I'm sorry, Godslayer. I should go. I've taken up enough of your time already, and you've been very kind."

A coil of sadness unfurls within me. I don't know what to say to her other than what I already have, so I settle on the only thing I can think of.

"Remember to bring Barra fish next time," I remind her. "And I would like to see your sketches, if you're inclined to share them."

Carolissa stares at me in disbelief, but she's far too polite to decline, and so she eventually musters up the courage to nod. Then she offers me one last curtsy, this one smoother than the others, and retreats down the aisle toward the yard.

I watch her go.

It's the first time I've felt any sort of camaraderie with any of the ladies of the Celestial Court. It was a pleasant, if brief, experience, and

I wonder what would happen if I were to seek out Carolissa's company in the future.

She's interesting, if not a little strange, and she wasn't afraid of the kelpie. And after a few minutes, she wasn't afraid of *me*.

I smile up at my trusted companion.

Perhaps a friend of Barra's could one day be a friend of mine.

CHAPTER 6

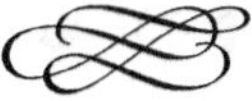

SYRAN

Lyanndra is right.

Ressa is dangerous, and we have no idea what she's capable of or what she wants. The blinking shadow, too, troubles me more than I want to admit.

What is it?

What part does it play in all of this?

Coupled with this morning's disastrous oversight from Orobos, I fear that I've disrespected Lyanndra. She did advise me that my top pick for general was unsuitable, and if I had listened to her earlier, we may have already found Ressa.

And I'm well aware that my focus on my former betrothed must make Lyanndra uncomfortable, even if my crossed star doesn't show it. Does she somehow think that my drive to capture Ressa is due to affection rather than alarm?

The thought curdles in my gut, and I suddenly feel the need to find my future queen, to make sure that she knows the truth of my motivations and the wholeness of my devotion to her.

But where is she?

It's been several hours since the Godslayer departed for the stables, and I have not seen her since. It's possible that she's still out riding, but perhaps I'll find her somewhere else, such as in the library or at the training grounds.

Yet, when both of those searches prove fruitless, I make my way to the yard beyond the barracks. She must still be tending to that great beast of hers. If I have to camp out amidst the muck and mire of the stables to wait for her return, so be it. It's a small sacrifice to make sure my crossed star knows just how much I care for her.

But as luck would have it, just as I round the side of the palace, I catch sight of her. Her windswept hair is loose, framing her face in a honeyed cascade. She's wearing a baggy tunic–*one of mine*, I realize–tucked into a pair of simple trousers.

Need rushes through me as I drink in her casual appearance. There's a fresh ease about her, I observe, and I'm glad to see her in better spirits after such a fraught morning.

When she notices me, her hazel eyes light up, and both my chest and trousers tighten further. How fortunate am I to have a creature as fierce as the Godslayer gaze upon me with such passion?

It's all I can do not to run to her as we close the distance between us. But my control snaps once she's within reach, and I instantly sweep her into a tight embrace. To my delight, she melts against my chest and draws her arms around my torso before letting out a relieved sigh, like she's glad to see me.

We stand like that for a long time. Though I wish we could linger, the feeling of her pressed against me, and the way she smells of leather and horse is driving me wild. I know that if I don't pull away now, I'll end up throwing her over my shoulder and carrying her to our chambers, where I'll show her exactly how enticing I find her.

So I step back, allowing cool air to rush into the sudden space between us, and offer her my arm instead. "Walk with me?" I request.

She nods and tucks her hand into the crook of my elbow. I'm glad to see that the skin of her knuckles is mostly healed, though some of the scabs remain. Her wrist, too, looks better.

For a few minutes, we're content to stroll through the palace grounds. I lead her past the barracks and into the cobblestoned courtyard, where several other Demigods and Starless are occupied with idle chatter. Seeking a little more privacy, I guide us to the training grounds, which stand empty while the guards are out on patrol.

"Did you enjoy your ride?" I ask once I'm satisfied we're alone.

Lyanndra nods.

I was hoping that she'd have more to say, if only to delay this difficult conversation, and now I find myself at a loss for words.

"I owe you an apology," I manage after a few uncomfortable seconds. "I fear that I dismissed your counsel too easily, regarding both Ressa and the matter with the generals. I haven't given you the respect you deserve. I... I'm sorry."

Her eyes widen at my words, and I struggle to read her reaction. Does she accept my contrition? Or does she think me a fool?

"The truth is, I'm afraid," I admit, unable to stop myself now that I've started. "I worry that I made the wrong decision in sparing Ressa, and that the deaths of those guards are my fault. What if she hurts more people? What if she hurts *you*?"

The question strips me bare, down to the very bones.

Because I'd let Ressa murder a hundred soldiers or raze entire villages if it meant I could keep Lyanndra safe. If the kingdom crumbled to ash around us, if Alastria burned until there was nothing left but stardust, I would let it, if I could spare her.

I meant what I said to her here on the training grounds only a few short weeks ago.

For her, I will always yield.

"Syran," she murmurs in a voice so quiet that I barely recognize my own name on her lips. She brings both her hands up to cup my cheeks as her eyes seek out mine. What does she see in them?

The shadow of my father?

A weak, frightened man pretending to be king?

But then she stretches up and presses her lips to mine, and the doubts wash away in a tidal wave of heat.

I cling to her like a miracle.

She's moonlight in my hands, radiant, guiding me home. Her mouth molds to mine as she forgives me with all that she is, and I am lost to her.

I need her.

I ache for her.

I want to drive my name from her lips again and again until she knows no other.

I lo–

I'm distracted when Lyanndra breaks the kiss only to drag her mouth across the sharp angle of my jaw, and I groan as her teeth graze my skin. And when she nips her way down the hollow of my neck, something curled deep within me ignites.

Striking fast, I spin her in my arms so that her back is flush with my chest. From the way she squirms against me, I'm absolutely certain that she can feel the hard press of my cock as I roll my hips into hers. She tips her head back and lets out the most sinful sound I've ever heard, and I implode.

"Do you know what you do to me, Lyanndra?" I hiss into her ear. "Do you know how I burn for you?"

"Show me," she pleads.

That's all the invitation I need.

I want to scoop her up in my arms, but I have enough blood left in my brain to remember that she prefers her privacy, so I refrain. Instead, I step back from her and once again hold out my arm.

She stares at me for a moment, her pupils blown with want and her face flushed a delicious shade of pink, before she folds her hand into my elbow.

Unspoken need blazes between us as we walk, arm in arm, back around the front of the palace. When we reach the courtyard, none of our subjects pay us any more heed than a passing nod or curtsy, and if they notice the way I attempt to hide my arousal with my free hand or the unmistakable desire sparking in Lyanndra's eyes, they have the good sense not to acknowledge it.

We're just about to pass through the grand doors of the Celestial Court when a commotion sounds at our backs.

The golden gate that separates the palace grounds from the city of Nexus clangs open, and I turn swiftly enough to see a rider burst through. He's not a Celestial Knight, but the white mantle he wears about his shoulders indicates that he's a messenger. His traveling clothes are rumpled, and his body is slumped with exhaustion.

How far has this Demigod come? What urgent matter would have him ride to the point of collapse?

Lyanndra glances over at me, concern quickly chasing the lust from her eyes. "Ressa?" she wonders aloud.

But when the messenger dismounts and pushes through the growing crowd of onlookers toward us, I'm gripped by the terrible suspicion that this is something worse than one madwoman's rampage.

When he reaches us, I hold up one hand, silencing the speculative murmurs of the assembled Demigods.

"Your Highness," the messenger says. He drops his head in a respectful nod. By the way he sways on his feet, I determine that this man's journey has been long and arduous.

"What news do you bring?" I ask.

"I ride with word from the Southern Caldera," he tells us. At my side, Lyanndra tenses. "This morning, a great trembling of the earth was felt in the villages closest to the mountain."

This morning? I'm aware of how fast the messengers work, but this Demigod's skill is most impressive. In turn, I will make sure that he eats well and rests for as long as he desires.

"Were there any casualties?" Lyanndra questions. There's an edge to her voice that makes me nervous, like she knows something I do not.

"Dozens," the messenger replies. "Probably more. The destruction is widespread. Several Starless settlements were leveled by the quake."

She stiffens further, and I'm surprised to hear panic laced into her next inquiry. "Which settlements?"

"Gry, Breem, and Loryn took the most damage," he explains. "Ryv and Sheel escaped the worst of it."

The report is nothing short of terrible. That kind of ruin in the three Starless villages closest to the peak of the Southern Caldera is a tragedy for the entire the kingdom. We will have to send out an aid caravan as soon as possible. If messengers run ahead to the many settlements along the route, perhaps other support can get there sooner. And we can spare a battalion of Celestial Knights to help restore order and assist with rebuilding.

"Thank you," I offer to the Demigod. "You may find quarter in the palace. Whatever you may need, you only have to ask."

To my surprise, the messenger shakes his head. "That's not all, Your Highness," he says.

Lyanndra narrows her gaze onto him once more. While I know that her loyalty to the Starless, and to Alastria, runs deep, she's more agitated than I've ever seen her. There's fear in her eyes, raw and wild, and that delightful blush that crept over her features just minutes ago has faded to a worrying shade of white.

Once again, I feel as though I'm missing something that she sees with crystal clarity. Then it strikes me.

Does she have some connection with the Southern Caldera?

I know that she traveled across most of the continent in her time as a soldier and then later as the Godslayer. I recall that, when I first came upon her in the snowy tundra of the north, she wore a piece of the hammered bronze armor favored by the Starless of the Caldera.

But she's never mentioned the sunbaked landscape of Alastria's southernmost reach, and she certainly doesn't sport the brown skin and black hair common to those who herald from the shadow of the mountain.

So why does her voice shake when she prompts, "What? What else?"

The messenger hesitates for just a moment, and then reveals, "The reports... they're strange. Unreliable."

"Tell me," Lyanndra insists in a tone that leaves no room for argument.

"There was a noise," he says, "just after the ground shook. I was told that it sounded like shrieking. Like a roar."

"A roar?" I repeat. "From what?"

"Something big," the messenger replies.

Lyanndra, who's gone so pale that her face is practically gray, looks up at me with wide and frightened eyes. And when she speaks, a thrill of terror traces up my spine. "Something old," she whispers. "Something that was supposed to be sleeping."

And when she finally pulls her eyes from mine, this time casting her horrified gaze over to the southern horizon, I am certain that she knows more than she's letting on.

"It's waking up," she mutters. "By the stars, *it's waking up.*"

CHAPTER 7

Lyanndra

Breem.

Years have passed since I last heard the name of the village that lies closest to the towering peaks of the Southern Caldera, and it's been longer still since I left that place for what was supposed to be the final time.

Yet, I can picture the cracked and arid landscape perfectly in my mind. It's hard to forget the ancient black rock of the cliffs that rise up to blot out the sky, nor the vast network of caverns and tunnels that honeycomb the sheer sides of the dormant mountain.

How many times did I climb those craggy outcroppings as a girl? And what wonders I found in the many caverns dotting the mountainside! From steaming springs to strange white lizards that were so accustomed to the dark that they had no eyes at all, there was always some new curiosity to uncover. Back then, I thought that I would never tire of those explorations.

I recall a particular adventure, the one that changed everything, where I stumbled upon the entrance of a new cave on a scorching afternoon. Eager for relief from the sun's unrelenting glare, I ducked into the cool darkness of the earth's embrace. I expected to see stalagmites and stalactites yawning from the rock like the teeth of some petrified beast, and I was not disappointed.

But I had not expected to find something old.

Something sleeping.

The vague, molten shape of it is seared into my mind, some great, slumbering thing barely comprehensible to my youthful mind.

I ran from it then, and I never told anybody what I witnessed. Some animal part of me understood that this thing was not meant for Starless eyes, and if anybody were to wake it up, the consequences would be dire.

And so I kept my terrible secret.

And so the thing beneath the mountain slept.

Until now.

"Many of the Starless homes nearest to the Caldera are no longer habitable," the messenger explains to Syran, drawing me back to the present. "The buildings that still stand may not survive the aftershocks."

"We'll need to send aid out as soon as possible," my crossed star comments. "I assume that there will be refugees seeking shelter and food?"

The exhausted Demigod nods. "Yes, Your Highness."

"How many?"

"Several hundred, at least," he replies. "More, if the quakes worsen."

I know from experience that the possibility is more likely than not. I remember how the minor shifts in the earth would rumble through the very rock beneath my feet in the shadow of the Caldera, rattling every object in the homestead and sending treacherous showers of shale raining down from the sides of the mountain. They would rarely come alone. Sometimes, the shaking would roll through the village over a span of several hours or even days.

As a result, the many structures in those Starless settlements, from barns to houses, are built to withstand such tremors. The fact that so much destruction has occurred is a testament to the severity of this latest quake.

What could have caused such a dramatic disaster?

My first thought is the thing under the mountain. Did its sudden stirring prompt the earth to churn around it?

But the messenger said that the roar happened after the quake, not before. Perhaps the creature woke from the force of the tremor, not the other way around.

My mind then turns to Ressa.

She's the only Demigod I know of that holds dominion over the rocks and minerals of Alastria. The last time I saw her wield her abilities, she was barely able to throw a few chunks of stone over a short distance. But while I don't deny that her powers are dangerous, especially after she dispatched those two guards down in the dungeons with such ferocity, I don't believe that she's capable of something of this magnitude.

But if not her, then what?

At this point, does it even matter?

The messenger's news replays through my head.

A great tremor of the earth.

Dozens of casualties, probably more.

A roar.

Something waking up.

For the first time in many years, I allow myself to picture what I left behind in the village of Breem so long ago. Guilt bubbles up in my throat like bile.

I know what I have to do.

"I must ride to the Southern Caldera immediately," I say aloud. There's no taming the panic in my voice, not when it thunders through my blood and grips my fraying nerves with razor-sharp talons.

Syran turns to me, his face fraught with confusion and concern. "Let's discuss this inside," he urges quietly. I follow his gaze to where various guards and courtiers gather around us, eager to eavesdrop, and nod. He offers his arm, and I take it, allowing him to lead me into the palace while our people mutter and speculate in the courtyard at our backs.

We don't speak as we navigate the now-familiar route up to Syran's chambers. Beneath the seething fear, my whole body feels numb. Why is this happening now, when I've finally found my place in this kingdom at my crossed star's side?

Why is this even happening at all?

I have no answers. All I can do is picture the faces of those I left behind and hope to the stars that they're unharmed.

Once we're safely sequestered in the privacy of Syran's chambers, I drop my arm from his and slump down onto the edge of the bed. I can guess the kinds of questions he will ask, and I want to answer none of them.

Sure enough, he immediately demands, "Lyanndra, what is going on?"

"I need to go to Breem," I insist.

"Breem?" he repeats. "The whole of the Southern Caldera is crumbling. Why is that one village so important?"

A sliver of me wants to tell him, but I've held it close for so long. Breem isn't supposed to be a part of me anymore. I left it far behind to become a knight, the Godslayer, and, now, Queen of Alastria.

And yet, I can't escape it now.

All I can say is, "I have to go."

"This is madness," he argues. "We'll send soldiers out to help. An aid caravan and a battalion can do more than either one of us alone."

"It's my duty as the Godslayer," I push back, but the statement lacks my usual conviction, even though there is some truth to it. Of course, I should go and assist my people during this terrible time. Seeing me, their Starless hero, would give them hope.

But that's not the real reason why I must do this.

I have to go to Breem.

"Maybe," Syran says. "But I know you, Lyanndra. I know how dedicated you are to our people. And I also know that you aren't telling me the truth."

His words sting, because he's right. Tears gather in the corners of my eyes, and it's all I can do to blink them back. I can't even look at him for fear of what I'll see on his face.

He knows I'm keeping something from him. Does he hate me for it? And if I tell him, will he think me deceitful?

But to my surprise, he drops to his knees before me, forcing my eyes to meet his. I'm shocked to see that there's no judgment there, only distress. He reaches out and curls his fingers around mine. His skin is warm with the heat of the midnight flame that burns within him, but even his black fire can't chase away the terror that wells in my chest.

"Please, Lyanndra," he begs. "Please, talk to me."

I shake my head, and this time, I can't stop the tears from rolling down my cheeks. I don't even understand why I'm crying. Guilt? Fear? Something else entirely?

And when Syran speaks again, it somehow makes me feel even worse.

"If you need to go, I won't stop you," he says in a tone so gentle it skewers me right through my heart. "I'll always chase you, wherever you wander, but I won't imprison you again. Go if you must. But I just want to know *why*."

Something inside me gives. A sob rips from my chest before I can stop it, and then I'm past the point of no return.

Syran tugs my hands, drawing me down from the mattress and onto the cold marble floor of his chambers. He gathers me into his arms and holds me tight against him, as though he's afraid I'll disappear if he lets me go for even a moment. I bury my face into his chest and breathe in the ashen scent of him.

What will he think of me when he finds out the truth?

The panicked part of my mind whispers that his opinion of me will falter, that he'll judge me for where I came from and what I did.

But he already knows that I'm Starless, and, by extension, common. He's seen me with blood on my hands and has tasted every inch of me. Wouldn't he accept this aspect of me too? Wouldn't he accept my greatest shame?

There's only one way to find out.

I am the Godslayer.

I have faced the divine and walked away victorious.

And before I can remember that I am also, in fact, a coward, I force myself to speak.

"Something sleeps beneath the mountain," I whisper.

Syran stiffens against me. "Under the Southern Caldera?" he asks.

I nod into his chest, still not ready to meet his gaze. "I saw it," I say. My voice, which once rang across the battlefield as I announced the death of a king, sounds thin and muffled as I press deeper against the front of my crossed star's tunic. "I was just a little girl, but I never forgot."

"What did you see?" he presses with tenderness I do not deserve.

I think about that for a moment before I realize that I don't have an answer for him. Even when I shut my eyes and try to draw the memory closer, all I recall is the way the molten shape pulsed with heat as it slumbered deep beneath the earth. And I can still taste the fear of it, of knowing that the thing I was looking at was so wholly unnatural that I wouldn't be able to describe it adequately even if I tried.

"I don't know," I tell him finally. "But it was big. And if it wakes..." I shake my head. "It could destroy not just the village, but the whole region."

"This is bad," Syran breathes, and I'm inclined to agree with him. Then he muses, "But if this thing had already woken, the messengers would have brought us reports of it by now. Perhaps it was roused but not fully awoken. Perhaps it will simply fall back asleep."

It's reasonable enough, though something in my gut tells me that it's only a matter of time before the situation worsens. Who knows how long this thing has been sleeping, undisturbed, beneath the Caldera? Maybe it's taking its time, stretching and yawning until it's ready to come out and devour us whole.

"Lyanndra?" My name on Syran's lips finally draws my eyes to his, and when I meet his gaze, I know what he's going to ask next. "Why Breem?"

"I...."

For a moment, I freeze.

If I tell him now, I will never be able to take it back. Out of all the people in Alastria, Syran knows the most about me. We've danced and laughed and fucked. He knows all of my favorite foods and the books that I like and the noises that I make when he laps at me with his wicked tongue. He's seen me at my very weakest, when his poisoned flame nearly killed me, and he's been by my side as I've felled our enemies in a bloody cascade.

I will trust him with my past.

I will trust him with my shame.

Sensing the shift in my resolve, Syran cups my cheeks in his hands and presses his forehead against mine. "Tell me," he pleads. "Give me all of you."

And I do.

"I herald from Breem," I admit. "I abandoned my family there."

And then I utter the words I promised myself I would never again say aloud.

"I left them there to die."

CHAPTER 8

Lyanndra has a family.

I don't know why that admission shocks me, but it does. I've always thought of her as a lonesome creature, a woman more suited to solitude than society. It's even harder to picture her as somebody's daughter or sister, especially when I visualize her in her tarnished armor and golden helm. When she's the Godslayer, she's untouchable, unreachable by all arms except for mine.

But here, in my embrace, she's just Lyanndra. She's stripped bare, naked without her steel shell and monstrous greatsword.

Tears streak down her face, and her eyes are wide with desperation. Looking at her now, it strikes me that this is the first time I've ever seen her cry. Even when she was recovering from what should have been the fatal blow of my flaming sword, when the pain must have eaten her from the inside out, she did not crumble.

How long has she been holding this in?

How many years has she carried this guilt?

"I left them there to die," she repeats. Her eyes search my face as though she thinks I'll pull away from her, but she will not be rid of me that easily. "Do you understand?"

"I don't," I answer honestly. "But I want to, whenever you're ready to tell me more."

She draws in a shaky breath, and I take that moment to consider what I know about her.

Back before she accepted me, before I even knew her name, I sent Torran to find out whatever he could about the Godslayer. I wanted every whisper and every rumor, anything he could dig up. But when we finally had a chance to speak of his journey after the failed coup, he could reveal nothing to me that I didn't already know.

He couldn't find out who she was or where she came from. As far as I know, he still doesn't even know her name.

By all rights, she should feel like a stranger to me. After all, we've barely known each other for a year, and she wished me dead for most of that time.

But I know her.

I *know* her.

She can't hide the honor with which she meets her enemies on the battlefield or the gentleness in her hands when she lies in bed beside me. I've seen her show mercy and rage, grief and ecstasy.

She is the Godslayer.

She is Lyanndra.

She is my crossed star, the woman I will make my queen.

Whatever she did in her past, whatever she went through, it brought her to this place. How could I ever think less of her for becoming better than what she once was?

And while there's still so much I don't know about her, I am absolutely certain that I want all of her, every secret and every flaw, all that she is.

Lyanndra shifts in my arms so that her head once more rests against my chest. I don't like that she feels the need to hide from me, but I can't deny that the way she burrows into my embrace for comfort warms my heart more than any flame.

"Even when I was very young, I knew I didn't belong in Breem," she starts. Her voice is soft and resigned. "My parents took me in from a traveler when I was just a babe. I was different right from the start."

That explains her ruddy features and her golden hair, which are so unlike those native to the Southern Caldera.

"I never wanted what was expected of me. I would rather explore the caves or wander by myself than help the other women tend to the homestead," she continues. "I always dreamed of running away and making a different life for myself."

"You did," I murmur. "You became a knight."

"Eventually," she agrees. "But not soon enough." She sighs, and, from the wetness seeping through the front of my tunic, I surmise that the tears have started once again. I bring one hand to the small of her back and press my palm against her spine, holding her close. With the other, I draw slow, soothing circles in the space between her shoulder blades.

"What happened?" I ask.

She seems to shrink further into me as she answers. "I became a woman. Or at least, I started to. As was the custom, my parents arranged a betrothal to a boy from a merchant family that settled in the village a few years before. The dowry was promised, and the date was set."

I do my best not to let Lyanndra feel how I tense against her. I am acutely aware that the events of which she speaks likely occurred well over a decade ago, but the mere thought of her being promised to another man churns the flames in my chest to rage.

But I don't want her to think that my anger is directed at her, so I force my body to relax as she continues her tale.

She doesn't seem to notice my shift in mood. Instead she says, "I told the boy that I didn't want to marry him. I was young, and stupid, and I thought that would be enough."

"But it wasn't?"

She shakes her head against me. "He told his father, and he, in turn, threatened my family. He said that if I didn't honor the betrothal and raise the dowry, he would harm them." Shame floods her voice as she finishes. "So I ran, and I left them to their fate. I left them there to die."

"Did they?" I ask. She finally pulls away from my chest to stare at me with eyes swimming in guilt and confusion, and I add, "Die?"

The question seems to take her off guard. She pauses for a moment before she replies, "I don't know. I never went back. I *couldn't*. If he did kill them, how could I face that?"

I watch her for a long moment.

Is this really the dark and looming secret that's chewed upon her conscience for all these years? It seems so silly that Lyanndra, the fiercest warrior I know, would be frightened of learning the truth. If this happened to her today, she would slay that merchant where he stood without a second thought.

But then I try to see it from the perspective of her younger self. She wasn't a battle-hardened knight back then. She was just a restless child. I can imagine her at that age, her face softer and without the crows' feet that gather at the edges of her eyes when she smiles. She was trapped in a life she did not want, bound by the ceaseless expectations of others.

"You did what you had to do," I say softly. "You made your choice, but so did your parents. They must have known that wasn't what you wanted."

"It was just the way things were done," she replies.

"That doesn't mean they were right."

"And I was?" she argues. "They never mistreated me. They were never cruel. They considered me their own blood, and I betrayed them. I ran because I was selfish."

"You ran because you were afraid," I point out. "And because you wanted more than they could give. Is that so wrong?"

She doesn't seem to have an answer for that. Instead, she just continues her story where she left off. "The night after the boy's father came to the homestead and threatened my parents, I stole my own father's armor and one of the horses from the barn. There was a band of soldiers passing through. I found them where they were camped on the outskirts of town and simply disappeared into the midst of them. Nobody ever questioned me."

"And you became a knight," I say.

She nods. "I did."

"And you never went back."

She shakes her head.

"So your family could be alive and well?" I challenge.

Her eyes widen, as though she's never actually considered that possibility before. But then her expression darkens, and she snaps, "Why are you defending me? What I did was unforgivable."

"It was human," I say. "And in the meantime, you've sent yourself to the gallows for a crime that might not have even come to pass." Softening my tone, I reveal to her, "There are things I haven't told you, either, things that bring me more shame that I care to admit."

That gets her attention. Her gaze sharpens, and I can feel the question building behind her eyes even before she asks, "What could you possibly be ashamed of?"

I draw in a deep, unsteady breath. Lyanndra was brave enough to share the worst of herself with me. Now, I must show her the same devotion.

"When I was about the same age as you were when you left Breem, I held certain beliefs that… that haunt me." It takes great effort to continue. "Like my father before me, I was convinced that the Starless were nothing more than animals. I thought they should be eradicated."

Now, I understand why Lyanndra hid her face from me earlier. It wasn't that she didn't want me to see her. She was afraid of what she'd find written on my features. The same urge fills me now, but I do not give into it.

"What made you change your mind?" she breathes, as though she can't believe that I once held such hatred in my heart.

"I stepped past the walls of Nexus," I explain. "I spoke with the Starless and found them to be no different from me, at least in any of the ways that truly matter. And I started seeing my father for who he was: a cruel, isolated man who mistook fear for power. But I am still ashamed of the way I was, even now."

Lyanndra takes my hand in both of hers. "You were young," she murmurs.

"So were you," I counter. "Perhaps it's time that both of us stop punishing ourselves for what we did in ignorance."

For a moment, I think she's going to agree, but then she shakes her head. When she speaks, her voice is full of tired conviction. "I have to go back to Breem. I abandoned my family once. I can't do it again."

I want nothing more than to keep Lyanndra here at my side. But I swore that I would never hold her back again, and I know that she would easily best me if I tried. So I reply, "Then don't. Go to them."

Lyanndra's eyes widen in disbelief, but I'm not quite done yet.

"Will you ride with a host?" I request. "For my peace of mind?"

She hesitates for only a moment before she nods. Relief wells in my chest. I expected her to push back against this compromise, but I'm pleasantly surprised that she's so quick to meet me in the middle. While I don't want to see her go, I would rather she have a battalion of Celestial Knights at her back than nobody but Barra to keep her company.

I lean down and brush my lips over hers before bringing my mouth to the shell of her ear. "And don't beseech me to come with you," I plead. "After what happened with Kartas, one of us needs to stay here to guard the throne. But I'm powerless to resist whatever you may beg of me, so please, do not ask this of me."

Lyanndra shivers against me. The thought of losing her to Alastria, if only for a short while, makes me want to clutch her tight and never let her go. But she is the Godslayer, and she was never meant to be caged.

She will come home to me.

And if she doesn't, I will make good on my vow.

I will chase her, wherever she may roam.

To the very stars.

"Wait for me here," she breathes. She makes no effort to hide the pain in her voice, even as she honors my request. "And know that my heart will remain with you, no matter where I go."

I rest my forehead against hers, sealing our pact. "Always."

"Always," she agrees.

And then I kiss her like it's the last time. I want to memorize the shape of her lips against mine, the curve of her tongue as she yields her mouth to me, the very taste of her grief. Now that we have heard each other's shame, there is no barrier left between us. She is mine, and I am hers–completely.

Lyanndra is the first to pull away. Her face is once again flushed, this time from desire rather than tears. "You don't hate me?" she asks.

"I could never," I assure her. I want nothing more than to kiss her again and show her just how much I mean those words, but I hold myself back. Though I now know the truth of her connection to Breem, she still has not explained what, exactly, she saw beneath the mountain. So instead of crushing my lips to hers, I ask, "What of the creature?"

She shakes her head. "I've never seen, or even heard of, anything like it since," she replies. "I don't know *what* it is."

Then her eyes sharpen, and she's once again the fearless warrior I'm used to.

"But I know somebody who might."

CHAPTER 9

Lyanndra

Guilt claws at me with vicious talons.

Even though Syran has absolved me, I cannot seem to forgive myself.

As I lead him out of his chambers and down to the library, where I hope to find the one Demigod I know of who's interested in the vast array of creatures that call Alastria home, the sour dread doesn't leave me.

I have no choice but to go to Breem and attempt to atone for my sins. But what will I encounter once I arrive there? Will I find graves instead of familiar faces, bloodstains instead of my brothers and sisters?

A fresh wave of regret shatters over me when I consider the possibility that my family is somehow still there, intact and unharmed.

After so many years, will they even remember me? Will they hate me for how I left them? Do they even realize that I became the Godslayer and will soon be Queen of Alastria?

Even worse, what if they survived my betrayal, only to perish in this latest disaster?

The questions plague me in a noxious cloud. I'm so consumed that I barely pay any mind when Syran tugs me to a halt in order to instruct a nearby guard to find Torran and direct the old Demigod to meet us in the library with the greatest of haste.

"Breathe, Lyanndra," Syran murmurs in my ear once the task is done. His hand tightens in mine. "We need our wits about us."

I nod, though I do not feel any calmer.

The rest of our journey through the glowing corridors of the Celestial Court is a blur. It isn't until we step into the warm silence of the library that the world finally seems to slip back into full focus.

Golden evening light filters in through the stained glass windows, painting a vast patchwork of colored motes along the marble floor. Shelves, each laden with more books than any person could possibly read in one lifetime, rise up in terraces to kiss the eaves. It's my favorite place in the palace, aside from the silk sheets and wicked pleasures of Syran's bed.

A handful of courtiers and off-duty guards lounge in plush chairs or linger between the shelves. I scan their faces as we pass, but I don't spot the one I'm hoping to see.

"Is she here?" Syran asks, keeping his voice low so it doesn't ring throughout the cavernous space.

I shake my head. "Let's try upstairs."

We climb the golden staircase to the second level of the terrace, but she's not there, either. It isn't until we reach the third and final story that I catch a glimpse of brown hair and that sharp nose buried in a book.

"Lady Carolissa," I say.

She jumps at the sound of my voice, and I immediately feel bad. I didn't realize how consumed she was in her reading, and frightening her even more than I did down in the stables earlier today was never my intention.

But she recovers soon enough. After a few shocked seconds and a wide-eyed glance at Syran where he lingers at my back, she stands and curtsies like she did before. "Godslayer. Your Highness."

"We have no time for formalities, my lady," Syran interjects, waving away her bow. "We need your help."

Panic flashes over Carolissa's delicate features. "Help? From me?" She gasps.

I nod and take a seat at her table. Only when Syran claims the chair beside me does she sink back down into hers. "We're trying to identify a creature," I tell her. "Something… unusual. Do you think you could assist us?"

"Oh." She taps her nails, which are painted the same deep ruby shade as her dress, nervously against the cover of the book she was reading when we so rudely interrupted her. There's a drawing of some fanged beast inlaid upon the cover, which only bolsters my hope in this strange but endearing Demigod. But then my heart constricts as she murmurs, "Wouldn't you rather ask one of the scholars?"

"Are you not a learned woman?" I push back. "If I wanted to speak to some musty old man, I would have done so."

Her eyes fix on something behind me and widen even more, now to an almost comical extent. She opens her mouth, and then shuts it again quickly.

"And here I thought my presence was requested." A thin, brittle voice chuckles from over my shoulder.

I nearly shrivel up and die from embarrassment as I realize that Torran has come to join us, as Syran asked. Trying to save face, I swivel in my seat and say, "Old? Perhaps. But never musty. You're most welcome at our table, Torran."

The ancient Demigod laughs again and accepts my invitation. As he lowers himself down into the last remaining chair, I marvel at how quickly he arrived, especially after climbing all of those stairs with only his gnarled cane for support.

"Is the news true?" he asks once he's settled. "There was a quake in the Southern Caldera?"

"Unfortunately, yes," Syran confirms. "We're told the damage is both devastating and widespread. But that's not all. There are reports that the villagers heard a great roar echo through the land shortly after the tremors began."

Carolissa latches onto that detail immediately, asking, "A roar, Your Highness? From what?"

"That's what we're trying to determine," he says, "and what we're hoping you can help with."

Doubt creeps across her face. "I… I don't know much," she stammers. "I'm not sure how well I can assist you."

"Will you at least try?" I request. I keep my tone as gentle as possible, but still, she blanches.

"Torran is far more knowledgeable than I," she demurs.

But the old Demigod shakes his head. "I may be a scholar, Lady Carolissa, but I am no expert in the myriad fauna of Alastria. You, on the other hand, have read every bestiary in the library no less than twice."

A red flush tints the young woman's cheeks, as though she's not used to receiving compliments where they are due. But Torran's words are enough to break her resolve, for she sighs and acquiesces, "Very well. I shall do my best, though I can make no promises."

"That's all we ask," Syran assures her.

Carolissa draws in a deep breath and then asks, "What do you know of this creature?"

Syran turns to me. I accept the silent invitation to speak and say, "I saw it once, but it was many years ago. The memory is… unclear."

"Legs?" she asks.

I blink.

"How many?" she clarifies after a long moment.

"It was hard to tell," I admit, feeling decidedly unhelpful. "Arms, legs—there were a lot of them. And its body was… molten. Like rock."

"Did you see a face?" she inquires.

I close my eyes and try to recall the details. I have the impression of features, but they're not clear in my mind's eye. I'm starting to get frustrated.

After several painful seconds, Syran seems to pick up on my

growing exasperation because he suggests, "Perhaps you could draw it."

The idea comes as a relief, and I nod in agreement. But once I have a quill in hand, I find myself struggling with this task too. My best art is forged on the battlefield, not on parchment. Yet, I do what I can, even if my crude rendering of the creatures comes out blotted and misshapen.

When I'm done, I pass the rudimentary sketch over to Carolissa. To her credit, she has enough decorum not to laugh at it, though I can't help but catch Syran's smirk out of the corner of my eye.

He may be my crossed star, but he is also an ass.

Resisting the urge to glare at him, I instead watch Carolissa. Just like when we talked of Barra in the stables, she's completely focused on the drawing as though it's the single most interesting thing in the kingdom.

"Molten," she mutters under her breath. "Elemental, maybe? And limbs like those…" Her face pales, and she immediately glances to Torran. "Elemental. Do you understand? I… I fear I know what this creature is, but… I may not speak of it."

The ancient Demigod's expression darkens. "Let me see," he urges, reaching for the sketch. I don't miss the way Carolissa's fingers shake when she passes it to him. Dread curls in the pit of my stomach as horror clouds Torran's usually placid features. "By the stars," he whispers. "This is… impossible."

"What is it?" Syran demands. I can tell from his clipped tone that he feels the same anxiety I do.

"Lady Carolissa, will you fetch me a tome from the Archive Room?" Torran requests. He speaks in some ancient language that I don't understand, but she seems to recognize it easily enough. Across the table, the King of Alastria bristles, never one for being ignored, but his advisor continues to do just that.

The young courtier does as Torran asks. She rises quickly and scurries off down the golden staircase, presumably to ground floor, where the Archive Room is tucked away in a shadowy corner beyond the shelves.

"What is going on?" Syran presses in the meantime.

Torran refuses to meet his eye and only shakes his head in response.

Tense silence settles down upon us in heavy drifts as we wait. I, too, burn with curiosity, but I'm well aware that Syran's most trusted advisor is also a stubborn old man. If we want answers, we will have to be patient.

My crossed star, on the other hand, seethes.

He isn't used to being kept in the dark.

At long last, the click of heeled slippers against the stairs announces Carolissa's return. She appears holding an ancient, crumbling book in her arms. I recognize the binding as dragonhide. How old must the tough material be to degrade to such an extent? And when Torran accepts the volume and flips it open on the table, I consider how many people before us must have read these pages, and I shiver. Suddenly, it feels like there are far more than four of us here.

But this is no time for superstition. Shaking off my ghosts, I ask, "What language is this?"

"Ancient Alastrian," the old Demigod replies. "An early dialect, at that." He flips through the pages until he finally lands on one particular illumination. He taps a bony finger against the drawing. "Is this the creature?" he asks.

Fear surges through me as I instantly recognize the beast that cavorts across the crumbling parchment.

"That's it!" I gasp. "That's what I saw!"

Syran leans over to study the illustration. "What is it?" he questions. "I've never seen the likes of it."

"Nor has anyone," Torran explains. "At least, not in this age." He glances at Carolissa, who can't seem to take her eyes off the drawing. "Would you like to explain, my dear?"

She shakes her head. "I cannot," she whispers. "It's blasphemous."

Torran sighs. "Very well." Then he turns his attention back to Syran and I, and begins, "This thing is called an Ushum."

Instantly, Syran recoils.

Confused and outnumbered, I ask, "A what?"

"Ushum," Torran repeats. "Are you not familiar with the stories?"

I shake my head. I'm Starless, and, while I certainly know many of the Demigod customs, I didn't grow up with the same devotion that most of them did. The majority of their more archaic legends are unknown to me, including this one.

"There are things in our religion that are canon," Torran explains, "and things that are not. One of those rejected beliefs is that, before the rise of the Celestial Gods, something else ruled in their stead."

"The Ankir," Syran interjects. "The Old Gods."

The wizened Demigod nods. "The Ankir were thought to be primitive, elemental deities heralding from beyond the very heavens. Some of the more heretical scholars even theorized that the fallen stars from which the Demigods originally drew their abilities were remnants of the slain Ankir that fell to earth after the Celestial Gods rose to power."

Dread once again pools in my veins. "And what of the Ushum?" I ask. "Is it one of the Ankir?"

"In a way," Torran replies. "In our canon, the Celestial Gods are pure and righteous. But in some of the lesser texts, it is said that the Celestial Gods and the Ankir were not always at war. Legends speculate that their unions produced bastard offspring, known as the Ushum. When the Ankir fell, the Ushum were banished to the earth so that the new order did not have to face its shame."

Finally, I understand Syran's horrified reaction and Carolissa's stark refusal to even voice this creature's name. "If this is an Ushum, are you saying that it's been sleeping beneath the Southern Caldera since the rise of the Demigods?" I question.

"If it's truly molten, as you say, perhaps it is the *reason* for the Southern Caldera in the first place," he speculates.

I think of the old stories I grew up with, of how long ago lava flowed from the mouth of the mountain. It's said the smoke was so thick that all of Alastria was blanketed in ash, and even the snow in the north turned black. Has the Ushum really been slumbering since then? And if it wakes again....

"We have to kill it," I state. "For the safety of the kingdom."

"I agree," Syran adds without hesitation. "But how does one destroy the divine?"

His eyes land on me.

I am the Godslayer, after all, but the Flaming God was only ever a man. This Ushum is far more than that. The power of the former king was likely a mere shade of this thing's ferocity.

"Torran?" I ask.

The old Demigod drags his finger down to the bottom of the page. For the first time, I realize that there's a second drawing underneath the sketch of the Ushum.

"This," he says. "This is said to be the only weapon that can kill the Ankir and, by extension, their children."

I squint at the tiny illustration. For a second, I don't understand what I'm looking at, but then it strikes me.

The curving outline is that of one of nature's most effective weapons.

It's the shape of a sharp and wicked fang.

CHAPTER 10

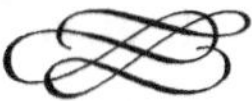

"A fang?"

My voice rings through the stunned silence that's descended over the table. Lyanndra is leaning so far over the crumbling old book that her nose is practically buried between the pages. Lady Carolissa, on the other hand, seems so frightened of the mere drawing of the Ushum that she hasn't even taken her seat again.

"That's what most of the scholars think," Torran says, meeting my eyes over the top of Lyanndra's bowed head. "In fact, it's one of the few things they all seem to agree on."

"A fang from what, exactly?" my crossed star asks without looking up.

Torran sighs. "Now, *that* is a good question. Do you see this text?" He points to a line of barely legible script that furls into the curve of the illustration. When Lyanndra nods, he reads the words aloud. The sounds make absolutely no sense to me, and when she repeats them back to him, it's clear that she's just as lost as I am.

"What does it mean?" she questions.

"I don't know," the old Demigod replies. "Nobody does."

Lyanndra finally tears her gaze from the page to stare up at Torran. She doesn't make an effort to disguise her disbelief as she asks, "Excuse me?"

"It's never been translated," he explains. "This dialect is so old that the only way to decode it is to use accounts from other scholars. But because the Ushum are considered a blasphemous topic, many of those texts were either never written or long since destroyed."

Unsatisfied with that answer, The Godslayer turns to Lady Carolissa next. "Out of all of us, you know the most about the animals found throughout the kingdom. Do you have any idea what this might say?"

The young Demigod peers down at the mysterious text. In those few seconds, I am filled with the feeble hope that she's able to do the impossible and come up with a reply, but then she shakes her head. "All I can offer is that I know the translations for most of the creatures that roam Alastria, but not this one. I do not recognize the shape of the fang, either. It comes from no creature I know."

"Nor do I," Lyanndra admits. "And I have seen a great many beasts in my time, both living and dead."

"Perhaps this creature is not from Alastria," Torran suggests.

Frustration rises in my chest as I join in the fray. "So you're telling us that the only weapon that can kill the Ushum is a fang from an animal that's completely unknown to us?"

"An animal that we do not have a translation for," Torran corrects, but the nuance matters not to me.

This is utterly ridiculous. The quakes in the Southern Caldera are bad enough. I'm going to have to make arrangements not just to send aid out to the impacted area, but to welcome refugees into Nexus if necessary. My crossed star is about to leave me for what could easily stretch on into months. Adding some legendary, heretical beast to the mix just feels like the stars have forsaken us.

And what if the Ushum wakes up?

From my many history lessons with Torran, I know that the Caldera last erupted several hundred years ago, or perhaps even further back into antiquity. Aside from the catastrophic damage to the immediate area, the cloud of ash emitted in the explosion was thick enough that it blotted out the very sun. That, in turn, ruined the year's crops, resulting in a kingdom-wide famine that decimated the population over the course of the next decade.

I will *not* let that happen under my rule.

"We need to find this fang," I state. Turning to Torran, I add, "Whatever you require to translate the text, you shall have."

My advisor nods, but his face remains grave. "I must warn you, Syran. Drawings of this weapon appear repeatedly in the text, and while I may not have a direct translation regarding its nature, I can share some of the myths surrounding it." When I nod in acquiescence, he continues, "Do you recall that I once told you that you and your crossed star are equals in power?"

"Yes," I say.

Lyanndra glances up at me with interest, and I know she wants to learn more, but there's no time for that now. She must understand because she doesn't interrupt Torran when he begins to speak again.

"The same is true for killing a god. At least, that's what the scholars propose."

"The weapon must be of equal power to that which it destroys," Lyanndra murmurs.

Torran's blue eyes flash to the Godslayer, and I catch a flash of admiration in his gaze as he confirms, "Well said."

I frown. "Does that mean that the only thing that can kill the divine is also divine?"

"I am inclined to say yes. But remember that you are a Demigod, and your equal in power is Starless. So there is a possibility that there are similar forces at play here," he points out. "Then again, the myths say that the fang may have been the weapon the Celestial Gods used to defeat the Ankir in the first place."

Once again, I feel that this situation just keeps getting worse. Now, we're looking for the fang of a divine creature in order to destroy one of its kin?

The old Demigod meets my gaze. I'm overcome with the sensation that he's not looking at me so much as *into* me, but then he blinks and the moment passes.

"If the fang is real, we will find it," he vows. "But be prepared that it may truly be nothing more than a myth."

"The Ushum are supposed to be creatures of legend," Lyanndra argues. "So perhaps there is some truth to the fang after all. Regardless, I ride to Breem at first light, with or without it."

I want to stop her, but I know she will go nonetheless, even if she has to fight me to do it. Yet, she can't face the Ushum on her own, not without the fang.

"Locate the Ushum, but do not engage it," I tell her. It should be a direct command coming from the King of Alastria, but the plea behind my words undermines every ounce of my authority. "I will track down the fang and come to you as quickly as I can."

Lyanndra considers this carefully. While neither of us want to leave the throne unattended after what happened with Kartas, this plan is not without its merits. She'll have time to take stock of the damage in the Southern Caldera and to check on her family. While there, she can find the creature and assess the level of its threat. If we're lucky, I'll be able to bring the fang to her, and we can end the Ushum together.

"How do you propose to find the fang?" she asks after a long moment.

"I will work on the translation," Torran chimes in. "Lady Carolissa can help me, if she is willing. It will be nice to have a young brain around me instead of ones so *old* and *musty*." He looks right at Lyanndra as he says it, and I'm relieved to see her match his smirk.

"I'm willing, in service of Alastria," Lady Carolissa says.

I've never paid her much mind until today. She's rather young, barely just slipping into womanhood. Her hair is a rich shade of brown, and she has sharp, birdlike features that somehow seem in stark contrast with her youth. I struggle to remember which family she hails from, but the rich red of her dress indicates that she works with life energy.

More importantly, Lyanndra seems to like her. Though they only just met, I'm surprised that my crossed star interacts with the younger woman in such an easy manner. I hope that they might become friends in time. It would be nice for the Godslayer to have more allies around the palace.

"Thank you, my lady," Torran nods. "And I think we can safely assume that the Ushum has not yet fully woken up, though it has clearly been disturbed."

"If what you say is correct, that the Southern Caldera formed around it, then I must agree," Lyanndra says. "If the creature was truly active, we would know. I will find it and make sure that it continues to sleep until we can kill it."

"Please, just be careful, Godslayer," Lady Carolissa warns. "The legends about the Ushum all describe them as dangerous. We don't properly know *what* they're capable of."

Lyanndra nods.

Now that it's settled, I turn back to Torran. "We should start our hunt immediately. What do we need to begin?"

As the old Demigod lists off a series of book titles that he requires for the translation, I copy them down beneath Lyanndra's crude sketch of the Ushum. It strikes me that I've never seen her draw before now, and I find it deeply amusing that she isn't particularly good at it. This woman could cut down any foe on the battlefield and wields her blade with frightening precision, yet she holds a quill like a child just learning their letters.

I think I shall keep this little piece of art.

Once the index is complete, I rise from the table to go fetch the tomes. Lyanndra stands at the same time. She shadows me as we pass Torran and Carolissa, leaving them to discuss the nature of the mysterious fang, until we descend the first flight of stairs. Then she reaches out and weaves her fingers through mine.

We don't speak until we reach the Archive Room, home to the oldest and most decrepit texts in all of Alastria. As soon as the heavy door shuts behind us, I whirl around and pull her in for a clandestine kiss.

Lyanndra returns my passion with equal fervor. When I bring my hand up to her chest, where she still wears my pilfered tunic, I can feel her heart thrumming against her ribs, desperate to escape to me.

When we finally break away, I lean my forehead against hers and capture her hazel eyes with my green ones. "I don't want you to go," I whisper against her lips.

"I know," she breathes back.

"Promise me you won't do anything reckless," I beg.

"Like what?" she asks with a grin. "Like following somebody into the woods, getting chucked off my horse, and being eaten by strix?"

I narrow my eyes at her. "No. More like challenging somebody to a duel to the death and losing."

"I only lose when I want to," she smirks. "But you already know that."

I silence her impertinence with another kiss. A strange sort of grief rises in my throat as I realize that, after tomorrow, I'm going to have to wait far too long to do this again.

And if we only have less than a day before she leaves, then *fuck it*.

I'm going to make the most of it.

Before she can object, I sweep Lyanndra off her feet and up onto the square table at the center of the room. It's a small mercy that there are no manuscripts lying around, for I couldn't care less about priceless tomes and archaic knowledge right now. All I can think about is the way my crossed star gasps, "Syran!" as I work her trousers and smallclothes down to her knees.

She eyes me hungrily as I kneel before her. I think about how she once paid fealty to me as her king here amongst the shelves and shadows of this very library.

Now, I will worship on my knees before my queen.

I cannot stop myself from tasting her, and she immediately wraps her legs around me as I do. Her hands curl into my hair, gripping at the roots. I groan against her slick heat at the slight burn of it, and that alone causes her to gasp again. The sound spurs me on. Everything about her, from the way she pulses on my tongue to the battlefield scent of her, stronger now than ever, drives me wild.

I want to memorize every inch of her, and so I do.

And when she shatters on my face, it's my name on her lips and my hair in her hands. It's my neck she squeezes with her powerful thighs.

And I am hers, completely and without question, down to the stardust in my veins.

CHAPTER 11

Lyanndra

Syran is naked.

I watch him as he stalks toward the massive copper tub in which I lay, his eyes fixed on the place where the soapy water covers the swell of my breasts. It's the last bath I'll get before I return to the road, but I suppose I'll be content to share it with him, so long as he pays the right price.

He's certainly well on his way to doing so, having already ruined me once with his mouth in the Archive Room and then again on his cock when we returned to his chambers yesterday evening.

When he finally reaches the edge of the tub, my favorite part of him level with my hungry gaze, he asks, "May I join you?"

I grant his request by inching forward and giving him just enough space to slide into the water behind me. In spite of the warmth of his perpetual flame, I shiver as he wraps his arms around my waist and pulls me into him. Still, I'm content to lean my head back against the broad width of his chest, close my eyes, and sigh.

"Will you think of me while you're gone?" Syran murmurs in my ear as his hands begin to explore.

"Yes," I whisper as his fingers graze over my nipples. The first thrills of pleasure course through me at his gentle caresses.

"And will you touch yourself as you do?" he asks. This time, while one palm remains cupping my breast, the other ventures down lower, though he never quite reaches the place I want to feel him the most.

"Yes." The word falls from my lips as I squirm beneath his teasing hands.

"Show me," he commands.

I can't help but obey. Before I even have time to feel shy or embarrassed, my fingers are already pushing his aside, seeking the warmth of myself. This isn't something I do often, but I try my best to copy how he's touched me in the past.

But it's not enough.

"Please, Syran."

"Tell me what you want," he demands. His breath fans over the shell of my ear, and I instinctively roll my hips back against his. I can feel the length of him pressed against my spine, so close, yet just out of reach.

His hands draw to my waist and hold me still. The press of his fingers into the muscles there, and nowhere else, drives me wild. When I'm finally able to voice my desire, I plead, "Show me I'm yours. Make me remember, no matter how far I go."

A growl rumbles through his chest, and then he stands suddenly, dragging me with him. Water sloshes over the sides of the tub and onto the marble floor of the washroom, but neither of us care. All I can focus on is the way I fit so well in his arms as he carries me into the main room of his chambers.

I assume he's going to bring me to the bed, but he doesn't. Instead, he releases me just long enough to pull open the balcony doors before he continues our journey outside. There, he pins me against the cold, sturdy iron of the railing.

The new day has barely begun, and the world is still swathed in shadow. The last glimmer of the moon hangs over the horizon, the only witness to what comes next.

"This is where we first met," Syran says as he spins me in his arms so that I can look out over the gardens and the flat plains of the midlands beyond. "Do you remember?"

"I do," I murmur. I recall, in great detail, how sure I was that it was all just a dream. I was frightened, yes, but something within me knew even then that I was safe with Syran.

His hand slides down between my thighs, and he hisses as he feels how ready I am for him. "Look out upon your kingdom," he demands. "This is yours, Lyanndra. *I* am yours."

"Yes," I moan as one finger slides inside of me. It's everything I wanted from him just a few moments before, but now it still isn't enough.

I need more.

I need *him*.

My fingers grip the intricate iron railing as I rock into his hand. I can feel him stroking himself behind me, and I can't wait any longer. I reach back and grip his cock in my palm, guiding it to where I long for him the most.

I let out a sinful moan as Syran pushes into me. He's so much taller than I am, and I have to stand on the very balls of my feet in order for him to take me like this. And once he starts to move, I'm forced to brace myself on the railing in order to keep some semblance of my balance, even as he draws an arm around my middle to hold me steady.

The rhythm he sets is cruel and delicious. At this angle, every stroke has me gasping and panting off into the darkness. My thighs shake and my calves scream from the effort of holding myself upright, but I will not give into the exhaustion, not until we both get what we want.

It doesn't take long for me to reach that precipice I so desperately yearn for. And when Syran's hand roams down, and his fingers circle that electric place just above where our bodies meet, I can't hold on for any longer.

I cry out as I shatter on his cock.

Yet he does not stop.

"Come home to your kingdom," Syran growls in my ear as his hips begin to stutter. "Come home to *me*."

And when I vow, "Always," he finally finds his release.

Afterward, we stand together on the balcony, Syran with his arms around me and me with his essence dripping down my thighs, and we look out over our land.

Our home.

I've never had one of those before.

But now, pressed against the only man I have ever trusted fully with myself, I know that my home isn't a place, not fully. There is somewhere I'll always belong, and that is by Syran's side.

No matter how far I wander or where I roam, I will always come back to him.

We linger there, basking in the glow of each other, until the edge of the sky begins to lighten. Only then do we venture back inside.

I clean myself up as Syran dresses and gathers my armor. By the time I leave the washroom, he has my dragonhide leathers ready and waiting for me. I don them over my smallclothes. They feel like a different kind of home, like slipping into a second skin.

Next, Syran takes his time buckling on each piece of my tarnished armor, his fingers drifting restlessly over my body as he goes. Every touch feels like a goodbye, and by the time I'm fully strapped into my familiar steel shell, I don't even bother to hide the tears that slip down my cheeks.

"Do not weep for me," he murmurs as he wipes them away with trembling hands. "Please, I cannot bear it."

I shake my head but say nothing. There are no words that will mend the way my heart splits at the thought of leaving him. Every ounce of my being longs to stay here with him, to remain by his side and in his bed, but I know that I have a duty to my people and to my family.

To myself.

I have to go.

"Wait," Syran requests as I reach for my golden helm where it sits atop his sheets. He crosses to the desk, where he retrieves something that shimmers enticingly in the dark glow of his flame. And when he drops to one knee and holds it out to me, I recognize it for what it is.

It's a token.

The silk fabric is like molten gold seeping through his fingers. Black stitching ebbs and flows over the gleaming surface, and, when he smooths out the long strip of material, the image suddenly slides into clarity.

It's the curling black snake of his sigil, the same one that adorns the rings that bind us.

"Will you accept this token of my affection?" he asks in a voice so quiet that I can barely hear it over the thundering beat of my heart.

"You would give me your token, as a maiden would to her champion when he rides off into battle?" I tease, though the gentleness of my tone betrays the honor I feel.

Syran's green eyes flash and he challenges, "Are you not my champion?"

"Are you not my maiden?" I jest in return.

He leans forward to steal a kiss before replying, "I am whatever you ask of me. I am yours, completely."

"As am I," I declare. "I will wear your token with honor."

Satisfaction flashes across his fine features as he ties the strip of black and gold fabric around my left arm, closest to my heart. There is no missing Syran's claim upon me. I'm proud to know that, even when my gauntlet and the dragonhide glove layered beneath obscure my ring, everybody will know who is waiting for my return.

Something swells in my chest, that warm, glowing thing that I have yet to give voice to, and I'm overcome. It's as though I have no choice but to close the distance between us and capture his mouth with mine.

He meets me without compunction. He engulfs me, conquering me with his tongue as he draws the most wicked moans and gasps from my lips.

But we break apart when the morning bells begin to toll, signaling the start of the day.

It's time.

I finally retrieve my golden helm and, with one last, longing glance at Syran, I slide it on. Though I'm certainly capable of buckling the strap beneath my chin, I welcome his quick fingers as he reaches up to fasten the clasp in my stead.

"You're beautiful," he murmurs as he steps back.

Beneath my helm, I blush.

All that's left to do is don my sheathed greatsword and my cloak. Then, we leave Syran's chambers for what feels like the last time and descend, arm in arm, down to the courtyard.

I'm surprised to see how many members of the court have gathered to see us off. Torran is there, with Carolissa at his side. Both dip their heads respectfully as I pass, and I return the gesture easily. I surmise that the rest of the courtiers are in attendance for the host, which is comprised of several dozen Celestial Knights. Clad in gold and sitting astride their handsome mounts, they glimmer in the early morning light like fallen stars.

It's difficult to differentiate between the warriors, but I manage to pick Mallan, Irtas, and Orobos out of the crowd by the colors of their mantles. At my insistence, Wayre and Noros will stay behind to assist Syran.

And at the front of the company, Barra is waiting.

We haven't gone on a proper journey in many months, and now, she paws her great hooves against the moonstone cobbles in barely restrained excitement. I offer her a quick scratch behind her massive ears before I wedge my foot into the stirrup and hoist myself into the saddle. Even after Syran painstakingly inlaid golden scales into the worn leather to match my armor, this seat still feels the same.

I yield Barra with my legs, pivoting her hindquarters until we're facing Syran.

The last time I left the palace on horseback, I was fleeing from him and everything I thought he stood for. Now, my heart pounds out the same frantic tattoo, but it is not fear that I feel.

Syran nods once. His features are composed, but his eyes burn for me.

I nod back.

And then we turn, and the palace is behind us.

Barra's long strides echo over the cobblestones as the host parts, allowing me to lead the way through the golden gates of the Celestial Court.

Away from my crossed star.

Away from my heart.

CHAPTER 12

Syran

Lyanndra is gone.

She and her host have long since disappeared through the gates of Nexus, yet I remain in the courtyard, watching the spot where my crossed star once stood. While I understand how necessary it is for her to go to Breem, both to find the Ushum and to face her past, I already ache for her.

And beneath the yearning, a deep sense of unease yawns to life, stretching and roaring like the great beast that sleeps under the crest of Southern Caldera.

Have we made the right choice?

Logic says we have, but my heart insists otherwise.

I'm so consumed by my troubled thoughts that I barely notice when Torran joins me. It isn't until he rests one frail hand on my shoulder that I fully acknowledge his presence.

"All will be well," he assures me. His blue eyes sparkle in the fresh sunlight, but the familiar sight does nothing to put me at ease.

"I'm worried," I confess. "For her and for me." I don't tell him how lost I feel without Lyanndra. I already miss the calm surety of her presence at my side and the rattle of her armor, her gentle kisses, and her heated touch.

And some insecure part of me longs for her counsel.

Before her, I had Kartas to rely on. Now, I am alone with only my own judgment, however unreliable it might be.

I was too much of a fool to see through Kartas' plots and Ressa's machinations. How does anybody expect me to sit on the throne and rule as King of Alastria when my own poor choices have already put my people at risk?

For the first time, I realize how much Lyanndra has tempered my decisions. She speaks her mind and does it well, and her eye for strategy is comparable to my late cousin's. She would have impressed even my father, if he ever would have seen past her Starless nature.

Torran squeezes my shoulder, distracting me, if only for a moment, from my many inadequacies.

"Keep faith in the stars," he urges, "and keep faith in the Godslayer." He doesn't advise me to keep faith in myself, but I hear it all the same, woven between his words.

Plagued by the sensation that I have somehow shown too much of myself to my advisor, I nod and then promptly change the subject. "Have you found anything new regarding the fang?" I inquire.

While Lyanndra and I spent one last night together, Torran and Carolissa remained in the library, pouring through the tomes we brought them earlier from the Archive Room. I don't expect that they were able to uncover much in such a short time, but any information is better than none at all.

"Come, and I'll show you," Torran replies.

A dim flicker of hope alights in my chest at his words. The sooner we're able to find the fang, the quicker I'll be able to go to Lyanndra. If luck is on our side, perhaps this ordeal will be over in a matter of days.

I follow Torran into the palace and through the winding corridors until we reach the library. Instead of climbing up to the highest terrace where we convened the previous day, we make our way through the shelves and situate ourselves in the Archive Room. I school my face into the most neutral expression I can muster as we sit down at the same table where I had buried myself between Lyanndra's legs just hours ago.

Instead of my crossed star, the only things adorning the surface now are books. Most of them are so old, I'm worried they'll disintegrate if I even glance at them for too long, though I spot a few more modern bestiaries among the mix.

Once Torran is settled in his chair, I prompt, "What did you discover? Do you know what animal the fang belongs to?"

"If only the stars would bless us so." He sighs. In that instant, any optimism I hold for finding the mysterious weapon in a timely fashion is well and truly dashed. But then the Demigod continues, "However, I did find another legend that addresses the fang."

I'm not normally interested in such archaic tales, but I also understand that any piece of information, however small, might lead us in the right direction, so I say, "Tell me."

Torran drags one of the newer books toward us, and I'm surprised to realize that, for once, I can actually decipher this text. It's not modern Alastrian, but it is an older dialect that I've seen before.

"The Blaspheme of Lyrtas," I read aloud.

"Very good," my advisor remarks on my translation. "Are you familiar with Lyrtas?"

I nod. "He was originally a disciple of the Celestial Gods. But he disagreed on what texts should be considered canon, and so he was declared a heretic by the other disciples and banished from Alastria."

"He was also a great scholar, and, by all accounts, quite mad." Torran flips forward a few pages in the book before he passes it back to me. "In his time, he produced many works, including one about the fang. Though the text itself is thought to have been destroyed upon his exile, mentions of it still crop up from time to time."

And, indeed, the words before me are evidence of that. "Lyrtas spouted many blasphemes. Perhaps the most famous heresy is his claim that the greatest of celestial weapons was prophesied to return to the seat of Alastria at the end of days, heralding the fall of the Demigods, and thus, the fall of divinity."

The fine hairs on the back of my neck prickle to life as I process the words I've just uttered.

End of days?

The fall of divinity?

But when Torran speaks, he focuses not on such dismal qualifiers. Instead, he repeats, *"The greatest of celestial weapons."*

"The fang?" I ask

He nods. "It must be. From what little I've been able to translate from the older texts, that same language appears around several illustrations of the fang."

While any mention of the object we so fervently seek is worth investigating, I don't see what this particular account offers, aside from perhaps giving me nightmares of my kingdom collapsing into ruin.

Torran seems to pick up on my confusion because he recites a longer section of the passage this time. "The greatest of all celestial weapons *was prophesied to return to the seat of Alastria.*"

It finally dawns on me.

The seat of Alastria.

Nexus.

The Celestial Court.

"You think the fang is *here?*" I gasp.

"Maybe not presently," he clarifies. "But perhaps in the future."

"A dismal future where Alastria falls," I point out.

"One that is hopefully many years from now. But this is the only mention of a location I've uncovered so far. We must be scholarly about this, Syran, and learned men do not dismiss such things out of hand."

I want to snap at him that I am no scholar, but I hold my tongue. This situation is not of Torran's making, and it would be unfair to treat him with such little respect. After all, this Demigod took an arrow for the kingdom–and for me.

Drawing in a deep breath, I request, "Pass me a book. Let's see if we can find anything else about this wretched prophecy."

We spend the rest of the day sequestered in the stuffy box of the Archive Room, engrossed in our search. Lady Carolissa joins us when the midday bell tolls, and I'm relieved to find that she's brought an urn of strong, black tea and a plate of dried meat, bread, and cheese with her. After a quick break to eat, we resume our hunt.

While Torran deciphers some of the more ancient texts with Lady Carolissa's help, I scour maps of the Southern Caldera and sift through several bestiaries for more information on the Ushum—or how to kill one.

But our hands are still empty by the time the evening bell peals through our secluded corner of the library, and I send the two Demigods off to dinner with a heavy heart.

I slump down in my chair and rest my head in my hands.

How are we supposed to find this fang?

The animal it belongs to could be anywhere in Alastria, or even beyond it. And I don't even want to consider what it would mean if the weapon were to find its way to the Celestial Court.

Part of me wants to stay here forever, but I'm far too tired to engage in more research, and the sour taste of failure dissuades me from joining the others in the royal dining room. Instead, I make my way down to the training grounds.

Perhaps a good fight will distract me from my frustrations.

But when I arrive, it's to find that all of the Celestial Knights left with the evening bell. All that remains are the targets they must have used in their afternoon drills. It seems that my only opponents tonight will be the thick slabs of painted wood.

I'm disappointed, but I shall make do. Perhaps it will even be better this way. After all, I don't have to worry about burning any soldiers with my poisonous flame.

Eyeing the targets, I decide it's time to coat this place in ash.

My midnight flame surges forth from my hands, licking out at the painted wood of the closest target with glittering ferocity. It goes up immediately like kindling in a bonfire.

Before that first fire can die, I incinerate the next target in the line.

Heat curls through my body, comforting and almost conscious, and I call it–screaming–to the surface.

Every time the black blaze erupts, I imagine the feel of Lyanndra against me, her breath on my neck, her gasps in my ear. I let the flame consume me as she does, until there's nothing left on the training grounds but smoldering embers.

Spent and panting, I coax my fire back and survey the damage.

I grin into the growing darkness. The training grounds are destroyed.

It felt good to ruin something.

But ruining Lyanndra would be even better.

A groan rises in my throat at the very notion of taking her. How is it that she's only been gone for a few hours, and already I'm undone without her?

My grin flips to a scowl as I leave the ashen remains of the targets behind and retreat back into the palace. Though my stomach growls, I abandon all hope of a late dinner and instead climb the tower to our chambers, where I can be alone with my roiling thoughts.

It's all I can do to keep my head above the rising tide of my need as I shed my armor and the clothes I wear beneath. But even the loose pair of sleeping trousers I change into feels far too constricting. Still, I attempt to ignore the discomfort and instead slide into bed, where the sheets are cold and lonely without my crossed star.

I wave one hand, extinguishing the black flames that light the room, and then settle back against the pillows. Maybe if I close my eyes and will sleep to come, the night might pass faster.

But as I drift off, Lyanndra is there, engrained in the dark space behind my lids.

How far away is she now? Is she still pushing her host forward through the dark, or have they stopped to make camp for the night? The questions muddle together in my drowsy mind.

I imagine her sitting at the cooking fire, silent and watchful while the Celestial Knights banter around her. Or perhaps she is already lying in her bedroll with her monstrous greatsword sitting within reach and her wicked dagger tucked away in its sheath at her thigh.

Is she thinking of me? Does she long for me the way I yearn for her?

I remember the first time we were apart, when she fled the palace and sought refuge in the shadowed valleys of the northern mountains. The pull to her had been strong, but we had not yet consummated our bond.

Now, she leaves behind negative space. There is no one and nothing that could ever fill it.

By the stars, she has brought me to my knees.

I picture her in my mind's eye.

The Godslayer, in her tarnished armor and golden helm with my token tied around her arm.

Lyanndra, in a forest green dress spinning in my arms on the Winter Solstice.

My crossed star, naked beneath me, clutching me in the wickedest of ways.

Unable to control myself any longer, I reach down and unlace my trousers with shaking hands. My cock is already hard just from the thought of her, and I hiss in pleasure as I close my hand around myself.

But even as I pump my length within my clenched fist, I can't help but wish it were her palm against my heated skin. I imagine her leaning over me, her mouth closing over the tip of my cock, and my hips jerk at this phantom sensation.

Am I awake? Is this a dream?

I cannot tell.

I do not care.

A groan pulls forth from my chest as I–as she–brings me to my release. And then I'm undone for her, my very essence spilling out onto the black silk sheets as I cry out both of her names.

And once I've spent myself, sleep snatches me away with quick and nimble talons.

As I slip into the darkness, I feel the weight of her ring on my finger, the only sign that she was ever here at all.

CHAPTER 13

Lyanndra

The first time I left Syran behind, I was desperate to be free of him and the way he always seemed to beckon me further into his burning orbit.

Now, I long for him, so much that it causes a physical ache in my chest. The pressure only grows as the days blur on, though I have done my best to keep myself distracted.

I've pushed the host hard. Several of the knights who ride at my back have survived many seasons of battle, but a good portion of the others are as green as they come, only having seen haphazard combat in the fight to reclaim Nexus from the usurper. They're not used to grueling days in the saddle and long nights on the ground.

Still, we're making good time. After just over a week of travel, we're almost halfway to Breem. The very tip of the Caldera looms over the crease of the southern horizon, but already, I notice signs of the destruction the messenger heralded.

Two days ago, we passed through a village that reported feeling the tremors rippling through. Thankfully, their buildings held and their people survived. Yesterday, we came upon the first refugees journeying down the road. Most of them were unharmed, though some had treatable injuries. I sent them to the town from whence we came, along with a handful of Celestial Knights, to await Syran's aid caravan.

And today, we ride toward the settlement of Sheel, the first of the five villages most impacted by the quake.

It's immediately obvious as we reach the outskirts of the town that this place did not fare so well as the last.

The first structure we pass was once a lean-to designed to shield livestock from the elements, but it's entirely collapsed now. The damage is sobering, a grim portent of what's to come. Though the less experienced members of the host continue to chatter idly amongst themselves, us veterans fall silent.

We know what lies ahead.

An hour later, I smell the first body before I spot it sprawled in a ditch beside the road.

It's hard to tell whether the corpse was once a man or a woman, though I suspect the former based on the height and width of the shoulders. Given the level of decomposition, there's also no way of knowing how this unfortunate soul died, and I am not in the mood to speculate.

Behind me, one of the newer soldiers retches from the stench.

I continue to guide us forward.

The closer we get to the heart of Sheel, the worse the situation becomes. Many of the buildings, from barns to houses, are collapsed or leaning. I spot cracks running through the stone and wooden beams of several of the ones that remain standing, a sure sign of weakness. One more good tremor, and those, too, will come down.

But the Starless toll is the most significant. There are a dozen more bodies amassed in the center of town, awaiting burial. Family members and friends, dressed in black and sobbing quietly, mourn there. Others work to repair their homes, and I spot several injured individuals languishing in the doorways of ruined buildings where they once dwelled.

There is none of the usual chatter or bustle I've come to associate with a village of this size. The market is empty. The tavern is quiet. There is only death and ruin here now.

My stomach churns. Out of the five affected villages, Sheel is the farthest from the Southern Caldera, which seems to be the epicenter of the quakes. If the conditions here are so bleak, what will we find when we reach Breem?

I don't have the chance to ponder this question further, for the Starless villagers have caught sight of my golden helm. Guilt slides through my veins as their faces lift with hope at the mere glimpse of me. How can I possibly help these people? This is no monster to be slain or villain to be stopped. What use am I here?

My unease only grows as the people crowd around us, all talking at once.

"Godslayer!"

"She's here!"

"The stars are merciful!"

If I were on my own, I would simply dismount and do whatever I could, whether it be hauling rubble or treating wounds. But I have a host at my back, and those hands could do far more work than just my own.

"Irtas," I call over my shoulder.

The Demigod guides his horse forward. The gelding eyes Barra warily and paws the dry earth of the road but holds steady.

I don't know Irtas well, aside from when we've met on the training grounds. He strikes me as rather bland and uncreative, which is exactly what I need now. This isn't the time for Mallan to push back against my orders or Orobos to glare at me like I'm unworthy of my reputation.

"We will stop here and render aid," I tell him. "Your company will gather anybody who requires treatment for their wounds. Mallan's men will assist with repairs. Orobos will deal with the dead."

"Yes, Godslayer," he acquiesces. He turns his horse around and barks out my orders. And while I know the candidates for general do not think highly of me, the devastation around us is enough to encourage their compliance.

As the soldiers begin to break away with their companies, I consider what role I should play. The Demigods with healing abilities are best suited to treating the wounded, and burying the dead alongside their mourning relatives requires a gentleness I do not possess, so I decide to join Mallan's men in helping with repairs.

But before I can slip down from Barra's back, a villager pushes through the front of the crowd and hails, "Godslayer!" His clothes, which are quite fine by Starless standards, indicate that he's well respected in this community. The others part to let him through. When he stands before me, he says, "Sheel thanks you for your aid."

Beneath my golden helm, I nod.

When I add nothing more, the man continues, "As you can see, our situation is grim. But the refugees we've received from Ryv, Loryn, Breem, and Gry report much worse. Even the road isn't safe."

I tilt my head and consider that statement. Have fissures opened up in the ground, making travel difficult? Or are the problems of a more human nature, such as looters or other opportunists?

But then the nature of the danger becomes clear as he states, "Every night, the lycan comes."

I'm filled with a strange mix of dread and relief at his words. Lycans are vicious, and it's no surprise one has been drawn to this area given the stench of death and decay that lingers like a caul over this place. They're scavengers first and foremost, but when there's enough blood in the air, they tend to be less discriminatory between the living and the dead.

Yet, this is a beast that bleeds, a tangible threat that I can defeat with arrow and blade. Is that not what I'm good for? Hunts such as this are the very bones of the Godslayer, of who I became in the wake of the battlefield. And it's been far too many months since I fought a true opponent with the full weight of my greatsword.

I'm itching to begin even before the man finishes explaining the locations of the lycan attacks. It's already late afternoon, and soon the darkness preferred by the creature will descend.

Should I go alone, as I used to? Or shall I make use of this host?

Each company can spare a few soldiers, I decide. There's no need to take unnecessary risks.

"Will you do it, Godslayer?" the man asks, once again grabbing my attention and drawing me back from my schemes. "Will you help us?"

After the war, I never turned down a plea for assistance, and I am not about to start now.

I nod.

The man's face sags in relief, and his expression is echoed across the villagers close enough to hear his request. I don't blame them. Lycans are hungry creatures, and when this one is finished devouring the dead and the easy targets that travel along the road after dark, it'll only push closer to the heart of the village if it isn't discouraged.

I won't let that happen. I won't allow these people to suffer more than they already have.

And I won't deny myself the fight I seek.

With nightfall closing in, I waste no time in pulling soldiers from the ranks. I take five men from each company, choosing carefully as I go. Lycans are fast and agile. Their snapping jaws can easily pierce flesh and shatter bone, and they can overwhelm their prey with little effort. The Celestial Knights I assign to my makeshift hunting party are all light on their feet and quick with a blade, and, most importantly, have fought such beasts before.

Neither Irtas nor Orobos voice any objection as I poach their soldiers, though the latter rolls his eyes as soon as he thinks I'm no longer paying attention. Mallan, on the other hand, poses a problem.

"I'm coming with you," he declares after I inform him of the hunt.

Hidden behind the visor of my golden helm, it's my turn to roll my eyes. When he steps up to me, trying to intimidate me with his superior height, I close the distance even more until our armor is nearly touching. He instinctively leans away, and I grin.

"You want to be a general?" I ask him.

"Yes," he says eagerly.

"Then follow your orders, soldier." I punctuate my statement with one more pace forward, forcing him backward in spite of his size.

He scowls but does not argue further.

Frustration claws at me as I gather up the last of my chosen knights and assemble them at the mouth of the southern road. When Syran speaks, his tone leaves no room for argument or challenge. But I am the Godslayer, not a king, and I was not born with a crown upon my head. These men, even the Starless ones, do not respect me.

I am the Godslayer.

I am a woman.

They do not want me to be both.

Gritting my teeth, I climb back astride Barra, where I tower over even the tallest of the mounted Celestial Knights, and peer out into the gathering dusk.

As if on cue, a lone howl shivers through the twilight.

The horses behind me snort and dance, their ears flickering back and forth in panic. Barra, too, shuffles restlessly beneath me, but I know it's not fear that drives her to paw at the sunbaked ground.

She wants her dinner.

It would be rude of me to keep her waiting.

I pull the greatsword from the sheath at my back. Tense silence ripples out behind me as I hold the blade up into the darkening sky. Then I point it forward in a silent command.

Let the hunt begin.

While Barra attempts to surge forward, I hold her back. This is not a charge into battle. As long as we're on this road, the lycan will come to us. Still, the kelpie strains against me, hungry and eager.

As we trot southward, the howling becomes louder and more frequent. But I know that it's scented us when the cries in the distance abruptly cease.

Somebody with less experience might think they were safe and that the creature had moved on, but I've encountered enough of these beasts to recognize that this is the way they hunt. Right now, it's cutting silently through the darkness as its nose leads it in a deadly sting toward us.

In a matter of minutes, it will be here.

We will be ready.

At my back, the schiff of iron on leather tempers the night air as the Celestial Knights draw their blades. I ready my own greatsword, already planning my first downward slice.

For a long moment, we wait. The road is silent, save for the restless shuffling of the spooked horses. There isn't even a breeze.

And then, just a few feet away, I spot something low and lithe darting from shadow to shadow. It looks, upon first glance, like a strange, hairless hound. But then it stands up on its hind legs and sniffs the air, and there's something so terribly human about the set of its shoulders and the way its pointed snout turns toward us that I almost–*almost*–gasp out in horror.

The lycan.

On all fours, it appears deceptively small. But erect, it's easily the size of a grown man. I've seen quite a few of these horrible little bastards over the years, but they never fail to make my hair stand on end and the blood freeze in my veins.

And when it charges, there's no howling fanfare. It's just a silent shadow, its eyes shining faintly in the dark, its powerful jaws stretched wide.

I expect it to pounce toward me first. But it seems to want to avoid Barra, so it skirts just out of range of her stomping hooves and around the side of the hunting party, which is the worst thing that it could do.

The horses immediately go wild, and the night descends into chaos.

Several Celestial Knights are immediately unseated, flying unceremoniously off the backs of their mounts and hitting the ground with varying amounts of grace. The ones that remain on their steeds swing wildly, unsure of where the beast went.

I pivot Barra so that I'm facing the hunting party and turn just in time to catch a glimpse of the lycan as it darts easily through the fray. It seems to be fixed on one particular soldier who landed on his back and is struggling to even sit up. His sword is nowhere to be seen.

He's dazed and defenseless, and nobody but the lycan or I seem to notice. Its canine eyes fix upon the fallen knight, and I swear I see that thing grin.

No.

I won't let this happen.

I don't think. I just slide down from Barra and run. The distance is short, but the creature is faster. If it reaches him before I do, it will tear him to shreds before anybody can even react.

Just as I skid within range, the lycan pounces. It leaps at the knight with its maw spread wide, and the man lets out a strangled, terrified sound, the type of noise that a person makes when they're staring death directly in the face.

Horrified, I swing my greatsword.

For a moment, I think that I'm too far away, that the trajectory of my blow isn't wide enough, but then the lycan collides into the steel with a wet thump.

Shockwaves rattle through my arms at the impact. Blood mists in the air between us, and I turn my head away. The creature whimpers once. Then it slides loose from my blade with a nauseating sloughing sound that reminds me of that day in the throne room.

The day I killed the usurper.

Hot bile rises in my throat at the memory, and I force myself to look down at the dead lycan, if only to prove that it's a beast that bleeds out upon the road before me, not a man.

Not Kartas.

Behind me, the soldier lets out a low sob, and I draw in a rattling breath.

I didn't just kill a man.

Tonight, I saved one.

CHAPTER 14

Syran

The first wave of refugees arrives fourteen days after Lyanndra rode south with her host.

In that agonizing fortnight since her departure, I've spent countless hours toiling away in the Archive Room with Torran and Lady Carolissa, trying to track down any more information regarding the fang. But all we've found so far are breadcrumbs of myth and speculation that only ever seem to lead us in circles.

Why can't the stars bless us with something useful, like a map that guides us directly to the weapon we seek or a codex to aid in our translations of the ancient texts?

At least my crossed star seems to be having more success than I.

Even from where I stand just beyond the threshold of the throne room, I can hear the murmurs of the Starless refugees within, though I cannot make out their words. I know the Godslayer sent them, however, from the reports of the Celestial Knights who accompanied this group of asylum seekers.

She helped these people.

She felled a great and bloodthirsty beast.

She saved one of her soldiers from certain death.

The Godslayer is a hero.

Pride swells in my chest as I recall how the knights spoke of her. They were impressed and respectful, clearly in awe. Yet, that satisfaction is tempered by an edge of yearning that licks up in a jealous flame.

I wish I could have been there to witness her kindness and fury. From the way the men described it, I can almost see her standing there above the soldier, her golden helm gleaming in the darkness as she struck the lycan down on the wicked edge of her blade.

It evokes the memory of the night she saved me from the strix all those months ago. I can still recall the iron taste of fear on my tongue as I braced for the inevitable, but then she was there, materializing through the blizzard like some fey, forgotten god with moonlight in her eyes.

Longing tugs deep inside of me at the vision, but I force it down. As much as I crave Lyanndra and everything she is, there is no time for pining, not when my people are waiting for my aid.

I draw in a deep breath and then step into the throne room.

Silence ripples through the grand space as I enter. Nobody announces me.

Nobody needs to.

The crown on my head speaks for itself.

I've chosen to forgo my ceremonial armor today, instead opting for a simple combination of a tunic, trousers, and boots. Thanks to Lyanndra, I've had the opportunity to experience how her Starless brethren normally live, which is a far cry from the opulence and wealth of Nexus. The Celestial Court is probably foreign enough to them as it is, and I do not seek to alienate these people further.

On any other occasion, I would proceed down the aisle to where my throne awaits upon the dais at the head of the room. But I do not want to appear cold or uncaring, nor do I want to linger alongside my crossed star's empty seat, so instead, I turn to the nearest Starless—a round woman who's clutching the hands of two small boys–and bow my head in respect.

"Good evening," I say. "I welcome you to the Celestial Court. You will be safe here. Whatever aid you require, you only need ask."

When I finally look back up at her, I'm surprised to see shock plastered across her features. Her mouth works, and then finally she musters her voice to ask, "Are… are you not the king?" Then, in case her assumption is correct, she quickly adds, "Your Highness."

"I am," I confirm.

A flurry of hushed whispers echoes through the space, and I strain to hear them before they're swallowed up into the crowd. I catch the words, "bow," and "Starless," before the woman captures my attention once again.

"Thank you, Your Highness," she murmurs. Her eyes are wide, as though she still cannot quite believe that I have spoken to her.

"You are most welcome," I reply. My eyes flicker down to the boys. They look to be no older than five. Crouching so that we're eye to eye, I nod solemnly to each of them, though only one returns the gesture, while the other hides behind his guardian's skirts.

When I straighten up again, I realize that every single person in the room is gawking at me, and I can't help but wonder if I've made some grievous mistake. Is there some Starless custom I overlooked? Have I offended them?

But when I move on to the next refugee in line, a man with his arm in a sling, he does not meet me with malice. Instead, he sticks out his uninjured hand with his palm extended toward me.

For a moment, I don't know how to react. But then I recall seeing Lyanndra do this once or twice with some of the Starless Celestial Knights, and I realize that it must be a greeting, or perhaps a sign of respect. And if these people can journey here, where our customs and lifestyles are so different, then I can certainly meet them in the middle.

I raise my arm and clasp the man's hand.

"Thank you, Your Highness," he says.

"There is no need to thank me," I assure him. "It is my duty to help. I stand by the oath I swore to my kingdom and my people."

Another round of murmuring sweeps through the throne room, and once again, I'm out of my element. Is this how Lyanndra felt when she first arrived at the Celestial Court? Like an exotic creature on display? I didn't pay much attention back then, but now, I realize that perhaps I should have.

I try to appear unperturbed as I continue to greet my subjects. Thankfully, it doesn't take long for my unease to settle, and for the precarious tension in the room to subside. I even manage to smile once or twice as I speak with each of the refugees in turn.

Such interactions are necessary but exhausting. By the time I've received every one of the displaced Starless and promised them the aid they deserve, I want nothing more than to retire to my chambers and get some much-needed rest. After all, sleep has been hard to come by without the warmth of Lyanndra's body against mine. I find myself growing more exhausted by the day.

After instructing the guards to escort the refugees to the temporary quarters I've arranged for them throughout the city of Nexus, I take my leave. Yet, when I finally reach my chambers, change into a pair of comfortable sleeping trousers, and collapse into bed, I find that I'm unable to drift off.

The sheets are too cold. When I stretch my arm out, my fingers brush only silk, not calloused skin or golden hair. The room is strangely silent without Lyanndra's soft snores and the muttered sounds she sometimes shouts out in the middle of the night.

This place is empty without her.

I am empty without her.

Frustrated, I sit up and try to rub the exhaustion from my eyes with the heels of my hands. Perhaps I should sift through some of the maps I brought up from the Archive Room earlier today. That would certainly bore me to the point of sleep.

Not wanting to risk crumpling the documents in my bed, I get up and make my way over to my desk. I slump into the chair and stare down at the parchment on top of the pile. The lines of the navigational chart seem to squiggle and blur together beneath my drowsy gaze. Focusing is a challenge. And while I do make a valiant effort, it's not long before my eyes begin to wander.

I spot a leather strip, the kind that Lyanndra uses to tie her hair back, curled beside my quill, and one of her fletching feathers sticking out from between two tomes. Several of the wooden carvings I've made for her dot the surface of the desk like tiny sentinels, though I'm pleased to see that the one of Barra is missing. She must have taken it with her.

There are so many reminders of my crossed star here that it's hard to pay attention to anything else. Yearning, raw and hot, creeps its fingers around my heart and squeezes. And even as my head bows and I begin to doze, I retrace the lines of her face in my mind until it's almost like she's standing before me, like she's here, like she's….

My eyes snap open.

I'm not at my desk anymore, nor am I even in my chambers.

Barren, tawny rock stretches in every direction. Twisted shrubs and thick tufts of umber grass seem to be the only things that will grow in this arid landscape. In the far distance, the craggy tooth of a mountain juts up over the horizon.

The Southern Caldera, I realize. *This must be a dream.*

I've never been this far south. How is it that my mind conjured up this scene? Yet, while this place is strange to me, the night is the same as the one I fell asleep to in the Midlands, clear, cool, and doused in starlight.

"It's beautiful, isn't it?" a familiar voice asks from my right.

Something deep within me, dark and sparking, stirs as I turn to face the speaker.

Lyanndra stands at my shoulder, as fierce and stunning as she was when I last saw her. She wears a simple black nightdress embroidered with gold, one of the ones I recall her wearing, and, more interestingly, taking off, back in the comforts of the palace. Her hair is loose, and her feet are bare. When her hand finds mine in the space between us, I feel the warm press of her ring against my skin.

"Yes," I breathe. "Beautiful."

She smiles at me, and I am unbound.

"I've missed you," I murmur as I step closer. More than anything, I want to sweep her into my arms and remind her that she is mine, and I am hers. But a part of me is terrified that this is just a dream, that if I touch her further, she might vanish beneath my fingers like she was never here at all.

"And I, you," she whispers back. Her hazel eyes shine with need, and I know she speaks the truth.

"Is this real?" I ask. "Tell me. Tell me you're here with me now."

She closes the distance between us and reaches up to press her palm against my cheek. Instinctively, I lean into the warmth of her, desperate for more. When neither of us disappears, explodes, or turns to ash, she smiles again and questions, "Does it matter if this is real if we're together?"

I shake my head.

Because it doesn't matter, not when I can feel her skin against mine. Not with the desire that's written so plainly across her striking features. Not with the way my trousers tighten at the mere sight of her.

"No, it fucking doesn't," I say.

Then I do what I've longed to since the moment she left.

I claim her with a bruising kiss.

Whatever she was about to say is lost as her lips surrender to mine. The taste of her drives me wild, and I'm surrounded by her battlefield scent, stronger now that she's been on the road for so long. When she gasps against me, I take the opportunity to explore her with my tongue and nearly combust on the spot when she returns the favor.

By the stars, I've missed her.

And whether this is a dream or some half-scape like the first time I took her the night we were crossed, I will not let this opportunity pass us by.

Breaking the kiss, I trail my lips down the line of her jaw until I reach her ear, where I promise, "I'm going to ruin you, Lyanndra. I'm going to fuck you until you shatter on my cock. Is that what you want?"

She lets out a low moan as she nods into the crook of my neck.

"Say it," I demand. "Order me."

Her eyes flash as she tips her head up to look at me.

"Take me," she commands.

I do not have to be told twice.

I sink down, dragging her with me, until I'm sitting on the rocky ground with Lyanndra straddling my lap. The delicate fabric of her nightdress pools around us, and, as much as I want to see her bare, my need to be inside of her is far more pressing.

It takes a moment, one that feels far too long, to pull myself free from my trousers, and then another to skim my hands beneath the raised hem of Lyanndra's skirt. I groan aloud as I realize that she wears nothing underneath.

I can't wait any longer.

Wrapping one arm around her waist, I use my free hand to align the tip of my aching cock between her legs. She doesn't wait for me to press into her. Instead, she sinks slowly down onto my length, gasping as she goes.

By. The. *Stars*.

A choked and needy sound, one certainly unbefitting of a king, works its way from my throat as she seats herself upon me. For a second, I think I might unravel there and then, but I force the rush of pleasure back. As much as I want to find my release inside of her, she gave me an order, one that I have no plans to disobey.

I shift my hands to her hips as she once again tucks her head against my collarbone. "Look at me," I urge.

She meets my gaze with hungry eyes. When I'm sure she's paying attention, I roll my hips into hers.

"Syran!" she pants.

The shape of my name on her lips is everything. It's the feeling of her body around mine, the moonlight that filters down across this strange and barren landscape, the very spark that flickers in the heart of me. She is all that I want, all that I am.

Mine.

Gripping her hips, I drive myself into her in one powerful thrust.

Mine.

She rocks against me, begging and moaning until I once again give her what she desires.

Mine.

Over and over again, I strike myself into her. At first, she rides me, matching my pace, but, as her limbs start to tremble and her tight heat begins to flutter around me, she simply clutches my shoulders as I do as I promised.

I ruin her.

Twice.

And then I can't hold back any longer, and it's my turn to shatter.

In the aftermath, before our breathing evens out and our heartbeats return to normal, I simply hold her. Because this is a dream, even if it is real, and we're both going to wake up eventually.

Yet, my heart still crumbles when the first tendrils of dawn curl across the horizon. Even in my arms, Lyanndra's form grows hazy, and I know our time is short. I press my forehead against hers.

"Come home to me soon," I whisper.

She smiles, but her expression is tinged with the same grief that now stings the back of my throat and the corners of my eyes. She opens her mouth to reply, but it's too late.

The night is over.

Dawn has arrived.

And when I jerk awake in our chambers with my cheek pressed against the surface of my desk and the maps crumpled from where I fell asleep upon them, my eyes are wet.

I tell myself they're not tears.

But that, too, is only a dream.

CHAPTER 15

Lyanndra

I wake with the sun–and with a mess between my thighs.

My body is deliciously sore from the way Syran ravaged me in our shared dream. Did it actually happen? Something deep within me whispers that last night's vision was no illusion. It was a place in between this world and another.

Not quite real.

Not quite a dream.

But there's little time to ponder it further. My gaze slides along the lightening horizon until it lands on the crest of the Southern Caldera. The jagged mountain is so close now. If we leave early, we can reach Breem by late afternoon.

I take a moment to stretch my shoulders, which ache from the way I gripped Syran as I lost myself to his frantic thrusts and growling breaths, and then I crawl from my bedroll to find a few knights of the host already awake. It strikes me as strange that none of them seem to meet my eye, but no matter. After strapping on my armor with practiced, efficient hands, I clear up my little rectangle of camp before ambling over to where the others are gathered around a cooking fire.

One soldier passes me a tin cup full of tea. He also doesn't look at me, but I take the offering all the same.

None of us speak.

That's normal for me.

It is not normal for everybody else.

After the lycan attack in Sheel, the Celestial Knights have grown more comfortable around me. The soldier I saved, a young Demigod by the name of Jurlan, was relatively unscathed, aside from his wounded pride and a pair of soiled trousers. Now, he follows me about like a shadow, never far from the protective range of my greatsword.

I can't say I blame him.

And when we returned from the hunt with the creature's pelt as proof of its demise (Barra took care of the rest of it, much to the disgust of the party), word of what I did spread quickly throughout the host. Shortly after, Orobos found me on the outskirts of the village, where I was attempting, with little success, to calm my fraying nerves. He brought with him a bottle of unidentifiable alcohol.

Puzzled, I watched in silence as he sat beside me. For a while, neither of us spoke—until, finally, he confessed, "Jurlan's my nephew. My sister's only boy."

I said nothing.

"Is it true?" he asked. "You saved him?"

I nodded.

"He said you threw yourself in front of him. That you were ready to die for him."

They weren't exactly questions, but I nodded again anyway.

Orobos fell silent then, too. The only sound was the liquid sloshing inside the bottle as he took a swig and then passed it over to me. I accepted it, drew in a sip (it was ale, not great but not the worst I've had either), and then gave it back to him. We drank late into the night, as only soldiers who have seen too much can.

He hasn't glared at me since.

It didn't take long for the rest of the Celestial Knights to follow his course. First, Jurlan's friends within his company came by to thank me. Then, the more seasoned soldiers, who knew what it meant to stand in the way of a blow intended for another, suddenly seemed to have room for me at their cooking fires, where they chattered enthusiastically and long into the evenings.

And now, a week since we left Sheel, I no longer feel like an outsider in my own host. I'm reminded of my old battalion, the one I was part of when I felled the Flaming God. They didn't know I was a woman then, and the camaraderie was easy.

Now, these men are well aware of what lies beneath my golden helm, and they have accepted me in spite of it.

So why will nobody look me in the eye this morning?

I'm halfway through my cup of tea when I realize.

Syran once told me that Torran and Kartas knew he found me in our dreams the night we were crossed because they heard us. Or him, at the very least. From how he described it, the noises he made during our spectral encounter carried over into the waking world.

And did Syran and I not meet in such a clandestine way again last night?

My face flares with heat as I finally understand why these men are awake. They're not early risers who are eager to get started with their day.

I woke them.

With noises.

Unspeakable noises.

By the stars, it takes every ounce of my self-control not to fling myself directly into the cooking fire and just be done with it all. At least the soldiers are wise enough to keep their mouths shut as they continue not to look at me. I knock back the rest of my tea in a single, burning gulp and shudder, wishing it were something stronger.

Poison, preferably.

"More?" one of the knights asks.

I nod. He ladles another measure from the kettle over the fire and into my cup.

He doesn't look at me.

I don't look at him.

Maybe Barra will eat me, if I ask her nicely. That's one way to be rid of this shame.

But I do not throw myself into the fire or drink poison or prostrate myself in front of the kelpie. Instead, I drink my second cup of tea and pretend, very hard, not to exist.

Finally, one of the men brandishes his horn, inlaid with gold and poached from one of the uncomfortably large hares that wander the western shores of Alastria, and blows it.

The camp springs to life in a sudden frenzy as soldiers jolt awake, cursing. It's enough of a distraction that I can slip away, leaving the empty tin cup behind. I busy myself with fetching my bedroll and securing it to the back of Barra's saddle. Then, I whistle for my old friend, who thunders in from the fields, where she likely spent a good few hours terrorizing the local goat population.

She stands patiently as I first check her hooves, then run the thick bone comb I keep in the saddlebags through her tangled mane. After a quick brush down of her sealskin hide, I begin the process of tacking her up. The actions are soothing and methodical, and I almost–*almost*–forget about my eternal and unending embarrassment.

By the time I'm done, the rest of the soldiers are nearly ready. Tents and bedrolls are stowed away. Horses, resplendent in golden plates and colorful banners, paw at the rocky ground. Curls of smoke rise from the extinguished cooking fires as the last stragglers secure their armor and climb upon their mounts.

Within minutes, we're ready to go. I lift my greatsword high, capturing the host's attention, and then thrust it forward toward the rising spire of the Southern Caldera.

Breem is on the horizon, and with it, my reckoning.

My earlier mortification curdles to shame as we push onward.

After we left Sheel almost a full week ago, we stopped in Ryv, the smallest outpost in this part of Alastria. The settlement, for it could not even be called a town, was destroyed. No buildings stood, and few people were left. The ones who remained were badly wounded and unable to travel. We did for them what we could and loaded them on wagons borrowed from Sheel and bound for Nexus. I only hope the refugees survive the journey.

Two days after that, we came upon Loryn, a place that always seemed so exciting and exotic to the young, frustrated girl I was. But we found the colorful markets collapsed and shuttered, and the once friendly people grim.

The destruction was remarkable. Even the ground there wasn't spared. Certain patches were loose and crumbling and would shift underfoot when we walked. Others were simply not there at all, collapsed into sinkholes that were so deep that, when Jurlan dropped a pebble down one, we never even heard it reach the bottom.

Now, as we ride toward Breem, putrid steam rises from the fissures that have opened in the rocky landscape. Sweat builds in the small of my back beneath my armor, and it has nothing to do with the sun that beats down upon us. No, it's the scent that turns my stomach now. It's the smell of the Ushum, pulled from a memory long past and buried deep.

My unease grows as we close in on our destination. The land here is broken and smoldering. Several times, we have to stray from the road in order to avoid the jagged cracks in the rock. It should be a relief once I spot the first buildings in the distance, but the dismal state of them only heightens my anxiety to a point of sharp, steel-tipped fear.

It's strange, coming back to this place after so long, only to find it in ruin. When we finally enter the village proper, I can't help but stare. There are homes I remember and ones that I don't, but the road is the same, and the way the shadow of the mountain caresses the ground with shady fingers is so seared into my memory that I suddenly feel out of time. I'm just a girl again, coming home from the market in Loryn in the back of my father's wagon.

Yet, everything is crumbling. The road is a mess of debris. Several of the buildings in the town square are partially collapsed, though the tavern still stands strong amidst the sagging frames. And, like all of the other settlements we've passed through, there are the dead lined up, waiting to be buried.

Hot dread churns in my gut as we linger in the center of Breem.

Even if Syran was right, even if my family made it through my betrayal all those years ago, how could they have possibly survived *this*?

I need to see for myself.

I need to *know*.

The villagers who gather round us barely register in my brain. When Irtas asks me what each company should do, I mutter out the orders automatically, not really hearing myself. Whatever I said must have made sense, since each candidate for general splits off with their men in tow.

And then, before anybody can waylay me, or I can change my mind, I do what I came here to do.

I go home.

At first, I keep Barra at a neutral trot. People wave and point as we go by, but I ignore them. In spite of the heat of the afternoon, I'm grateful for the weight of the golden helm upon my head. Nobody can see the fear on my face. Nobody can see my shame.

But as the seconds tick by, and my heart beats harder and harder against my ribs, I urge the kelpie to a canter, and then to a full gallop. I know the way to the homestead by heart. How many times have I come this route? Hundreds? Thousands?

And then it's there, a long, reinforced house rising up from the rock with shocking familiarity. The weathered boards are bleached like bones from the sun. Waxed paper covers the many windows to keep the bugs at bay. The roof, thatched with coarse grass and sloped at an angle, is patchy but otherwise the same as I remember.

It's still here.

Not crumbling.

Not a ruin.

And there are people here too. They're hard at work clearing debris from the yard. Do I recognize any of them? I squint through my visor. They're still too far away.

But there's no hiding my identity, even at a distance.

One of the men glances up at the sound of Barra's thundering hooves, pauses, and then shouts, "Godslayer!" The others look up then and hail me, and there's no turning back now.

Barra skids to halt just outside the yard. The men working there drop their tools and approach. But before any of them can say anything further, the door to the homestead bursts open to reveal a tall, matronly woman in a stained apron and a brown smock.

Beneath the golden helm, I blink.

That glossy black hair.

Those brown eyes.

I'd know her anywhere.

"What's all this fuss about?" my mother shouts at the group. She crosses her arms in front of her chest as she fixes the closest man with a glare that could rival the heat of the Caldera itself. Aside from the fine lines on her forehead and around her mouth, she looks exactly as she did all those years ago when she'd yell at me for staying out too late.

And, most importantly, she's alive.

Not murdered.

Not dead beneath a pile of rubble.

Alive.

She doesn't seem to notice me. Her attention is focused on the man closest to her.

"The Godslayer!" he announces. "She's here!"

My mother rolls her eyes. "Don't be ridiculous," she scoffs. "Why would she come *here?*" But then she follows the line of the man's gesturing arm to where I sit astride Barra at the edge of the yard, and her mouth falls open.

I freeze.

Does she know?

Does she recognize me?

There's only one way to find out.

I reach up and, with shaking fingers, unbuckle the clasp at my chin. Then I pull the golden helm from my head, revealing the terrible truth of me.

For a moment, my mother simply blinks, as though she can't believe what she's seeing. But then something sparks behind the shock, and she breathes, almost too softly for me to hear, "Lyanndra?"

Tears well in my eyes.

"*My* Lyanndra?" she gasps, louder now.

And then I'm sliding down from Barra and running toward her with the golden helm tucked in the crook of my elbow, not caring about anything other than the way she opens her arms as I approach.

And when she finally catches me in a tight embrace, the tears come in earnest.

"Lyanndra," she whispers into my ear, her voice shaking with emotion.

And I'm home.

I'm *home.*

CHAPTER 16

"You look quite pleased with yourself."

I glance up at Torran, who smiles placidly over the table at me. The steam from the tea, black as my flame and served in two ceramic mugs, distorts his face, but there's no mistaking the flicker of humor in his bright blue eyes.

How am I supposed to respond to that? There isn't exactly a polite way to tell him that yes, I *am* quite pleased with myself because I made my crossed star chant my name like a prayer last night as I fucked her into oblivion, so I simply say, "I slept well."

"It sounded like you did," Torran hums in agreement. Before my brain can fully process what he just said, he continues, "I hope you don't mind that I asked you all the way out here this evening. I fear I'm quickly tiring of the library."

"You and me both." I sigh. If I have to spend one more hour in the stuffy box of the Archive Room, I think I may just spark my midnight flame and let it all burn.

As such, Torran's hut is a fine reprieve.

It's more of a cottage, really, though the walls are earthen and the ceilings are so low that I have to stoop at the shoulders to avoid bumping my head against the rafters. Bundles of herbs hang from the beams above. Their aromas mingle into an odor that should be foul, but inexplicably isn't. And the old Demigod has a bed here, though I suspect he also sleeps somewhere in the castle most nights, along with a small kitchen that's reserved for brewing tea and mixing potions rather than any normal sort of cooking.

It's been a while since I last visited, but it's just as I remembered. Somehow, in all the bustle of Nexus and the Celestial Court, this place always stays the same.

I recall coming here, to this quiet sanctuary in the little patch of woods beyond the palace, as a boy. My mother brought me at first. She would stand with Torran at the kettle, and I would half listen as they spoke of poisons, antidotes, tinctures, and poultices. Mostly, I spent my time gazing about at the herbs and charms, awestruck and curious, and maybe a little frightened too.

Later, I would seek out his kindness after fights with my father. And when the Flaming God met his end, I came to Torran for his wisdom and guidance.

Now, I'm in dire need of all three of those things.

"I take it you didn't invite me out here for tea?" I ask.

Torran shakes his head. "Alas, no."

"Then you've found something?"

The old Demigod steeples his fingers around his mug and replies, "Yes and no." I'm in no mood for riddles, and it must show on my face because he explains, "While I haven't quite figured out what the fang *is*, I have discovered what it *is not*."

That certainly sparks my interest. My curiosity only grows when he pulls a surprisingly small book from within the folds of his robe. The tome is old, the leather flaking, and the whole thing is about the size of my palm. I think the cover was gold at some point, though the luster has long since worn away. The inlaid text on the front is barely legible. The markings remind me of the ones of the moonstone basin that sits in the chapel, the one used in the Ceremony of the Crossed Stars.

"Do you know what this is?" Torran inquires. His voice is low, conspiratorial, almost electric, and he suddenly seems more alive than I've ever seen him.

"No," I reply.

His eyes glitter in thin evening light. "You must swear to me, Syran, that you will not forsake me if I tell you, for I am about to confide in you the deepest of heresies."

Something stirs in my chest, though I cannot say if it's fear, dread, or excitement. Whatever it is, I manage to assure him, "Never, old friend."

He offers me a tight smile. "I will hold you to your word."

I nod.

"We're in the presence of a great wonder," he says. "This book is, as far as I know, the last surviving copy of the *Blaspheme of Lyrtas*."

Shock crashes over me in a cold wave. While I've never put much stock in the religious underpinnings of the Celestial Court, my father certainly considered himself devout. I don't believe, not the way he did, but I also never questioned the veracity of the stars too deeply.

Until Lyanndra, I realize.

And now again, when I'm faced with perhaps the unholiest relic I have ever laid eyes upon, this small gold book clasped in my advisor's hand.

But didn't Torran tell me that the works of Lyrtas, a mad Demigod who was turned away from the disciples as a heretic, were destroyed long ago?

For a moment, I don't even know how to respond. Then finally, I choke out, "I… I thought it would be bigger."

The old Demigod laughs. "You sound like a maiden on her wedding night, and here I thought you'd send me straight to the dungeons!" He shakes his head, and then his expression sobers. "No matter. I picked this book up on my travels when you sent me to trace the Godslayer's lineage," he continues. "I didn't bother translating it at the time, but after so many hours researching the fang, I realized that a tome as old as this one may well hold some secrets."

"You were right," I comment.

"I was," he agrees. "Imagine my surprise when I realized what was contained within these pages!"

I can acknowledge how thrilling it must be for a scholar such as Torran to uncover such a thing, but at the same time, I'm starting to grow impatient. "Does it speak of the fang?" I ask.

"Indeed," he confirms. "According to Lyrtas, the fang is of no beast found in Alastria or anywhere on this earth." His eyes seem to glow in the evening light as he leans forward and says, "It is of the *stars*."

Of the stars?

Even as my brain works to fathom this latest revelation, Torran continues, "Lyrtas believed that the falling stars that gave the Demigods their powers were actually pieces of the slain Ankir, thrown down to earth by the Celestial Gods. He theorized that the weapon the Celestial Gods used to destroy their predecessors–the fang–was banished here, too. After all, what beings would allow such an artifact, one with the power to slay their own kind, to exist among them?"

It's ridiculous.

It's preposterous.

It's *blasphemy*.

And yet, something about it echoes within me, etching deep into my bones in a way I cannot fully explain. It's the truth, even if it's heresy of the highest order. I know it as surely as I know Lyanndra is mine.

It is written in the stars.

Across the table, Torran's face creases with concern. "Are you well, Syran?" he asks.

"Quite," I say. We both ignore how my hands shake as I reach for the ceramic mug in front of me and lift it to my lips. The tea is hot and aromatic, and when I take a sip, the burn of it on my tongue is unexpectedly grounding.

Silence veils the space between us as I gather my thoughts.

Blasphemy aside, is this not a good thing? If Lyrtas' theories are to be believed (and I *do* believe them, with frightening surety), the fang is somewhere here in Alastria. And if it's here, that means I can find it.

As though he can sense the trajectory of my thoughts, Torran slides the book back into his robes and advises, "Do not celebrate just yet. There is more, and it is less savory than the news I've already shared."

"Less savory than heresy?" I ask.

He smiles, but it doesn't quite reach his eyes. "What do you know of the Moon Prophecy?"

"Only what you taught me."

I think back to that night in the woods, so long ago now, when Lyanndra and I ate roasted rabbits together in the glow of my black flame. I recall how I told her the story of the Moon, who disagreed with the Celestial Gods' choice to reward the Demigods with fallen stars. For the Goddess' impudence, the other deities banished her to live amongst the Starless, so she cursed them with a prophecy.

Two sisters would be born from her bloodline. One would have the power to save the Demigods, and the other would have the power to destroy them.

The gods would have to make an impossible choice.

The wrong one would mean their demise.

But it's just a story, one that never made the canon for the obvious fact that the moon remains in the sky overhead, among the stars.

"Lyrtas wrote that, if the Celestial Gods failed to favor the sister that would save the Demigods, the other would usher in the end times," Torran says.

"The Moonlit Age," I murmur. I don't know where those words come from. Cold roots of fear spread in my chest at the realization.

The old Demigod's eyes sharpen in the growing gloom of the evening. "Where did you hear that?"

Thoroughly unnerved, I shrug. "I must have read it somewhere."

But I know that I haven't. The phrase came from somewhere else, something forgotten and buried. Something old and far away, something dry and whispering that flexes out in the stars and inside of me, and….

"Syran, are you all right?"

I start at Torran's voice. For a moment, his face waves in and out of focus, but then it snaps back into place, and that far-away feeling inside of me is gone.

"I… I'm fine." As if to prove it, I take another sip of tea, though I doubt either of us is convinced by my charade. Once I'm certain the strange spell has passed, I ask, "What does the Moon Prophecy have to do with the fang?"

Torran stares at me as though he thinks I might pass out or burst into flames. When I do neither, he sighs. "Just as the text we found the first night suggested, Lyrtas thought that the discovery of the fang would usher in the Moonlit Age. He's not exactly clear on the details–something about serving a goddess, he really was quite mad–but he's very insistent about that."

"The Moon Prophecy is just a legend," I state.

"So is the fang," Torran replies.

"Yes, but pardon me for not considering the ramblings of a blasphemous lunatic to be entirely accurate," I argue. "These are stories, nothing more."

Torran shakes his head. "Just because Lyrtas was mad doesn't mean he was wrong. Perhaps some details have been lost to time and translation, but we'd be fools not to consider the possibility."

"The possibility of what?" I challenge.

"That perhaps the fang should *stay* hidden."

The words hang between us like a shadow.

My first instinct is to push back, to raise my voice like my father would have done and insist that this whole thing has gone too far. But then I realize that, as much as I hate to admit it, Torran has a point.

What if Lyrtas was right?

What if the fang is somehow an omen or a catalyst of the Moonlit Age?

If I find it, I could go to Lyanndra. We could kill the Ushum.

Yet, I could also usher in the end of my kingdom, of my people, of the very stars.

But then I recall the stories of the cataclysmic eruption that devastated Alastria centuries ago. I think of Lyanndra, powerless to stop the Ushum on her own, camped out in the barren shadow of the Southern Caldera. I think of the innocents, Starless and Demigod alike, who would perish if the great beast were to wake.

"My duty is to my people," I state firmly. "Not to the superstitions of dead men."

Torran's expression is unreadable. "Even at the price of your kingdom?" he asks. "Even at the price of your crown?"

His words remind me of the weight that burdens my temples. I've gotten used to it in the months since the coronation, but at times like these, I wonder how any of the kings before me could bear it for long.

"This crown is worthless if I hide behind it," I say.

I swore an oath to protect Alastria and the souls that inhabit it. The words of the dead will not make me falter.

I will find the fang.

I will put an end to this.

CHAPTER 17

Lyanndra

The homestead was never quiet.

Between ten siblings and the bustling lifestyle of Breem, there was always somebody shouting, or rattling pots, or churning butter. Even at night, when everyone was asleep, it was impossible to escape the snores and mutterings of the others.

But now, for possibly the first time in this building's long history, everything is silent.

Sitting at the massive table in the middle of the kitchen, I feel distinctly out of place in my tarnished armor and the velvet cloak that bears the shining sigil of the Celestial Court. My golden helm sits on the wooden surface at my elbow, a stark reminder of who I have become.

I am not the same woman who left this place over a decade ago.

There are scars on my body and lines on my face. No longer do I run from those who would threaten me. I was forged in the fire of the Flaming God, a soldier turned something more.

I am the Godslayer.

And soon, I will be queen.

"Lyanndra," my mother says.

She hasn't released my hand since she led me inside and sat me down at the table, in the same spot I claimed as my own when I was just a girl. Has anybody taken this chair since? Something about the way she stares at me now, as though she can't quite believe that I'm here, tells me that this seat has remained empty for quite some time.

"Lyanndra," she repeats.

I know I should say something.

Anything.

Back when I first left, when the guilt was a raw and open wound, I would lie awake at night and think of what I would tell my parents if only I had the chance. Sometimes I imagined crying and apologizing, begging them to take me back.

Other times, I was sure that I'd meet them with anger. Why did they have to drive me away? Why couldn't they accept that I would never fit into their shape of the perfect woman, the perfect wife, the perfect mother?

Yet, time dulls all wounds, a lesson I learned well through my years as a soldier. Eventually, I assumed that my family was lost, and so there was no point dwelling on a past I could not change. Still, on long rides, on nights where the wind howled and kept me from the slender grasp of sleep, I would sometimes think, *What if? What would I say to them, if I could?*

But words fail me now.

My mother opens her mouth, presumably to say my name for a third time, but she doesn't get the chance.

The kitchen door flies open, revealing a small, wiry man silhouetted against the bright afternoon. The sun has etched deep furrows into his forehead and around his mouth since I last saw him, and his braided black hair is graying at the temples now, but he is unmistakable. He takes two steps into the room before his eyes land on me.

He freezes.

"It's true." My father gasps. "It's *true.*"

Fresh tears brim in my eyes, but I blink them back. It's not lost on me that I've cried more in the last month than I have in years.

"You're here. You're back." Even thick with emotion, his voice is exactly how I remember it. His eyes, deep brown, slide to my armor–*his* armor once, though it hasn't been for a long time now–and then to the golden helm that sits before me on the table. "You're... you're the *Godslayer*."

I nod.

His mouth opens, then closes, and then opens again. "You killed the Flaming God."

I nod.

For a moment, he says nothing. He just stares, his gaze flickering between my face, my armor, and the helm. Then he surges forward, and I have just enough time to stand before his arms are around me, pulling me into him.

I can't stop the tears from coming now.

I don't even try.

"By the stars, Lyanndra," he whispers into my hair as he holds me close, "we thought you were *dead*."

Even though my face is buried in the crook of his shoulder, I manage to shake my head. The angry girl who left Breem behind may be gone, but the woman I've become is here, and breathing, and *alive*.

After a few breaths, my father pulls away, though his hands linger on my shoulders as he studies me once more. "You've taken good care of this," he comments, brushing the edge of my armor with his fingers. Then his eyes land on the raised seam where Syran's fiery blade sunk through the plate, and he frowns. "Is it true what they're saying? That the king nearly killed you?"

I nod. Syran personally repaired the damage, welding the slice shut with the heat of his midnight flame. But even the fine golden inlay he added cannot hide the evidence of our battle.

My father's eyes narrow. "And you are to be his queen?"

I nod again. I seem to be doing a lot of that today.

"Lyanndra," my mother interjects. Somehow, she's still clutching my hand like a lifeline. "*Why?*"

The question twists in my mind like a serpent. Why did I abandon them? Why did I become a knight, and later, the Godslayer? Why am I marrying my sworn enemy?

For the first time since I arrived at the homestead, I speak.

"I'm sorry."

My mother's fingers tighten over mine, and her eyes shimmer with tears as I turn to face her. "Why did you leave?" she demands. A thread of anger weaves through her words. I find I cannot blame her. "We thought you were *dead*, and all this time–*all this time!*–you never once thought to let us know you were alive? Not *once?*"

"I...."

My voice trails off into nothing. There's no excuse I can make. There's nothing to justify what I did.

"Ashya," my father says in an attempt to soothe her. "Sit. I'll put on the kettle, and then Lyanndra will tell us everything, starting with the night she left." He shoots me a look that leaves no room for argument.

I nod.

Only after I sink down into my chair does my mother do the same. As my father bustles about the kitchen, drawing water for tea and stoking the fire beneath the large black pot hanging in the hearth, she does not release my hand. Neither of us speak. By the way she clenches her jaw and stares at me from the corners of her eyes, I can tell she desperately wants to.

Finally, my father returns with two steaming clay mugs. He places one on the table before me and hands the other to my mother. Then, he retrieves his own before he takes a seat beside her.

There's no point in delaying the inevitable any longer, I suppose. Ignoring the tightness in my chest and the panic that creeps along the tips of my nerves, I do as he requested.

I start at the beginning.

"Aaro," I say. It's a name I haven't spoken aloud since the night I left.

Both of my parents stiffen in their chairs.

"It was already too much," I confess. My voice is quiet and thin. It sounds far away, somehow, as though I'm not fully attached to myself.

Still, I force myself to keep talking. "Life here. What was expected of me. All of it. And when you betrothed me to Aaro, I just… I *couldn't.*"

"But your sisters would never…" my mother starts, though her voice trails off when my father shakes his head.

I stare at her for a moment.

What I did to my parents was terrible. They have every right to hate me.

But they're not innocent, either.

How many times did I tell them that the life they planned out for me was not what I wanted? Would they rather I made myself small for them instead of carving out my own place in this kingdom, one that I paid for in blood and ash?

I am the Godslayer.

I will be queen.

Is that not enough?

And when I finally continue, my voice is stronger, more akin to the one that orders soldiers and speaks as equal to the king's.

"I am not my sisters," I tell her firmly. "I never was. *That* is why I left."

My mother's eyes widen.

My father's expression does not change.

"You took my armor," he says.

"And your horse," I reply evenly. When he doesn't interject, I continue, "The night Aaro's father threatened us, I snuck out once everybody was asleep. I joined up with the battalion that was passing through."

"And you became a knight?" he presses. "With no training?"

"I taught myself."

It's true enough. When I explored the vast warren of tunnels and caverns that run beneath the Southern Caldera, I would use whatever I could find as a makeshift weapon. Stalactites and stalagmites became enemy soldiers to be defeated. Patches of moss were great, slavering monsters with jaws stretched wide. Against such opponents, it was impossible to lose.

But that didn't mean I wasn't knocked on my ass the first time I sparred with the Starless soldiers who would later die beside me on the battlefield. I was weak compared to the others, and small. Yet, I improved quickly once I built up the muscle for combat, and especially when I realized that my lack of formal training made me unpredictable, and therefore, confusing to my opponents.

His voice draws me back to the present. "And you killed the Flaming God?"

He already asked that, but I nod all the same.

My mother, having gotten over the initial shock of my words, takes over once again. "Why didn't you come back?" she demands. "Why didn't you let us know you were okay? You left us wondering if those soldiers snatched you up in the night and…" She draws in a deep breath and finishes, "Why, Lyanndra?"

Guilt churns in my chest as I admit, "I was ashamed."

The truth settles between us like a stone in shallow water.

This is it. This is the phantom that has haunted me for so many years.

I refuse to let it torment me a moment longer.

"I thought Aaro's father would make good on his threats when he found out I ran," I lay bare. "I thought he would kill you. I left you all to die. How could I ever come back after that?"

Surprise flashes across both of their faces at my answer. I wait for their anger, for their hatred, but it doesn't come. Instead, my mother stares at me the way she used to when I'd do something particularly stupid as a child. My father lets out a snort that sounds suspiciously like a laugh, which is somehow even worse.

Confused and uncomfortable, I stare down into my mug of tea and wait.

Finally, my father reaches over and takes my free hand. "Lyanndra," he says, drawing my eyes to his. There's no trace of malice in his voice, only regret. "Aaro's father made threats, yes, and he did try to act on them. But there was one of him and seven of us."

As his words sink in, I realize that there's no need for any further explanation. Suddenly, the way my mother stares at me makes complete sense.

Why did I ever think that Aaro's father would stand a chance against the men in my family? Against six brothers and my father, who was a soldier before he settled down on the homestead, he wouldn't have been able to do much damage.

For the first time, I see the situation not through the eyes of a frightened girl, but with the assessing gaze of a knight.

My family was never in any mortal danger.

"I am a fool." The words slide from my mouth before I can stop them. "How can you ever forgive me?"

My mother is on her feet before I even finish the question. For the second time that day, she sweeps me into her arms and holds me close. I let her.

"I'm so sorry," she whispers. "How can you forgive *us*?"

"We may not share blood, but I've always held you in my heart," I say. My voice cracks with the tears that once again threaten to over-flow. "Leaving you the way I did is my greatest shame. I am *your* greatest shame."

Though I cannot see him with my face pressed against the front of my mother's smock, I don't miss the way my father rests his hand on my armored shoulder.

"How could we ever be ashamed of you?" he asks. "I've heard the stories about the things you've done, and not just how you slayed the Flaming God or the usurper. You help people. You bring peace in your wake."

Then he, too, wraps his arms around me. I'm clasped between two people I thought I'd never see again, who would forgive me, who would love me unconditionally and never let me go.

Out of all the enemies I've ever faced upon the battlefield, my guilt was the fiercest.

But the specter of my childhood fear is vanquished now.

The shame within me starts to unravel.

I am home.

Finally, I am free.

CHAPTER 18

I'm going to burn it all to the ground.

Midnight fire sweeps from my outstretched fingers and snatches at the hem of my opponent's mantle. He dodges away, but not before I manage to singe the dragging edge of the fabric.

The soldier curses and holds his hand out toward the charred spot. A second later, a thin trickle of frost sizzles down to choke out what's left of the smoldering flame.

Fuck.

Resisting the urge to snarl, I keep my face composed and my sword swinging. The knight must have been expecting a second fiery attack because he tracks my free hand as it sweeps in one direction, but doesn't seem to notice the way my blade arcs toward him from the other. It'll be a clean hit to the shoulder.

Disarming, in more ways than one.

But at the last possible moment, a flash of steel interrupts the blow and forces my blade off course.

Fuck.

I nearly forgot about the second soldier.

He moves faster than his companion, and when he alights back from me after the parry, I realize that he's attempting to copy the Godslayer's fighting style. But he doesn't possess her infuriating grace, nor her keen and nuanced judgment on the battlefield.

He'll fall soon enough.

Fire licks my free palm. The warmth is comforting and familiar. It tugs at something deep within me, the same sparking flint that connects me to Lyanndra. It whispers and begs at me to flare the embers into *more*. The call is strong, like ash on my tongue.

I am inclined to meet it.

Drawing on that deep well of fire, I summon my midnight flame. It twists into a serpentine blaze that weaves through my fingers and down my arm like it's alive, like it knows what I want from it and it chooses to listen. Dimly, I think this new awareness should alarm me, but it doesn't. Instead, I'm filled with the hot surety that this is somehow *right*.

I do growl then, composure be damned.

The knight opposite me blanches, but he does not lower his sword. At the same time, his companion, now recovered, steps up beside him. They're shoulder to shoulder, a wall of gold, but I am the Lord of the Midnight Flame, and I will not be extinguished so easily.

Heat shimmers through the air as I unleash upon the soldiers. Black fire strikes from all angles. The one with the charred mantle desperately tries to lower the temperature with his powers, but I am stronger than him, and even as he manages to snuff out a single lick of flame, five others lash out in its wake.

And just before the maw of my midnight blaze closes around him, he throws down his sword and yells, "I yield, Your Highness! I yield!"

The second knight, who lingers just outside the range of my fire, has enough sense to do the same.

I draw the flames inward, coalescing them once again into that dark and hidden place at the heart of me. I lower the blunt sparring blade I carry and step back to survey the two candidates for general I just defeated.

Noros takes his helmet off first, revealing a layer of sweat-streaked ash caking his skin and panic in his eyes. While his skills in physical combat left much to be desired, he used his powers well, as weak as they are.

But he is no general.

When he stoops to grab his sword from the ground, I turn my attention to the other Celestial Knight.

Wayre, unlike his counterpart, doesn't seem unnerved by my poison flame. He's grinning when he pulls his helm from his head in spite of the soot that coats his face. "Well met, Your Highness," he says with a respectful nod. From his tone, I surmise that he rather enjoyed the fight, whereas Noros looks positively spent.

Interesting.

I recall how Lyanndra told me that Wayre was her top pick for general. Now that I've fought him, I think I'm starting to understand what she means. He's decent enough in combat, nothing special, but I do appreciate that he's tried to learn from his many spectacular losses to the Godslayer. He seems even-tempered. And, most importantly, he knew to yield before he was in mortal danger.

But even as I consider the possibility of promoting Wayre to general, Kartas' face flashes in my mind's eye.

A pang of grief skewers my chest. I think of how easily Kartas slipped between his role of friend and general. None of these men could ever fill that void.

Yet, Kartas was never really who I thought he was. I remember how he fooled me the night Lyanndra was attacked by his courtiers in the infirmary, and rage surges up to join my sorrow.

Lies filled Kartas' lungs like air. He was willing to kill me to take the throne and follow my father's blood soaked legacy. He was willing to kill *Lyanndra*.

I shouldn't be comparing these Celestial Knights to him, but my dead cousin's face still haunts me as I dismiss both Noros and Wayre back to their barracks. I keep picturing Kartas as he was on the throne room floor, cleaved nearly in two and staring at me with unseeing eyes. It's the death he deserved, but part of me still recoils in horror at the memory.

Sighing into the dusky air, I retrieve my blunt sword and heft it onto my shoulder. There's no point in ruminating on the usurper any longer.

The evening bell will ring soon, and the promise of a hearty meal entices me to abandon the training grounds for the comforts of the palace. If I'm lucky, Torran will be off researching, leaving me alone to my food and my thoughts. After all, the last thing I want to do is discuss world-ending prophecies and the elusive fang over supper.

And it seems the stars are on my side today, for nobody bothers me as I weave my way through the marble corridors of the Celestial Court.

By the time I reach my destination, I find the royal dining room blissfully empty with several steaming platters waiting upon the table. I flop down into my chair and reach for the nearest dish. In my rush to fill my plate, I nearly miss the letter, sealed in black wax with our joint sigil, sitting beside my napkin.

My heart stutters when I notice it. It could only be from Lyanndra.

Abandoning my dinner, I use a butter knife to slit the seal before unfolding the parchment. Sure enough, the page is filled with her familiar, spiky penmanship.

I scan the letter, eager for any details on her condition or whereabouts. I'm relieved to hear that she's made it to Breem and found her family unscathed, but the damage to the Southern Caldera is great, as we feared. There is no sign of the Ushum.

And she writes other things, too, things that make me shift in my chair as I struggle to hide my growing excitement and tightening trousers. I read the passage once, and then again, where she details what she wishes to do to me upon her return to the Celestial Court, and I am hopelessly undone.

Feverish yearning fills my chest. I wolf down my dinner, barely tasting it, and then carry the letter and my goblet of wine with me as I bid a hasty retreat back to our chambers. There, I draw myself a bath.

Once I've heated the water with my midnight flame, I set the goblet and the parchment down on the windowsill beside the tub before stripping down to nothing. I'm already uncomfortably hard just from reading Lyanndra's words. If she insists on teasing me so, it's only fair that I bring myself some relief.

A low hiss escapes my throat as I sink down into the scalding water. It's nothing compared to the heat of my crossed star, but I can't deny how much I enjoy the way the warmth seeps into my muscles and melts away the tensions of the day.

The fang can wait.

The would-be generals don't matter.

Kartas' ghost can haunt somebody else tonight.

It's just me and Lyanndra's wicked words now.

I sigh and close my eyes, picturing the wonderfully vulgar things she wrote of in her letter. At the same time, my hand dips down beneath the surface of the water to close around my aching cock.

"Lyanndra," I moan out into the empty washroom. I imagine her hand against me, small and calloused, as I begin to pump my fist over the velvet skin of my length. If she were here right now, she'd look at me with mischief in her eyes and a smirk upon her lips while coaxing me closer and closer to the edge.

Heat rushes through my veins as my mind wanders. Did she touch herself while she wrote that scandalous letter? Did she imagine my fingers inside her instead of her own? And when she found her release, did my name spill from her lips the way it did in our dream?

Each question drives me further to ruin. My hand moves faster beneath the water as I think of her panting and hungry for me. I recall the dream we shared, how she sank down on my cock like she was made for it, and I groan aloud.

By the stars, I would give *everything*—my kingdom, my crown, my flame—to be with her right now, to hear her moans in my ear, to feel her shatter against me.

And when my hips jerk and the pleasure peaks, I growl out her name as I spill myself relentlessly to the very thought of her.

She doesn't leave my mind when I finally come back to myself. I redraw the bath and wash myself properly this time. After, I dry off and drain the last of the wine from my goblet before retiring, naked, to our bed. I tuck her letter beneath the mattress, as though that will bring her closer to me still.

Then I close my eyes and invite sleep to come.

But the night is cruel, and I find myself turning beneath the sheets as I struggle to get comfortable. Thoughts race through my mind at such a dire pace that I barely have time to consider one before it's overshadowed by the next.

Is Lyanndra camped out with her host, or is she staying with her family?

Were they glad to see her? Will I ever meet them, or will they hate me for being a Demigod, as she once did?

Does she think of me often?

Does her yearning for me match mine for her?

Somehow, I think it does. I feel her need somewhere deep within me, in that same dark place where my fire sparks and whispers and writhes. And now, as I straddle the veil between sleep and wakefulness, it strikes me that perhaps I can call to her the way I summon my midnight flame.

Will she answer?

There's only one way to find out. With nothing to lose, I reach for her.

At first, nothing happens.

But then, little by little, I feel that tug in my chest that I've come to associate with our bond, as though there is a thread that ties us to one another, and all I have to do is *pull*.

So I do.

The effect is instant. The room melts away, and for the briefest moment, I am nowhere and everywhere all at once. But then the world, or some approximation of it, coalesces around me, and though I have no way of explaining how I know it, I am absolutely certain that I have achieved my goal.

Yet, my heart drops when I realize where I am.

I am standing on an ashen battlefield. Bodies, mangled and unrecognizable, twist up from the drifts in a terrible tableau. Acrid smoke hangs low in the air. And in the center of it all, there lies a corpse clad in gold and crimson, its green eyes lifeless and tilted toward the sky.

Panic claws at my throat.

I'd know those eyes anywhere.

My father.

But he's not the only person I recognize in this horrendous place. A familiar figure kneels before the fallen god, her shoulders shaking as she struggles to catch her breath.

Lyanndra.

And I realize with growing dread that this is no dream I have invaded.

No.

This is why she tosses and turns at night. *This* is why she sometimes shouts herself awake.

This is no dream.

I have stepped directly into a nightmare.

CHAPTER 19

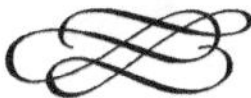

Lyanndra

No.

No, no, no, no, no, no.

Ash rains down from the sky in a perverse mockery of snowfall. Smoke, black and acrid, stings my throat as I fight to draw in a single breath. Panic scrabbles at my ribs, and I want to close my eyes, to shut out the sight of the Flaming God prostrated on the ground before me, but I can't.

I *can't.*

And even if I could, I would never be able to escape the smell. It's impossible to forget it, the stench of charred bodies, overheated metal, and blood, so much blood....

I stare down at the man who once was king.

His eyes are green.

Empty.

Gone.

My stomach churns. I think I might vomit, but I know it'll be clotted and black, so I swallow it down. How long will I have to pay for my sins? Haven't I already given enough?

"You're dead," I snarl down at the corpse. "And I'm not, and this isn't fucking *real*."

I know I'm right. This is a nightmare, but my awareness doesn't make the miserable dream any less excruciating. Even if it's all just an illusion, the taste of bile in my mouth is genuine.

So is the fear.

So is the panic.

I've never told Syran about these terrible visions. On the few occasions when I woke from them, confused and shouting in his bed, he drew me into his arms and held me close without question. He knew I would speak of it when I was ready, but how could I ever explain to him that it's the lifeless corpse of his father that haunts me so?

Yet, I long for my crossed star now. I want him to shake me awake and kiss my forehead while he whispers in my ear that he's here. I want the hot pressure of his hands splayed across my back and his arms around me. I want his fire and his safety, everything that he is.

Thinking of him grants me enough strength to finally force my eyes closed, though it doesn't pull me from this dreadful place entirely.

At least in the darkness, I can imagine that Syran is with me. My tortured mind conjures the warmth of him at my back, and I can practically feel the phantom weight of his hand curl over my armored shoulder as he murmurs my name.

"Lyanndra."

My eyes snap open.

No longer am I stuck on the smoldering battlefield, surrounded by the dead. The air is clear of ash. The burning heat quickly dissipates into a mild chill that prickles along my bare arms. I'm standing in the yard outside the homestead in the shadow of the mountain, but I know this is still a dream by the way my armor melts seamlessly into a fine nightdress as the landscape settles into silence around me.

And I know that—somehow—I am not alone.

Syran is *here*.

Part of me dreads that this is another nightmare, another trick, but the urge to see him is stronger than my fear.

I turn around.

He stands before me, his body bare beneath the silver moonlight, his flaming hair unbound and swept by the breeze. He's so close that my breasts brush the broad plane of his chest as I tip my head up to meet his burning gaze.

How long has he been here? How much did he see? What must he think of me, kneeling before the body of his slain father?

I worry that he will judge me for it, but then he closes the sliver of distance between us and takes me in his arms, and there's only the familiar comfort of his body against mine. I melt into him.

"Syran," I breathe.

He draws one hand down to my waist, pinning me solidly against him, while he slides the other to the nape of my neck. "I'm here," he assures me. His velvet voice rumbles through his chest and reverberates into me. "I have you."

We linger like this for a long time, until my limbs stop trembling and my heartbeat slows. Only then does he pull away.

"Is that always what you see?" he asks quietly, his eyes searching mine. "The battlefield? My father?"

I nod.

"Can the dead not leave us in peace?" Fire seethes behind his green gaze, but I know him well enough now to understand that I am not the target of his fury. "Why must they bedevil us so?"

It strikes me then that I am not the only one of us who's steeped in blood. And while Syran's nights pass peacefully aside from the occasional bout of insomnia, I realize now that perhaps his personal phantoms plague him in his waking hours, instead of in sleep. So I question, "What ghosts do you see?"

Grief creeps across his face in a torrid wave. "Kartas," he utters.

A sharp blade of guilt twists within me at his admission. I open my mouth to say something, to lay the blame at my feet, but he cuts me off before I can speak.

"Don't," he warns, his eyes flashing dangerously in the moonlight.

"My father and Kartas chose their own paths, and they paid the price for their misdeeds. I will not have them haunt you for it."

"What if I deserve it?" I challenge.

"You don't," he says firmly. "And I will spend every second of my life proving that to you, if you'll let me." He presses his forehead against mine and implores, "Ask this of me, Lyanndra. Allow me to take this burden from you, to carry it with you. *Please.*"

I stare up into his blazing eyes, searching for any sign of dishonesty. But I feel it deep within me that he speaks only the truth, even if I cannot yet see it.

"Prove it to me," I tell him. "Make me believe it."

"Until the stars fall."

And then he seals his vow with a burning kiss.

My lips meet his with a hunger that reflects how much I've longed for him these past few weeks. This is still a dream, yes, but it is also somehow real, and I refuse to wait for him to show me just how serious he is about keeping this promise.

He seems to feel the same, if the hard press of his cock against my stomach is any indication. I can't help but gasp as the sensation. Dimly, I'm aware that there's some reason why I should be quiet, but the heat of him is far too distracting for my mind to dredge it up.

But as a moan builds in my throat, I remember how my soldiers wouldn't meet my eye the morning after Syran first visited me in our dreams, and I freeze.

"Wait!" I hiss.

Syran tips his head and fixes me with a questioning look.

"The noises," I whisper. Embarrassment heats my face as I explain, "Whatever sounds we make in our dreams, we make in reality."

He considers this for a moment before his eyes alight with mischief and a smirk creeps across his face. "You'd best be quiet then."

And before I can object, he's down on his knees and throwing the hem of my nightdress over his head. Then his mouth is on me, and his tongue is inside me, and I am lost.

Bolts of pleasure surge through my veins as he grips my hips hard, encouraging me to ride his face like I would his cock. I just manage to slap my hands to my mouth before I cry out.

By the stars, this man will be my undoing. And I will let him unravel me, thread by thread, until he has seen all that I am. There is nobody else I trust. No other would look upon such dark and rotting parts of me, only to take me like this beneath the quicksilver coin of the moon.

And as I reach my peak upon his face, it is all I can do not to howl out his name.

Syran.

My crossed star.

My equal in power.

The man I will marry and rule beside.

My legs tremble from the intensity of my pleasure, and I lean heavily against him as he surfaces and draws me into his arms once more. He pulls my hands from my mouth, only to capture me in another searing kiss. This time, I can taste myself on his lips before he breaks away.

"Have I convinced you yet?" he whispers in my ear.

It's my turn to smirk. "Not entirely," I reply. "Perhaps you should keep trying."

He laughs, and the sound does absolutely nothing to quell my rising desire. But before I can act on it, he kneels again, this time pulling me with him. I let him drag me down onto the umber grass and pin me beneath the hot weight of his body, where he lines his cock up with my core.

Then, as he enters me in one powerful thrust, he growls, "I wish you could view yourself through my eyes." He rolls his hips, and I remember to stifle my moan with my hand just in time. "When I look at you, I see the moon. Even when you're just a shadow of yourself, the tides still bow to you. The night holds its breath when you speak. Fuck the Celestial Gods. You are of the heavens, Lyanndra, and you are the only star I need worship."

And he does worship at my altar then, as devoutly as he is able, and I need nothing else, crave nothing else, *am* nothing else.

I am his, completely.

And he is mine.

We are bound together. We are inseparable. And when we finally unravel, it's together as one with my name as a benediction on his lips.

Only after, when I'm settled in his arms awaiting the inevitable arrival of the dawn, do I think to ask, "How did you find me? In my nightmare, I mean."

Syran presses a slow kiss to my temple and answers, "I was thinking of you, and there was this *pull*. It felt like calling upon the flame, in a way."

"Could you do it again?" The notion of having Syran here with me in this dreamscape is tantalizing, especially with so much physical distance between us.

He seems to come to the same conclusion, for he grins. "I shall certainly try, if it means I can have you like this once more."

"You can have me any way, if you succeed," I promise.

"Then consider it done." He presses another kiss to my forehead, and I nestle deeper into the unyielding comfort of his arms.

At some point, just before the sun rises, I slide off into a doze. I'm barely aware of how he dissolves in the thin morning light, but I don't miss the way his lips brush mine one last time.

A second later, I blink, properly awake this time.

I'm back in my bedroll in the field just beyond the homestead, where my parents insisted my host make camp. A quick glance around reveals that, while the usual early risers are already milling about and stoking the cooking fires, nobody appears to be staunchly ignoring me. Satisfied that I did not repeat my past shame, and with the way Syran indulged me, I decide not to linger here any longer.

There is much to be done.

Like the other settlements this close to the Southern Caldera, Breem is in dire need of assistance. While I want to start my search for the Ushum as soon as possible, I'm also concerned that the damage to this town's structures will only worsen if there are more tremors to come. Our priority has to be shoring up the homes here first, then the barns and outbuildings. If the creature is indeed waking, it will serve us well to limit the immediate destruction from any quakes it might cause.

Tomorrow, we will form a search party to locate the Ushum's lair while the rest of the Celestial Knights continue to render aid to the villagers. According to Torran and Carolissa, the beast has been sleeping for a thousand years. Hopefully, it can rest for one more day.

I stand and stretch, relishing the delicious ache between my thighs, before donning my armor. Not wanting to disturb my parents, I forgo the homestead for the nearest cooking fire, where I procure a strong cup of tea and a ration of hard cheese.

Prizes in hand, I wander over to one of the nearby fields and clamber up onto the fence to look out across the arid landscape.

Everything here is some tone of brown, from the chestnut tint of the ancient rock to the tufts of tawny grass that peek out from the cracks in the stone. The sky sits in shocking contrast, as blue as the oceans and the lapis lazuli found in the marketplaces of the Eastern Roosts.

It's peaceful.

There's beauty here, if you're willing to wait for it. As I sip my tea, I catch sight of a small brown lizard zigzagging between the knots of grass. Tiny, ground-dwelling birds, pleasingly round and fooled by my silence, seem to pop out of nowhere to peck at the rocky ground. A large green dragonfly that drips with dew flits in front of my face before droning off into the distance.

I smile into the placid morning. The only way this could be better is if Syran were here beside me to enjoy it.

But, like all quiet moments, this one, too, must come to an end.

My serenity is shattered by the sound of footsteps pounding against the hard-packed earth at my back.

Instinct overtakes my previous indolence, and the world around me snaps into sharp focus.

There is only one set of footfalls. I like those odds.

But even with my greatsword strapped to my back, my hands are full of tea and cheese. And while the latter will do little in combat other than play, perhaps, into the element of surprise, the former is scalding and the tin cup will do some damage if used creatively. I hope that will give me enough time to free my hands and draw my blade

With my strategy determined, I jump down from the fence and turn to face my opponent.

The man who approaches is tall, slim, and strangely familiar. I'm certain he's not one of my Celestial Knights, and, given the simple jerkin he wears, I assume he must be a villager. Is it possible that this is somebody I knew before I left?

I grow sure of this when he stops a few feet away. His face is soft and round, and his long, white-blond hair is braided back in the typical southern style. Yet, his features betray his origin, and I think that I *do* know this Starless man. Or at least, I did.

He seems to recognize me, too, for his blue eyes widen, and his jaw drops. I stare, trying to place him, as his gaze trails down along my tarnished armor and then back to my face.

"It really is you," he murmurs. "I heard them talking in town this morning, and I couldn't believe it. I just… I had to see for myself. And it *is* you, Lyanndra, isn't it?"

For a moment, I'm stuck.

But then my stomach drops as cold realization floods my veins.

That pale hair. Those blue eyes. The dimpled cheeks that always made him appear so much younger, even when we were children.

Dread squeezes an iron hand around my lungs. I haven't seen him since the night I left, when he and his father came over to the homestead to threaten my family.

Aaro.

The boy I was supposed to marry.

And in spite of the years that have gone by and bad blood between us, I have a terrible, sinking feeling that he's not quite done with me.

Not yet.

CHAPTER 20

Syran

Something is wrong.

Even as I make my rounds through Nexus, where I check on the refugees and oversee the preparations for the next aid caravan, a sour pit of unease swirls in my chest. It wasn't there when I woke from the dream I shared with Lyanndra. In fact, I felt satiated and at peace when I opened my eyes.

But shortly after I rose for the day, I noticed this strange sense of disquiet, which has now grown into something I can no longer ignore.

The most unnerving thing about it is that I do not think this emotion is mine.

I think it belongs to Lyanndra.

While I'm satisfied that she's not in any true danger, questions still haunt me while I go about my morning duties.

How is it that I can feel this echo of her? I imagine it must have something to do with the bond of the crossed stars. After all, this isn't the first time it has happened. Didn't I feel with frantic surety that she was heading toward the Celestial Court–toward *me*–after the Ceremony? And I knew she was in danger in the infirmary, though I was never able to explain how.

Perhaps by going to her last night as I did, I opened up some greater channel between us.

Yet, that still does not address my biggest concern, which is that if this sensation originated with Lyanndra, something must have happened to make her feel this way.

Is it a remnant of her nightmare? I think back to the horrific tableau that haunted her so. It was a facsimile of the battle where she killed my father, and I will not pretend that it was easy for me to bear witness to such a sight. But still, I do not, and will not ever, blame her for what she had to do.

I meant what I said to her.

My father tried to pull out the beating heart of Alastria and burn it to ash.

The Godslayer made sure he met a fitting end in turn.

And as terrible as the vision was to behold, it was far worse to realize that Lyanndra has been battling such phantoms alone for so long.

I want her to lean on me, to do as she asked and allow me to shoulder the pain and the guilt that she carries within her. After we consummated our vows, I hoped that she would understand that as long as there is air in my lungs and fire in my soul, she will never have to suffer in silence.

So it wounds me more than her monstrous blade ever could to consider that she might doubt me still.

No.

I refuse to believe that.

Lyanndra is fierce and steadfast. When she makes a promise, she intends to keep it, and she would never play with my heart that way, even unintentionally. No, something else must have happened in the short time after we woke, something unnerving enough to rattle even the Godslayer.

Was it the Ushum, stirring beneath the Caldera? Or was it something else?

Anxiety swirls within me throughout the rest of the morning. By noon, I can bear it no longer, and I return to the palace intent on finding some answers. I've never heard of this sort of bond between crossed stars, but if there's one person in Alastria who might know of the secrets of this ancient magic, it's Torran.

Predictably, I find him in the library. He's tucked away in the Archive Room, sifting through several sheaves of old parchments, while Lady Carolissa flips through a tome on mythological beasts at the table beside him.

The young courtier jumps to her feet as I enter, curtsies, and mumbles, "Your Highness."

"Please, my lady. There is no need for such formality," I remind her, as I do every time our paths cross. I wonder if she bows to Lyanndra too, or would if my crossed star were here.

She curtsies again. "Yes, Your Highness."

Fighting the urge to sigh, I turn to Torran. "I could use your wisdom, if your papers can spare you for but a moment," I say.

The old Demigod peers up at me, his blue eyes brilliant even in the low light. "I think they could be persuaded." He nods to Lady Carolissa and asks, "Would you mind giving us some privacy, my dear?"

She nods and does as he requests. Once she's gone and the door is shut firmly behind her, I slide into the nearest chair at the table.

"I take it this isn't about the fang?" Torran inquires.

I shake my head. "No. I was wondering if you knew anything more about the bond of the crossed stars."

Torran raises an eyebrow. "Trouble?" he asks.

"The opposite," I reply. "The bond between the Godslayer and I is… strange. Most welcome, but strange."

"How so?"

I hesitate for a moment. Lyanndra may be forthcoming with me, but she's also solitary by nature, the type of person who values her privacy. I do not want to violate her trust by sharing details with

Torran, but I also desperately need some answers. Finally, I settle on, "We visit one another in our dreams."

A strange expression passes over my advisor's face, though it's gone in an instant. Then he asks, "Does this happen every night?"

"No," I tell him. "Only sometimes."

"And is it random?"

"It was," I say.

"Was?" Torran repeats.

I feel my face grow warm as I admit, "Until last night."

"Ah," he replies with a knowing grin. "I see."

"I would much rather that you didn't," I grumble.

The wizened Demigod wheezes out a laugh and then leans back in his chair. "I can't say that I'm surprised by any of this," he reveals. "While I do not yet possess the explanation that you seek, I would be lying if I told you that I didn't expect curious things to happen between the two of you."

"What do you mean?"

"You're a Demigod. The Godslayer is Starless. That alone is most unusual." He fixes me with his vibrant gaze once again, and not for the first time, I feel that he's looking through me rather than at me. "Does it not follow that the bond itself would be of a similar nature?"

I nod in agreement.

"And would we not expect it to be powerful?" he continues. "You possess great strength, Syran. I don't think even your father understood the fire that burns within you."

"And what of the Godslayer?" I ask.

His face alights once more. "Something burns within her, too, I think. Though what it is, I'm not sure anybody knows."

That dry, ancient thing at the heart of me whispers that he speaks the truth, and I find myself nodding again before my mind can catch up.

Torran's brow furrows. "Are you feeling quite yourself, Syran?"

"Yes," I answer quickly. "I'm just tired." It's not a lie, but it's not entirely accurate either. And while I'm fairly certain that the old

Demigod sees right through my deception, he at least possesses the decency to pretend that he doesn't.

"Once I solve the riddle of the fang, I will turn my attention to the bond," he promises.

Grateful for the change in subject, I reply, "Thank you. And speaking of the fang, have you any news?"

He sighs and gestures to the various parchments that are spread across the table before us. "The little I've found so far only supports our prior theories," he explains. "As you know, Lyrtas the Blasphemer thought that the fang was a divine weapon used to kill the Ankir."

I ponder this for a moment and then frown. "If it can slay a god, does that not mean that the fang must be of equal power?"

"That is *exactly* what it means," Torran confirms. "And because the Ankir were, according to legend, elemental in nature, I believe that perhaps the fang is, too."

Elemental?

It's an interesting theory to consider, especially in the context of Lyrtas' mad ramblings. I take it a step further and muse, "If the pieces of the Ankir *were* the fallen stars that gave the Demigods their command over the natural forces, what if the fang was also found by our people?"

Torran tilts his head. He's clearly intrigued. "Are you suggesting that the fang has already been uncovered?" he asks.

All I can offer him is a shrug.

"It is certainly possible," he concedes after a thoughtful moment. "Maybe the weapon we seek has been under our noses this entire time."

"Wouldn't we have heard of such an artifact?" I challenge, even though it was my own heretical pondering that brought rise to the suggestion in the first place.

"Only if those Demigods knew what it was when they found it," he replies. "Consider this, Syran. There are researchers from the Eastern Roosts. They call themselves *archaeologists*—a mouthful of a word, if you ask me—and they dig up great swathes of old riverbeds and forests. They find all sorts of odd things. Some of them are identifiable, like arrowheads carved out of stone."

"How inefficient," I remark.

"Quite," he agrees. "But we know the purpose of an arrowhead and can recognize one regardless of the material. Yet, some of the items are simply a mystery to us: strange bits of twisted metal, preserved footprints belonging to no man or beast known to us. Those are pieces of history that, without context, we have no name or label for."

"Am I to understand that you think the fang could have been treated like one of those objects?"

Torran shrugs. "Perhaps."

I take a moment to contemplate this idea. If the fang was indeed uncovered long ago by the ancient Demigods, where would it be?

The cathedral is my first guess, but I quickly dismiss that idea. While the holy space is filled with all manner of ritualistic items, I don't recall ever seeing anything resembling the weapon we seek within the house of worship.

But what about underneath it?

"The reliquary," I blurt out.

The old Demigod's face lights up. "Of course!" he murmurs excitedly. "If anybody found the fang all those years ago, they may not have realized what it was, but they might have had enough sense to store it in the reliquary!"

I think about the cramped, dusty catacombs that stretch beneath the cathedral and suppress the urge to cringe. Cobwebs and old, decrepit relics do not instill any particular sense of terror within me, but there's something about the space that reminds me of the dungeons, and that does give me pause. Still, if there's even the slightest chance that the fang is down there, I must go after it.

"We shall start the search immediately," I tell Torran as I rise from my chair.

He smiles sadly. "As much as I would like to accompany you, I fear these old bones are far too brittle for such an adventure." Before I can argue, he suggests, "Why not take Carolissa with you? I am confident that she would be able to identify the fang if she were to see it. The stars know she's spent long enough staring at the drawings of it."

While my hubris would rather that I make the journey alone, I have to agree that he does have a point. "Very well," I acquiesce.

"And take the map," he cautions. "You'll find it behind the altar in the cathedral, by the entrance to the reliquary. It's a maze down there. I would hate for you to get lost."

"Thank you." I offer him a nod and start toward the door, but before I can even reach for the handle, Torran pauses me once more.

"Take care in how you speak of this to Carolissa, Syran," he warns. "The things which we have uttered here today are blasphemy of the highest order. You and I may not be concerned with such heresy, but not everybody will feel the same. The fang, and our hunt for it, goes against every teaching of the Demigods."

I recall how Kartas and Ressa manipulated the courtiers into thinking that Lyanndra bewitched me and how my cousin was willing to die for his twisted beliefs.

As much as I hate to admit it, Torran speaks only the truth, so I say, "I shall heed your counsel."

But he has one last question before I go.

"Are you sure you want to do this, knowing the price you may pay?" he asks.

I meet his electric gaze with all the fire I can muster. "I have no choice."

He sighs and nods. "I thought you might say that. But remember, Syran, to reach beyond the stars is to defy them."

Something Lyanndra said to me long ago in anger surfaces, and finally, I understand what she meant.

"I will not bend a knee so easily to the stars," I growl.

I will forge my own path for this kingdom.

I will bow to nothing.

To nobody.

Nobody except my queen.

CHAPTER 21

Lyanndra

"How can I help?"

I stare at Aaro. My expression is stony, rivaled only by the jagged peak of the mountain that rises up in the distance, though not by much.

Did he not understand what my silence toward him this morning meant?

Was walking away and leaving him alone in the field not enough?

Around me, I can feel the shifting eyes of my men as they try desperately to seem as though they're not paying rapt attention. It was a shock for my host to realize that I herald from Breem. Now, the nearest Celestial Knights eavesdrop with shameless abandon, eager to feast upon the scraps of my old life.

"Please," Aaro insists. "I can be of use here."

He's right.

I can think of several uses for him, mainly feeding him to the Ushum when I find it. With any luck, it will succumb to indigestion and die.

But I am, unfortunately, the Godslayer, and as much as I'd like to refuse him, this village is suffering. There's rubble to be hauled and foundations to be shored. Every pair of hands will make a difference.

So, it's with great effort that I nod once before immediately turning away. I don't care to see whether triumph or satisfaction creep across his face. Instead, I catch the gaze of Mallan, who works beside me, and jerk my head in Aaro's direction. The candidate for general knows me well enough by now to understand the silent command.

"Come with me," Mallan instructs. Thankfully, he has enough sense to send Aaro far away from where I'm filling the cracks in this house's foundation with coarse, brown mortar, saying, "We could use another body running timber from the caravan."

The two men stride off.

In an attempt to turn my thoughts from Aaro, I focus back on what still needs to be done.

We're lucky that Syran's aid arrived within days of our host reaching Breem. No trees grow this far south, and the lumber we need to reinforce the structures here cannot be found locally. The wood that was delivered from Nexus with the caravan is invaluable.

The convoy also brought much-needed food, water, and medicine. Presently, Orobos' company is tasked with handing out supplies to the villagers in need, leaving Mallan and Irtas, along with their men and any of the townsfolk willing to help, to the manual labor.

With so much assistance, I expect that we'll finish securing the town's dwellings by nightfall. Tomorrow, I'll direct Mallan's company to work on the barns and other outbuildings while I'll lead Irtas and his soldiers on the search for the Ushum's lair.

Not for the first time, I consider what to do when we locate the creature.

Killing it is not yet an option.

If it slumbers, even restlessly, I suppose we should simply leave it alone.

But what if we wake it? What if it rises before we're ready, before we have the fang?

Perhaps it would be wise to evacuate the village, or at least prepare for such an event. Most of these people have never ventured further than Ryv or Sheel, let alone the midlands of Alastria, and we would need to secure supplies and shelter for them before undertaking such an effort.

I'll write to Syran tonight, I decide. I'd rather we be ready for the worst than scramble in the face of disaster.

With my plan in place, I let myself fall back into my work. There's nothing complicated about this current task, and it's soothing in a way that allows my mind to wander while my hands take over. But my relative peace is once again disturbed when Mallan returns.

He glances at me in a decidedly unsubtle way as he reclaims his spot along the foundation and picks up his trowel. I can practically feel the questions buzzing off him. To his credit, he manages to keep his mouth closed for at least a full minute before he blurts out, "Who was that?"

I don't even bother looking at him.

He must be feeling particularly bold today because he presses, "He said he knows you."

When I continue to ignore him, he finally seems to take the hint, for he falls silent, though his eyes still dart over to mine every now and again.

Internally, I seethe.

Who is Aaro to claim that he knows me? Even as children, he, like my parents, always seemed to have an idea of who I should have been, but never who I actually was.

Yes, there were times where we snuck out into the fields, friends in tow, with bottles of pilfered mead, or rode horses together across the arid landscape. We had fun. But other, more tenuous memories overshadow those unfettered moments.

How many times did Aaro ask me to kiss him? Was one refusal not enough? And when my words no longer worked, I quickly picked up on the way he would pass me the mead twice as much as he would the other girls, and I started bringing my own bottle.

I did not fall into that trap.

He did not give up.

In the mornings, he brought me soft rolls baked by his mother or handfuls of wildflowers picked from the thin soil at the base of the mountain. It didn't seem to matter that I rejected his gifts every time. If I stayed out late, he would try to walk me back to the homestead. He chatted with my parents and helped my brothers in the fields.

They liked him. They thought I should, too.

And it culminated, of course, in the disastrous betrothal.

I never wanted to be trapped in a marriage with Aaro, but he was overjoyed when he found out about our parents' schemes. He told me that I should be happy, that he would honor me and provide for our family, whenever it grew.

The very thought made me sick.

My stomach still turns at the mere memory, even though over a decade has passed.

Does Aaro understand why I left? Did he think that, when I told him that I would never marry him and he went to his father in an attempt to force my hand, I would simply crumble before him? Would he have smiled as he gathered up the pieces of me, forming them into the wife he so desperately wanted?

I think he would have.

Yet, a long time has passed since then. I am not the same as I was. Perhaps I am not the only one.

Syran's words, spoken on our last full day together, echo in my mind. He told me how he very nearly followed in his father's bloody footsteps, that he almost became the hateful, rotting thing he fights against now. And I cannot deny that I assumed this of him when we first met. In fact, I despised him for it.

So I ponder now whether it's fair for me to judge Aaro for his behavior back then. Like me–like Syran–he was just a child. He was under his father's influence as much as my crossed star was.

Is it possible that Aaro has changed since then?

The question lingers in the back of my mind as the morning slides into afternoon.

In spite of the cool shadow of the mountain at our backs, the air is alive with dry heat. Sweat pools at the base of my neck and beneath my arms, soaking through my smallclothes and causing my dragonhide leathers to stick uncomfortably to my bare skin. Several of the Celestial Knights shamelessly strip down to their tunics and, in a few cases, their trousers.

As a woman, I do not have that luxury.

Still, I'm used to this heat. I grew up in it, though it's not in my blood, and I know all of the tricks to keep myself from succumbing to the sun's ire. While I work hard, I take frequent breaks and make sure to visit the well often, where the water is cloudy with sediment stirred up by the quakes, but drinkable yet.

It's during one of these lulls that I turn from drawing a bucket up from the depths to find a very pregnant woman staring at me from the road.

She wears a simple yellow smock and a plain apron atop it, a style favored by many of the Starless in this region. Her hair, long and glossy black, is braided to her crown.

This, amongst everything else about her, is what causes me to freeze.

For I wear my hair in the same manner.

I have since the first night I left Breem. My golden curls were too unruly to fit beneath my father's stolen helm, and I couldn't quite bring myself to cut them, so I wove them tightly to my scalp the way one of the other girls my age taught me when we were younger.

And now she's in front of me once more, strangely unchanged after so many years aside from her swollen stomach and the way her face has thinned with age.

What was her name?

For a moment, I struggle to remember, but then it surfaces to my lips before my mind can catch up. I say, "Aminnya?"

Her eyes widen. "It *is* you," she gasps. "I saw you ride into town, but I never thought..." Her gaze drags over my tarnished armor, where the golden scales glisten in the afternoon heat. "You really are the Godslayer."

I nod.

Aminnya surveys me carefully, fear and awe flickering across her face in turn, and I take the opportunity to study her. I remember her as a gentle, quiet girl who would blush when any boy–Aaro especially–would look her way. Didn't she always speak of settling down and building a family of her own? By the looks of it, she has accomplished her goal, and I find that I'm quite happy for her.

"The armor suits you," she comments after a few more seconds of awkward silence. Then, as her eyes settle on Syran's golden token on my arm, she adds, "Your Highness."

"I am not yet queen," I inform her.

"But the rumors are true?" she asks. "You're to marry the king?"

Once again, I nod.

Shock flashes across her features, as though she can't quite reconcile the woman who stands before her with who I was before. Her mouth opens, closes, and then opens again. "But... he's a *Demigod*. And you're... *you*."

"Yes," I say. "I am aware."

I am also aware of how, much like the Starless of the north, the people of the Southern Caldera have little love for those who consider themselves blessed by the Celestial Gods. While I would like to think that my impending marriage to Syran will be seen by all as a show of peace and unity, I am not so much of a fool to believe that none will consider it akin to an act of treason.

It is unclear to me where Aminnya stands in that debate until she leans closer, as she used to when imparting rare bits of gossip, and drops her voice low. "Is he as handsome as they say?" she questions in a conspiratorial tone.

An image of Syran, his flaming hair loose about his face and his green eyes flashing above me as he thrusts his hips into mine, courses through my mind. Heat creeps up my cheeks at the mere thought.

My reaction must be telling enough because the last of her trepidation melts away, and she smiles. "You look well, Lyanndra. Truly."

"As do you," I reply. "I am glad we have both found our paths."

We stand together, there at the well, Aminnya with the wide curve of her stomach and the tiny life inside, and me in my armor with my greatsword at my back. How is it that we both started out in this place, yet ended up choosing such different destinies?

But I do not have long to contemplate this question, for, even as we linger, the water in the bucket I hold begins to tremble.

I have just enough time to grab hold of Aminnya's shoulders before the ground shudders beneath our feet. She clings to me as the earth heaves. Shouts rise from elsewhere in the village, and somewhere in the distance, a splintering crash indicates that another building has collapsed.

And at the worst of it, when I can barely keep up both of us upright, a sound echoes through the quaking afternoon.

A roar.

A snarl.

A grief-stricken wail.

The vibration curls around my bones, and I instinctually cringe. It's like nothing I've heard before, yet somehow I know what it is.

I *know*.

And even after the keening cry fades and the earth stills, the cacophony still echoes through my ears like a battle cry.

It's the shriek of the Ushum.

It's waking up.

We're running out of time.

CHAPTER 22

SYRAN

"Are you sure about this, Your Highness?" Lady Carolissa asks.

No.

I am not.

I peer down into the dark, yawning abyss beyond the open door of the reliquary and resist the urge to shudder. A waft of dry air, tempered by eons of dust and rodent droppings, swirls up from the depths to assault my nose.

"I could just stay here," the courtier suggests. She lingers behind me, peeking around my shoulder as though she expects some monster to come barreling up the marble stairs at any moment.

I sigh. At our backs, the gloomy cathedral is, comparatively, a paradise. I suppose I could leave her up here and return with anything that looks even remotely like a fang for her to inspect.

But then, I realize that there may be ancient texts to read or deci-pher, ones beyond my comprehension, and I shake my head. "I am sorry to ask this of you, my lady," I tell her, "but if there's any hope of finding the fang, it must be done."

She grimaces. "Very well, Your Highness."

Still, neither of us moves.

The seconds drag on in silence as my thoughts turn to Lyanndra. She wouldn't hesitate to march down those steps and into the labyrinthine chambers that stretch far beneath the footprint of Nexus. I visualize the look she'd give me, her hazel eyes glimmering and one brow raised in a silent challenge. *Are you coming?* she would ask. *Or is the great and mighty King of Alastria scared?*

"Imagine what the Godslayer would say if she could see us now," I muse. "She would think us cowards—or fools. Perhaps both, if she were feeling uncharitable."

Lady Carolissa's grim expression lightens, if only for a moment. "I have heard tales of her adventures," the young woman says. "She is fearless, and so should we be."

I nod.

Yet, that is not entirely true, is it? I know what horror looks like written across Lyanndra's features. I've held her to me while she's trembled and have kissed away her tears.

No, she is not above the same terrors that plague us all, but she faces them with steadfast determination. It is that, her insistence on staring down those who seek to torment her, that makes her who she is.

The Godslayer is not fearless.

She is brave.

"So should we be," I murmur.

Before I can change my mind, I conjure a flicker of midnight flame in my palm and step forward into the darkness.

Lady Carolissa follows closely on my heels.

My black fire throws the walls of the catacombs into shocking relief. Our shadows bend and twist at our sides as if they have lives of their own, and I do my best to ignore the disconcerting illusion as we descend into the reliquary. The silence, too, becomes harder to disregard. It chews up our footsteps and spits them out as unnatural echoes that sound, at times, as though somebody else is in here with us.

Relief pools in my chest as we finally arrive at the bottom of the marble steps. It's so dark down here that the light of my flame just barely penetrates the shadows. Though it's been many years since I last visited this sacred place, I remember that there are sconces lining the walls, just waiting to be lit. With a flick of my hand, I ignite them all in a blazing cascade.

Behind me, Lady Carolissa gasps.

While this place does bear some superficial resemblance to the dungeons, the differences are noticeable enough to bring me some comfort. The stone here is clean and glittering. Even in the flickering gloom, I can make out the sigils carved into the marble walls.

"Protective wards," the courtier whispers as she runs curious fingers over the etchings. Confusion creeps across her features. "What are these for?"

I glance over my shoulder at the antechamber, where several corridors snake off into the darkness. This place thrums with primal magic. It's so heavy in the air that I can practically taste it, like ash on my tongue.

Does she not feel it too?

Something deep within me seems to shift. Blood rushes through my veins in a sudden torrent, urging my heart into a pounding tattoo as the embers of my soul ignite with searing black heat.

Every flame in the room shudders and flares in response.

"Your Highness?" the young Demigod asks. She makes no effort to hide the alarm in her voice.

"I'm fine," I insist, though it spills out as more of a hiss than anything. "Just… do you not feel it?"

She shakes her head. "No, Your Highness."

I close my eyes and let out an unsteady breath.

The strange sensation is already starting to recede, though my heart still races beneath my ribs. Whatever it was that came over me is likely a product of one of the artifacts stashed away in this dismal place. There is, after all, a reason for those protective wards, and it has nothing to do with keeping anybody out.

Some of the things down here belong in the dark.

And some of them want to *leave.*

But I will not fall victim to such folly, so I rally myself and turn back to Lady Carolissa. Her expression is discomposed, bordering on fear, and I worry that I have rattled her far more than anything we might find in this cursed place.

"Expect clever tricks," I warn her. "There are things down here that are best left forgotten, and we cannot let ourselves succumb to their power. Do you understand?"

"Yes, Your Highness," she replies, but I can tell from the way her brow furrows that she does not.

No matter.

She'll find out soon enough.

Using the map from the cathedral as a guide, I steer us down the first corridor to the right of the stairwell, where, according to Torran, the oldest artifacts are kept.

For several minutes, we walk without exchanging a word, but, when we reach the first roomful of relics, Lady Carolissa exclaims, "By the stars!"

She rushes forward, her previous trepidation all but forgotten. I find the sight strangely endearing. There's something about the way her eyes widen in wonder as she drinks in the surrounding curiosities that makes me realize why Lyanndra seems to like her so.

"Look at this!"

The young woman holds up a large jar filled with murky fluid. Within, I can just barely make out the hazy shape of some sort of pale, swollen lizard folded in on itself. My face twists in disgust, but Lady Carolissa seems wholly unperturbed.

"This is a basilisk," she explains. "A baby, of course. They were supposedly eradicated centuries ago, but the pattern of spikes along its spine is unmistakable."

She hands me the jar before I can draw my arms away. I stare down at the bulging white eyes of the lizard—the basilisk, I correct—and cringe. Yet, even as I replace the vile specimen back where the courtier found it, she's already onto the next grisly relic.

"These are from an herbivore, I think," she murmurs, pointing down at an open velvet box that rests inside an alcove. The deep blue material is scattered with various teeth, though they are too small and dull to be the fang we seek.

I grimace.

Why can't we focus on the nice, normal relics, like the golden candelabra in the corner or the great oak bow mounted upon the far wall?

From where she rummages in yet another alcove, Lady Carolissa excitedly proclaims, "More teeth!"

"Great," I grit out.

But those, too, are not what we so desperately search for. They are indeed fangs, but the edges are serrated and look nothing like the one in the pictures I've seen.

It takes us about an hour to work our way through the entire room. Aside from some minor objects of interest, such as a crown wrought in silver and braided through with dried flowers, a strange iridescent orb that seems to glow in the semi-darkness, or an ivory cameo of a man with an exceptionally large nose, we find nothing more of note.

As we return to the corridor once more and navigate toward the next chamber marked on the map, Lady Carolissa sighs. "It's sad, in a sense, to think of all these wondrous things locked away down here," she says.

"Some of these relics are stored in this place for a reason," I caution.

"So you say," she replies. Her expression turns wistful as she continues, "But imagine venturing out across Alastria to collect such rarities!"

While I know little of these matters, I recall something Torran told me and relay, "There are people from the Eastern Roosts who do just that."

Her eyes shimmer in the glow of my midnight flame. "I can think of nothing more exciting," she murmurs. "In my dearest dreams, I picture myself traveling around, as the Godslayer does, to catalogue all the living things within the kingdom."

I check the map briefly before glancing over to her and inquiring, "Have you not petitioned to join the palace scholars on their expeditions?"

The young Demigod's stride falters, and she fixes me with a look of such astonishment that I, too, pause. "Surely, you jest?" she gasps.

"I speak with all seriousness," I assure her.

"It… it is not proper." She punctuates her words with a shake of her head. "It is not what is expected of me as a lady of the Celestial Court."

And in that moment, I truly understand Lyanndra's strength. Here before me stands a young woman, only a few years older than my crossed star was when she left her family behind to pursue her future as a knight, who is stuck within a treacherous web of presumption.

The passion that burns within Lady Carolissa is vibrant, yet she tamps it down. For what? For others to gaze upon her and reduce her to embers?

I will not have it.

"Petition the scholars," I tell her. "I will see to it that you shall have a place within their ranks."

Conflict rages across her avian features as she hesitates.

"Think on it," I say, a little less forcefully.

A delicate pink blush rises in her cheeks and she nods, though she doesn't quite meet my eye. It seems that is the most I will pry from her today, for she once again falls silent at my side.

And it's in this lull that I notice a sound in the distance.

It's quiet, indistinct, but I'm certain it's no trick of the ancient, echoing corridor.

At my shoulder, Lady Carolissa pauses. She tilts her head to the side and then whispers, "Do you hear that?"

But even as she speaks, the noise grows louder. I recognize it now as a dry sort of rustling that makes me think of scaled creatures shifting through dead grass. Nothing grows down here, though, and there should be no beasts in this place, aside from the ones pickled in jars.

"Your Highness," the young Demigod mutters. She lifts one shaking hand to point at something far off in the darkness.

I raise my arm and summon my flame.

Eyes glimmer from the shadows.

Not two.

Not four.

Eight.

And then that number doubles, and triples, and suddenly there are countless shining orbs staring out of the dark. And there are legs, too many to count.

My stomach drops.

Eight eyes. Eight legs. Bulbous bodies.

"Arachnae," I snarl.

"Amazing," Lady Carolissa whispers.

Deadly is the word I would choose for these particular creatures, but there's no time to argue. The eight-legged fiends seethe forward as one, the wiry hairs of their legs swishing against the smooth marble of the corridor to create that terrible rustling.

"Go," I command, pushing the courtier back the way we came. "Go!"

The urgency in my voice breaks her out of her thrall, and she does as I order. She stumbles off toward the antechamber. I waste no time in joining her.

At our backs, the arachnae skitter across the smooth marble. They're faster than us, but they don't seem to like the light of my midnight flame. They shy away from the licking blaze I hold in my palm, though they take advantage of the shifting shadows to try to force their way closer.

We streak past the chamber we already searched, the one most likely to hold the fang, and then burst into the antechamber. All we have to do is make it to the steps.

But the stars do not favor us this afternoon, for arachnae pour out of the other passages in glittering droves.

They're everywhere.

The antechamber is a sea of writhing legs and staring eyes. They block our only escape, and they seem to know it because they close in tightly, forcing us back against one of the sides of the space.

I shove Lady Carolissa behind me and use my back to press her flat against the wall. "Close your eyes!" I order. I don't wait to see if she obeys.

I unleash.

Black flame pours from my outstretched palms in a heaving torrent. The arachnae closest to us are incinerated instantly. The rest of them skitter over one another, desperate to escape, but it's too late. I push the fire ever outward until the entire antechamber is swathed in shadowy death.

An acrid scent, like that of an empty kettle left over a hearth for far too long, fills the air. Smoke chokes my lungs, and behind me, the courtier coughs. But I do not relent, not until the charred bodies on the floor cease their twitching.

And then finally, I call the fire back into myself.

It's done.

I am the first to move. I step away from Lady Carolissa and peer down at the nearest of the arachnae. It is little more than charcoal. The others fare no better, aside from some of the corpses at the far end of the antechamber.

"By the stars," she gasps. She stares out at the morbid scene, her eyes wide with fright and something else entirely. I only recognize it as keen interest when she kneels beside one of the more intact bodies and studies it closely.

"We should go," I tell her.

She shakes her head. "I must take one of these with me," she insists. "Very few people have the opportunity to study arachnae." Before I can stop her, she gathers the charred shell of the creature in her arms.

I am in no mood to argue, so I simply wait for her to step over the remaining bodies and start up the stairs. At the top, a rectangle of light welcomes up back to the open door and safety of the cathedral.

But as we climb the steps toward the surface, I can't help but recognize that, unlike Lady Carolissa, my hands are empty.

Lyanndra placed her full trust in me to find the one weapon that could destroy the Ushum.

Yet, I still do not possess the fang.

I have nothing to show for this journey.

I have failed.

CHAPTER 23

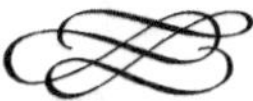

Lyanndra

We are running out of time.

It's early evening now, and while the ground no longer quakes, the aftershocks rattle through my mind without respite.

The Ushum is waking.

We are running out of time.

I stare down at the two lines I've scrawled across the parchment. How soon will this letter reach Syran? I can only hope he's had better luck finding the fang than I've had attempting to reinforce the buildings here.

Before I etch my signature onto the page, I add one last sentence.

Come to me soon.

He will understand the double meaning behind my words.

Bring me the fang so we can end this before it begins.

Bring me your heart so that mine can be whole again.

Beneath the missive, I sign my name and then fold closed the corners of the paper.

Finally, I rise from the bale of hay I've been slouched upon for the better part of an hour. My muscles are sore from the day's work, and I take a moment to stretch before descending from the loft and into the main aisle of the barn.

My parents keep goats here mostly, though my father's two geldings hold vigil in the stalls farthest from the door. Barra, too, has taken up residence, if only to keep her from devouring any more of my mother's chickens, though she is not enthusiastic about her confinement.

I glance around the familiar space. As a girl, this is one of the many places I fled to when the homestead grew too loud or too crowded. The smell of mingled straw and manure is comforting. Even the rustling of the animals and the unhurried sighs of their breath soothe me.

It's no wonder I returned here to pen my letter to Syran. The events of this day left me feeling conflicted and unbalanced.

Syran's unexpected appearance in my dream should have, by all rights, fueled me through the daylight hours. But Aaro's abrupt arrival this morning counteracted the glow of last night's encounter in a way that drives me to turmoil. Coupled with the stirring of the Ushum, I am paralyzed, trapped between my duty, my past, and my future.

These thoughts churn within me as I make my way over to the lit lantern that hangs beside the stable doors. I pull the stick of black sealing wax from where I tucked it into my boot earlier and hold it to the flame. As the substance melts, it falls like ashen tears onto the seam of the parchment, binding it closed.

Before it can cool, I turn over my left hand and press the smooth onyx face of Syran's ring into the wax to brand it with the symbol of our union.

A fresh pang of yearning needles my heart at the sight.

It is not enough to have Syran in my dreams, I realize. It is not enough to wear his ring on my finger, nor to wind his token around my arm. I want him here with me, real and burning. I want…

"Lyanndra."

The voice snatches me from my thoughts, and I glance up to find my father lingering in the doorway before me. He follows my gaze down to the golden band upon my finger before his eyes drag upward to meet mine once again.

"Will you break bread with us tonight?" he asks.

I shake my head. "I eat with my men."

"Then you will go hungry, by the looks of it," he replies. "Your soldiers have long since finished their suppers." He nods behind him toward the cooking fires that glow like beacons in the gathering darkness.

Is it really that late already? How long have I stood here like a fool?

"It will make your mother happy," he adds, and my resolve wavers even further.

Until now, I've staunchly refused my parents' offers of food and a bed in the homestead. While most of the Celestial Knights have realized my connection to this place, I do not want it to appear that I think myself above them, so I've insisted upon sleeping in my bedroll beneath the stars and sharing the same thin stews and meager rations as the rest of the host.

Yet, surely they won't begrudge me one meal?

Part of me wants to resist solely on principle, but the combination of guilt and hunger that swirls within my chest prompts me to sigh and relent, "Very well."

My father waits as I stash my quill, ink, and wax back in Barra's saddlebags, which are slung over the door of her stall. I pause to run my fingers over the soft sealskin of her nose before tossing her a hunk of dried mutton.

"Where in the stars did you find that wretched thing?" my father asks as we retreat from the barn.

"She found me," I reply.

We say nothing more as I track down a messenger and hand him my letter. There's no need to tell him it's for Syran. The black seal of his crest speaks for itself. Only when that task is done do I follow my father back to the homestead, where the evening's meal has already begun.

Stepping inside is like sliding back in time.

A fire blazes in the hearth of the kitchen. The many candles and lanterns strewn about the room cast a cheery glow, so different from the flickering darkness of Syran's midnight flame. My mother bustles around with platters of food while my sisters, grown now, assist.

My brothers already sit at the table. Several have wives beside them, one of whom is clearly pregnant. A myriad of small children play at their feet or clamber in their laps, and it strikes me that these are my nieces and nephews.

And then there's Aaro.

He's sandwiched between two of my siblings, and he smiles and laughs as though he's one of them. Rage flares in my chest, but I tamp it down. While I won't ruin my mother's dinner, perhaps I can retreat, unnoticed, back to camp. I'd rather go to bed hungry than spend another second with my former betrothed.

But, alas, I am spotted before I can enact my plan.

"The great and terrible Godslayer!" Aaro heralds from the crowded table as he catches sight of me. "Tired of soldier's fare?"

Resisting the urge to roll my eyes, I resign myself to this wretched fate and drop down into my old chair. I lean over to place my golden helm and gauntlets on the floor at my feet. When I straighten up, I find the room has gone rather quiet.

"Is that Father's old armor?" one of my brothers asks.

I nod.

"I barely recognized it with those scales," he comments. "When did you add them?"

"I didn't," I reply.

My mother, who comes by to drop a steaming circle of flatbread onto my plate, inquires, "Then who did?"

"Syran." My crossed star's name slips out before I can stop it, and the effect is immediate.

It's as though I uttered a curse.

Everybody in the room seems to freeze, except to glance at one another in disbelief. My father, seated at the head of the table, clears his throat, while my mother's knuckles tighten over the platter she holds.

Is it my familiarity with the King of Alastria that shocks them so?

Or is it because he's a Demigod, and we are Starless?

Aaro is the first to speak. His eyes flash as he quips, "Does the king do that for all the Starless women he tries to murder, or just you?"

It takes every ounce of my self-control not to launch myself over the table and show him exactly what I think of his quick tongue. Instead, I simply glare at him, my eyes blazing and my fists clenched.

But the moment, however, does not last long.

Outside, a shout arises.

A horn, signaling danger, sounds seconds later.

I'm out of a chair in an instant. Before anybody else has even made it to their feet, I'm already pulling on my gauntlets. I don my golden helm as I barrel for the door, not willing to waste any time.

I burst out into the night to find chaos on our doorstep. My eyes dart over the scene as I struggle to make sense of it.

Blades flash beneath the moonlight. Celestial Knights, resplendent in gold, cry out as they meet their opponents in battle. The enemies—for the way they slash at my men indicates that they're certainly no friends of ours—wear dark cloaks and a strange mix of armor. They don't seem centralized, but they fight with some skill.

Marauders, I realize.

I estimate four dozen, almost equal in number to my host.

Beneath my golden helm, I snarl.

"What in the stars is going on?" my father asks, coming up behind me in the open doorway.

"Back inside!" I shout. "Now!"

He stares at me.

Though he can't see it through the visor of my helm, I fix him with the fiercest glare I can muster. "Wield your sword. Hold the line at the door. You do not come out until the horn sounds."

His mouth opens to argue, but I cut him off before he can form the words.

"I am the Godslayer," I bark, "and that is a fucking *order*."

For a second, I think he is going to disobey, but then he simply nods and retreats back inside. I wait until I hear the door latch behind him.

Then I join the fray.

It's dark. The marauders have the advantage out here in their shadowy cloaks, while the Celestial Knights shine like constellations in the night. But in my tarnished armor, I'm in my element. I slide through the carnage like a ghost with my greatsword drawn and swinging, picking men off one by one as I go.

My heart thunders against my ribs as I dance between skirmishes.

I slash out at two opponents simultaneously. My blade slices cleanly through their armor, which wails almost as loudly as they do before both sounds abruptly cut off.

Next, I take down a mercenary with a straight, flat sword. He moves the weapon through the air with beautiful skill, but, when it flashes down against my greatsword in a screaming arc, the steel snaps on my blade. The impact topples him backward, where a Celestial Knight runs him through the gut.

I move on.

A man gripping twin blades, both curved and gleaming in the moonlight, turns toward me. His eyes widen as he recognizes the golden helm I wear.

"Godslayer!" he cries. "Godslayer!"

Panic erupts.

Some of the marauders throw down their weapons instantly, while others rush closer still, eager to draw legendary blood.

I deal with the twin blades first. Luring the man's blows up to meet my greatsword in a half-hearted swing, I wait until his steel hits mine before I raise up my boot and kick him squarely in the thigh. He grunts and falls to one knee, and I take the opportunity to bring my weapon down upon him.

He does not get up again.

Even as he crumples, still more men come. I cut through each one, sometimes with the help of my knights, sometimes on my own. I'm panting now, struggling to draw air into my burning lungs, but I will not stop.

I *cannot* stop.

Out of the corner of my eye, I catch sight of Mallan, distinguishable by his yellow mantle, battling three marauders at once. Irtas, his helmet lost somewhere in the fray, attempts to join him, but the Starless knight shoves the Demigod back.

"I can take them!" Mallan yells over the cacophony.

Irtas stumbles.

"No!" I bellow as I watch the Demigod wheel into one of the mercenaries, who turns to meet him first with surprise plastered across his face, and then with the edge of his blade.

Steel sings through the air.

Irtas' eyes widen.

The mercenary strikes true.

Irtas falls.

Rage, as hot and deadly as Syran's flame, explodes in my chest. A battle cry rips my throat, and something deep within me ignites.

I am unbound.

The mercenaries nearest to me bear the brunt of my onslaught. I hack through them without hesitation. There is no mercy here, no grace. There's only the hiss of my greatsword and the iron stench of blood, the shudder of each hit rumbling up my arms and the screaming of my muscles as I unleash upon my enemy.

And it is only when the last of them lay dead at my feet that the red haze lifts and the world rushes in, funneling down until I'm clawing at the clasp of my helm, needing it *off* so that I can breathe.

Cool night air surges over my heated skin. Sweat drips from my brow to sting my eyes. I can taste it, along with blood. For the first time, I realize that my lip is split.

When did that happen?

I find that I don't particularly care.

Somewhere to the right of me, the horn sounds, signaling the end of the battle. I pay that no mind, either. I'm too busy scanning the bodies that are scattered around me in a grisly fractal, searching for gold, for the deep blue of the mantle I seek.

And then I spot it, closer than expected.

"Irtas!" I rasp. My voice is hoarse. My throat burns.

The man does not move.

I stagger over to him and drop to my knees by his side. Blood leaks out from the edges of his armor and from the thin wound in his gut. His eyes stare up at me, wide and vacant.

Empty.

Gone.

Numbness floods in to replace my rage as I gaze down upon the fallen soldier. He's not the only Celestial Knight to die tonight, and he wasn't even my friend. But he was mine to command, mine to defend.

I failed him.

By the fucking stars, I *failed*.

Bile rises in my throat, but I force it back down. Instead, I struggle to my feet. My legs shake beneath me, and I wish Syran were here. He would know what to say to the men who stare at me now, awaiting my orders.

And he would know what to do about Mallan.

The Starless knight stands a few feet away. His helmet is off, and he grips it between trembling hands as he dips his head down and casts his eyes toward the ground. I'm not proud enough to mistake this as respect or deference.

I know shame when I see it.

"It's my fault," he whispers. "It's my fault."

And when I take a step toward him, he drops to his knees.

"I as good as killed him," he sobs. Beneath his armor, his shoulders shake. "It may as well have been my sword that ran him through."

A murmur ripples through the Celestial Knights. Every one of us knows that the penalty for such a crime is death.

Does he think that I will execute him?

I consider it.

I have dispatched others for less.

But then I remember how young he is, barely a man at all, and I think of how I left my family to die. I bore my shame, and I became better for it.

So I force my aching legs to carry me forward until I stand just before Mallan's dipped head. His breaths come in panicked gasps as I loom over him. When I reach out and grip the scruff of his mantle in my gauntleted fist, he shudders.

The Celestial Knights freeze.

I raise my greatsword.

And when I bring it down, it slices only through yellow fabric.

Mallan chokes out a strangled noise. His shoulders sag, and he finally gathers the will to look at me. I meet his eyes with an empty stare.

I drop the shorn mantle down on the bloody ground in front of him.

"Earn it back," I command.

And then I turn and walk away.

CHAPTER 24

SYRAN

Lyanndra is in pieces.

The shattered edges of her, sharp and insistent, slice me anew with each passing second.

I am powerless to soothe her pain.

Ever since last night, I've been awaiting word of the tragedy that has surely befallen the village of Breem, for something terrible must have happened to plague my crossed star so. Her rage, frightening in its blazing intensity, was the first to hit me, with sick grief following closely on its heels. Now, there is something else in its place, something numb and hollow that scares me more than even her brilliant fury.

And this, I cannot abide.

I slouch deeper into my throne and glare out at the empty room. Where in the stars is the messenger? I am certain one must be on the way.

This delay would be more bearable if I managed to visit Lyanndra in her dreams last night. Did I not swear it to her that I would try?

But when I reached for her in the dark, my call went unheeded. It took me an hour of fruitless attempts to realize that she must have forsaken sleep altogether.

So I am paralyzed. All I can do is sit upon this cursed throne with the burden of the kingdom bearing down upon my throbbing temples, and wait. And wait. And, by the *fucking* stars, wait.

The minutes ooze by, and still nobody comes.

A fresh wave of dread churns within me. What has happened out there in the shadow of the mountain? Has the Ushum risen from its ancient den? Does it ravage the southern frontier with gnashing teeth and molten claws? Or is this a tragedy of a more mundane nature?

Whatever occurred, it was powerful enough to rattle even the Godslayer.

I think of Lyanndra and how she met me in battle so many months ago. I lashed out upon her with fire and steel, but she did not flinch. She did not falter. Even at the edge of death, she glared at me with such defiance that the ghost of it torments me still.

She is unmovable, as unyielding as the moon and as terrible as the very stars. No enemy can sneak up on her. She turns her back on no foe.

So how is it that she is broken by whatever has happened? How is it that my moon has lost her luster?

My scowl deepens.

Time slides ever onward, in spite of my misery, and, just as I think that I should give up on my vigil and return to my hunt for the elusive fang, footsteps sound just beyond the threshold of the throne room.

I regain my royal posture as the double doors swing open. The man who hurries inside wears light golden armor over his traveling clothes. A white mantle swirls at his shoulders.

Finally.

The messenger has arrived.

He stops before me and drops his head in deference. "Your Highness," he says. "I travel from the Southern Caldera and carry with me word from the Godslayer."

My heart thuds in my chest as I ask, "What news do you bring?"

"Two letters, Your Highness," he replies. He draws a pair of notes from a pouch at his belt and steps forward, holding them out to me.

I will my hand not to shake as I accept them. As much as I want to immediately tear open the seals and pour over my crossed star's words, I resist the urge. I want to be alone when I read them. Something tells me that whatever Lyanndra has written, it was meant for no eyes other than mine.

Before I can prompt further, the messenger continues, "I regret to inform you that there has been a great loss among the host, Your Highness. Eight men fell to marauders late last night. Commander Irtas is among the dead."

Shock needles my spine.

Irtas? *Dead?*

"What of the Godslayer?" I demand as anxiety swells within me.

"She is unharmed," he answers, and I don't even bother to hide the way my shoulders sag with relief at this news. "I am told she fought fiercely, like a great warrior of yore. At least a dozen men fell to her blade."

Having experienced a mere fraction of her wild fury, I have no doubt that this Demigod speaks the truth. Yet, there is something missing. Irtas' loss is a blow to our forces, yes, but as far as I know, Lyanndra was not particularly fond of him.

"Is that all?" I ask.

He shakes his head. "No, Your Highness. There has been a demotion amongst your ranks."

"Who?"

"Mallan," he replies. "The Godslayer stripped him of his mantle. It is said that he was, in part, responsible for Commander Irtas' demise."

Ah.

There it is, that missing piece.

I wait for the messenger to speak again, but when he doesn't, I say, "You are most welcome to rest here in the palace. Whatever you require, you shall have. Dismissed."

"Thank you, Your Highness." He bows his head once more and

then retreats the way he came, drawing the doors behind him as he goes.

Only when I'm sure that I'm finally alone do I study the letters I hold in my hands.

One is a thick sheaf of parchment, folded into thirds and sealed with black wax. The other is thin, only one page, the corners carefully tucked in and bound by our royal sigil.

It is the smaller of the two I choose to open first. Not bothering to draw my dagger, I use my flame to melt away the seal until the edges of the missive unfurl, revealing my crossed star's words.

The Ushum is waking.

We are running out of time.

Come to me soon.

Dread and longing twine around my heart and squeeze.

Our worst fear is realized. According to Lyanndra, the Ushum is no mere legend. And if it is indeed stirring, I need to find the fang. There is no room for failure. I *must* complete this task, and I must do it soon.

But I cannot shake the bitter foundering of my most recent attempt to procure the celestial weapon. After yesterday's search of the reliquary, which I resumed with a small army of Celestial Knights in tow, I am sure that the fang is not down there.

So where is it?

And I will not–cannot–go to her without it. Lyanndra has put her trust in me to complete this hunt.

I will not fail her, even if I have to defy the very stars.

Yet, her last line haunts me even as I place the parchment on my lap and break the seal of the second letter.

Come to me soon.

"Soon," I whisper to the throne room. But there is nobody here to behold my vow.

Disquieted, I unfold the other bundle. Lyanndra's script is the same as always, but there's something cold in the way her letters are scrawled upon the page, something distant.

Here, she writes of the skirmish that took place in Breem last night. She tells me, in that strange and detached way, that Mallan's recklessness sent Irtas to his doom. Instead of executing Mallan, she tore away both his rank and his mantle. That, I decide, is a decision I will not question. Additionally, she's sending the dead back to Nexus with the next caravan of refugees and requests that the fallen soldiers receive full honors upon their posthumous arrival.

And with her signature, the note ends upon the very first page.

This does nothing to quell my growing unease. I thought I would receive more from her, some profanity or some passion, anything other than this flat missive.

As it turns out, the rest of the package contains the letters and writings of the dead Celestial Knights. I start to skim the first of them but then stop myself a few lines in. Just as Lyanndra's words are for me alone, these pages belong to the families of the lost.

I will not read them.

I will do my fallen men this one last honor.

With grief and longing pressing hotly against my ribs, I descend from my throne and stride to the doors. My feet, unattached from my thoughts, carry me through the glittering halls of the Celestial Court and out into the afternoon.

I will have to inform the widows of the dead, I realize with a woeful pang. While I could easily delegate the unpalatable task to Torran, Wayre, or Noros, I resolve to take care of it personally.

These men are—*were*—my responsibility.

My steps falter as it strikes me that perhaps Lyanndra feels the same. Before she was the Godslayer, she was simply a rank-and-file soldier of little renown. Other than our battle against Kartas, she has never led an army. She has never held the responsibility of command.

She has, in all likelihood, lost more brothers in arms that she can count. But it's different when those knights are under your injunction. It's different when your decisions determine whether men live or die.

Lyanndra does not grieve Irtas because he was a friend.

She mourns him because he was hers to protect.

Fresh sorrow rushes through my veins at this dreadful understanding. And as though my body already knew what my mind did not, I look up to find myself at the stables.

I pause in the doorway and wrinkle my nose in distaste as I breathe in the equine scent of this place. Why does Lyanndra love it so? Sometimes, she truly is beyond me.

Still, I find some comfort knowing that this is one of her favorite places to go in times of turmoil.

With a sigh, I step into the dim aisle. Several horses lift their heads above their stall doors to whicker and stare as I pass. I catch sight of one, a bay mare with her ears pinned back and her teeth bared, and muster up a tired smile.

"Hello, old friend," I murmur as I reach out to stroke her nose, only to draw my hand back a second later when she snaps out at my fingers.

This is the horse gifted to me by the Starless of the north. She carried me well across Alastria and through the battle of Nexus. I wonder, dimly, if she ever had a name.

Perhaps I should give her one.

Lyanndra would like that, I think.

A thin voice calls out from behind me, shaking me from my reverie. "There you are, Syran." I turn to find Torran standing at the mouth of the aisle. "I thought I might find you here."

"Did you?" I muse.

He nods. Even in the low light, his eyes sparkle like gemstones. "When I spoke to the messenger after he left your audience, I was worried that you might do something foolish."

I offer him a tight smile and ask, "Like taking a horse and riding off after the Godslayer?"

"Something like that," he says.

"I want to, more than anything," I confess with a sigh. "But I can't go to her. Not yet. Not without the fang."

"I am working tirelessly on the translation," he assures me.

The truth behind his words is plain. How many hours has the old Demigod spent holed up in the library, poring over arcane texts with

Lady Carolissa? I can see it, too, in the purple shadows beneath his eyes and the way he leans heavily on his gnarled cane.

Guilt creeps through my chest as I say, "I fear that we will be too late."

"To kill the Ushum before it wakes?" he challenges. "Or to ease what ails your crossed star?"

I consider what will happen if the creature rises from its unholy slumber. The destruction will be catastrophic. The eight lives lost in yesterday's skirmish are nothing in comparison.

But then I think of Lyanndra, of her earlier unease, and her rage, her grief, and her emptiness, and I utter, "Both."

Because aside from the Ushum and Irtas' demise, I feel certain that there is something that I'm missing.

Something is wrong.

CHAPTER 25

Lyanndra

"There is a prayer we recite for the fallen," Orobos says. "Will you bear witness?"

I drag my eyes away from the dead—preserved by the healers and wrapped in the shrouds that will cradle them on their final voyage back to Nexus—and turn to face the Demigod.

He stands behind me with the visor of his helm lifted. His eyes are hard, but, when they shift to meet mine, they don't hold the judgment I expect to find there.

And while I do not think myself worthy, I nod anyhow.

He draws in a deep breath and then begins to chant in a rich, velvet voice that rolls over the hushed fields here on the outskirts of Breem. "O stars, hear our plea. Accept now the blood of our brothers, spilled in wrath and taken in fury. They are of you. May the heavens embrace their spirits. May death deliver them unto the gods."

The invocation carries on the thin breeze and fades into the afternoon sky.

If the stars heed his words, they give us no sign.

There is only the silence of the shadow of the mountain, the quiet before the rolling storm.

The dead do not stir.

I do not speak.

In the distance, the remaining Celestial Knights work to bury the bodies of the felled marauders.

I left only four survivors in my rampage. They had enough sense to throw down their weapons upon hearing my name, though I don't remember sparing them with any clarity. And yet, I must have; for, they still breathe.

They told us that they came from the west after hearing word of the tragedy that had befallen the Southern Caldera. They expected easy looting with little resistance, and certainly did not foresee a bloody skirmish with a full host of Celestial Knights, let alone the Godslayer.

But what good was I, if I could not protect my own men?

"There is something we Starless say to honor the dead when the gods so cruelly snatch them away," I mutter.

Orobos starts, as though surprised to hear my voice at all, but recovers quickly enough to reply, "I would like to know of it."

I turn my face up to the heavens and growl, "Fuck you."

He stares at me for a long moment. I can't tell if he thinks me mad, blasphemous, or honest. But then he blinks, looks up into the uncaring blue sky, and utters, "Fuck you."

Maybe I was wrong about Orobos.

Perhaps he will make a decent general yet.

We stand the remainder of our vigil in silence until the wagon arrives to collect the dead. I've assigned two Celestial Knights, all we can spare after such heavy casualties, to ride with it. While I've never been one to suffer the living in favor of the departed, it feels important to make sure this precious cargo has an escort.

"Did you send word to His Highness?" Orobos asks once the wagon creaks off down the road.

I nod.

By the positioning of the sun overhead, I expect that Syran must have received my letters by now. Dread twists within my gut at the very thought.

Does he think less of me for my failure?

I am a soldier, and a lonesome one at that. I know how to fight and keep myself alive, and I help when I am able. Never have I hidden any of these things from my crossed star.

But this calamity reveals something new about me, to the both of us.

I am no leader.

I am no queen.

And even though I voice none of this to Orobos, it must pass across my face because he drops the heavy weight of his gauntleted hand upon my shoulder. "This wasn't your fault, Godslayer," he says.

The line of my jaw tightens, both from my guilt and the audacity of the knight's touch. "I think Irtas would disagree."

"I think he would slap Mallan upside the head for his reckless-ness," he counters. "But he would not blame you. There is no easy death for a soldier, and none of us expect one. You, out of all of us, know that."

"I should have demoted Mallan sooner," I spit. "I should have been out there when the marauders attacked."

He shakes his head. "You tread a treacherous path, Godslayer. How sure are you that Mallan's foolhardiness would have been curbed by a reprimand? Would he not have railed against such an act in an attempt to prove his worth to you?"

I hear the truth in Orobos' words, even though I don't want to.

Still, he continues, "And if you were out there with us when the horn sounded, how do you know that the fiends wouldn't have caught you unaware and struck you down?"

"Set your reasoned tongue on somebody else," I snap, though my words lack the teeth to rend or tear.

Orobos' hand squeezes lightly atop my armor before he with-draws it. "Think on what I've said, Godslayer. But regardless of your conclusions, the blame is not yours to shoulder."

"If not mine, then whose?" I challenge.

He has no answer to offer.

His silence says enough.

I cast my eyes out to the horizon, where the jagged tooth of the Caldera rises up against the sky. As much as I would like to linger here and wallow in my shame, we are in this place for a reason. My shortcomings will not extend to neglecting my duty.

"Are the dead marauders buried?" I ask.

"Yes, Godslayer."

"Then organize the search parties," I instruct. "One for each quadrant of the mountain. I will gather any villagers willing to help us. We must find the Ushum's lair tonight."

Before another tremor destroys Breem for good.

Before anybody else dies on my watch.

"Yes, Godslayer," Orobos acquiesces. He spares me one last look before he flips down his visor and marches off in the direction of camp to rally the remaining Celestial Knights.

I follow behind him, taking my time as I pick through the fields toward my family's homestead. Sour guilt churns in my chest at the thought of facing my soldiers once more. In spite of my abject failure, they still looked to me for guidance all through the night.

Do they not understand how lost I am?

Yet, I can't abandon them.

It doesn't matter that I stayed awake until dawn, barking orders and interrogating the survivors. It doesn't matter that exhaustion presses heavily against my temples now.

I will see this through because it must be done.

I must locate the Ushum.

I must end this before it begins.

While Orobos organizes the Celestial Knights, I make my way over to my parents' homestead, where I plan on asking them to help me recruit any of the townsfolk who are willing to assist us in our search for the Ushum's lair. But fresh fingers of trepidation creep around my heart as I approach.

They must have seen my rampage last night, or at least the aftermath of it. And I spoke to my father the way I would my knights. Not as his daughter, but as the Godslayer.

What will they think, now that they have witnessed the brutal truth of me?

There is only one way to find out.

I push open the door of the homestead and step inside.

My gaze lands upon my mother first. She sits at the long table in the center of the kitchen, and I notice that she wears the same faded smock and apron, still stained with splashes of dinner, from the night before. When her eyes dart up to meet mine, it takes everything in me not to visibly recoil.

She stares at me like she's never seen me before.

Like I'm a stranger.

Like I'm somebody to be feared.

Some foul, unnamed thing blooms in the pit of my stomach as I realize that my own mother is scared of me, of what I've become.

This is why I left, I want to tell her. *There is something inside of me that is not like the rest of you.*

But the words do not—will not—come, so I say nothing at all.

My father rises from his chair at the head of the table and regards me with an unreadable expression. Then he leans down to my mother's ear and says, in a voice so low that I barely catch it, "Ashya, let me speak with her alone."

She nods and then stands. As if she cannot bear to walk past me, she instead shuffles off deeper into the kitchen, where she disappears through the curtained doorway leading off to the bedrooms.

Once she's gone, my father gestures to my empty chair. "Sit," he says. "I'll make us tea."

I want to reply that I don't have time for such trivialities, but he doesn't wait for me to answer. He simply bustles off toward the kettle, which is already boiling away over the hearth, leaving me to linger awkwardly by the table.

"It's true, what they say about you," he remarks as he busies himself crumbling dried leaves and petals into each brown, earthen mug.

I try not to let my tone waver as I ask, "And what is that?"

"That you're a fierce warrior. That you fight well and with honor." And when he glances up at me, I'm shocked to see that his eyes glisten not with fear, but with pride. "That you protect people."

"I lost eight men," I choke out.

He shakes his head. "And how many more did you save? If you weren't here, those marauders would have massacred every last one of us."

My first instinct is to argue with him, as I did earlier with Orobos, but I swallow back the urge. This isn't a perspective I considered before. Perhaps I'd do well to think on it later. But for now, I came here with a purpose, and it wasn't to drink tea and nurse my injured pride.

"There is more ruin to come, unless I can stop it," I say. "You heard the roaring during yesterday's quake?"

"Aye."

"Then you know that there is something stirring beneath the mountain. I'm here to find the creature's lair while Syran tracks down the weapon that can kill it. I must be ready for when he comes."

"Syran...." My father shakes his head. "You speak of the Demigod King as an equal. Yet, you do not deny that he tried to take your life?"

"He did," I confirm.

"And you wish me to believe that you are marrying him at your own behest?"

Anger flares against my ribs, and this time, I don't bother trying to tamp it down. "Yes," I reply hotly. "I do."

He sighs. "Lyanndra, he is a *Demigod*. You, of all people, should know that they do nothing but lie and scheme in order to destroy our kind."

"As you schemed to betroth me to Aaro, against my will?" I snarl. "What right do you have to judge me? To judge *Syran*? He has seen me. He has fought beside me and has not *once* flinched at the things I've done. I killed his father because nobody else would, and he does not hate me for it. How is it that he can embrace all that I am when my own mother looks upon me with fear? What does it say about you that Syran, who was once my sworn enemy, can honor me when my own family cannot?"

Shock strikes across my father's features like a backhanded slap. I can practically hear the ring of it echoing in the silence between us.

I will not give him a chance to argue. I will not allow him to make me small again.

"When I find the creature, Syran *will* come," I hiss. "And if anybody dares to raise a blade against him, I will cut them down as surely as the moon rises each night. You have my word on that, as your daughter and as the Godslayer."

He doesn't answer my challenge. He simply stares at me with that same surprised look. And then, when I think that the only thing left for me to do is rise from the table and storm out to meet my host, he crumbles and asks, "What do you need of me?"

I draw in a deep breath, pushing my fury down. "Men," I say. "Or women. Anybody willing to help us in the search."

"I will do what I can," he promises.

And he makes good on his vow.

Within an hour, three dozen townsfolk have abandoned their duties to trudge up and down the steep sides of the mountain. They place golden flags at the entrance of any caves they find, and I send two soldiers into each opening with hopes that one group might get lucky.

It's as I'm waiting for a pair of Celestial Knights to emerge from one particular cavern that somebody hails at my back, "Godslayer!"

I turn to meet the call, only for my earlier anger to flare once more.

Aaro stands before me, his white-blond hair shimmering in the sun, and his blue gaze fixed upon mine. My ire must be plain on my face, because he holds his hands out and says, "I mean you no harm. I came only to apologize."

I narrow my eyes at him and say nothing.

"I'm sorry," he tells me. His voice is earnest, his eyes pleading.

I don't trust it for a second.

"My behavior last night was…."

"Treasonous?" I offer.

Color rises in his cheeks as he mutters, "I was going to go with *uncalled for.*"

My glare deepens, and he flinches.

"I just... I thought you were *dead*, Lyanndra," he confesses. "I thought those soldiers took you. And now I have to face that you just left me like that, for all those years, not because anybody made you, but because you *chose* to. You *chose* to break our betrothal."

Is he just now realizing this?

Was the fact that I told him I didn't want to marry him not enough of a hint?

Or was it Syran's ring upon my finger that finally guided him toward the truth?

Unaware of how unimpressed I am with his tirade, he continues, "I don't understand why you never came back, but you're here now. And after last night, I know that you're... not the same as you were. But I want to know who you are *now*, not cling to the memory of who you used to be."

And when, still, I say nothing, he adds, "And I would like to help with the search, if you'll allow me."

Once again, I want to turn him away. Or, better yet, assist him in losing his balance on his way down the mountain.

But I've failed enough for one day, and I cannot afford to be so reckless, so I sigh and relent with a curt nod.

I only hope that this, too, is not a mistake I'll later come to regret.

CHAPTER 26

SYRAN

"For the love of the stars, Syran, would you *please* stop pacing?"

My eyes snap over to Torran, who peers at me from over the top of a tome so ancient, it looks like it might disintegrate just from mere perception alone. Beside him, Lady Carolissa sits with shock plastered across her aristocratic features, as though she cannot believe that the old Demigod dared to impart my given name.

"Apologies," I mutter.

But I do not stop patrolling the edges of the small space.

The walls of the Archive Room close in like a tomb. The air is thick with dust and the smell of crumbling parchment, and I think that if I have to gaze upon one more bestiary or map, I might simply perish.

I've been sequestered away in this dismal place since Torran found me at the stables earlier. His optimism in puzzling out the translation, however, seems to have been gravely misplaced. It's been hours, and he still has not cracked it. With every passing second, I feel more and more trapped, like an animal stuck in a cage far too small.

Is this what Lyanndra endured when I kept her locked away in the infirmary?

The question hits me like a blow from her hulking greatsword.

While such times feel like a distant memory now, I still hate knowing that I ever caused her pain. After everything I put her through, it's a wonder that she forgave me at all, let alone agreed to rule by my side.

And while I cannot change how I treated her in my misguided arrogance, I can hold fast to the vows I made to her.

I *will* find the fang.

I *will* go to her as soon as I am able.

I *will* put an end to this.

"You *will* stop pacing, Syran, or else I shall drive you out of this place with my cane." Torran interrupts me in an uncanny echo of my thoughts. He brandishes the implement in question, though I can tell from the way his eyes sparkle with humor that he is not serious.

At least, not completely.

And then his face softens, and, in a gentler tone, he suggests, "Why don't you take a turn of the grounds? Perhaps that will do us all some good."

I want to snap at him that nothing will do us any good at all if the Ushum wakes up, but I hold my tongue.

Torran is trying his best. He's already surpassed all expectations by identifying the fang in the first place and piecing together the archaic patchwork of legend and myth that will, hopefully, lead us to it. If I can be of no help here, the least I can do is let him work in peace.

So I sigh and say, "I think I shall. But alert me immediately if you discover anything."

"Of course," he replies with a nod.

I bid him and Lady Carolissa good evening and then head out into the library. The gathering darkness filters in through the stained glass windows, spilling into a mosaic of muted shadows that creep upon the floor. Soon, the whole room will be bathed in moonlight. And while I dread to see another day pass without news of the fang, the impending night does, at minimum, promise another attempt at reaching Lyanndra through our bond.

Anticipation thrills through me at the notion.

I want to see her again. I want to take her in my arms and tell her that what happened was not her fault, that she is not less than what she was before. I want to show her that I will desire her in all of her failings, all of her secrets, and all of her flaws.

Eight dead men will not change that.

Nor would a hundred.

Lyanndra is mine.

And now that I've basked in the moonlit glow of her, I will never let her go.

But the night has yet to quicken over the midlands, and I fear that it will be hours still before I have any chance of seeing my crossed star once more, so I retreat to the training grounds with the intention of burning time away.

I begin with drills. It's easy to lose myself in the rote movements, ones ingrained so deeply within me over years of practice that they come now without thought or reason. And as I cycle through endless sets of forms and strikes, my mind wanders to Lyanndra once again.

My yearning for her is like a living thing that writhes and stretches in my chest. It drowns me until my lungs burn, and my very soul aches, but I will not divest myself of this terrible desire, for to do so would be to forsake a part of myself.

Is this, too, a symptom of our bond?

I know not.

I care not.

Because what I feel for Lyanndra cuts deeper than lust or mere affection. It is as soft as a gray dawn, as brilliant as the silver wash of the full moon. It burns like the fire at the center of all that I am, hotter and blacker than any midnight flame I could ever hope to conjure. It is the power behind her blade, the glimmer in her eyes, and the very taste of her, like starlight on my tongue.

And I am certain, of this more than anything else in my entire existence, that I can name the twisting, glowing thing that steals my heart away.

Love.

I *love* her.

Warmth surges through my veins at this realization.

"I love her," I whisper into the swirling evening. *"I love her."*

And, as if my own flame agrees, a new heat rises within me, dry and ancient and strangely familiar.

It's the sensation I felt that late afternoon in Torran's hut when he told me about the fang's potential connection to the Moon Prophecy, the same one that struck me in the Archive Room, on the training grounds, and then again in the reliquary.

It's as though, for a breath of a second, that something is reaching for me from across a great distance, as I did to Lyanndra a few nights prior.

But it is not her.

It is not her.

This is something different, something old and sinuous. I feel a tether, thin and tremulous but *there*, like a slim black thread, boundless, stretching off into an eternity I don't understand. And I wait for the pull of it, for the tug that will send me flying off into the dark, and, in that horrible, fleeting moment, I am both fascinated and frightened.

But there comes no heaving force along the line, no rushing blackness or endless void.

There is only the sensation of something stirring and then settling, both deep within me and very far away.

Not yet, it seems to whisper from the dark flint at my heart.

Not yet.

And then my eyelids, which I don't remember closing, fly open, and my gaze meets the familiar constellations of the midland sky. I'm sprawled on my back, though I know not how I ended up there. Midnight flame flickers from my palms to pool around me like a pyre, and my breath comes in panting gasps.

Everything within ten feet of me is ablaze.

Hot fear slides across my ribs and squeezes.

Did I do this?

I must have.

The dread does not leave me as I call the fire back. I sit up and glance around the empty training grounds. There's nothing here to tell me what happened, other than the ash that coats the hard-packed dirt.

And what *did* happen?

I remember the swirl of love I felt for Lyanndra, which is enough to chase away the worst of my distress. But after that, it's as though I lost myself for a moment, as if I was somehow pulled away from my own being.

Whatever that was, whatever caused such disarray within my mind, I have no wish to repeat it.

Rattled and wary, I survey my surroundings once more. Did anybody see me succumb to that moment of madness?

But there are no shouts from the palace, or guards swarming to assist me. Nobody sounded the alarm.

There's only the low hum of nocturnal insects and the background bustle always present at the Celestial Court.

There's only the night sky.

There's only me.

I draw in a deep, shaking breath and then climb to my feet. My legs tremble beneath me. The beating of my heart thunders in my ears. For a moment, I sway where I stand, but then the world shifts again, and I am myself once more.

My first instinct is to go to the infirmary and seek help, but I quickly dismiss that foolish notion. I can't have my healers thinking I'm weak, or worse, succumbing to madness, not when I've finally claimed the throne as my own.

Shall I turn to Torran?

But even as the idea rises, I push it back.

Torran is pouring everything he has into translating the text around the fang in hopes that it will unravel this cursed mystery. I cannot afford to bother him with such a thing when victory is so close at hand.

And if I were to confide in him, what would I say? That I was overtaken by the bond of the crossed stars? That something whispered inside of me? I cannot explain what happened to myself, let alone to another.

No.

I will keep this to myself.

Resolute, I do my best to tamp down my disquiet as I stalk across the shadowed training grounds toward the palace. The marble walls of the Celestial Court welcome me with their familiar glow, and I find that I am glad for their embrace after such a strange and inexplicable spell.

I take a quick, silent meal by myself in the royal dining room before returning once more to the dust-drenched corner of the Archive Room. If Torran picks up on my unease, he says nothing of it. He just seems content that I'm no longer pacing.

By the midnight bell, I retire to my chambers. The lure of seeing Lyanndra is stronger now, and I cling to the memory of her as I change into my nightclothes and slide into bed.

I close my eyes and delve into myself, feeling blindly for the bond that tethers us.

For a moment, I fear that I will not find it, and that I will somehow pull that terrible black thread instead. But then I sense her within my flame, and I'm so overcome with relief that I think I might weep.

"Lyanndra," I whisper as I reach for her.

The bedchamber melts away, and, just for a second, I am in that nothing place. Then the cool night air, tinged with sulfur, flushes over my skin, and she's there in front of me, a vision swathed in moonlight.

"You came," Lyanndra breathes.

At first glance, she looks just as she did the last time I saw her. She's clad in a black nightdress laced with gold, and her feet are bare. Her honeyed hair tumbles loose over her shoulders. Yet, her eyes are tired, and her face is grim, and I am reminded anew of the death that plagues her.

"Did I not swear it to you?" I ask as I step toward her. "Am I not a man of my word?"

"I thought…." Her voice trails off to nothing, and, when she meets my gaze, shame brims in her eyes.

"That I would forsake you?" I finish.

She nods, and my heart shatters.

"Never," I vow as I wrap my arms around her. I press a kiss to the crown of her head, and, at that, she sags into me.

"It's all my fault," she murmurs into my chest.

"No," I state, drawing back so that I can once again look her in the eye. I need her to see that I mean what I say, that I never doubted her, not even for a second. "There are choices a leader can make that put their men in danger. Foolish choices. *Deadly* choices. But you did not cause this bloodshed. You were not responsible for it."

"Eight men died under my command," she argues, but her tone is more tired than furious.

"And so will many more."

She blanches at that, though she doesn't pull away from me.

"Any knight who wields a blade knows the cost of it. I have lost hundreds of soldiers, Lyanndra, too many to count." It's a grim confession, one I am not proud of. But it's the nature of war and of keeping the peace, and she needs to hear it. "Irtas and those men died defending their people and their kingdom. Do you think that their sacrifice makes you unworthy of leadership? Of the throne?"

"Does it not?" she challenges.

I shake my head. "You are a cunning warrior with an eye for strategy that puts mine to shame, yet you cannot see what's right in front of you."

"Then enlighten me, O great and wise Lord of the Midnight Flame," she snaps.

I grin.

There's the Godslayer, all passion and hot fury, dredged up from the depths of Lyanndra's brooding self-pity.

"Did you know I spend most of my time wondering if I am fit to be king?" I ask.

Genuine shock flashes across her face.

"Every day, I feel sure that somebody will look upon me and realize that I am no better than an imposter," I continue. "I was born to sit upon the throne. I did not earn it, not as you have. But I have come to think that perhaps the sign of a just ruler is not confidence, but the willingness to question every action, every choice. Perhaps the guilt we feel keeps us true to our joint purpose. Perhaps that is what makes us fit to wear our crowns."

"I do not yet wear one," she states.

Love—for it can be nothing else—surges through me as I dip my lips down to brush against hers. I hope she feels it. I hope she understands that my flame burns only for her, from now until the stars fall.

"Soon," I promise her.

Even if Lyanndra does not believe it now, I will do as I vowed.

I will shoulder her burdens.

I will show her that she's worthy.

I will make her my queen.

CHAPTER 27

Lyanndra

Something has changed.

I sense it in how Syran's mouth captures mine and in the way he curls his arms around me to draw me close. He pours this new and tender thing into me with a desperation that pools in my core and sets my blood aflame.

This is more than need or desire.

This is *devotion*.

And with it, the barb that's readied on my tongue melts away.

A moment later, he breaks the kiss to catch my gaze once more. His green eyes, so vibrant against the endlessly brown landscape, glimmer as he murmurs, "There is nothing you could do that would ever drive me away."

He skims one hand down my spine to rest at the small of my back, and I shiver.

The ghost of his previous confession looms in the small space between us. It's hard to believe that this Demigod, who rages with the blazing heat of very stars, could doubt himself so. Does he really think that he is unfit to be king?

I open my mouth to tell him that his insecurity is nothing more than passing madness, but then I pause.

Everything I could say to him, could he not repeat back to me?

For all of the reasons I have faith in him, should I, too, have faith in myself?

Disquiet ripples through me as I realize that maybe Syran speaks the truth. Maybe I've been a fool.

As if sensing my crumbling resolve, he presses his forehead against mine. "There will be times," he whispers, "when we fail. There will be moments we later come to regret. But we will have each other to lean upon. Neither of us need carry the weight of our sins alone."

My very nature urges me to rage against him. I've always existed apart from everybody else, even when I was young. As a knight, I kept to myself, not out of want but out of sheer necessity and fear of what would happen if the truth of me were to be discovered.

And though Syran asked this of me before, and I agreed, I didn't fully understand the scope of his vow.

Now, I stand and wonder what it would feel like to allow him to truly walk beside me, to know that whenever I falter, he will be there to hold me until my balance returns.

Something far more powerful than guilt or grief quickens within me at the thought.

I want to know, I realize.

And then, as the ferocity of the decision grips me, I ask, "Do you truly mean it? For if you don't, speak now, before I'm trapped upon a throne with a crown as my shackle."

"Yes," he says, eyes blazing in the darkness. "I mean it—with everything that I am. You are my star, and I am your moon, Lyanndra. I orbit you, helplessly and completely. There is no power that could tear me from you now, no storm that could separate us. Do you not feel it? Do you not see that I was yours from the very start?"

Something within me releases at his words.

It doesn't snap or splinter. It simply eases, like the sigh of a breath held for far too long, and fills me with a sensation so warm and so gentle that my entire being bends from the softness of it.

"I do," I confess. "I feel…."

But my voice trails off into nothing, not because I don't possess the words to speak of it, but because I can't reveal this tender truth to him.

Not yet.

Not like this.

When I tell Syran that I love him, it will not be in a dream. It will be with him standing before me, solid and real, where he can't dissolve away into the dawn.

And when I glimpse the way his midnight flame flares behind his eyes, I know–*I know*–that he feels the same.

In place of the words, he claims my lips once again in a bruising kiss. His hold on me is tight, as though he's afraid I'll vanish if he lets go, and I melt into it, into *him*. The ashen scent of his fire swirls through the cool night air, and I'm struck with a pang of longing so sharp and sudden that I fear I'll never recover if I do not have all of him tonight.

And when I pull away from him, he growls at the sudden loss. The sound travels straight to my core.

But his resistance softens as I sink to my knees before him, hooking my fingers at the waist of his trousers and dragging them with me as I go. His cock, already hard, is level with my face. I waste no time in darting out my tongue to taste him.

He gazes down at me through dark crimson lashes and groans at the sight. "By the stars, Lyanndra," he chokes out as his long fingers twist into my hair. "Do you know what it does to me, seeing you like this? Knowing that I am at your mercy?"

I draw him further into my mouth, savoring the way his thighs shudder under my hands. His reaction emboldens me to swirl my tongue over the tip of his cock, and he rewards me with a moan so salacious that even I blush. I continue this ruinous torture until he finally pushes me, firmly, but gently, from him.

Though part of me would like nothing more than to see him come undone from my mouth alone, I allow him to tug me back to my feet and steal another kiss.

I want him–badly. And when he slides one hand between my thighs and finds the wetness pooled there, he murmurs, "Let me take you, Lyanndra. Let me show you that I'm yours."

"Do it," I command.

And he does.

Within seconds, he's divested me of my nightdress. I don't know, or care, where it goes. All that matters is that he lays me down upon the ground and covers my body with his own. He pushes into me, groaning as he does, and I only just remember to stifle my own gasp against my palm as he fills me.

"I will walk with you," he promises as he rolls his hips into mine. "I will be whatever you ask of me. I am yours, in every misfortune. In every miracle. In every lifetime. In every constellation."

Mine, I think. *He's mine.*

And something stirs deep within me, quiet and watchful, but it's gone as quickly as it comes, and then there's only Syran's blazing heat, consuming me, branding me.

He brings me to the very edge like this, teasing me with his mouth and his cock and his wicked fingers until I unravel beneath him. A second later, his body stutters, and he, too, is ruined. Like the last time, he doesn't leave me. As soon as he returns to himself, he rolls to the side, only to pull me into the warm slope of his chest a moment later. He trails one hand up my side and to my breast, where he traces a lazy circle around my nipple.

I shudder in pleasure.

He flashes me a positively rakish grin in return. Without stopping his idle torment, he dips his mouth low to my ear and purrs, "It's not enough to have you in our dreams, Lyanndra. Just think of all the ways I'll fuck you when we're finally together."

Longing surges through me at the thought, and I shift in his arms to face him. "I miss you," I breathe. "I'm glad to see my family safe and unharmed, but they...."

The words die in my throat. How do I even finish that sentence?

They're scared of me?

My own mother looks upon me like I'm a monster?

My father thinks you'd like nothing more than to slice me open and bathe in my blood?

Finally, I shake my head and tell him, "I wish I never came to Breem. I wish that I remained by your side, where I belong."

Syran presses his lips to mine with such tenderness that tears, unbidden, sting my eyes. "Soon," he assures me. "Torran tells me that he's close to finishing the translation, and when he does, I will hunt down the fang and come to you. I swear it."

"I have yet to find the Ushum," I confess. "But it's here, Syran, and it's waking up."

His mouth sets into a stubborn line. "We will put an end to it," he vows.

I wish that I could match his fierce conviction, but my hope is waning, and I worry that time is not on our side. This fear burdens me even as we lie together and stare up at the southern sky, until the first rays of dawn chase away the moon, and my crossed star with it.

And when I wake in my bedroll in the field beyond my family's homestead, it's with tears coursing down my cheeks and an ache in my chest so deep that I wonder if there will ever be enough time with Syran to fill it again.

This weight doesn't leave me as I wipe my face on the edge of my bedroll and then rise to start the day. I allow myself a quick cup of tea and a roll, pilfered from the homestead window where they were set out to cool, and then gather the Celestial Knights to resume the search for the Ushum's lair.

But this morning, like yesterday, yields nothing but shallow passages and yawning caverns that culminate, always, in dead ends.

Several times, I take it upon myself to duck into the previously searched caves in hopes that I might see something the others missed, something to spark the fading embers of my memory once more. Yet, the rocky walls all look the same (brown), and every stalagmite is of a similar shape (pointy), and I can't even perceive any differences in the tiny lizards (white and eyeless) that skitter down here in the dark.

By the time I emerge from one craggy opening to find the first smoky tendrils of dusk creeping across the horizon, I have nothing left to offer my host than disappointment, frustration, and an order to retreat back to camp for the night.

After I give the command, Orobos falls into step beside me as I pick my way down the mountain. "We may not have found the beast," he says, "but we made progress. Every cave we've searched and marked off narrows it down. We're getting close. I'm sure of it."

I level him with a flat look, one that would rival even my mother's worst stare, and he shuts his mouth. For the rest of the journey, he has enough sense not to test my ire.

He's right, though.

I think on his words as I navigate through the bedrolls, tents, and cooking fires that litter the camp. When I pass by one orange blaze, Jurlan hails me. At first, I consider ignoring him, but then he enthusiastically shouts, "Godslayer! Some of the villagers brought us meat pies!"

And when he holds up not one, but two, steaming pastries, I cannot refuse.

I sit with them for a short while, as long as it takes for me to devour my dinner. It's the best meal I've had in quite some time, though it doesn't compare to the palace fare I've grown used to over the past few months.

For all of the faults of the Demigods, at least they know how to cook.

The company, too, isn't bad. Jurlan's friends among the host, Demigod and Starless alike, are young and raucous. Their humor does leave something to be desired, considering that most of it centers around bodily functions, but the easy way in which they speak reminds me of the many pleasant nights I spent with my old battalion.

I linger until the noise grows too much and the fatigue sets in, and then I take my leave with a silent nod.

From there, I wander.

The landscape here is almost exactly as I remember. I make my way across several fields, heading over to one in particular where we used to drink and tell stories late into the night. I clamber over several fences, which I used to vault on my father's stolen horses, and recall how my mother would come out and shout at me for being so reckless.

I grin.

Perhaps I was the Godslayer even then.

Perhaps I just didn't know it yet.

When I reach my destination, I flop down onto the rocky ground. There's a bare, burned spot here in the center of the field, proof that the delinquent youth of Breem still gather here from time to time. But it's blissfully empty this evening. I sit, admiring the stars and thinking of how Syran will come to me tonight, and I am at peace.

That is, until a voice calls from the far edge of the fence, "Lyanndra!"

I glance over and immediately recoil. Even in the moonlight, the figure is unmistakable.

Aaro.

Does he have to spoil every quiet moment I manage to steal in this interminably brown and wretched place?

If he notices my distaste for him, he pays it no mind. Instead, he clears the fence with a fair amount of grace and jogs over to me. When he gets closer, I catch sight of an object in his hand—a bottle, two thirds full and sloshing with amber liquid.

"Mead," he says, as if it's not evident. "Your favorite."

It's not, but such trivialities have never stopped him before.

He settles himself down on the ground beside me, uncorks the bottle, and takes a deep swig. "Do you remember when we were kids?" he asks after he swallows. "We'd come out here and get so disgustingly drunk that we'd have to prop each other up on the way home."

I don't bother acknowledging his reminiscence. Instead, I reach for the mead. I'll certainly need it if I'm to listen to him blather on about the desiccated corpse of our shared past for any length of time.

He grins and hands over the bottle. I take a sip, and then another for good measure, before I pass it back to him. The token on my arm flashes like molten gold beneath the stars as I move, and I don't miss the way his eyes narrow upon it.

"You really are going to marry him, aren't you?" he asks.

I nod.

"Why?"

The question hangs in the night air between us. I don't owe Aaro an explanation, but still, I admit, "He sees me."

"And I don't?" he challenges.

Anger licks up my ribcage like black fire, and I shake my head.

"I couldn't give you a palace," he says, his voice wavering. Hurt creases across his tanned features. "I couldn't give you a crown. But we could have been happy, Lyanndra. How can you possibly think you'll have that with him?"

Aaro is past the point of listening, and there's no use in arguing with somebody who's so intent on remaining so spectacularly dim, so to that, I say nothing at all.

But he must take my silence as permission or hesitance because he leans in toward me with his eyes half-lidded and his lips parted.

"No," I state firmly. I push him back, not hard, but not gently either. The scent of alcohol lingers heavily on his breath, and, in one last attempt to be charitable, I add, "You're drunk, Aaro. Go home, sleep it off, and never speak to me again."

Resentment pools in his eyes as his face twists into something unrecognizable. "Listen to yourself, Lyanndra!" he snarls. "You ran off because you were a fucking coward, and now you come back here wearing your armor and that helm and his *fucking* token, and you think I should just, what? Let you ruin your life even more? Let you degrade yourself so you can become the favorite plaything of the Demigod king?"

Something cold snaps into place inside me. And this time, when Aaro grabs my wrist and tries to kiss me again, I do not hold back.

My former betrothed is bigger than me, but he's stupid, drunk, and slow.

I wrench my arm from his grasp and scramble to my feet. Before he can even react, the sole of my boot connects with his chest, sending him flying backward into the rocky dirt of the field.

The air leaves his lungs with a satisfying *whump*. I know I should probably just leave him like this, sprawled and gasping for air, but the oldest wound inside of me is open and weeping, and I think I shall make him feel it too.

So I kneel with my knee in his neck. My greave, inlaid with Syran's golden scales, presses into his windpipe, not enough to cut off his air completely, but enough to make him struggle. He claws at my legs and arms, whatever he can reach, but I do not move.

I am the Godslayer.

I do not falter.

"You think me weak?" I growl, baring my teeth. "You think me a coward?"

His eyes widen in fear, and it's my turn to grin.

"Know this," I hiss. "I am *nobody's* plaything. I was brave enough to shed the skin of all that held me back–of *you*–and forge my own path. This is the life I chose for myself. I *chose* to be the Godslayer. I *chose* Syran, even if the stars had to force me to see him." I punctuate the Lord of the Midnight Flame's name with a flash of pressure on his throat. "You should be grateful that I choose now to let you live. But heed me, Aaro: I will not be so merciful if I see you again."

And with that, I finally release him.

I leave him like that, pathetic and flailing and clutching at his neck in the middle of the field where he first tried to make me smaller than I was.

And when I storm back to camp, it's with the rage of the stars burning in my chest and a wound, open for so long, finally starting to heal.

CHAPTER 28

SYRAN

I have not yet found the fang.

It's an admission I make to Lyanndra nightly in my visits to her dreams, one that shames me more with each passing utterance. And while she still has not located the Ushum's lair, her lack of progress doesn't hold the same weight as mine. We know, at least, the beast's general location. But the weapon we seek could be anything or anywhere, buried beneath centuries of rock or hidden in plain sight.

Time is not on our side, and I fear that the Ushum will wake before I complete my duty.

Yet, even as I stare down my impossible venture, my crossed star's task seems to close in on her like a vice. During the days, I can feel the echoes of her frustration and discontent across the vast distance of our bond. At night, she grows quieter and more thoughtful, which only makes me miss her all the more.

I long to come to her in her waking hours and search with her. We may still fail, but at least we'd do so together.

And something else burdens her, too.

The night after our tender encounter where I vowed, once again, to remain by her side, she met me with such ferocity that I thought I might melt from the heat of her. She all but pushed me down and straddled me, kissing me with a burning fury that had me gasping and panting beneath her.

In that quiet moment after she debased me so thoroughly as to have me calling her name out into the night, I asked her, "What happened?" For something surely had.

When her hazel eyes met mine, I found only firm resolution there.

"I took care of it," she said.

Now, almost two agonizing weeks later, I still cannot scrub her expression from my mind. I hate knowing that something chews at her thoughts, and that, even after everything, she does not feel like she can share with me whatever plagues her so.

But I remind myself that she is a solitary creature, one used to secrets and subtlety. While I grew up with advisors and Kartas to confide in, Lyanndra had nobody.

She speaks not of her siblings, though I suspect she has many, and, from the way she avoids talking of them, I surmise that she is not particularly close to her parents. Her friends, it seems, are limited to me and her monstrous steed, who, to my knowledge, is not the chatty sort.

So I understand that I ask a lot of her. It must be difficult for her to change her ways. I only hope that in time, and perhaps with some gentle encouragement, she will learn that she should not fear unmasking herself to me, for I shall accept her secrets with honor.

After all, what greater gift could such a lonely being bestow upon me than her trust?

But until that day comes, I will be patient.

Today, however, my tolerance runs low.

"He insists on meeting with you, Your Highness," Noros says for the third time in the last hour. He speaks of a stranger who seeks my audience and who cannot seem to accept my repeated refusals.

From where he sits in a high-backed chair to my left, Torran suggests, "Perhaps indulging him would put an end to his efforts."

"Throwing him in the dungeons would have much the same effect," I snap. "My answer remains unchanged. If he wishes for me to hear him, he must wait until tomorrow."

But the old Demigod does have a point. If I don't put a stop to this, how many more times will this man—whoever he is—come to the palace gates?

The first occurrence, the guards stopped him and asked his business, and, upon learning that he would seek an audience with me, informed him that it would not be possible until the following day.

The second, they marched him off in what I hope was a mildly threatening manner.

At this third and current instance, Wayre took it upon himself to hold the man at the doors of the palace while his counterpart ran to me for further instruction.

But before I can send Noros back to once again dismiss the stranger from the palace grounds, the doors to the throne room part to reveal a throng of guards led by Wayre. They escort a man in their midst.

He's Starless, by the looks of it.

He wears a plain, rough spun tunic and trousers that are worn and patched at the knee. His skin is tan, and his blond hair, so fine that it appears almost white beneath the afternoon sunlight, is tied back in a series of intricate braids. I recognize the technique as the kind favored by the men of the Southern Caldera.

Interesting.

I think, at first, that he must be a refugee, but I do not recall welcoming him to Nexus. Has he just arrived? And if so, why is it so dire that I hear him?

His blue eyes find mine and widen.

Stretching to my full height upon my throne, I arrange my features into a blank mask. I watch him carefully as the odd party stops just across the threshold. As Wayre breaks away from the group to approach the dais where I sit, the stranger's gaze does not break from mine.

"What is the meaning of this?" I demand.

Wayre bows his head in respect. "My apologies, Your Highness, but I did not think it wise for him to remain where others could hear," he murmurs. "He is making… claims, Your Highness."

"Claims?" I repeat. "Of what variety?"

"The most vicious sort, Your Highness," he replies. He glances over his shoulder at the man, and I have spent enough time in this knight's company to recognize the ripple of distress that creeps across his features. "I think, if I may be so bold… perhaps it would be best that he tells you directly?"

I do not care to hear this stranger's clandestine whispers. Rumors are passed through the halls of the Celestial Court like currency, and while some of them may hold a kernel of truth, all are designed to rend reputations and draw the blood of courtiers. Such pathetic machinations are below me.

Whatever this Starless stranger has to say, it is of no concern of mine.

So when I speak again, I do so loudly. "I am in no mood for rumor and scandal. If it is aid he seeks, see to it that he receives it, and send him on his way." It will not be said of me that I didn't show this man some kindness, even at his dismissal.

Wayre nods. "Yes, Your Highness."

But, just as he turns to leave, Torran reaches out a frail hand toward him. "Wait," he says.

I glare at the old Demigod. There is no need for words. My distaste for his insubordination is written plainly across my face.

He focuses his gaze, bright and depthless, upon me, and, while his expression remains neutral, I do not miss the quiet weight in his voice as he states, "I should like to hear his wild claims. Indulge a bored old man's curiosity, Your Highness. You know how I enjoy hearing such tales."

My eyes narrow.

For I happen to know that Torran does not, in fact, enjoy dipping his toes into the noxious pool of palace gossip.

What are you playing at? I wonder. *What do you see that I do not?*

There is only one way to discover the answers I seek.

"Very well," I relent, directing my words at Torran but raising my voice slightly so that it rings through the throne room.

Only then do I turn to the man, whose eyes remain fixed upon me.

I adopt my most imperious tone and order, "Approach."

At my words, the guards part to allow the Starless stranger passage toward the throne. He hesitates for a moment, and I'm pleased to see a spark of fear ignite in his gaze. But then he musters his courage and strides forward.

When he reaches the dais and bows his head in deference, I take the opportunity to study him.

He looks quite well for a refugee. There's no sign of malnutrition or illness, and he appears uninjured aside from an angry bruise that yellows at his neck. At first glance, there is nothing at all remarkable about the contusion, but then he raises his head once more and I notice an odd pattern pressed into his skin.

It reminds me of something, I realize.

In fact, I am sure I have seen that design somewhere before.

But *where*?

Yet, my thoughts scatter when the man speaks. "Thank you, Your Highness, and my apologies for so rudely interrupting you. Please know that I would certainly have waited for tomorrow's audience if the matter wasn't so very urgent."

If what he's come to tell me is of such great and timely importance, then why can't he simply get on with it? Thoroughly unimpressed, I reply, "Speak of it quickly, if your business is so pressing."

Once again, he hesitates.

Fighting the urge to scowl, I open my mouth, fully intending to send him on his way, but then he breaks his silence.

"I am Aaro, Your Highness, and I come bearing grave news from Breem."

Icy fingers grab my heart and squeeze.

My first, panicked thought is that something terrible has happened to Lyanndra, but I quickly push that away. I saw her last night in our dreams, and aside from her growing frustration, she was well.

Is it the Ushum, perhaps? Is it finally awake?

But then I realize that the man who stands before me is no messenger. Even if the Ushum rose from its slumber this very minute, it would take him a fortnight to reach me with the news.

No, this is something else.

As if sensing my sudden distress, the Starless stranger–Aaro, he called himself–continues, "I must speak with you about the Godslayer, Your Highness." Then he glances over his shoulder at the Celestial Knights lingering at his back, and adds, "Alone."

I consider this for a moment.

There is something about Aaro that gives me pause, and I do not like the thought of turning away any of my sworn swords. Yet, I suspect he will be more agreeable to sharing if I grant him this request, so after a long moment of thought, I glance at the guards gathered in the center of the throne room and command, "Leave us."

They obey without question. Even Torran rises from his chair and shuffles from the dais.

As soon as the doors shut behind them, I order, "Speak."

Aaro swallows and nods. "I know Lyanndra," he says. "From before."

My fingers tighten around the arms of the throne as I lean forward. He must speak the truth, since she has, to my knowledge, never shared her given name with any other since starting her journey into knighthood.

"We grew up together," he continues. His voice is hoarse, probably as a result of whatever happened to his neck, but still, it rings throughout the throne room like a death knell. "We knew each other... quite well."

Suspicion creeps across my ribs and I ask, "How well?"

He shifts from one foot to another before stammering, "We were... we were betrothed, Your Highness. We were to be married."

Ah.

My gaze sharpens as I imagine him, younger but still annoyingly handsome in his simple sort of way, trying–and failing–to woo Lyanndra.

My Lyanndra.

From the way she spoke of Aaro, she never harbored feelings of any kind for him, aside from general disdain. Didn't she say that she left Breem because of the betrothal, after all?

So I state, in a burning tone so dangerous that I'm surprised he doesn't smolder where he stands, "I know who you are."

Fear flashes across Aaro's face, and he takes a step back. "Please, Your Highness," he begs. "I come to you not as a rival but with a terrible truth. If you must strike me down, then so be it, but heed me first! Please!"

His piteous scrounging is enough to stay my hand, not that I was planning on killing this fool. If he ran across Lyanndra in Breem and she did not see fit to dispatch him, then I shall respect her wishes on the matter, as much as it pains me to do so.

In my silence, he ekes out, "Lyanndra sought me out upon her arrival to the village. We spoke, and I thought that we were friends again. A fortnight ago, we shared a drink and she…."

I stare at the man, daring him to continue.

"She said that her betrothal to you was purely political." His voice is so low with terror that his words are just barely audible. "And I had drunk so much, and was just so glad to have her back that…."

"You laid with her?" I finish.

"*She* laid with *me.*"

Rage, blistering and endless, explodes in my chest.

How dare he?

How *dare* he!

I want to call my flame and broil him alive. I want to reduce him to a pile of ash. I want to throw him in the dungeons so that Lyanndra, when she returns, can pull him apart, piece by fucking piece.

But I do none of these things, for I am the King of Alastria, and I shall act like it.

It takes every ounce of my control to rise from my throne to loom over Aaro and hiss, "These are treasonous allegations. What proof do you have to back them up?"

Because I already know that there is no evidence. There is nothing he could possibly produce that could convince me of Lyanndra's deceit.

Yet, fresh dread rises in my lungs as he pulls something forth from the pocket of his trousers.

For the object he holds shimmers like liquid gold in the sunlight.

Unmistakable.

Undeniable.

Aaro raises my token aloft, and I know, with burning horror, that he could have only gotten this from one person.

Lyanndra.

CHAPTER 29

Lyanndra

There's been no sign of Aaro since that fateful night in the field.

By all rights, that should be a good thing, and, for the first few days, it was.

I wasn't constantly looking over my shoulder while climbing endlessly up and down the sides of the mountain, waiting for him to appear akin to some unwanted phantom. No longer did he hover by my parents' homestead in the evenings or join them for dinner.

It's as if he simply vanished into the darkness like the shadowy figure that plagued us in Syran's chambers so many weeks ago, never to be seen again.

Yet, I still do not feel comfortable here in Breem.

I wish, more than anything, that I could return to Syran's side. But I am nothing if not resilient, and I will complete my task. I tell myself that soon, he will come. Soon, I will have him once more. And in the meantime, I manage by stealing away a slice of silence in my parents' barn every now and then, where I'm suitably hidden from prying eyes.

It's where I find myself tonight as the last dregs of evening light start to fade, along with my hopes of ever finding the Ushum's lair. And aside from my most recent failure, I'm plagued by a feeling that I'm convinced is not my own. An echo of anger seethes deep within me. It writhes like a serpent, tight and sinuous, and each time I reach to grab it, it wriggles away further beneath my skin.

Is this Syran's rage?

I think it must be.

My chest tightens at the realization. What drives him to such burning fury? Has some calamity struck the Celestial Court? Has the fang slipped through his fingers?

Or worse, has some harm befallen him?

There's no way for me to answer these devilish questions, not until Syran visits me tonight in our dreams. But, even as the shadows of dusk lengthen over the worn boards of the hayloft, that seems an eternity away.

So I sit and I wait, and my mood sours further with every passing minute. Not even the tin cup of watery stew I clasp between my hands can cheer me up, as dinner usually does.

Then, to make matters worse, I catch the shuffle of footsteps brushing against the straw-strewn ground down in the aisle of the barn. A second later, a familiar voice calls, "Lyanndra?"

I lean over the edge of the hayloft to see my father standing just below me. His face is hard to distinguish in the gathering darkness, but I can just make out that he holds two bowls in his hands. Steam rises from them, carrying the tantalizing spice of my mother's cooking up to where I sit.

My stomach growls. I glance down at the stew, which is beige and slightly congealed on the top, and sigh.

"Here," I call.

"I thought this might tempt you," he replies. "You always did like your dinner."

He passes both bowls up to me before he climbs the short ladder that leads to the loft. The ceiling here is low, and the dimensions are cramped, but I shuffle over far enough so that he's able to settle in beside me with his back against the wall and his legs dangling over into the aisle.

Once he's situated, I hand him his food. He nods down at the cup of forsaken stew near my feet and says, "I don't envy those days of cooking fires and rations."

I answer with a shrug.

At the moment, I don't particularly want his—or anyone's—company, not with Syran's anger surging through me. But my father and I have barely spoken since our argument over my crossed star, and, as much as I understand that my parents may never see me as I am now, I still hold out hope that something redeemable will blossom out of this journey to Breem.

So I'll let him say his piece, and I'll do him the courtesy of listening. Any more than that, however, I cannot promise.

"I imagine the food at the palace is decent, at least," he muses as I tear off a piece of steaming flatbread and use it to scoop up some curry. When I bite into it, warm spices dance across my tongue, and I sigh. It's such a nostalgic taste, one that I didn't even know I missed until just now, and I find myself wondering if anybody in Nexus might be able to help me recreate it when I return.

My father, too, dives into his bowl. We eat in silence for a few minutes before he asks, "Is the Celestial Court as grand as they say?"

When I nod, his eyes widen.

"Gold?" he presses. "Gemstones?"

Again, I nod, thinking, with a pang of sadness, of the way the corridors of the palace glitter in the sunlight and about the silken sheets of Syran's bed. But even as I miss the place that once served as my prison, I'm reminded of how the Demigods still have so much while the Starless hold so little.

What else can I do to help my people? How can I ever give them the justice they deserve?

Beside me, my father's shoulders tense. "And do you... are you allowed to wander?"

I stare at him for a moment and then nod.

Does he really think that Syran keeps me locked away like some precious little pet?

But then I remember how the king *did* confine me to the infirmary for so long and concede that I cannot fully blame my father for his unfair assumptions.

He shakes his head. "The way you struck down those marauders… you were terrifying to behold. Impressive, but terrifying." Even in the growing darkness, I can feel his eyes slide to mine. "Has he seen you like that, Lyanndra? Does he truly understand what we, the Starless, mean when we call you Godslayer?"

I draw in a shuddering breath and reveal, "He was there that day. He saw what I did."

"What?" my father gasps.

"Syran saw me kill his father. He watched as I slid a knife between the Flaming God's ribs and bled him like he did our people. Syran knows who I am. *What* I am." I turn to face him, though he's just an outline now in the gloom. "Do you?"

"I know that you are brave," he replies quietly. "I know that you have earned your title. And I know that I am proud of you and the things you have done."

Something hot rises in my throat. It's such a foreign emotion that I can't even tell if it's good or bad, or if I'm worthy of it.

In the darkness, my father finds my hand. His palm is ridged with callouses and the scars of labor, but it's familiar and warm, even after all this time. Though he must feel the band of Syran's ring where it rests against my finger, he says nothing of it. And when he squeezes, I return the pressure.

"You're my daughter, Lyanndra," he says in a voice barely louder than a whisper. "I don't wish to fight you. The stars know that I'd lose. But if you are to marry him, please–*please*–tell me that this is what you want. Tell me that if he tries to harm you, you'll strike him down and put an end to his kind's bloody reign."

"Don't," I warn. "He is not his father. He would die before hurting me."

His hand tightens over mine. "Are you sure of that?"

"Yes."

He sighs at the fiery resolution in my tone. "I fought against his kind," he says after a long moment. "I remember the bloodshed and the slaughter. It's been decades, but still, I dream of the battlefield some nights, of the horrors I saw and the ones I wrought."

"As do I," I murmur.

Again, his fingers squeeze mine. "I notice that you no longer wear his token. Have you doubts about this union?"

Shame and longing muddle within me at his words. I wish I knew where I lost the golden scarf, which I tied so securely around my arm each morning until it went missing a few weeks ago. It must have been in one of the caves, for I searched the encampment and the surrounding fields thrice over to no avail.

Does nothing in Breem wish to be found?

Yet, I say, with as much conviction as I can muster, "I have no doubts. I *will* marry Syran. I *will* be queen."

And finally, I withdraw my hand from his.

Silence falls between us.

Somehow, it seems larger in the dark.

When I'm relatively certain that my father's finished speaking, I return to my food. The curry is a little cold now, but the bread beneath is still warm, as is the spice that flickers across my tongue like tiny embers. I eat slowly, savoring every bite.

What will Syran think of such fare, I wonder, when he joins me here in the shadow of the mountain? I don't think he's ever tasted anything quite like this. Will he be overcome by the sharpness of it, or will his fiery nature welcome the heat?

Slowly, the quiet fades into something more comfortable. I find that I'm content to sit up here in the hayloft with my father by my side, even if he doesn't understand what I see in my crossed star.

But then, just as my guard starts to falter, my ears catch a low sound rising in the distance.

At first, it's a deep whine that reminds me of the buzz produced by the fingernail-sized, bloodsucking gnats that plague the swampy lands to the southeast of the kingdom. But it's too dry for them to reproduce this close to the mountain. And when the droning grows louder, I know that no insect is behind this.

"Down the ladder!" I bark, shoving my father toward the edge of the hayloft. "Now!"

He follows my order automatically. Perhaps he never really stopped being a soldier, even after putting down his sword.

But there's no time to dwell on such thoughts, for, even as I drop down after him into the aisle, the sound swells into that same grating wail as before.

I know what's coming. I grab my father and pull him to the door of the nearest stall just as the ground starts to shudder beneath our feet. It's not the sturdiest portion of the barn, but it will have to do. The framing of the threshold will hold.

"Stay here," I shout over the dissonant howling of the Ushum.

"Lyanndra!" he yells, but I'm already gone.

The floor of the barn churns. Dust rains down as the boards above splinter and grind, but I do not falter. The goats shriek, and the horses scream and kick at the walls. When I reach the door of Barra's stall, it's to find the kelpie's red eyes rolling in alarm as she pins her ears and snaps her jaws in the air.

Gripping the door with one hand to keep myself upright, I fumble at the latch with the other. After a long few seconds, it springs free beneath my fingers, and I haul the door open as much as I can amidst the quake.

"Go!" I urge my mount.

Something at the far end of the barn collapses with a great rending crash, and that is all the encouragement the kelpie needs. Barra flies from the stall, her great hooves slapping against the roiling ground, and disappears out into the night.

"Lyanndra!" my father calls. "Where are you?"

"Stay there!" I bellow back, for the safest place he can be is in the doorframe of the stall where I left him. At least that way, the roof can't fall on him.

And even as I say it, a portion of the ceiling in front of me caves.

I fling my arms up in front of my face as I shy away from the destruction. The air itself seethes with dust and debris, and I can barely see. The floor bucks and cracks, forcing me to crouch low in order to keep some semblance of balance, and the whole time, the sound, *that dreadful fucking sound*, yowls away in the distance.

If this goes on for much longer, the whole barn is going to collapse.

But that's not my biggest concern.

Is this it?

Is this the moment that the Ushum finally wakes and bursts free from the ground to lay waste to the Southern Caldera?

Have we failed?

But the earth's spasms grow no worse. And after several tense, agonizing seconds, the tremors come fewer and far between, and the creature's cry lessens until it's once again just a whirring hum in the distance.

Then it's gone completely, and the ground stills.

The quake is over.

The Ushum has yet to rise.

I stand, coughing and squinting amidst the dust, and survey the damage. The main ceiling of the barn has collapsed completely, though the framing of the stall kept me safe.

"Lyanndra!" my father calls once again. His voice is thin with the grit of the air, but, to my immense relief, I detect no notes of pain within it.

"Here," I shout as I squeeze out through a gap in the debris. Moonlight pours in through the splintered roof, which at least allows me to see as I pick my way over to the stall where I left my father.

He's shaking and covered in dust but appears otherwise unharmed. His face crumples in relief when he catches sight of me. "By the stars," he gasps as he draws me into his arms. "By the *fucking* stars."

We don't linger there for long. The roof creaks ominously overhead, and, as I guide my father around the worst of the damage, I realize that the entire hayloft has folded. I see him to the doors first, ushering him out into the comparatively clear night air, before heading back inside, for I can't imagine leaving the goats and horses in here if the structure splinters any further.

After bringing out the animals and handing them off to my brothers, who have gathered around the damaged barn, I return to my host.

There are few casualties, but those who were injured sport bruises and abrasions, nothing of concern. I'm relieved to see the homestead still standing, seemingly untouched, though from the smoke that rises near the center of Breem, I suspect that the rest of the village was not so lucky.

And later, after aiding the townsfolk as best as I'm able, I collapse into my bedroll just as the moon hits its peak in the southern sky.

I close my eyes, but I do not allow myself to sleep quite yet.

Instead, I remember.

I send myself back to when I was a girl, when I would scuttle like a mad little spider all over the mountain without a care in the kingdom. There's no particular recollection in my mind of the opening, or of the cave itself, but the smell comes back to me now: sulfurous, woolen, and something else, something that turns my stomach even in this moment, something ancient and very far away.

Retching from the mere memory of the stench, I sit up in my bedroll and wipe my hand over my mouth. The onyx ring, etched with the coiled serpent of Syran's crest, flashes in the moonlight. I focus on it, on *him*, as I draw in a deep breath, and then another.

But the phantom scent still lingers. Even as I settle back into my bedroll and drift off to sleep, it doesn't leave me.

The cave I seek is out there. It has to be.

And I need to find it, fast, before the worst happens.

I need to find it before the Ushum wakes completely.

CHAPTER 30

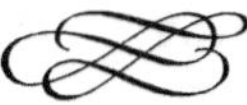

SYRAN

Rage.

It festers inside of me, clawing at my ribcage and gnashing at my insides with teeth of midnight fire. I feel nothing else. I know nothing else.

It's swirling.

Endless.

Devouring.

And while I'm lost to it, my body seems to move of its own accord. I pack without thinking, stuffing trousers and tunics into the pair of saddlebags slouched against the foot of the bed. There's already a crumpled heap of maps inside, along with a few weapons and a parcel of jerky, dry biscuits, and hard cheese I took earlier from the kitchens.

A knock sounds upon the door and echoes through the chamber.

I ignore it.

But when Torran's voice, high with alarm, calls, "Syran!" from beyond the threshold, only then do I pause.

After Aaro's terrible revelation earlier this afternoon, I snatched the token from his hands and left him in the custody of Wayre and Noros. No longer could I stand to look upon him. If I remained there one second longer, I would have turned him into naught but ash.

I stormed past Torran, who attempted, in vain, to stop me, and marched immediately to the kitchens, where I procured the rations I'd need for the journey south.

Now, I prepare myself for travel. Or at least, I was trying to before my advisor came pounding on the door.

"Leave me," I growl. I have no time for his silver tongue and knowing looks. I must leave for the Southern Caldera immediately.

Fang or no fang, I *will* track down my crossed star.

"Syran, don't be a fool!" Torran admonishes from the corridor. "I wish only to aid you!"

A fresh wave of anger rises to join the flood. It fuels me as I stalk over to the door and throw it open, revealing the wizened old Demigod who awaits beyond. He's as composed as ever, with his neat silver hair and the effortless drape of his deep purple robes. Yet, his eyes are creased with worry, and, I think, something else.

Anxiety?

Excitement?

It matters not. I *care* not. All that concerns me is getting to Lyanndra as soon as possible. Dreams won't suffice, not now. I must see her in person, face to face, *real*.

Before I can shut him out again, Torran ducks into the chamber, where his eyes immediately drift to the hastily packed saddlebags. "You plan to leave?" he asks, as if he doesn't already know the answer.

"Do I have any other option?" I snap back. I chart a course around him toward my desk, where I grab several bestiaries and a book on the topography of the Southern Caldera. Those, too, find a home in the bags, though they barely fit on top of the balled-up tunics.

"Perhaps," he says. "Perhaps not."

I roll my eyes. "More riddles?"

"A riddle has but one answer. Here, you have several to choose from," he replies.

Fire, hot and dripping with venom, prickles my palms as I spin around to face him. "What choice do I have?" I hiss. "Do you know what that Starless bastard claimed? Do you have any idea of the proof he presented to me?"

"No," Torran states patiently. "Because you ran right past me instead of seeking my counsel. What do you think I am, Syran? A mind reader?"

I stare at him, long and hard.

He meets my gaze and holds it.

"Don't play games with me, old man," I snarl. "I am in a dangerous mood."

"Then tell me what has happened."

For a moment, I hesitate, trying to find the words. Then I utter, "The Godslayer heralds from Breem. That man, Aaro, was betrothed to her when they were but children. He says now that they laid together only a fortnight ago."

"Preposterous!" Torran scoffs.

But when I pull my golden token, the one that should be, by all rights, tied around Lyanndra's arm, from my pocket, he blanches.

"No," he says, shaking his head. "That's not possible. She would never...."

I grit my teeth together as the rage rises once more.

When he catches sight of my reaction, his eyes widen in shock. "You don't truly think this of her, do you?"

"I *think* that I must ride to Breem," I retort. "Immediately."

Distress flashes over Torran's features. It's like watching parchment crumple. Perhaps, if I were in a better state of mind, it would send a pang of regret through me, but my fury overshadows everything, his feelings included.

"You do not have the fang," he states.

"I do not," I agree. I punctuate this statement by tossing an errant dagger into the nearest saddlebag.

Because right now, I don't give a single, Ushum-shaped *fuck* about the fang. The bastard god can rise from the ground and devour the kingdom whole, for all I care, so long as I reach Lyanndra before it grinds us both between its jaws.

"What about Alastria?" he asks. "What about the throne?"

"Fuck the throne," I spit. "It means nothing–*nothing*–without her."

Torran sighs, and I can practically feel the wave of defeat that radiates off him. "Do you trust Wayre and Noros to hold the line? If you think them up for the task, I shall ask it of them. And I will, of course, remind them what happened to the last general who thought he could claim the kingdom when you were away."

I want to snap at him to do whatever the fuck he pleases, but then I pause.

Through the midnight blaze of my rage, a memory comes to me.

Kartas.

Dead.

Sliced nearly in half, bleeding out on the throne room floor.

The crown on my head suddenly weighs more than I ever thought possible, and it's this burden that urges me to nod and acquiesce, "Do what must be done."

He bows his head in respect, though I do not, in this moment, deserve it. "I will see to it." Then his electric blue gaze fixes upon mine once more, and he adds, "I will take my leave now, for I, too, must prepare for the journey."

I narrow my eyes. "Speak plainly."

"Do you really think I'll let you go off on such an irresponsible and reckless pilgrimage on your own?" he asks. "I will accompany you, and I will bring the texts on the Ushum with me. My translation is nearly complete. With any luck, I shall decode the writing on the way, which may reveal something useful to us upon our arrival in Breem."

"Absolutely not," I counter, shaking my head. Torran is old and frail, especially after Kartas put an arrow through his leg. He'll only slow me down.

But he's more stubborn than he looks, for he argues, "I shall go with you, or I will inform the guards that you've gone mad and have you dragged to the infirmary."

"You wouldn't dare," I hiss.

"I would, and you know it." When I take in the unyielding hardness in his gaze, I believe him. "Do you hear yourself, Syran? You're raving. And I understand why, truly I do, but if you insist on succumbing to this insanity, at least let me be there to keep you on your path."

I glare at him, the flaming green of my eyes meeting his cool blue. I should argue with him. I should have him thrown into the dungeons for his threats, which would be considered treasonous at the best of times.

But I am not so far gone as to miss the wisdom in his words, so it is I who looks away first.

"So be it," I mutter. "Now go, old man, before I change my mind. Meet me at the stables at the tolling of the midnight bell. But be forewarned: if you do not arrive by the last knell, I shall leave without you."

He nods once again. "Thank you, Syran. And I shall not be late. You have my word."

With that, he sweeps from the room, finally leaving me to burn once more in the blistering fire of my rage.

As soon as he's gone, my thoughts turn to Lyanndra yet again. I stare down at the token I still hold in my hand and bare my teeth. The swathe of fabric shimmers a brilliant gold, but there are a few brown smudges upon it that look like dried blood, though some attempt has been made to clean them up. There's also a slight tear, as though the tip of a blade sliced through it.

This should be on her arm.

I shouldn't be holding this.

I shouldn't be holding this!

The spiral of outrage that accompanies this thought leads somewhere dark and fathomless, and I fear that if I were to fall into it, I might never claw my way back out again.

So I force myself to shove the token back into my pocket, as if that could trick the flame that writhes within me, and focus on the task at hand.

There isn't much more to pack. I toss the last few items into the saddlebags and then use my weight to flatten everything enough so that I can clasp them shut. Then I sling them over my shoulders and make my way out into the corridor.

At this late hour, the halls of the Celestial Court are mostly empty. Guards bow their heads in respect as I pass, but they know better than to question me. I make it all the way until the front doors of the palace before I meet an obstacle.

Wayre and Noros linger upon the threshold. Both nod as I approach. When they look up at me once more, I surmise that Torran has already gotten to them.

"Is it true, Your Highness?" Noros asks. "You're journeying south?"

"Yes," I say.

"It's an honor to keep watch over the kingdom in your absence," Wayre states.

I want to tell him that this honor is due only to Torran's machinations, but instead, I tell the Celestial Knights, "Maintain order while I'm away. Quell any sign of insubordination swiftly and without mercy. We cannot risk another coup. And remember: the last of my generals who stood against me met his end in front of the very throne he sought to conquer. It would be a shame if another were to succumb to his same fate."

Noros pales at my words, while Wayre grimaces.

"Yes, Your Highness," they say in unison.

"I ask one final thing of you before I depart," I continue. "Bring Aaro to the stables at the tolling of the midnight bell."

"Yes, Your Highness," they repeat as one.

With that, I bid them both farewell, and then I stride off into the night.

The air is cool and smells faintly of the flowers that grow in the sumptuous gardens behind the palace. I pause long enough to breathe it in deeply.

It's been a while since I left Nexus. In fact, the last time I passed through the archway separating the city from the rest of Alastria, it was to pursue Lyanndra in her flight up north. That feels so long ago now.

And in two short weeks, I shall see my crossed star again, albeit under very different circumstances.

But I cannot afford to tarry long. The midnight bell will soon sound, and there is still much to be done.

Fueled by the unending inferno of my anger, I stalk through the courtyard and around the side of the palace. Most of the barracks here are dark, though candles burn in a few of the windows. I pass by them, not caring whether the Celestial Knights within take any notice, and head toward the stables.

The yard, too, is quiet and dark. A lone lamp hangs just beyond the mouth of the stable doors, beckoning me. It's far too late for any of the grooms to be awake, but this isn't the first time I've had to saddle my own horse.

And I know exactly which beast I shall choose as my mount.

My favorite bay mare is dozing when I find her in her stall, but she's easily roused with a few handfuls of oats. I manage to coax her out into the aisle and tack her up without getting bitten, which is, I think, a feat.

After, I pull out two other horses and do the same. I'm just checking the girth on the final steed when the first peal of the midnight bell rolls out over the sleeping palace.

For a moment, I think that Torran won't come.

But then he materializes from the dark beyond the stable doors, his silver hair streaming out behind him and his eyes glittering in the low light of the single lantern.

"Were you hoping I'd be late?" he asks as he bustles past me to the second horse. He wastes no time securing his own bags to the creature's saddle.

"If only," I grumble.

A few seconds after that, Wayre and Noros arrive, escorting Aaro between them. The man glances nervously between the horses and me.

"What... what is this, Your Highness?" he asks. There's no mistaking the threads of trepidation that weave between his words. "Are you going somewhere?"

"No," I say. "*We* are."
Aaro's jaw drops. "Where?" he utters.
I fix him with a burning stare.
"The Southern Caldera," I tell him. "Breem."
We're going to see Lyanndra.

CHAPTER 31

Lyanndra

"That's the last of them, Godslayer, or at least the ones we could convince to leave," Orobos states.

I nod at the Demigod. He stands beside me as we survey the caravan that rolls slowly but steadily along the northern road out of Breem.

It's a solemn procession.

Carts and wagons, loaded to capacity and pulled by drays, make up the bulk of the convoy. Starless refugees, some on the backs of horses or mules, others traveling by foot, are interspersed between. Most of them are silent, though I pick up on hushed murmurs and the cries of an infant every now and then.

Guilt churns in my gut as I watch them pass. I should have found the Ushum's lair by now. I should've been able to keep my people safe.

But with the tremors getting worse and no word from Syran on the fang, I cannot risk putting these people in danger.

"How many left in Gry?" I ask.

The remote village sits just before the southern border of Alastria, hidden behind the jagged peak of the mountain. Breem is closer to the Caldera, but the journey between the two settlements takes days, and even with the superior speed of Syran's messengers, we would never be able to warn them in time if–*when*–the Ushum rises.

"About a dozen," Orobos replies. "Mostly men."

I shake my head. "Fools, the lot of them."

Yet, I can't completely blame them for wanting to stay behind. Many of these people have never left Gry for any significant period of time, and they hold little love for Demigods. For those who chose to stay behind, dying at home might well seem like the better alternative than placing any trust in the Celestial Court.

Now, after ordering the evacuation earlier in the week, the refugee caravan is finally passing through town on its way to Nexus, where the displaced Starless will be able to find food and shelter. Tomorrow, we will send the residents of Breem on the same path, my family included. It's too dangerous to allow them to stay, not with the way the Ushum pitches and keens beneath the ground as it struggles against centuries of slumber.

But even as I know that these people will be safe, my heart breaks for them.

For I know what it means to leave a home behind.

Anxiety, hot and sour, rises in my throat as I think of Syran. He hasn't come to me in our dreams, not since the night before my parents' barn collapsed, though I can feel his anger still seething deep within me, squirming and writhing like a living thing.

Is he well?

I think he must be, for I can detect no physical pain hidden within the swirling mass of his rage. Yet, my nightly calls across our bond go unheeded, and the few letters I've sent with the messengers fare no better. I can think of nothing I did to warrant such disdain, so I choose to believe that some terrible betrayal has befallen Syran, and that he wishes to brood on it, undisturbed.

Still, a vicious part of my mind whispers that he's forsaken me.

No.

I refuse to accept that.

Syran swore to me that he is mine, and I am his, completely. I will not let such foolish insecurities distract me from his devotion. He will find the fang, and he will come. I just wish I could speak to him, if only for a moment, if only so that I could understand what torments him so.

And, as if the stars themselves deem fit to answer my call, a lone rider appears on the northern horizon. Even from this distance, the white mantle that streams out behind him gives away his identity.

A messenger.

But with what news?

My heart shudders as the Demigod approaches. He skirts around the caravan, guiding his horse carefully over the steaming fissures that opened after the latest round of tremors, before he finally reaches us.

His traveling clothes are rumpled, and the skin beneath his pale eyes is a deep purple. It's clear that he's traveled over quite some distance, though I still have yet to understand the specific magic that allows these couriers to fly across the land in so little time.

He halts his horse before us and dips his head respectfully. "Godslayer."

"Do you bring word from the Celestial Court?" I ask after returning the gesture. If so, this will be the first time in weeks that I'll hear from Syran. Perhaps I'll finally learn the source of his ire.

"Yes, Godslayer," he replies. "I was instructed not to deliver this until now." He withdraws a letter from his satchel, and when he passes it down to me, I notice the seal is a deep shade of purple instead of the black I expected.

A pang of disquiet needles my heart.

Grateful for my golden helm, which hides the trepidation that surely flashes across my face, I thank the messenger and bid him to make his way to camp to rest. Then I slide the dagger from its sheath at my thigh and slice open the unfamiliar seal.

But when I unfold the parchment, it's to find that the handwriting within is instantly recognizable. The loopy, elegant script is one I've seen often: Torran's.

Godslayer, the old Demigod writes. *When you receive this letter, over a week will have passed since we journeyed through the gates of Nexus. I accompany His Highness on the road to Breem. Have hope, for we will arrive within days.*

I should be relieved.

I should be elated.

But it's unease, not joy, that twines along my nerves now as I stare down at the missive.

Have they found the fang? Why did they wait so long to inform me of their travels?

And why did Torran write this note when Syran could have done so himself?

The questions burn through me, but I have to concede that there's no use in speculating. I'll find out soon enough.

Beside me, Orobos shifts. His glance toward the parchment I hold isn't subtle, though I suppose I can't hold his curiosity against him. "What news does he bring?" he asks.

"The king rides to Breem," I tell him. "He will arrive within the next few days, with Torran at his side."

Relief settles into the lines of Orobos' face. "Thank the stars," he sighs. He knows as well as I do that the Ushum's grumblings have grown longer and more frequent. We'll be lucky to last another week before it awakens completely.

Then why do I feel so uneasy about Syran's impending arrival?

There's something wrong. I'm *sure* that I'm missing something, but every time I try to parse it from the tangled web of my thoughts, it slips further away, as though it doesn't want to be found.

This strange foreboding doesn't leave me even as the refugee caravan fades into the distance, or by the time Orobos and I return to join the others in the unending search for the Ushum's lair.

"How many caves can there possibly be?" one Celestial Knight mutters as we pass on our way up the mountain.

Too many, I think dismally.

The whole face of the Southern Caldera is riddled with a sea of black flags and a handful of golden ones scattered throughout. While the inky banners represent the caverns we've already searched, the others mark the passages we have yet to venture into.

However, there are some spots, especially on the far sides of the mountain, where the colored standards are sparser. It's to one of these areas I head, though I'm not entirely sure why.

I spend a little over an hour navigating the rocky outcroppings. Sweat prickles across my skin to pool uncomfortably under my arms and at the small of my back. At one point, when the sun is at its highest, I can no longer stand the oppressive heat within the confines of my golden helm, so I pull it off and secure it by the strap to the sheath of my greatsword.

From there, I venture into every crevice I can find, though most are little more than shallow indentations in the rock. The caves I do stumble across prove to be empty and unfamiliar. But as I continue to explore, I realize that the scent of the Ushum seems to be stronger now.

Is that because it's waking?

Or am I getting closer?

Tender hope dawns in my chest as I press ever onward. With every opening I find, I feel more and more certain that I'm going in the right direction, that, at any moment, I'll stumble upon the cave I so desperately seek.

But another hour passes, and then another. Frustration rises within me with each fresh failure, and by the time I stop amidst a rocky clearing to rest and drink some water from the bladder at my hip, I feel that if I don't find this cave soon, I'll burst into tears.

Or murder somebody.

Or both.

I flop down onto a relatively flat rock and stare up at the brilliant blue sky.

What will Syran think when he arrives with the fang, only to find that I've foundered so spectacularly at my task? And when the Ushum rises and breaks through the crust of the earth to wreak havoc on the innocent people of Alastria, it will be my fault.

That will be the legacy of the Godslayer.

"What a fine queen I'll make," I mutter aloud, "who would see her people become breakfast to a beast."

But there is still work to be done. Even if I don't locate the Ushum in time, at least I can say that I made a valiant effort, not that it will mean much when the great abomination swallows me whole.

At least I'll make a terrible meal.

After all, I'm far too sharp to go down easily.

At that, I rise from my rocky seat and turn to survey the area. There are barely any flags within view. I spot five or six black banners fluttering halfheartedly further down the mountain, but this area is clear. The soldiers should have swept this section already, but it's possible that they missed something.

Not likely, but possible.

With nothing left to lose, I resolve to search every inch of this place before returning to my host, even if it means picking my way down the mountain by the light of the moon.

I turn to do exactly that, only to catch a glimpse of *something* out of the corner of my eye.

Movement.

Adrenaline surges through my veins as I slowly swivel my head to focus on the area where I thought I saw… whatever the stars that was. At first, nothing stands out. It's just the same brown, rocky terrain sloping ever upward toward the crooked peak of the Caldera.

Perhaps it was just a bird, or one of those tiny jumping mice that root through the soil for crickets and other insects. I have a distinct memory of such a creature getting into the homestead when I was a child. It practically pinged off the walls while my mother stood on a chair and screamed as though it had pulled a dagger upon her and demanded all her silver. Ultimately, I managed to catch it in a pot and release it outside, and from then on, I held a certain warmth for the strange little rodents.

But this is no jumping mouse.

There, amidst the sharp angles of the outcroppings, is a flash of fabric.

Brown. The same shade as the mountain, barely perceptible, but distinct now that I've distinguished it from the rest of the rock.

A cloak?

Yes. I think that's *exactly* what it is.

And the person wearing it is watching me. I can't tell if it's a man or a woman, but the frame hidden beneath the hooded garment is certainly tall and slender. I'm careful not to turn toward them completely. It's better if they think I haven't noticed them.

Behaving as I normally would, I sigh–loud enough for them to hear but not so much that it appears farcical–and glance around. I purposely allow my eyes to slide over their cloak, as though to prove that I'm ignorant to their presence.

And, as soon as I shift my stance so that the figure is just barely within my line of sight, they move.

I spring into action.

"Halt!" I bellow.

The stranger bolts.

My body takes over as I give chase. I careen over rocks and boulders, ignoring the jagged press of them through the shell of my armor. But all the tarnished steel slows me down in this terrain, while the stranger slides gracefully over the outcroppings as easily as if they were passing through a meadow of grass and wildflowers.

Infuriated and panting in the late afternoon heat, it's all I can do to keep my eyes fixed upon them.

And, just as they slow and I think that I finally have them, they vanish.

I skid to a stop mere inches from where they stood. For a moment I wonder if this, somehow, is the same shadowy creature that visited Syran's chambers all those months ago, but then I push that thought aside. That thing was incorporeal. Whoever I chased up the mountainside is as solid and real as I am.

So where did they go?

My eyes skim the stone façade of the caldera for any clues. It doesn't take me long to discern a dark sliver in the earth a few feet away.

A cave?

No, it's more like a fissure, I realize as I creep closer. The ground within slopes downward at a steep, but not sheer, angle. And when I peer inside, another memory slithers back to me.

I remember, as a girl, half crawling, half sliding into the cool embrace of the earth (because it was hot, wasn't it?) to find a tunnel that smelt of something primal, something hidden.

"This is it," I gasp as I step down into the abyss.

This is it.

I take a step forward, eager to slip down into the darkness and finally–*finally*–complete my task, but then I pause.

Something about this is wrong.

It's almost as if that figure *wanted* me to see them. It's almost as if they baited me into giving chase. Why else would they lead me straight to the very place I've been searching for?

Realization, cold and cloying, runs an icy hand down my spine.

This is a trap.

The figure was bait.

I will not take it.

I'll signal the Celestial Knights–I'll start a fire, I decide, knowing that they'll surely come to investigate the smoke–and proceed with the utmost caution. I won't be played a fool so easily.

When I go into that cave, I'll do it with an army at my back.

When I go into that cave, I will end this, once and for all.

CHAPTER 32

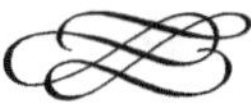

One more night.

It's a promise and a portent, one that besieges me without mercy as I tend to the horses beside our makeshift camp.

The looming peak of the Southern Caldera is so close now that the tip of its moonlit shadow only just creeps across the road. We're a day's ride out of the emptied village of Loryn, and we should reach Breem by sundown tomorrow if we hold our pace and leave with the dawn.

Behind me, Aaro assists Torran in setting up our meager camp.

While I don't like sleeping so near a main thoroughfare, there really isn't much choice. The ground here is perilous at best. Sink-holes and fissures, some so deep that they seem to drop off into the very heart of the earth, severely limit our options.

So, we end up settling in for the night on the rocky terrain just a little ways from the road. Once I'm done making sure the horses are cared for, I call forth my flame to light the cooking fire.

There isn't much in the way of game out here, so our dinner

consists of jerky and biscuits so hard that I think they'd be put to better use as flooring in the Celestial Court than attempted sustenance. But that doesn't stop Torran from filling the kettle with our water rations, adding dried leaves and herbs, and hanging the pot over the fire.

Soon, an aromatic haze of chamomile curls through the night, but even the familiar scent can't soothe the rage that coils and flexes in my chest.

Before Aaro's accusation, I thought I knew what it was to be angry.

Is that not what I felt, however misguided it was, when I watched the Godslayer fell my father in battle? And was my heart not filled with wrath when our blades clashed during our calamitous duel, or when she fled from me after the attack in the infirmary?

Yet, those are mere shadows compared to the fury that consumes me now. It's like a living thing, sinuous and spitting, pumping venom into me until it eclipses everything else.

One more night, I assure myself in an attempt to ease the torment. *One more night, and then I'll see her.*

And what will I say to her when she's finally standing in front of me?

She must have picked up on my rage by now, though I know not what she makes of it. Every night, when she tugs upon our bond, I retreat further into myself. I imagine she's sent me letters, only for them to arrive at the Celestial Court, where they'd fall into the hands of Wayre or Noros for safekeeping until my return.

Does she even realize that I'm no longer in Nexus?

Does she know that I reach for her now, not in a dreamscape, but with my hands, real and solid, as well as my fury?

"Tea?" Torran asks, jolting me from these bedeviling thoughts.

I shake my head.

He presses a tin cup into my palm anyhow.

A moment later, he does the same to Aaro. The Starless man absently accepts the offering before shifting his blank stare in the direction of the mountain.

It's been clear from the start that Aaro is far from a willing partici-pant in this journey. From the very first night when I all but threat-ened him to mount his horse, he's been quiet and sullen. Now, as we grow ever closer to our grim destination, his mood reeks of fear.

Is he worried about our proximity to the Ushum? The tremors as the thing yawns and shifts beneath the earth are admittedly alarming, and I would not blame him for that particular cowardice.

Or does he dread what awaits him in Breem–Lyanndra, and my wrath?

Whatever plagues him, he does not speak of it, or of anything. He simply sits by the fire, his tanned face wreathed in midnight shadows, as he keeps vigil over the Southern Caldera.

Torran, however, is far more invested in the Ushum's activity. He limps over to me now, leaning heavily on his cane as he goes, with a large book tucked under his free arm. I recognize it as the illuminated manuscript he originally used to identify the beast. He lowers himself with painful care down onto the rocky ground beside me, and, not for the first time on this venture, I feel a pang of guilt that I did not insist he stay behind.

The ride so far has not been kind on the old Demigod. Though he doesn't complain, I suspect his leg ails him greatly after so many days on horseback. Yet, he seems in good enough spirits, especially now as he balances the tome on his knee and opens it to the image of the Ushum.

His eyes flicker briefly to Aaro before his gaze lands on mine. "I'm almost there," he whispers, leaning in so that our traveling companion cannot overhear. Torran's shared the same sentiment before, but there's a strange, frantic energy to his tone that gives me pause.

Is he actually close to translating the text?

Or is this just another false alarm?

As though sensing my hesitation, he slides the book over to me. "Look here," he directs as he trails one finger over the arcane script nestled in the wicked curve of the illustrated tooth. "That, I think, is the word for *fang*. In fact, I'm positive it is."

I nod, though I don't see how this helps. Didn't we already know that particular nature of the weapon?

Still, I do my best to follow as he continues, "These letters repeat in the phrase written here. And if we assume that these longer words are the name of the beast the fang belongs to, that means we can fill in the gaps."

"So it's a puzzle?" I ask.

"Exactly." He slides a piece of parchment from his sleeve. On it, I recognize the same script as the ancient lines written in the book, which he's copied onto the page in deep purple ink. Beneath, he's listed out the start of the translation. "Any ideas?"

I squint down at the characters and try my best to make sense of them, but every time I think of an animal, it has too many letters or not enough of them, or the ones we know end up in all the wrong places. After several agonizing minutes, I shake my head.

"I've no idea," I admit.

"Nor do I," Torran says with a sigh. "I thought a pair of fresh eyes might help, but alas." He secrets the parchment away once more and then shuts the book with a dusty snap. "I think I shall retire to my tent for the evening. Perhaps a change in scenery might whet my mind."

We bid each other good night, and I watch as he hobbles away toward the shelter, which is little more than a golden sheet held up by some sticks that Aaro hammered into the hard soil. I know I should probably do the same and retreat to my bedroll, but the idea of chasing sleep when Lyanndra is *right there* is laughable.

There will be no rest for me tonight, not when tomorrow's reckoning is so close at hand.

Instead, I sit before the fire. I long to draw my token from my pocket, but I do not wish to brood so openly in Aaro's presence. While a journey such as this does tend to build a certain level of familiarity, however unwanted, I have not grown to like this man any more than when I first laid eyes upon him.

Let me remain the King of Alastria to him and nothing more.

Soon enough, Aaro, too, adjourns for the night. He disappears off into the darkness behind Torran's tent, and though I can't see him, I wait until I hear the sound of his bedroll unfurling before I finally allow myself to succumb to my base desire.

A fresh wave of rage surges through me as I pull the token forth. The shadows of my midnight flame cavort in a flickering waltz across the fabric. In the moonlight, it appears to shift between silver and gold, the moon and the sun. My sigil is a black slash across the iridescent banner, as dark as the flint at the heart of me and the fury that burns there.

"One more night," I vow to the shadows.

I don't know how long I linger there, but at some point, I must have drifted off into a doze, for a short time later, a sound—a low grunt of pain, or something close to it—jerks me awake.

My heart beats wildly in my chest as I scramble to my feet. Instinctively, I summon my flame and survey the camp.

At first glance, everything appears normal.

Torran's tent is dark. I can see the outline of Aaro's bedroll just beyond it, though it looks rather flat.

I frown.

Where in the stars did he go?

But when a knife slashes at my ribs from behind, rending between the plates of my armor, I have my answer.

Ignoring the pain that screams through my torso, I whirl on my heel to face him as black fire erupts from my fingertips.

For a moment, Aaro's face is frozen in a mask of shock and terror. He holds a small dagger—one of mine, I realize, probably pilfered from my saddlebags. Blood drips like ink from the cruel steel, too much to be from the slice he just inflicted upon me.

Torran, I realize with burgeoning horror. *What has he done to Torran?*

The fury that's been building since Aaro first darkened my doorstep overflows. It seeps into every part of me, into all the empty spaces, until it spills out in a roaring torrent of midnight flame.

I don't think.

I simply strike, as fast and as deadly as a serpent.

It wouldn't be considered a mortal wound, not even close, not if it was inflicted by anybody else. It's just a flickering tongue of fire that slices through the thin skin of Aaro's wrist. It isn't even deep enough to sever the tendons, though he drops the knife anyhow.

A second later, his face twists in pain.

I grin.

"My father's flame was normal," I hiss as I stalk toward him. "Do you know what makes mine different? Do you know what gives mine its most unnatural hue?"

Aaro, panting now, shakes his head. His eyes widen as I approach. It's more than fear.

It's terror.

When I reach him, I snake a hand around his throat and drag him close until our noses are almost touching. "Venom," I reveal. "It's not a particularly quick end, either. But is that not fitting, for a snake such as yourself?"

"Please!" he chokes out. "Please!"

"Did you beg like this," I continue, "when Lyanndra knelt upon your throat?"

His eyes seem to bulge from their sockets, but I do not know if that's from the pressure I exert around his neck as he claws uselessly at my arms or from the realization that I've caught him in his lie.

"Did you really think that I would be so gullible as to believe your little tale?" I snarl. "Or that I wouldn't recognize the pattern of her armor–the one inlaid *by my own hand*–on your *fucking* neck?"

Because I knew, from the moment Aaro uttered his loathsome deceit, that Lyanndra would never forsake me. And when I realized that the bruise he sported was the same scaled motif as her armor, there was no question in my mind that he had done something vile to her.

I wanted to burn the Starless interloper to ash where he stood, yet, there must be some reason why my crossed star showed him mercy.

No.

I would respect her wishes.

As much as it pained me to wait and keep up this farcical charade, I would bring him to her.

Then we would exact our justice on him—together.

But now that that is no longer an option, I can only hope that Lyanndra won't begrudge me if I have my fun now.

So I draw him ever closer and promise, "All I want to know is *why*. Tell me that, and I'll kill you quickly."

"Please!" Aaro gasps. "I did... I did only as she asked!"

"Lyanndra would *never* make such a request," I grit out.

He shakes his head, or at least tries to. "Not... her. Lady... R... Ressa."

Shock strikes me like a fist to the gut.

"Ressa?" I gasp.

How?

How could she be behind this treasonous plot? And for what? Did she really think that she could drive a wedge between Lyanndra and me that easily, when we're bound by the very will of the stars?

And if Ressa recruited Aaro for this scheme, she must have found him in Breem.

Dread builds within me as I realize that my former betrothed might be in the village right now.

With Lyanndra.

"Tell me what she's plotting," I demand. Though I want, more than anything, to wring the life from Aaro for his treachery, I loosen my hold upon him slightly, just enough so he can speak.

"She... she promised me a position in the court if... if I could seduce Lyanndra away from you," he admits.

"And did you?"

"No," he says quickly. "She nearly killed me. She... she's a fucking *animal.*"

Fresh rage, blinding in its intensity, rises in my throat. "She's my *wife*," I snarl.

Aaro has the gall to let out a gasping laugh. "She was supposed to be *mine*."

Mustering up the last dregs of my control, I do not crush his windpipe in my fist or set him ablaze. Instead, I speculate, "When Lyanndra bested you, Ressa sent you to me with your perfect little lie and a stolen token. Am I correct?"

The Starless man nods, and that is the last thing he does. For, before I question him any more, his face blanches, and his jaw goes slack. Only then do I remember the poison coursing through his system.

A second later, he falls limp, and I let him drop unceremoniously to the ground.

Is he dead?

I stare down at him for only a moment before I realize that it doesn't really matter. If he isn't, he will be soon enough. And perishing with my poison in his veins is about as far from a mercy as a death can get.

When I turn away from him, a flash of steel nearby catches my attention.

It's Aaro's knife, the one he stole from me, the one he used to slash my ribs. The wound stings with every breath I take, and I can already feel the blood pooling in my armor and soaking through my tunic beneath. But the red that lines the blade cannot all be mine, and I'm reminded that I've missed something important.

"Torran!" I shout.

But there is no answer.

I lurch toward the tent, desperate to reach him. From the outside, the makeshift structure seems untouched, but, when I pull the fabric back, I'm met with a horror that I can barely comprehend.

Torran is alive, but only just.

His eyes, once so vibrant, are dull with pain. His face is pale, and his purple robes are stained crimson.

How many times did Aaro stab him? Once? Twice?

I drop to my knees by his side. "Torran!"

"Syran?" he murmurs. His voice is so thin that it's a wonder I can hear it at all.

"Here," I assure him. I reach for his hand while I attempt to slow the bleeding. But the old Demigod is a healer, and he knows as well as

I that this is too much, far too much. Still, I ask, "Where's your bag? I can stop this. I can–"

"No," he whispers, cutting me off. "There isn't time."

Tears prickle the corners of my eyes as I insist, "Don't be a fool, Torran! Let me help you!"

He shakes his head and then grimaces. "Listen, Syran." His free hand clutches my wrist, leaving crimson smears along the surface of my armor. "The fang… I translated it."

I freeze.

"It means… the Midnight Serpent…." His features crumple as he draws in a shuddering breath. "Find it," he urges. "Find the fang… of the Midnight Serpent."

But even as the words slide from his mouth, his eyes drift off somewhere to the right of me, and his face relaxes. His chest rises one final time, then falls again.

And then he's still.

Then he's gone.

I am alone.

And the night is quiet once more.

CHAPTER 33

Lyanndra

We enter the cave at dawn.

"Are you sure about this, Godslayer?" Orobos asks as I hand him my lantern.

I stare down into the yawning abyss and nod. There is no doubt in my mind that this passage is the one we've so desperately searched for over these last few weeks. And, when I slide, feet first, down into the fissure, I know—*I know*—that this is it.

Gravel crunches beneath my boots as I land, mostly upright, at the bottom of the opening. Before me, the tunnel stretches away into grainy darkness. I squint into it.

Is the cloaked stranger there, waiting? Are they watching me at this very moment?

Not willing to take any chances, I draw the dagger from the sheath at my thigh and grip it tightly in my gauntleted palm. The passage I stand in is narrow. There's no room to even draw my greatsword, let alone swing it, so the smaller blade will have to do.

When nobody charges out of the gloom, I risk a glance back up toward the surface.

A thin sliver of light trickles in through the opening. I'm relieved to find that the rocky slope of the wall, while acute, appears climbable. At least we'll be able to scramble out of this tomb without much assistance if the need should arise.

Orobos' face, hidden by the visor of his helmet, appears in the aperture. "Godslayer?" he calls.

"Here," I heed. "Pass me the lantern."

He leans over the edge and lowers the lamp down to me. I'm just tall enough to grasp the bottom with the tips of my fingers, though the orange flame within gutters dangerously as I fumble for it. But then I finally manage to get a proper hold of it and steady the lantern before turning back to the tunnel to see what secrets the light will reveal.

Rocks.

Lots of rocks.

They look exactly the same as the ones aboveground, though these are occasionally interrupted by a patch of lichen or a trickle of moisture instead of the dusty brown grass found on the surface. Stalagmites and stalactites needle from the earth and remind me, uncomfortably, of Barra's teeth. I spot a single lizard clinging to the nearby wall. Bone white flesh stretches over its eyeless face like a caul. And then there's that smell, that musty, nameless stench that I know to be the Ushum. It's strong down here–not quite enough to make me gag–but almost.

Yet, there's no sign of the beast, or of the cloaked figure from yesterday. They must both remain hidden further in the tunnel, but they're down here.

They *have* to be down here.

"Orobos!" I herald over my shoulder.

"Yes, Godslayer?"

"I want you and half the company down here at my back," I order. "Jurlan will stay aboveground with the others. Leave any man who cannot abide small spaces behind." It'll be a tight enough squeeze in this narrow space with that many soldiers, let alone the full host. And besides, somebody needs to remain on the mountainside to meet Syran if he arrives today.

A thrill runs through me at the thought of seeing my crossed star once more.

I can't be sure if it's excitement or apprehension. The emotions that creep across our bond are a strange mix of rage, guilt, grief, and yearning, but I swear that I can feel him growing ever closer, as though we're two celestial bodies destined to collide. And last night, I thought I caught a flash of pain so bright and vivid that I sat up in my bedroll, panting and clutching at my ribs.

Was it a dream?

I want to believe that it was, especially when the phantom sensation of danger passed, but something deep within me remains unsettled.

Shaking my head, I force the unease back down.

There's no time to dwell on such things now.

I need my wits about me.

I keep my eyes focused on the tunnel ahead, ready to strike out at any sign of movement, while the Celestial Knights slither, one by one, through the crevice and into the dark.

Orobos is the first to join me. He peers over the top of my head at the dismal passage and mutters, "This is a deathtrap, if ever I saw one." His voice, even dropped to such a low volume, echoes through the cramped space.

I nod.

This is the perfect spot for an ambush.

The tight press of the walls will force us to proceed single file, and the longswords most of the soldiers carry will be useless in such close quarters. All it would take is one archer or bowman to pick us off. And stars forbid we should have to flee from the Ushum.

Yet, we have no choice.

If the creature does indeed slumber in this tunnel, we will do whatever it takes to find it, even if that means staring death in the face.

Gritting my teeth beneath my helm, I start forward into the dark.

The passage seems to stretch on forever. We move slowly and carefully, for the ground down here is as fragile as it is above. And though I rather like small spaces such as these, I worry that the tremors have weakened this cave far too much. One more quake, and the whole thing could collapse in on us.

It doesn't help that the rattle of our armor echoes off the rock walls in a raucous cacophony. I can barely hear anything over the racket, which only puts me further on edge. The cloaked stranger could be sneaking toward us right now, and I'd never be able to hear them over the noise. But aside from commanding the entire company to strip, there's little I can do. I'd rather these men be protected behind mail and plate than be rendered silent and, consequently, vulnerable.

As we press onward, I continue to train my eyes on the path ahead, even as my mind wanders. I think of Syran and his tempestuous emotions, and the bolt of pain I felt in the night. I can't fathom what's causing it all, but I know he'll be here to answer my questions soon enough.

The mere thought of him standing before me, not in a dream but *real*, feels like a promise too easily crushed. I hardly dare to let myself believe it, no matter how much I long to wrap my arms around him and breathe in his ashen scent.

Does he yearn for me the same way? Does it drive him now as he rides toward Breem, toward me?

I want it to.

By the stars, I want it to.

Beneath my golden helm, I set my jaw and resolve that, no matter what we face down here, I *will* return to the surface.

I *will* return to him, as I vowed.

But first, I must find the Ushum.

We're getting closer, I'm certain of it. The smell, dry and sulfurous, grows steadily worse the deeper we go. It prickles my eyes and grates at the back of my throat, and from the labored breaths and occasional gagging fit at my back, it's a safe bet that the others find the stench just as distasteful as I do. What will it be like when we actually reach the beast? I dread to think of it.

The miasma is distracting, and it's hard to tell just how much time passes as we pick our way through the tunnel. Eventually, we reach a section of the cave where the walls start to gradually taper on all sides, so much so that all of us are forced to crouch to make any progress. The squeeze is uncomfortable for me, let alone the taller knights who follow behind.

"Godslayer," Orobos says, making no attempt to mask the anxiety that drips from his words. "I fear that if I go any farther, I will be unable to turn around."

I pause. At my back, the soldiers, surprised by the sudden stop, shuffle into one another with muffled curses.

Orobos is right. When I turn my head to glance at him, my golden helm drags against the rock with a harsh, grating sound that I can feel in my teeth. The Demigod's face beyond his upturned visor glows faintly down here in the dark. *Perhaps his power is good for something after all*, I think wryly before he meets my eye with a grimace.

"I am no coward," he states, "but *this….*" He nods ahead to the dwindling space. "We cannot fit, Godslayer, and we would be fools to try."

"*You* cannot fit," I reply.

The Celestial Knights are all far taller than me, and broader about the shoulders. But I've been short all my life, and I remember the feeling of sliding through this place on my belly like one of those white, eyeless lizards, of the hard and unrelenting press of the earth around me before I spilled out on the other side as though born anew.

"No." Orobos shakes his head when he realizes what I mean to do. "*No.*"

There's no need for me to respond. We both know I'll attempt it anyway.

"If the king finds out that I stood by while you tried something so… so *hasty*, he will have my head."

Fixing him with a stony glare that rivals the very walls, I say, "*I* will take much more than that if you defy me. We have no choice. If we don't find the Ushum, we die anyway. The risk is worth it."

It has to be.

And I think he understands, if the grim resignation that settles across his illuminated features is anything to go by.

I turn back to the narrowing passage. It's a tight squeeze, just barely wide enough to accommodate the extra girth of my armor, but I can fit. I know I can.

I push the lantern in first. The flickering light does nothing to ease the hot dread that builds within me as I sheathe my dagger and drop down onto my belly. My armor scrapes the rocky ground. Loose gravel trickles down from the walls like crystallized rain, and dry dust billows with my every move.

And while I'm not normally bothered by confined spaces, I concede that I don't like this.

I don't like this *at all*.

Using the tips of my boots to propel me forward, I inch my way through the cloying gap. The flame of the lantern is hot against my face. Sweat drips from my brow. My heart pounds against my ribs, raging toward freedom. Every breath I draw presses me against the sharp rock, and I do my best to keep my inhales shallow and calm, even as panic creeps in around the edges of my vision.

How far have I gone?

The lamp blocks most of my view, and everything beyond it is simply black. It's like looking into the heart of Syran's flame.

It's like looking into the very abyss.

Was the tunnel always this long?

I don't know. I don't remember. This seemed like an adventure as a child, not the grueling experience it is now. When I was a girl, I wasn't worried about cloaked and possibly armed strangers, or blasphemous creatures slumbering in the deep, or such a mundane calamity as getting stuck down in the cool earth where nobody could hear me scream. At the time, it was *fun*.

But there is nothing fun about this now.

I shove the lantern a few inches into the darkness.

I pull myself after it.

Shove the lantern.

Pull myself.

Shove.

Pull.

Shove.

Pull.

I do my best to sink into the simple rhythm of it.

My armor grinds.

My heart pounds.

I draw in a breath.

I let it out again.

Soon, I tell myself. *I'll reach the end soon.*

And then it happens.

One last push of the lamp sends it clattering over some unseen edge. It's a sheer miracle that the fire doesn't snuff out as the lantern rolls across the ground, coming to rest on its side a few feet away. The light reveals a chamber, large enough for the entire host to fit in comfortably, and I feel like I might sob in relief.

I'm almost there.

The prospect of freedom drives me forward until at last, my fingers grasp the jagged edges of the tunnel's mouth. With this leverage, I'm able to drag myself along until my head is out, and then my shoulders, and then....

A low rumble sounds through the cavern. I feel it like a hum in the very earth as it rattles my armor and jitters its way up my bones. It's just a shadow of the power of the Ushum's tremors, but that doesn't mean this smaller quake isn't dangerous.

Because the ground is fragile.

These walls are weak.

And when the passageway starts to crumble at my feet, it's all I can do to scramble toward the cavern and the beckoning light of the lantern, toward relative safety.

I hiss in pain as a portion of the tunnel collapses onto my legs. For one terrible second, I think that I'm stuck, that I'm pinned here, but then I manage to kick free and draw myself those last few feet forward. And just as I slither completely from the narrow gap and tumble the short drop down to the cave's floor, the whole passage from whence I crawled falls in on itself with a crash so loud that it rings within my helm long after the sound ceases.

As much as I'd like to lie there on my back for a while, panting and waiting for my heart to stop racing, I scrabble up to my feet. At the same time, I fumble for my dagger.

For that quake was no accident.

I felt that force before, back during the Battle of Nexus. I'd know it anywhere, just as I should've recognized the cloaked figure who led me to this dreadful place.

It's no wonder she moved so gracefully across the rocky mountainside as I struggled to keep up. It's no wonder she lured me here, knowing that I would venture where the rest of my host could not.

So it's with no surprise that when I turn, it's to find her standing before me with her hair ragged and her eyes shining in the quivering glow of the lantern.

"Hello, Ressa," I say.

The Demigod noblewoman grins.

"Godslayer." Her smile widens. "I've been waiting for you."

CHAPTER 34

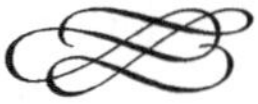

Torran is dead.

Lyanndra is in danger.

These two truths, terrible and undeniable, pulse through me with each beat of my heart and rush of air in my lungs. They hound me even as I urge my horse forward through the burgeoning dawn, toward Breem.

It matters not that blood trickles from the slash across my ribs, even after I attempted to cauterize the wound with my flame.

It matters not that I've ridden through the night without stopping.

I will not slow. I will not falter.

Not until I reach my crossed star.

Not until I've burned Ressa's rotten soul to ash.

If Lyanndra didn't previously know of the Demigod's treachery, I can tell by the way the bond between us stretches with taut urgency that she is now very much aware. This certainty spurs me onward over the cracked and steaming ground. It overshadows everything else, every thought and every feeling, every call that isn't hers.

And how could I have been so foolish not to see it before?

In hindsight, the threads were always there. They stole like wayward serpents through all of our plans and decisions, guiding us to this very point. Ressa must have awoken the Ushum with her powers, knowing that it would draw Lyanndra away from my protective grasp.

But why?

To destroy the kingdom? To lay waste to Alastria as I razed her heart?

But there are a thousand ways she could put an end to our reign. Why rely on the unpredictable nature of the Ushum to bring about our demise?

No, this is something else. I think of Lyanndra and how sure she was that a Demigod aided in Ressa's murderous escape from the dungeons and of the prisoner's mad ramblings of the blinking shadow that lurked down there in the dark.

Perhaps another hand was involved, I realize.

Perhaps the two threats are one and the same.

But if the shadowy figure that appeared to us in our chambers wished to cause so much strife, why didn't it just slay us that night as we slept, unsuspecting, in our bed? Why orchestrate such a plot?

My eyes, heavy and clouded from exhaustion and pain, fix upon the peak of the Southern Caldera as I struggle to find an answer. The mountain rises so high above that it appears to be almost falling toward the road, though I know it to be only a trick of the light and perspective. Below, Breem huddles in the cool embrace of its shadow.

It's hard to think of Lyanndra growing up in this place. It seems far too small for her, too shrouded. Is this what instilled the wandering spirit within her? Or was it always there, biding its time until she found her moment to step into something greater?

I picture her as she was when she first met my blade in the courtyard of the palace so many months ago. She was a legend come to life in her tarnished armor and golden helm, her greatsword flashing as she swung, not to kill, but to tease. My heart constricts at the memory.

She doesn't belong to a place such as Breem.

She belongs on the throne.

She belongs with *me*.

Hot resolves swirls through my chest as I push the bay mare faster. Even though I know that Lyanndra is a capable warrior who could best Ressa easily in combat, let alone any worthier opponents, there is still the Ushum to think of, and that shadowy figure.

At least Aaro is no longer a threat.

His corpse lies back at our makeshift camp, unmoved from the spot where he crumpled. There was no time for ceremony or burial, though I can't say I know much of how the Starless handle their dead outside of times of war. And is it not fitting that Aaro received such a riteless end? Given the scaled bruises Lyanndra's armor left upon his neck, I think she would agree.

And while I don't know exactly what the Starless man did to provoke my crossed star to such violence, I have some ideas. None of them are good. After all, Lyanndra would never tolerate the affections of another, not when she so fully swore herself to me. Fury rattles through me as the various possibilities flicker through my mind. What was it that she said to me?

I took care of it.

She started to, at least.

I had the dark satisfaction of finishing it.

In spite of my pain, I grin.

My heart holds no guilt for slaying Aaro in such a painful fashion. He deserved every second of agony for daring to touch Lyanndra. My only regret is not dispatching him sooner before he could prey upon poor old Torran, for my dear friend did not deserve to suffer such a cold and ungracious death.

Grief's unrelenting jaws grip my throat and squeeze as I clench my stiff fingers around the reins. Torran's blood remains laced across my bare palms, dry and itching now after so many hours in the saddle. I didn't bother to clean it before I jumped on my horse and flew out of camp in the direction of Breem. There was barely enough time to wrap his body in the golden fabric of the tent, let alone wash the gore from my hands.

Still, I should have done him the honor of praying over him or putting him to the pyre.

But he was already gone, where Lyanndra was–and still is–very much alive. All that matters now is reaching her. He would understand that, as practical as he was. He wouldn't want me to risk the woman I love for a dead man.

"I'll come back for you," I vow, more to myself than to his spirit. When this is over, I'll return to the campsite and take his body to Nexus. I'll lay him to rest in the heat of my fire and scatter his ashes in the forest surrounding his hut so that his memory can grow into something more.

Now, however, I must focus on reaching Lyanndra.

She's in danger. The surety of it screams and churns inside of me, fueling the flames that roil beneath the surface of my skin. Just like I know how to call the embers that smolder in my chest, I know it.

I *know.*

It's the same certainty that drove me to the infirmary in time to spare Lyanndra from Kartas' sinister plot, but it runs deeper now, as though the urgency is searing through my very veins.

Go to her, a voice seems to whisper. The words curl through my head and into the hot space behind my ribs, but they're also in my ear, dry and distant and very much outside of me. *It's almost time. Almost time.*

"Time for what?" I choke out, though no answer comes. The only response is a slight twitch of the bay mare's ears while her hooves clatter over the rocky ground, carrying me ever closer to Breem.

To Lyanndra.

I grit my teeth as something twists deep within me. I felt this before on the training grounds, and the force of whatever it was threw me flat on my back. That can't happen again, not when my crossed star's safety is at risk, so I do my best to push the writhing sensation back.

Still, I can't control the fear that twines through my mind.

What's happening to me?

Why was I too proud to seek Torran's counsel when I could?

Never again will the wise old Demigod affix his glittering blue gaze upon me. Never again will he sit in the Archive Room with his nose in a book and his mind in the stars. Never again will he listen to me confess my inadequacies, my doubts, and my blasphemies.

Never again.

A tear slides down my cheek.

It burns hotter than any flame.

I don't bother to wipe it away, nor the others that come after. Let them fall. Let them scald. For I know, better than most, that fire both destroys and purifies. Perhaps if I shed enough of them, they'll ignite this cloying grief and singe it away until it's naught but ash within me.

But the reprieve doesn't come. Woe remains lodged deep inside my chest, a rock thrown into a pool of desperate rage. My emotions swirl together into one suffocating mass until I can barely parse any from the others.

And the only thing that cuts through the noise and the seething darkness is her.

Lyanndra.

I'm coming, I pledge to her.

Can she feel the promise I've made?

Can she feel *me*?

Please, I beg of her. *Please know that I'm nearly there.*

A fresh wave of regret crashes over me. I should never have let her go to Breem alone. I should have ridden by her side. I should have done what I swore to her the first time I took her after the Battle of Nexus.

I should have chased her.

If Torran were still here, he would remind me that I stayed behind to guard the throne and search for the fang.

"Fuck the fang," I growl aloud. Did I not do everything in my power to hunt for it, to no avail?

And now, with the Ushum surely about to rise and Lyanndra at risk, I recall the old Demigod's last words.

Find the fang of the Midnight Serpent.

And how, exactly, am I supposed to do that? Am I expected to abandon my crossed star to track down some formidable snake I've never heard of? Such a beast doesn't exist. I doubt even Lady Carolissa would know of it.

Yet, there was a command in Torran's voice when he spoke, one that sliced through his caul of agony to strike me straight at the heart.

Did he understand something that I do not?

Of course he did.

The years may have dulled his body, but not his mind. Whatever secret lies at the center of this mystery, I'm certain he was aware of it. Now it curls with him into eternity, trapped forever in the thoughts of a dead man and the bloodstained pages of his books.

Anger surges now in a blistering swell.

Fire comes naturally to me. I can swing a blade like I was born with it clasped in my hands, and I like to think that I am fair and just.

But Torran was well aware that I am no scholar.

My mind is designed for war, not for the riddles and puzzles that he could solve as easily as breathing. He should have foreseen that I would not be suited to such cryptic clues. How dare he give me so little? How dare he do this, when he knew that if I failed to decipher his words, the whole kingdom could fall?

Or worse, that I could lose Lyanndra?

The mere notion is unbearable.

No.

I will not lose her.

I *cannot.*

I'll do whatever it takes. I'll die for her. I'll burn for her. I'll find the Midnight Serpent and slay it with my bare hands, if it means saving my crossed star.

Ressa won't claim her. The Ushum will perish before it touches her.

Lyanndra will not fall.

She is the Godslayer–unending, a living legend, the woman I'll love until the stars fade into nothing and darkness claims the sky.

And if she were to die?

Then I'll set the very heavens aflame until the Celestial Gods themselves tremble at the ferocity of my retribution. I will snuff out every star and every deity until only ash remains. There will be nothing left, nothing to rule over or to shape anew, nothing to rise or thrive or rebuild, for I yield to her and her alone.

So if the stars were to ever heed my prayers, I hope they hear me now.

I am the Lord of the Midnight Flame.

If Lyanndra falters, I will spare nothing, not even myself.

The world will be her funeral pyre, the gods her pallbearers.

"I swear it," I vow, and when that dry and ancient thing within me stretches and keens, I know that I've been heard, though by what, I cannot say.

Hot with the promise of vengeance and my desire to reach my crossed star, I set my sights on Breem.

The village is so close now that, in minutes, the shadow of the mountain will swallow me completely. I scan the edges of the settlement for a scout or lookout, any flash of gold that would indicate a Celestial Knight.

But nobody heralds me as I fly past the first few buildings. No shouts arise. No horn sounds.

Dread curdles in my gut.

Why is it so quiet?

Where is everybody?

I draw to a halt in the town center, which stands eerily empty. Was Breem evacuated? Yesterday, we passed the refugee caravan from Gry in the late afternoon before stopping to make camp—before Aaro murdered Torran in cold blood later that night—but the road was barren of travelers after that.

No, the villagers are still here.

But where?

My gaze flickers up to the rocky slope of the mountain. At first glance, it's as still and lifeless as the rest of this place.

But then, halfway up and on the farthest reaches of the peak, I catch a glint of gold.

Then another, and another.

Celestial Knights, I realize. Lyanndra's host, or what remains of it after the skirmish with the marauders and the men she sent to escort refugees back to Nexus.

And if they're up there, it's safe to assume that my crossed star is, too.

I've made good on my vow.

I've chased her to the ends of Alastria, even when the Ushum threatens to devour us all.

And once I find her, once I have her in my arms, I will never let her go.

Lyanndra is mine.

Not even the gods can take her from me now.

And I'll burn them if they try.

CHAPTER 35

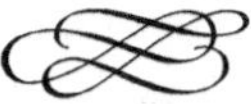

Lyanndra

Dust settles.

My mind does not.

Behind me, rubble obscures the narrow opening of the tunnel, sealing me in. I have no way of knowing how much more of the passage was damaged, or if my host managed to avoid the worst of the cave-in. I think of Orobos' face, luminous in the dark as he pleaded with me not to go, and anger creeps through my veins.

If Ressa's taken another general from me, I will show her no mercy.

Not this time.

"I dreamed of you," the Demigod murmurs, snatching my attention away. "Down there in the dark." That same festering grin stretches across her face, overshadowing her beauty and twisting her noble features into something grotesque. She's no longer the cold and preening vision that graced the shimmering halls of the Celestial Court.

Madness has had its way with her.

Her dark hair, snarled and uneven, hangs limply over her shoulders. Her eyes seem to glimmer in the light of the lantern, as though swimming in tears, though none fall. She still wears the same brown cloak as before. Beneath, I catch a glimpse of a tattered gray dress–Starless fashion, a far cry from the luxury once afforded to her as a courtier of Nexus–and the strange, vine-like scars left by Kartas' lightning that twine up her neck.

And in spite of the flare of murderous rage that thrills through me at the mere sight of her, I find my ire tempered by something else. Something gentler, but just as sour.

Pity.

How long has Ressa hidden herself away down here in the belly of the mountain?

Months, I guess, if the sorry state of her is anything to go by.

In a way, it's a fitting punishment. She's banished herself down here to the cool shadows of the earth, a place no more welcoming than the dungeons she fled from.

But why here? Why Breem, of all places?

Then it dawns on me.

"The Ushum," I gasp. "You woke it."

Ressa's grin grows impossibly wider. "I did," she confirms, her words soaked in pride.

Beneath my golden helm, I grit my teeth in a scowl. How many Starless have already died from the quakes? How many more will be slaughtered if the creature breaks free from the Caldera?

Quelling the urge to strike her down where she stands, I utter, "Why?"

"Why?" she repeats. "*Why?*" A laugh bubbles up from her throat, so delicate and refined, so at odds with the tattered state of her that I have to fight the urge to recoil. Then the levity on her face snuffs out in an instant, and she hisses, "Because of *you*. It's always you, isn't it? Kartas was *obsessed*. He was convinced that you were all that stood between him and the throne. And Syran...." She bares her teeth and snaps them into the air like a beast. "You *bewitched* him, didn't you?

You cast a loathsome spell upon him and stole him away from me. *You stole him away from me!*"

"I did no such thing," I say in the calmest tone I can muster, as though I'm speaking to some wild animal rather than a woman. "Syran's heart is his alone to give. If you truly care for him, you'll allow him that, even if doing so breaks yours."

Ressa hisses. At her feet, the lantern's flame gutters. "You know nothing of him. *Nothing!* I know all he's done, all the hideous truths he hides beneath those pretty eyes. I know what blood coats his hands. Would you still want him if you held his secrets?"

"Yes." My answer is flat, resolute. There is nothing Ressa could tell me that I would trust, and there's nothing in Syran's past that would change the man he is now.

"Liar!" she spits.

I shrug. She can believe what she wants. There's no use wasting my words on a woman whose mind is so frayed at the seams that I can see the stuffing spilling out from within.

But there are things that I do wish to know, ones that I hope are not yet beyond her, so once she finishes clawing the air and snapping her teeth in my general direction, I ask, "Why did you wake the Ushum?"

Her response, snarled out from her twisted mouth, is one I've heard before.

"Because of *you!*"

I already gathered that. Resisting the urge to roll my eyes, I press, "Yes, but *how?* How did you learn of the creature that sleeps beneath the mountain?"

"*He* told me," Ressa reveals. The grin splits across her face once more. "He knew you'd remember it. He knew you'd come."

Dread unfurls in my gut. I never once spoke of the Ushum, not until Syran all but pried the terrible truth from my lips. But he would never betray me like this, not to anybody and certainly not to Ressa.

Who, then?

One of the candidates for general? Torran?

But even as I consider the unspeakable possibilities, the disgraced courtier continues, "He needed you to come back to Breem, back to where it all began. Without Syran, of course. Never Syran. I wouldn't allow it. And when you fall here, it will be me who returns to him. It will be me left to reclaim his heart. I will be everything to him. *Everything!*"

It's my turn to sneer, though the golden helm hides my expression. Is Ressa really that far gone? Does she truly think that Syran wouldn't burn her to ash for what she's planning?

"Syran will learn of your treachery," I warn, though I doubt it will do any good. "He will not take kindly to it."

"Oh, but he will," she insists. Glee flashes across her features, which flicker wanly in the struggling light of the lantern. "For there are things in motion, Godslayer, that not even you foresaw."

Behind my visor, my eyes narrow.

"Imagine my surprise when I found out that before you sunk your fangs into Syran, you had spurned another."

My scowl deepens.

Aaro.

"I can't say I blame you for breaking that betrothal," Ressa says with another of those perfect, well-mannered laughs. "He hides a boor behind that darling face, does he not?"

It seems that Ressa and I agree on one thing, though it pains me greatly to admit it.

"But he was easy enough to twist around my finger. When he learned that you were coming here, he was all too eager to seek his vengeance. How pathetic he was, still yearning for you after all these years, only to find that you left him and willingly gave yourself to another. To a *Demigod*." The horrible joy melts into a glare. "You were *supposed* to lie with Aaro. You almost ruined *everything*."

"My apologies," I snarl. The memory of my former betrothed, his hands clawing at me as I knelt upon his neck and showed him mercy, swims to the surface of my mind.

I should have killed him.

I should have killed *her*.

After the Battle of Nexus, I should have run Ressa through with my greatsword where she fell in the doorway of the throne room. Syran would have understood. He would have forgiven me eventually.

Yet, here we stand. My fingers itch to draw my blade, to end this once and for all, but I abstain.

There are still questions that need asking.

There are answers she must give me before she dies.

But before I can prompt her, Ressa rambles on. "I was able to salvage the situation, no thanks to you. Aaro had the good sense to rip the token from your arm the night you rejected him. You were too busy spitting like the animal you are to notice."

Fresh anger seethes to the surface of my skin, burning as hot as Syran's flame and just as deadly. No wonder I couldn't find my crossed star's token. Aaro–that fucking *snake*–stole it from me.

"Why?" I grit out.

"I sent Aaro to Nexus, where he sought an audience with Syran," Ressa reveals. By the unhinged curl of her lips, she's taking great pleasure in this. "Aaro wove him a pretty tale of betrayal and seduction and produced the token as proof. And do you know what?" She leans in farther over the lamp, her eyes widening with bright glee. "Syran *believed* him!"

No.

No.

I think of the rage that screamed over the bond and of how his nightly visits to my dreams stopped so abruptly. His fury only intensified after that, roiling and curling within him like a creature vying for release, gnawing at his ribs and his heart as it echoed across the vast distance between us.

Now I know why.

Anger and betrayal run through my gut like twin blades.

How could Syran believe such a blatant and disgraceful lie?

How could he think I would ever crush his heart?

The pain turns to cold resolution in my veins.

When Syran gets here, I will make sure he learns the truth, even if I have to convince him with my greatsword pressed against his neck.

When he gets here, I will have Ressa's blood dripping from my hands and the Ushum dead at my feet, the fang be damned.

When he gets here, I will prove that my vow to him was not made lightly.

He will never doubt me again.

"How does it feel?" Ressa goads. "Do you understand how fickle Syran's heart is now? How much his fire *burns*?"

A growl builds in my throat as the rage storms upward, unable to be contained any longer. The logical part of my mind claws to the surface, whispering that I need to know who told her of the Ushum, who set this plot into motion.

But I'm consumed.

I'm undone.

I'm fucking *furious*.

So when I lunge for her, I don't reach for my greatsword, though I long to hear the satisfying thud of the metal rending through muscle and bone. Neither do I unsheathe my dagger, with its quick and wicked blade.

No.

I greet her in the way I did when we first met all those months ago.

With my fist in her fucking face.

For all her smooth elegance, madness has rendered Ressa slow. She only has time to widen her eyes before my knuckles connect with her jaw.

A satisfying crack reverberates through the cavern.

And now it's my turn to grin, even as my hand throbs in pain beneath my gauntlet. Ressa howls, her broken jaw hanging open as she clutches at it, her eyes wild in agony and disbelief.

"You *fucking bitch!*" she snarls.

I don't give her a chance to dart away or to use her powers. Instead, I reach forward and grasp her by the front of her cloak while she claws at my gauntlets. She's far taller than I am, but her willowy form didn't fare well during her time in the dungeons. She's got little muscle with which to push back. It's surprisingly easy to shove her up against the far wall of the cavern and pin her there with the bulk of my armor, even as she flails.

"Let me go!" she shrieks.

But I don't.

I won't.

Not until I find out what I want to know.

"Who put you up to this?" I demand. When she doesn't immediately answer, I jam my elbow into the thin ridge of her breastbone. I give her just long enough to let out of a pained yelp before I relent and hiss, "Who, Ressa? Who told you of the Ushum? Why did he need me to come to Breem?"

I expect the Demigod to thrash, to fight and spit like the mad dog she is. But to my surprise, she falls limp against me as her eyes shift to something over my shoulder, something at my back. Her face once again splits into that terrible grin, though it's crooked now, a reflection of her fraying mind.

"Why don't you ask him yourself?" she suggests.

A curl of dread snakes through me as the fine hairs on the back of my neck prickle to life.

I don't want to release Ressa. I don't want to turn my back on her. And isn't she known for her deceits? Her lies?

But something deep within me whispers that this is no trick. We're not alone down here.

Not anymore.

But I won't take any chances. Before Ressa can resist, I grab her arm and spin her into me so that her back is flush to my chest. At the same time, I clamp one elbow across her neck, forcing her to her knees. She can't kick out at me like this, and if she struggles, I can cut off her air before she even realizes it's happening.

From there, I pivot to face the cavern.

Lamplight flickers across the walls in serpentine tongues. Shadows shiver lithely over the ancient rock, locked in a dance that's entrancing, almost hypnotic. But there's no other movement, no silhouette in the encroaching darkness or whisper of footsteps along the dusty ground.

There's nobody here.

Yet, the sensation of being watched doesn't leave me, and I think, with growing horror, that I've felt this before, back in that stormy night in Syran's chambers.

"Show yourself," I command. "I know you're here."

For a moment, nothing happens.

Am I unraveling into nothing more than a mad fool like Ressa, shouting out into the empty darkness?

But then a shadow, deeper than the rest, shifts in a way so wholly unnatural that I *know* that my instinct is correct. It slides closer, lingering just at the edges of the lantern's light.

And when it opens its eyes, I shudder.

This is the figure I saw in Nexus, the one that helped Ressa escape from the dungeon. It guided her toward Breem and concocted this devious conspiracy. It had her wake the Ushum to draw me here. It set her to turn Syran against me.

Whatever this thing is, it's not natural.

And for some reason, it's here for me.

The creature fixes its colorless gaze upon me, staring even as I draw my free hand down to my dagger.

"Hello, Godslayer," it says in a voice that reminds me of the bitter wind that whips through the northern mountains.

And then it blinks.

It *fucking* blinks.

CHAPTER 36

"Is that really him? The king?"

"Your Highness!"

"He looks like his fucking father."

"His Highness has arrived!"

Shouts and murmurs erupt through the crowd that's gathered on the side of the mountain. The Celestial Knights immediately drop to one knee upon spotting me, though most of the Starless remain standing. Any other day, I might have cared. But now, I'm too busy scanning the faces of my soldiers and subjects, searching for the only one that matters.

All around me is a sea of brightly colored smocks and golden armor, of braided hair and fluttering mantles.

Yet I do not find the tarnished black steel or the distinctive helm I seek.

"Where is she?"

My voice slices through the noise, sure as any blade.

Silence ensues.

It's as if I cut the head off a great beast, muzzling it in one swift blow. And though I'm certain that every man, woman, and child assembled here needs no further clarification, I demand, "Where is the Godslayer?"

Desperation rises in my throat as the hush lengthens. Demigods and Starless alike look between one another with alarm and uncertainty plastered across their features, but nobody speaks.

What do they know?

What aren't they telling me?

Finally, one of the knights rises from his knee, though he keeps his head bowed. Dust cakes his armor, dulling its luster, and when I glance around at the others, I realize that several of the other soldiers seem to be in the same condition.

"Your Highness," the man says. His voice is hoarse, but I recognize it all the same.

"Orobos?"

The candidate for general nods and flips up the visor of his helm. Beneath, he appears grimy but otherwise unharmed. "Yes, Your Highness."

"Where is she?" I repeat.

"The Godslayer, she...." Fear flashes across his features before he continues, "I told her not to go, Your Highness, but she wouldn't listen."

My gaze sharpens upon him. "Go *where?*"

"Into the tunnel," he replies. "She found the cave leading to the Ushum's lair yesterday. She said she followed somebody there in the afternoon–a cloaked figure–but felt it was an ambush."

Ressa.

Orobos flinches at the sneer that passes over my face. My expression seems to urge him onward in his account, for he continues, "We entered the cavern at dawn. Half of us went with her. But the tunnel grew tight, and we could not fit, Your Highness. I swear to you that I told her not to go. I *swear* it."

She went in *alone?*

How could she do something so colossally stupid?

But then I think of how desperate she was to find the Ushum. Didn't she tell me that she was fearful of failing at her one task? Up until yesterday, I could feel her frustration trudging across our bond, and it couldn't have helped that I didn't visit her in her dreams these last few weeks. Did she think that I had forsaken her? Did I drive her to such recklessness?

Guilt flows between the cracks in my anger. Underneath, that sense that Lyanndra is in danger pounds in rhythm with my heart.

I need to find her.

I need to find her *now*.

"Show me this tunnel," I order. "I will follow her."

"You can't, Your Highness," Orobos replies. There's no defiance in his voice, only naked agitation. "It collapsed."

"Collapsed?" An image of Lyanndra, trapped and helpless beneath the mountain, flashes through my mind. Is it true? Is it possible? The rage and regret that swirl inside of me are joined by a pang of terror so deep that I feel it like a knife between the ribs.

"We've been searching for another entrance, Your Highness," the Demigod adds, as if that makes any difference to me now. "But it's been an hour."

An hour.

She's been entombed down there in the dark for *a fucking hour*.

Rage bubbles up to the surface. Heat simmers in my hands, and it's all I can do to keep my midnight flame from flaring in my palms. Losing control won't help me find Lyanndra any faster.

I draw in a deep breath.

"Ressa," I state through gritted teeth. "She's the one behind this."

Orobos' eyes widen. The blood drains from his face. Tracking down my former betrothed was his responsibility before he left to accompany the Godslayer to Breem. Does he understand what I'll do to him if his ineptitude results in any further harm coming to my crossed star?

Does he understand that he'll be the first to burn if she dies?

But I don't unleash upon him.

Not yet.

Every moment I linger here, Lyanndra remains in danger. I cannot afford to waste any more time, not now.

His shoulders sag when I release him from my burning gaze, but I pay him no mind as I once again study the crowd. Though the Celestial Knights have spent weeks scouring the mountain, none of them are likely to possess any deep knowledge of the tunnels and caverns that Lyanndra told me run beneath the Caldera. If I'm to find another way to the Ushum—to Lyanndra—I'll need the wisdom of a local.

And just as I'm about to ask for volunteers, a man pushes to the front of the crowd.

At first glance, he appears no different from the other Starless. His black hair, graying at the temples, is woven back into a series of tight braids not unlike Aaro's. He's rather small, though the wiry muscles that creep up his exposed arms bely the strength hidden behind his short stature.

But it's his eyes that hold my attention now.

They're a brown so dark they're almost black, so different from the flashing hazel of Lyanndra's. Yet, I see something of her in that gaze, something that transcends blood altogether.

Strength.

Determination.

Fury.

I know who this must be.

Lyanndra's father doesn't bow his head when he stops before me. He doesn't fall to his knee. He simply stares, a silent challenge written across his sun-worn features.

I meet his gaze with all the fury of my midnight flame.

So *this* is the man who drove my crossed star away.

This is the man who betrothed his own daughter, *against her will*, to the same Starless wretch who would later betray her.

This is the man who rendered the Godslayer to a sobbing mess in my arms, whose actions chewed away at her for so many years.

I should kill him.

It would be a lie to claim that I haven't thought of it, ever since that day in our chambers when Lyanndra revealed the truth of herself to me. For I know, intimately, the kind of damage a father can inflict upon his child. Mine paid the price for his many misdeeds. Why should hers evade such a tithe?

But even as the fire rages just below my skin, I tamp it down. There's something in the distressed set of his face and the way his eyes shine that gives me pause.

And as if he senses the danger that lurks in my palms, he snarls, "Burn me later, Demigod, if that's what suits you, but not before you find my daughter."

Ah.

So *that's* where Lyanndra gets her temper.

I'm reminded of the duel where I nearly killed her, when she let me believe that I had struck down the greatest threat to my kingdom in one fell blow. Upon waking, she regarded me with the same vicious glare that her father wears now.

I was so convinced that she would never see past my lineage, that she would never see *me*.

Yet, she warmed to me in time.

Will her father do the same? Is he even worthy of knowing me beyond the ghost of the Flaming God's features and the crown that now sits atop my head?

Perhaps that's not up to me, I realize. Perhaps this is Lyanndra's choice to make, her forgiveness to bestow. And if I were to unleash my flame upon him now, would I not just cement myself in the villager's eyes as the same monster my father was?

Wouldn't I prove to all present that I'm exactly who they think me to be?

No.

I will not become the former king.

So I force the contempt from my face and grit out, "I have no quarrel with you unless the Godslayer does. I'm here only for her."

Surprise flickers across her father's features, but it's quickly tempered by disbelief. "Do you think I don't know of the hold you have over her?" he spits. "Of the curse that binds you both? Her death would drive you to madness. You may have fooled her, but I know your kind. You'll save her, but only to spare yourself from the madness that would follow in her wake."

"You know nothing of me," I reply coldly. Isn't that what I said to Lyanndra so long ago in the infirmary?

He sneers. "I've killed enough of your kind to know how you Demigods think. Liars, every one of you."

"Then believe what you must. My heart and sword are hers regardless." I say it without thinking of the implications, without considering the burning truth that's woven between my words.

But Lyanndra's father doesn't miss it. His eyes narrow and he utters, "As if you have a heart."

Flames lick my palms, and I clench my fists in an attempt to hold them at bay. "I swore an oath to her," I tell him, dropping my voice down so that only he can hear. "And I intend to honor it. My word may mean nothing to you, but it means something to *her*."

He stares at me then with an unreadable expression, one I've seen on Lyanndra's face a thousand times before. It's disconcerting to catch the echoes of her on this Starless stranger's features. What else did she learn from him? Her skills with a blade? Her precision in battle? Her vicious tongue?

Finally, the man's posture breaks. It's barely noticeable, not quite defeat, but it's a victory all the same. "Prove it," he challenges. "Show me that you're a man of honor."

"For her, I'll do anything," I reply.

He holds my gaze for only a moment longer before he asks, "Do you know what it means to her? Being the Godslayer?"

I picture Lyanndra sitting astride her kelpie, her golden helm gleaming in the sunlight and my stolen velvet cloak fluttering at her shoulders. I see her shaking and lost after killing the usurper, and how she knelt before my father's corpse in the throes of her nightmares, and I nod.

I know what she is. I know the price of it.

"She'd die for Alastria. For its people," he says. "For *you*." His words sting like an accusation, as though I'm not worthy of her sacrifice, and they cut deeper still when I realize that maybe he's right. "If you want to convince me, then promise me this: *Do not let her*. I won't lose her again."

It's an easy request to make of me. Resolution burns through my veins as I vow, "The kingdom will burn before she falls."

Lyanndra's father searches my face, and he must find whatever he's looking for, because he holds his hand out to me. After receiving so many refugees in Nexus, I don't hesitate to extend my palm to his. If he's surprised that I would engage in this Starless custom, he doesn't show it.

It's only after he releases me that he says, "Come. We've been searching for another way into the tunnels, and I think we may have found one."

A soft pulse of hope alights in my chest as I follow him over the uneven ground toward a nearby outcropping, though the tender beacon is quickly overshadowed by my overpowering need to find my crossed star. The sense of danger is only growing, and I've already wasted enough time arguing with her father.

I have to find Lyanndra.

"Here."

At first, I don't understand what he's gesturing to. But then, as my eyes adjust to the rugged landscape of the mountain, I realize that there's a jagged opening in the rock hidden in a swathe of shadows, barely noticeable. A small golden flag flutters weakly in the breeze at its mouth.

"The scouts that explored the passage said that this cave seems to turn in the same direction she went," he explains. "It's our best chance."

It's also the only option left.

Turning, I face the opening. The tunnel yawns into darkness. Somewhere beyond it, Lyanndra is waiting for me.

I draw my sword in one hand and conjure my flame in the other. Fang or no fang, I will meet whatever I discover down there.

All that matters is that I survive long enough to reach Lyanndra. I have to find her, before it's too late.

CHAPTER 37

Lyanndra

"Who are you?"

My demand echoes through the vast cavern and tumbles off the walls in a hollow mockery of my voice.

The shadowy figure blinks.

Beneath my helm, I scowl. Is that all this abysmal thing can do?

But then, words slide from it, thin and reedy, as it croons, "A friend."

Liar, I think. Whatever it is, it is no friend of mine.

Ressa seems to share my disbelief, since she thrashes against me with such force that I almost lose my grip on her. In spite of the pressure I leaven against her throat, she manages to turn her head and snap her jaws inches from my chin. "I'm going to kill you, Godslayer!" she shrieks. "I'm going to tear you apart, piece by piece, until there's nothing left of you but your dirty Starless blood upon the ground!"

I roll my eyes, though I imagine the gesture is lost on her. However, the way I squeeze my armored forearm into the elegant column of her throat certainly gets the point across.

"Tell her!" Ressa gasps to the shadow.

A low, breathy laugh escapes it. "Have patience, Lady Ressa. Your moment will come."

The Demigod rends her nails against my gauntlet as she struggles to escape my hold. "You promised... that I could... kill her!" she wheezes. "You... promised!"

Interesting.

I think of how Ressa slipped so easily from the dungeons and of how the figure stole in and out of Syran's chamber without so much as opening the door. What deal did Ressa strike with her new companion? Did it tempt her with freedom in exchange for my death?

If so, why?

None of this makes sense. Why would it have Ressa lure me to Breem by waking the Ushum? What purpose does that serve?

And why me?

While the countless possibilities churn through my mind, the thing repeats, "Patience, dear lady. For now, I need you both alive."

Disquiet prickles across my skin as Ressa stills in my hold. "What?" she hisses.

I hate to admit that I share her curiosity, though I don't voice mine.

The figure shimmers slightly, and I get the sense that it's glancing between us, like it's searching for something. But it doesn't seem to find what it's looking for because it says, "Neither of you can die until I figure out which is which."

"Enough," I spit. Ressa flinches at the sound of my voice, but the thing doesn't move. "Speak plainly, or...."

"Or what? You'll throw your dagger at me again?" it interrupts. "You really are a beastly little thing, aren't you? A soldier, through and through."

My helm conceals the snarl that flashes over my face at its words. I'll show it what a beast I can be—once I figure out how to draw its blood.

"But it's no wonder," it continues. "You never stood a chance, growing up in this starsforsaken place. Not like your sister."

I stiffen. Sister?

"You don't know?" the thing asks. Genuine surprise wreathes its tone. "You haven't figured it out?"

"Figured out *what?*" I hiss. I'm not in the mood for whatever games this creature is playing. My fingers itch to close around the hilt of my greatsword. Will the blade cut through the figure? Probably not, but at least it would be satisfying to try.

It blinks. "The prophecy. The promise of the Moon."

I know the story. Syran told me of the legend while we wandered across Alastria, though I was much more preoccupied with the way his eyes burned into mine than with the tale he recounted at the time.

In front of me, Ressa lets out one of her perfect laughs. "You think *the Godslayer* is one of the foretold sisters? One of the daughters of the Moon?" She shakes her head as much as she's able given my arm around her neck. "A Starless whore like her?"

"How unbecoming it is," the thing purrs, "to talk of your kin in such a way."

Ressa and I freeze at his words.

Is he implying…?

No.

No.

Absolutely *not.*

I narrow my eyes down at the Demigod as I study her highborn features. Her skin was once perfect, but it's marred now by the memory of Kartas' lightning, and more recently by the bruise that spreads across her broken jaw like a thunderhead. Where my eyes are hazel, hers are a rich brown, like those of a doe. And her hair is nothing like mine, dark to my gold.

But do traces of each other linger in our faces? Certainly not in our noses, but maybe in the set of our eyes, or in the way our chins come to a point?

No.

No.

There's no way Ressa and I are sisters.

Absolutely fucking not.

She seems to reach the same conclusion, since she scoffs. "What insult is this, to compare me to a common harlot such as her?"

"There is nothing common about either of you," it says. There's a certain amount of glee in its voice, as though it's been waiting a very long time to reveal its secrets. "You were born of the same Demigod father, who carries in him the sacred blood of the Moon."

"Are you calling my mother an adulteress?" Ressa howls, once again writhing against me as I struggle to quell her rage.

For my part, I concede that I don't actually know who my true father is. According to my parents, a traveler from the north entrusted me to them as a babe, and I have no reason to doubt their story given my ruddy features and honeyed hair.

Is it possible? Was I sired by a Demigod?

I'm not so cowardly as to shy away from the prospect, as detestable as it may be.

Yet, I'm no Demigod. I have no powers, no spark bestowed upon me from the gods. I'm Starless through and through.

Aren't I?

Ignorant to my cascading thoughts, the thing speaks solely to Ressa. "Your mother was barren," it croons. "She could not bear a child, so she was given one to hide her shame."

"Preposterous!" she snarls.

I press my arm against her throat, silencing her once more. Over the top of her pitching head, I focus on the shadow and ask, "The sisters in the prophecy are twins, are they not?"

It blinks. "Yes."

"Ressa is a Demigod. I am Starless. I take it our alleged mother is, too?"

"Was," the thing corrects. There's something strange in its tone, something that I could easily mistake for sorrow if it were a man.

"We look nothing alike," I challenge.

"Not all twins are identical," it counters.

That's true enough, I suppose, but that doesn't mean that the figure isn't lying to us now. But its giddy eagerness makes me think that it actually *believes* the tale it weaves. Is this madness, or something more?

Because it can't be true.

It *can't* be.

Even if the prophecy is real, even if I somehow *am* one of the daughters of the Moon sent to test the gods, there is no *fucking* way that Ressa is my sister.

But I'll play along for now, if only to divine this horrible creature's plot, so I offer, "Let's say it's true. Ressa wasn't born under Syran's star sign, yet I was. How is it that I was crossed with him, and she wasn't?"

"Ah," it hums. "Twins are not birthed at the same time, are they? One must come first. Those precious minutes are all it takes for stars to align—or not."

I'm no fool. It's telling me half-truths, only what it thinks I want to hear. These answers come too quickly. They're practiced.

Rehearsed.

Like this thing has been waiting to recite its lines for a very long time.

But what did it call me earlier?

A beastly little thing.

Beneath my golden helm, I curl my lips into a humorless grin.

If that's what it assumes of me, then let it. Let it believe me to be no better than a mindless brute that can't discern candor from pretty lies. Let it underestimate me.

Let it learn what it means to cross the Godslayer.

Still, I have questions that need answering, so I ask, "Why does it matter who we are? What is the Moon Prophecy to you?"

"Everything," it rattles. "The Moonlit Age *must* come, and one of you will usher it in. One of you will obliterate the very gods. But which *one*?"

Does this thing not understand that I'm heralded as *the Godslayer*? Is it really so hard a mystery to parse?

But I won't give it the knowledge it seeks, so instead, I demand,

"Why the Ushum? What part does it play in all of this, aside from luring me here to Breem?"

"A test." The thing inches closer.

Ressa flinches.

"A trial."

I stand my ground.

"What better way to determine which of you is my champion than a fight against the divine?" it poses. "But whatever the outcome, the Moon Prophecy *must* be fulfilled."

And when it eases even nearer, Ressa hurls herself against my arm, causing me to slacken my grip just enough to allow her the air she needs to howl, "Deceiver!" She thrashes anew, and I'm reminded of how a freshly caught fish jerks and wriggles on the ground before it either suffocates or is granted mercy by its hunter.

If only dealing with the Demigod (who is definitely *not* my sister) would be so easy.

Yet, she's right.

This thing made her a promise. It's entirely beside the point that I would never let it keep it. And whether the shadow speaks the truth, or any version of it, only a fool would take it at its word.

So it's with great satisfaction that, when Ressa claws out at it and surges against my hold once more, I simply let her go.

She flies forward in a flurry of sharp nails and snapping teeth, which is quite impressive, considering her broken jaw. At the same time, the rock beneath my feet shudders. She's using her powers, I realize, but this time, I'm not on the receiving end of them.

Stalagmites and stalactites shake loose from her efforts. Ressa doesn't guide them with any precision, not like how she pierced those guards' throats in the dungeons of Nexus, but the intention is just as vicious. She hurls them at the shadowy figure in a quick barrage, leaving it no time to dodge or rally.

But it doesn't need to.

The projectiles pass right through it, just as my dagger and fist did in Syran's chambers. They shatter harmlessly against the far wall into splinters of rock and dust.

A shriek storms from Ressa's lips at the sight. She staggers forward with her arms outstretched, and I expect her to follow the trajectory of her makeshift weapons. But instead, the thing shimmers, its outline solidifying into the general shape of a man, before a piece of it—a hand—darts out to grab her by the wrist.

"Enough," it hisses. "Save your frenzy for the Ushum."

My gaze fastens on the place where the shadow holds her, and a wicked idea takes form in my mind.

Maybe it didn't kill us in Syran's chambers because it *couldn't*. What if its incorporeal nature works both ways? I couldn't hurt it, and it couldn't touch us, either. But now that it grasps her, does that mean I can do the same to it?

Does that mean I can make it bleed?

My grin widens.

I think I shall find out.

Ressa does a fine job of keeping it distracted while I draw my dagger from the sheath at my thigh. I'd much rather attack with my greatsword, but the motion of pulling it from the scabbard at my back would be less than discreet. It doesn't seem to notice as I heft the blade in the palm of my gauntlet. It's far too busy trying to hold the rabid Demigod at bay.

I wait for my opening. At any moment, it could look at me and fade away to nothing once more, but it doesn't. And then, when Ressa pulls at it, trying to yank her arm free, I take my chance.

The blade flashes in the flickering light of the lantern as I slash at the thing's wrist.

For a moment, I think nothing will happen, that the steel will just pass through it like it did that night in Nexus.

And then resistance shudders up my arm as the dagger slices deep, down to the bone.

Bone.

Perhaps this *is* a man, after all.

It releases Ressa and draws back to clutch its wrist. Blood spatters from the wound, materializing from its semi-corporeal flesh in a way that's both fascinating and horrible to behold. "You… you…."

"Beastly little thing?" I offer in the sweetest tone I can muster.

But it doesn't have a chance to reply.

Upon seeing that it can bleed, Ressa renews her attack with fervor. She alternates between hurling rocks and tearing at it with her nails, though neither type of blow does much harm.

The thing's grown wiser now, it seems, but so have I.

Brandishing the dagger, I dance in and out of the fray, aiming for the shadow's injured wrist. The wounded area doesn't fade with the rest of it, and I surmise that maybe it *can't*. I manage to get in a few good jabs, but Ressa doesn't distinguish between the two of us, and dodging her frantic hands and onslaught of stone keeps me from landing the damage I truly wish to.

I can't really blame her for her brutality, either.

The shadow promised her that it could kill me, and then denied her the very vengeance she desired. If I weren't actively attempting to sever the thing's tendons, I'd shake my head in pity. How many times do powerful men have to use Ressa to their own ends for her to understand what I learned as a girl?

The only shape a woman will ever fit into is her own.

And mine?

It's tarnished armor and a golden helm. It's a greatsword whistling through the air and a dagger, quick and vicious, between the ribs.

I am the shape of the Godslayer.

This is what I was made for.

My focus narrows.

I stare at the thing's wrist, a small target, easily missed. Keeping Ressa in my peripheral, I slide between them. There's just enough time for me to hack at its transparent limb, sending up a splatter of glistening blood, before the Demigod's next onslaught reaches me.

A rock the size of my fist thuds against the side of my helm. The impact doesn't hurt, but the force of it reverberates through the metal and rings in my ears until my teeth ache.

Staggering back, I tighten my jaw.

At least it wasn't a stalagmite.

But before I can jump back into the fight, a buzzing whine rises in the air, drowning out the aftershocks of Ressa's glancing blow until it fills the space like a swarm of insects.

"What...?" Ressa gasps, but the noise quickly surpasses the rest of her exclamation.

The sound pitches to a grating roar, and the whole cavern rumbles from the force of it. A waft of hot air, stagnant and ripe with that terrible, ancient smell, washes forth from one of the many openings in the side of the gallery. Ressa retches, but I swallow back the bile that rises in my throat.

The Ushum.

My gaze snaps to the tunnel from which the stench flows.

That's where it is.

But even as I come to the conclusion, a flash of shadow catches my attention. I flinch back, thinking it's going to strike me, but the blow never comes. Instead, the thing whips around and dodges past Ressa, only to disappear through the dark mouth of another passage.

"No!" Ressa screeches. "No!"

I hesitate.

I could chase after it, hunt it down and flay it with my dagger like the beast it thinks I am.

But then the keening wail sounds again, and I know what I have to do.

Prophecies and shadowy figures be damned, I'm going to find the Ushum.

I'm going to earn my title.

I'm going to slay a god.

CHAPTER 38

SYRAN

A sound shatters through the dark.

A wail.

A shriek.

A cacophony so jarring and fey that I lack the words or the thoughts to color it properly. The discordant cry stirs that ancient, clawing fire in my chest, and the sheer force doubles me over as my heart pounds and the wound at my ribs burns.

Then, before I can recover, the tremors come, rolling beneath my feet. Stone splits and rends from the earth's convulsions. The ground pitches. Dirt billows through the air, and chunks of rock, some bigger than my head, crash down from the walls and ceiling. It's as if the whole mountain is crumbling around me.

There's only one creature that could bring such violence in its wake.

The Ushum.

Fear races through my veins as the tunnel continues to quake. I've never felt the earth shake in such a way before, and I realize, too late, that I have no idea what I'm supposed to do to protect myself. Do I flatten myself against the wall? Do I remain, half-crouched, in the middle of the passage even as dust and fragments of brown stone rain down upon me?

But as quickly as it began, the shaking lulls, though the other-worldly sound doesn't die.

Not completely.

It remains at a low, whining hum that reverberates through the rock and the planes of my golden armor, stuttering up my greaves and coursing through my very bones until it reaches an almost unendurable throb. Dread threads between the vibrations as the noise—more felt than heard—persists.

And in spite of the torrid sweat that trickles down my spine, I shiver.

It's awake, isn't it?

The Ushum is *awake*.

Does my crossed star know? Is she getting ready to face it, to take her chances even without the fang? The thought of her standing her ground against that blasphemous beast is unbearable.

I have to find her.

I have to get to her before it does.

"Lyanndra!" I bellow.

But no answer comes over the harsh drone of the Ushum. There's only the groan of the ancient rock settling, the persistent dripping of water in the distance, and that infernal noise ringing through my head.

Summoning my midnight flame once more, I stumble further into the darkness. Shadows cringe away from the flickering light. At one point, I catch a glimpse of something quick and pale darting away from me—a lizard, I think, though none like any I've ever seen before.

It has no eyes, I realize with a grimace. But then again, I suppose it wouldn't need any down here in the dark where no light can reach.

Unsettled, I glance around at the close embrace of the mountain.

Did Lyanndra really wander these caves as a child?

I try to imagine her crawling through these tunnels, curious and unfettered by her parents' expectations. Did her love of solitude blossom down here in the gloom? Or did the stars simply fashion her that way from the very start?

Perhaps she was always meant to traverse such lonely paths.

Perhaps she was always meant to wander.

But not alone, I resolve. Not anymore. Not while she has me to stand by her side.

I'll find her. I'll make sure that she understands why I kept myself from her dreams, if only so that I wouldn't lash out against her in my anger. And I'll whisper my apologies as I supplicate myself to her, for she is the only star in my sky, and I will orbit around no other.

Will she forgive me?

I have to believe that she will. She has before, even when I didn't deserve it. Even when I couldn't absolve myself.

Fresh determination quickens in the hollow behind my heart. My vows to her echo through my mind as I press onward into the endless maze that runs beneath the mountain. Every step brings me closer to her. I can feel it in the thread that stretches taut between us, in the beckoning promise of our bond.

And it isn't soon after I heed her silent call that noises surface over the dull throb of the Ushum.

Shuffling.

Crashing.

Strange, animalistic howling.

I struggle to parse it all. Are people fighting up ahead? But I hear no clash of blades. And it's certainly not the Ushum, which buzzes frantically from somewhere deeper beneath the Caldera.

Is it Ressa?

Lyanndra?

Both?

I think of the courtier and the brutal way she killed those Celestial Knights back in the dungeons of Nexus. Is she attacking my crossed star at this very instant? Is she foolish enough to dare to take on the Godslayer?

For Lyanndra is no idle guard caught unaware. She was smart

enough to wait and bring her host into the cave with her after she spotted Ressa on the mountainside. And she suspected the courtier's involvement in Kartas' plot from the start.

From my crossed star's account, their battle in the courtyard outside the palace was dramatically one-sided, and Ressa was unconscious when Kartas perished upon Lyanndra's greatsword. Even when I dueled the Godslayer with the entire court looking on, she held back the sheer fury I saw her unleash upon my father the day she ended the war and claimed his helm as her own.

No.

In spite of all her scheming, Ressa's never borne witness to the true power of the Godslayer.

Ressa doesn't understand what Lyanndra is capable of.

She doesn't stand a chance.

Yet, the mere thought of my former betrothed harming my crossed star is too much to bear. Rage flares within me at the notion, and, this time, I don't even bother trying to push it back.

It spurs me forward into the yawning dark.

I have to find Lyanndra.

She's waiting for me.

She *needs* me.

Yes, something inside of me whispers. *Go to her. It's nearly time.*

My steps falter from the weight of the voice that trails along the edges of my mind. It seems to come from everywhere, nowhere, and that place deep in the embers of my being where my flame twists and writhes.

"What are you?" I demand.

The blaze I hold in my palm shudders high and scorches against the low ceiling of the tunnel. Heat builds within me as it did back on the training grounds and again on my ride to Breem, but this time, it doesn't overwhelm me.

Instead, it ignites in my chest, blistering through my blood and coiling in my veins.

You and I, wandering god, it murmurs from somewhere inside me and somewhere very far away, *We are one. Is this not what you asked for?*

Asked for?

"I don't understand," I choke out, though I can't fathom what, exactly, I'm speaking to or if it can even hear me.

You offered me your penance, did you not?

Penance? A memory, long forgotten, dredges to the surface of my thoughts.

"I offer my flame in penance to the stars," I recite. Those are the words Torran had me learn, the same ones I spoke at the Ceremony of the Crossed Stars. But they're just ritual, nothing more. They don't *mean* anything.

Do they?

Bind us in honor and in death, the thing inside me chants.

The next phrase is pulled from my throat, bubbling up before I can stop it. "In mind and in madness."

Behold us as one beneath your moon and sky.

"Behold us as one beneath your moon and sky."

We intone the last line together, our voices mingling in the flickering darkness of my flame. There's something so disturbingly *right* about the sound that I feel like I'm teetering on the precipice of a great and familiar void, on the very edge of sanity.

I consider its words for a moment before realization settles into my bones. "You bound us," I say. "The Godslayer and I. What *are* you?"

We are one, it repeats. *And I gave you only what you asked. A god for a god. Power for power.*

I whirl around, as though if I turn fast enough, I might discern the thing that speaks to me. "Why? What do you *want?*"

We. You and I. We want to burn *for her.*

I don't need to ask who it means.

It's always been for Lyanndra.

Didn't I know it from the moment the stars crossed us—and maybe even before? My poison couldn't fell her. Neither could my steel. Instead, she sparked the kindling at the heart of me and fanned it to life with her wildness.

My fire is hers.

I am hers.

And whatever stirs inside of me now, I feel the pull of it, that dark tether stretched taut into eternity. The thing at the other end flexes its sinuous, ancient body and sighs.

It's been waiting, hasn't it?

It's been waiting for a very long time.

Part of me wants to tug the thread that binds us, if only to glimpse what's on the other side, but I don't. Not yet. I simply stand there, my chest heaving and my breath coming in short, panting gasps as my flame pulses in my outstretched hand.

Will it pull me to it? Will it fling me into the rushing darkness so that I might finally see what's awakening in the midnight glow of my soul?

But it doesn't.

Nothing happens.

Like before, it bides its time.

"What are you waiting for?" I whisper. "When will I know to call you?"

But no words come in reply. There's only the dry, shifting feel of it within my chest and that shivering anticipation of what's to come.

And in spite of whatever this is that's taken root within me, I realize that it's not trying to hold my back from what I want most.

It wants her.

It wants me to *go* to her.

I hazard a step forward and then another. Lyanndra is somewhere nearby, I'm sure of it. It matters not what's happening to me, what I'm becoming. I'm not going to fail her now. I don't have the fang, but we can still fight the Ushum. And if we founder–if it rises from the ground to wreak havoc on Alastria–then at least we will meet our defeat together as one.

Hot resolve pools within me as I push onward. The sounds grow louder the deeper I go, though I can't tell if I'm getting closer to them or if the source is approaching me.

I only make it a few more feet when a dark figure darts forth from the tunnel directly in front of me. There's barely time to react before it barrels past me (through me?), and then it's gone.

"Halt!" I shout after it, but it's already vanished into the gloom.

My heart thuds wildly against my ribs as I struggle to process what I just saw. Was it a man? No, not exactly. It was….

A shadow.

A blinking shadow.

The same one that was in our chambers back at Nexus, the one that helped Ressa escape from the dungeons.

And if that thing is down here with Ressa, with *Lyanndra*….

Rage, black and blinding, explodes from me in a burst of flame.

I throw myself deeper into the dark, toward the drone of the Ushum and the promise of my crossed star. All I can think of is the Godslayer. I need to get to her. I need to protect her and fight for her, even though she's far more capable than I.

And as I pitch myself forward, the thing inside me urges, *Yes. Yes!*

Because I'm almost there.

I'm almost to Lyanndra.

I'm almost to my crossed star.

CHAPTER 39

Lyanndra

This is it.

Adrenaline pulses through my veins with each staggered beat of my heart. The stench of the Ushum is heavy, almost unbearable, a call to arms.

I'll heed it.

I'll see this through, no matter the cost.

The shadowy figure's flight is all but forgotten, and while I still keep Ressa in my line of sight, her howling madness pales in comparison to what awaits me now. Luckily, the Demigod seems far too occupied with shouting obscenities after her traitorous companion to pay me any mind. And it seems she's exhausted her powers, at least for now.

But then, as I sheathe my dagger and instead reach for my greatsword, she turns.

When her gaze locks onto mine, I pause. Her eyes are alight with gleaming madness. They glitter in the twisted glow of the lantern like twin gemstones, and for the first time, I wonder what she sees.

Does the world appear to her as warped as her mind is?

Does she even understand the true horror that lurks down here in the dark?

"Ressa," I say. I don't bother with her title. Any respect she might once have commanded vanished the second she chose to plot against Syran, against Alastria.

Against *me*.

She narrows her eyes and bares her teeth in a brutish snarl. "This is your fault!" she hisses.

"I don't think the Ushum cares which of us is to blame," I snap in return. "It'll devour us both regardless."

"I hope it chokes on you!" she rages.

Beneath my golden helm, I flash her a humorless grin. "Likewise."

We stand there for a moment, regarding one another with wary hostility. Sweat drips down her face. The fabric of her cloak is torn at the sleeves and hem, and beneath, her dress is in tatters. Her chest heaves with every wheezing breath she draws. At her sides, her fingers curl like claws as she tries to summon her powers, but nothing happens.

She's spent.

And when I see her like this, unbalanced and betrayed yet again, an idea flickers to life in my mind. Logically, I know there's little time for such nonsense. I'm aware of its absurdity, yet I consider it all the same.

"Help me kill the Ushum." The words tumble from my mouth before I can think better of them.

Ressa's broken jaw drops. If she feels any pain, it doesn't register in her face. And while she doesn't agree, she doesn't reject my proposal out of hand, either.

Emboldened, I ask, "Do you love this kingdom?"

The question seems to take her by further surprise, for she simply stares at me with those rabid, glinting eyes instead of answering. Then, slowly, as though suspecting a trap, she nods.

"Do you wish to rule?"

"Yes," she replies, eagerness curling through her voice.

"And what will you rule over if the Ushum breaks free?" I press. "What will be left of Alastria if it rises?"

Confusion crumples across her delicate features, followed quickly by cold fury. "Don't weave your foul enchantments over me, Godslayer," she sneers.

"This is no trick, Ressa," I insist. "Even if you were never given a choice before, you have one now. Help me fight the Ushum. Help me kill it."

"Never!" she snarls. Her tone leaves no room for reason or argument.

Did I really expect anything different?

I let out a resigned sigh. "So be it."

Reaching over my shoulder, I close my fingers over the hilt of my greatsword. When I pull it free of its sheath and brace my body against the familiar weight of the weapon, I feel more myself than I have since I left Nexus. A strange, calm surety washes over me at the realization.

I am the Godslayer.

I will keep my kingdom and my people safe, no matter the bloody cost.

This is all I was ever meant to do.

This is what I was made for.

My gaze locks on Ressa, who seems to have just enough of a grasp on reality left to recognize what I'm about to do. Her eyes widen in terror, and she lifts her hands, though I can't tell if it's to push me away, use her powers, or beg for quarter.

But I have no mercy left to give. Not for her. Not anymore. She had her chance to become better than what she was. I will not grant her a second one.

I heft the greatsword high, preparing to bring it down in a clean, precise cut.

"No!" Ressa shrieks. Her voice pierces through the lingering hum of the Ushum like a lance. In one last, desperate attempt to save herself, she flings her arms forward and calls to the rock.

And though she's too exhausted to do any real damage, she manages to fling a cloud of dust up into the air between us.

Debris pings off my armor and helm. She forces the grit up through my visor, where it stings my eyes and coats my tongue with ancient, sulfurous draff. Coughing and reeling, I stagger back, temporarily blinded.

I don't see Ressa run, but I hear her. Her boots—not the heeled slippers she wore back at the Celestial Court—slap against the stone as she flees. From the sound of it, I think she bolted down another of the many tunnels fanning off from the chamber, but not the one the shadow figure took, and certainly not the one that leads to the Ushum.

Some animal part of me longs to chase her, to pursue her into the dark and cut her down like the traitor she is, but there's no time.

I know what must be done.

Blinking the last of the dust out of my watering eyes, I draw in a deep breath and shoulder my greatsword. Though Ressa is gone, she left the lantern behind. It flickers forlornly in the middle of the cavern, and while I doubt there's much oil left to feed the flames, I grab it anyway. Then I turn to face the tunnel where the Ushum waits.

Darkness yawns at the mouth of the passage. The creature could be a stone's throw away, or a mile.

Either way, I'll find it.

Holding the lantern aloft, I creep forward into the abyss.

The scent of the beast swirls through the cramped space, growing stronger with every step I take. The temperature, too, intensifies. Sweat slicks my skin and drips into my eyes. While the dragonhide leathers I wear beneath my armor keep the worst of it at bay, the air inside the golden helm festers until it becomes unbearable.

Every breath I take burns. The stench of the Ushum, rank and woolen, churns my stomach.

Unable to suffer it one second longer, I drop the lamp down by my feet, strip off my gauntlets, and scrabble at the buckle of my helm.

"Fuck," I gasp as I finally manage to free the clasp and pull the piece of armor from my head.

Air, comparatively cool, rushes over my heated skin. But there's no time to savor the relief. I spare only a moment to secure the strap of the helm to the scabbard of my greatsword before reclaiming the lantern and continuing on my journey.

As I inch forward into the dark, I wonder how far under the mountain I am. Am I nearing the Caldera? I must be, if the dry, scorching air is any indication.

Time seems to stretch. Has it been minutes? Hours? There's nothing to mark the seconds except for the endless, hollow buzzing of the creature and the frantic pounding of my heart. And after a while, the light of the lantern dims and then dies, leaving me in a seething blackness so terrible and complete that I wonder if I'll ever find my way through this hellish maze.

But I did it once before, didn't I?

I came this way as a girl, before I ever donned my father's armor or learned to swing a sword. I wasn't the Godslayer then. I hadn't faced armies or the flaming purgatory of the battlefield, and the skin of my hands was not yet stained with red.

And if that child could reach the Ushum, then so can I.

I drop the lantern. There's no use for it anymore, not when I need two hands on the hilt of my greatsword in order to swing it effectively. Then I sidle over until my shoulder hits the wall of the tunnel. My armor scrapes against the jagged rock as I use the friction to guide me forward in place of my sight, though the raking sound is barely audible over the rising whine of the Ushum.

Step by step, I feel my way through the darkness.

And then, when I turn a corner, there's light.

It's just a faint orange glow in the distance, but it cuts the darkness like a honed blade, calling me into it.

As a moth to a flame, I quicken my pace. The rank stench of the Ushum is so strong that it's all I can do to swallow back the bile that rises in my throat. Heat roils through the air, on the edge of unendurable.

Ahead of me, the tunnel curves sharply to the left. Pulsing light spills from around the corner. And over the buzzing of the Ushum, so loud now that it rattles my armor, I can just make out the sounds of shuffling.

Dread grips me with freezing talons as I realize that the creature is *right there*.

This is it.

I close my eyes and draw in one last breath. My hands shake. Nausea writhes like a burning serpent in my gut, but I refuse to let my last act in defending Alastria be sullied by vomiting like a drunkard down here in the dark.

In an attempt to calm my racing panic, I think of Syran. Did he make it to Breem? Is he trying to find me? I have no way of knowing whether he's close, and I can't afford to wait any longer. My heart clenches as I picture his neat features and the flaming crimson of his hair.

"Forgive me," I whisper.

And then, before I can remember that I am, in fact, a coward, I ready my greatsword and step around the corner.

At first, I can barely comprehend what awaits me.

The sight is so familiar, like a remembered dream–like a *nightmare*.

A great, molten mass dominates the large chamber in front of me. It's not solid, exactly. It shifts and ripples beneath some sort of membrane, thin as parchment and utterly transparent. Black, root-like veins shoot through the yellow-orange bulk of its form, and they pulse in time with each whirring hum the creature emits.

And then there are the limbs.

Gaunt. Angled. Far too many, splaying out from its igneous body like those of an insect. My stomach turns at the sight. I realize each one ends in a foot or hand so horribly pink and elongated that they couldn't possibly be real, couldn't possibly be natural.

Yet, the Ushum *is*.

I understand now why Carolissa refused to speak of it and why

Torran was so rattled when he first identified the creature. Whatever this thing is, it's an abomination.

Blasphemous.

"Bastard child of the stars!" I shout. The rending drone of the Ushum is deafening, but the fury in my voice cuts through the cacophony. "Face me!"

For a moment, the creature doesn't react. Did it hear me? Does it even recognize a human voice?

But then, something shifts amid the shimmering heat. It's long and sinuous, about the thickness of my thigh.

A tail?

No, I realize with burgeoning horror.

A neck.

The appendage stretches from the thing's molten body, weaving toward me like a serpent ready to strike. There's a face, shockingly small for such a gargantuan creature, poised on the end of it, but it's hard to make out the features in the bending light.

Are those eyes?

Yes, and a mouth, small and toothless.

And soft, pink cheeks, such a stark contrast from the gelatinous membrane of its neck.

And....

Panic bubbles up inside of me. A scream catches in my throat. The Ushum is so close now that I could reach out and touch it, but I'm frozen in terror, for the thing staring back at me is so devastatingly ordinary that my mind can barely process what I'm seeing.

A face.

A human face.

An *infant's* face.

How can such innocent curiosity be plastered across the visage of such a towering horror?

How could this be?

How could this be?

For a moment, my mind is utterly blank.

Then I recall that the Ushum are said to be the offspring of the

Ankir and the Celestial Gods, only to have been banished in disgrace at the dawning age of the Demigods.

Is this creature just a babe, even after all these years? Was its slumber just a mere blink in the timeline of its existence? And does it rattle the earth now, not to destroy, but out of fear?

I think of what it must feel like, to be so young and awaken, only to find yourself utterly alone and in the dark. It's been sealed away down here for centuries, waiting for parents that will never come.

It's abandoned.

An orphan.

Alone.

Seemingly unaware of my turmoil, the thing stares at me. Its tiny features are shockingly emotive, and I think it looks surprised more than anything.

And the worst part of all is its eyes.

Green eyes.

Vomit forces its way up my throat, but I swallow it down. My heart beats so fast that my whole chest aches from the force of it. The chamber swirls around me.

But I can't look away. I won't.

I will do what I came here for, but not out of rage.

I'll do it out of mercy.

Something heavy settles within me. The bloodlust is gone, replaced by the weight of duty and a hollow sadness that fills the cracks in my horror.

"I'm sorry," I murmur.

I raise my greatsword.

But before I can bring it down to sever the thin stretch of its neck, its tiny features crumple with fear. It opens its mouth.

It starts to cry.

The wail is like nothing I've experienced before. It's as though every sound in Alastria is stitched together into one and raised to such a fevered pitch that it drives the very earth to shift in its wake. Pain spears through my head. Dropping my greatsword, I clap my gauntlets to my ears and fall to my knees.

The shriek seems to last forever. Blood, hot and vital, trickles from between my fingers. Great chunks of stone shake loose from the ceiling, and I'm surprised to see moonlight streaking in from above—we must be under the thin crust of the Caldera, I realize distantly.

And then finally, the Ushum falls quiet once again.

I barely notice as the neck retracts once more, bringing its face out of my blade's range. My ears echo and sting, and my whole body trembles from the force of the quake, but I don't remain on my knees for long. I grab my greatsword and brace myself against it as I struggle to my feet. Only then do I adjust my bloody grip.

The Ushum watches me with glittering interest. Its limbs scuttle through the rubble as the inky veins that run along its body pulse in a quick, staccato rhythm, but it doesn't approach.

Don't think about its face, I tell myself. Instead, I focus on its body, on the parts that can bleed. The membrane that holds its molten core together is thin, but I'm worried that if I pierce it, the burning insides will spill out and broil me alive.

It'll have to be the limbs, then.

Hot resolve flows through me as I stalk forward toward the beast. I'm acutely aware that I don't have the fang, but that doesn't mean I can't do some damage.

And when I launch myself at the Ushum, I don't cry out in fury or in wrath.

I howl for the unfairness of it all, for this scared and lonely creature that cowers away from me as I slice my greatsword out toward its trembling form.

My blade catches at the joints and cuts through them with brittle resistance. The Ushum wails in pain, but the sound is muffled by the blood that still leaks from my ears, and, even as it writhes, I continue to hack away at anything within reach.

The creature thrashes. I roll under one bony limb as the hand at its end crashes down where I was just standing. A leg flails in my direction, the foot aiming for the middle of my chest. I stumble away from it. Fingers, toes, and thin, crackling joints are everywhere, and I dance beneath the flurry as best as I can, dodging and carving at any opportunity.

But I don't notice the arm that swats at me from the side, not until it's too late, not until the unnervingly human nails connect with the side of my face.

Pain explodes across my cheek and temple. The force of the blow sends me flying across the length of the chamber, where I rag-doll hard against the ground.

Something sharp rends in my chest at the impact.

Blood pours down my face.

Agony sears through my eye socket and over the bridge of my nose.

But I'm alive.

I'm alive.

Hissing, I draw in a hot, cleaving breath in spite of the pain, and then another.

This fight's not over yet.

I refuse to die here down in the dark.

CHAPTER 40

Syran

"Lyanndra!"

My voice echoes through the crushing darkness, but the trailing end of the Ushum's wail quickly swallows it whole.

Even though she doesn't answer, I know I'm close now, so close that I can feel it in my bones, in that burning, searing place at the kindling of my soul. Fear, pain, and something else–something bright and primal–flare across our bond. The sense of danger is so strong that I can taste it like iron and ash on my tongue.

Desperation surges through my veins.

I need to get to her.

I need to reach her before it's too late.

And then, in the overwhelming blackness beneath the Caldera, I see a light.

It's surprisingly gentle. The orange haze might be mistaken for that of a fire, except that the glow is steady instead of flickering. The heat, too, is wrong. It's warm and somehow wet, and it plagues the air with a horrible, woolen stench that reminds me of clothes left far too long in the rain. Its sulfurous edge chips away at my composure, but there's no time to succumb to it.

Pushing back my disgust, I rush forward toward the beckoning light, only to find myself stumbling into a nightmare.

At first, I can barely comprehend the thing that looms before me.

My first thought is that the pictures in Torran's books didn't do the Ushum justice.

The second is that I understand entirely why the scholars deemed this beast a blasphemy.

It's massive, impossibly so. It takes up most of the cavernous space and fills the rest with that strange, pale light. Above, chunks of the ceiling have fallen in, revealing the star-strewn ink of the night sky. Watery veils of moonlight trickle down to mottle across its skin.

No.

Not skin.

Not exactly.

Dread writhes against my ribs as I face this forbidden relic of an age long past. The body of it seethes with liquid embers, held between pleading, pulsing fingers of blackened roots.

Or are they veins?

Or something else entirely?

Its mass rolls like fluid barely encased, like a molten drop of dew straining against the bonds of its shape. Thin branches of limbs trace from its sides, each one emaciated and oddly brittle for such a gargantuan form.

Are they arms?

Legs?

I can't tell.

I don't *want* to tell.

And then there's the great whip of its tail that lashes back and forth, high in the air. Something pale flickers on the end, something that, when it catches the moonlight just right, looks like….

No.

No.

I force my eyes away from the monstrosity before I can see too much. Part of me desperately wants to look–*needs* to look–but I don't give into the frantic temptation. I've seen enough horrors in my time, some wrought by my own hand, and I will *not* willingly gaze into the heart of another.

Not when it gazes back.

Not when it stares at me with green eyes from a young and line-less face.

Not when....

A groan, barely audible over the incessant buzz of the Ushum, steals my attention away. At the other end of a chamber, a shape on the ground shifts. Even caked in brown dust and spattered with crimson, I would know her anywhere.

Lyanndra.

Horror bubbles up in my chest. She lies on her back amidst the rubble, her golden hair pulled from its braid to fan around her and the cleaving length of her greatsword still clutched tightly in one hand. Blood flashes across her face in a great smear. From this distance, it's hard to tell what, exactly, the damage is, though I can feel the ghost of its sharp sting through the bond.

But she's alive. She's breathing. And when she sits up, I don't miss the hard set of determination in her jaw.

She isn't done yet.

This isn't over, not until the Ushum lies dead at her feet.

I want to go to her, to call out, to let her know that I'm here.

I do not possess the fang. Whatever the Midnight Serpent is, it's not within my grasp.

But I can promise her that she will never be alone again. Any enemy she faces, it will be with me by her side.

My sword is hers.

My flame is hers.

Every piece of me, every single spark of my being, belongs to the Godslayer.

Even facing death, I would not have it any other way.

Resolve burns through my veins with all the heat of my fire, and I reach for my sword, fully intent on slaying the beast that lumbers between us.

And then….

Time seems to slow.

Moonlight rolls in through the crumbled crust of the ceiling, and I pause. Is it night already? Wasn't it just barely dawn when I followed Lyanndra into the tunnels? Have the hours really passed so quickly?

A prickle of disquiet crawls across my skin, and it has nothing to do with grotesque monstrosity that shifts and buzzes down here in the dark.

Something is wrong.

Something is *right*.

Across the cavern, my crossed star struggles to her feet. Moving like a drunkard leaving the tavern in the early hours of the morning, she leans her weight into her greatsword as she pulls herself upright. A grimace of pain flashes across the half of her face that isn't painted with blood.

Lyanndra.

Her name builds in my throat, but my mouth won't cooperate. I should go to her. I should already be drawing my blade and flame to unleash upon the Ushum.

But I can't.

I *can't*.

My limbs are heavy and leaden. No matter how much I try to move, I'm rooted in place.

That ancient, curling thing within me stirs. It wraps its sinuous body around my heart, my lungs, my *soul*, and squeezes.

Watch, it whispers from everywhere at once. *Worship*.

And with blazing horror, that's all I can do as Lyanndra sways before the Ushum. At the motion, the creature's whip-like appendage unfurls in her direction, the tip coming to a halt just inches from her face.

It's *looking* at her, I realize with rising terror. The glimpse I caught of it earlier was no illusion.

That's not a tail.

That's a *neck.*

A *face.*

An impossible face.

But she doesn't blanche. She doesn't recoil in revulsion.

No.

The Godslayer plants her boots upon the dry rock and lifts her greatsword high until the wicked slab of steel hovers between her and her foe. Her one visible eye glimmers with burning defiance. Unwavering in her conviction, she stares at the towering blasphemy that rises up before her.

And she's afraid.

I can feel the panic coursing through her. It rides on the iron teeth of her pain, pulsing like a heartbeat, like a call to arms along the tether of our bond. Yet, still she stands with blood pouring down her face, matting the golden halo of her hair, and while her body may list slightly, her hands are steady upon the hilt of her blade.

Because even when she's tilting on the precipice of terror, even with agony streaking through her in vivid scarlet bolts, she is the Godslayer.

She does not falter.

She does not fall.

Not even a creature of the stars can bend her to its will.

The thing regards her for a moment. Will it strike out at her with those terrible, spindly limbs? I wait with panicked breath hitching in my lungs.

Then the Ushum opens its mouth and wails.

The sound is brutal. It echoes through the cavern in waves of shattered glass that break over me in a scathing tide. Whatever has a hold of me won't let me cover my ears, but by the fucking stars, I want nothing more than to drown out that noise, that shriek, that *rending fucking scream.*

Debris rains down from the ceiling and crashes down upon the ground in jagged explosions of shrapnel. Moonlight pours in through the fresh gaps to mingle with the orange light of the Ushum. Gold and silver meld as it cries, and cries, and cries.

And through it all, Lyanndra remains. Her face never changes. She doesn't flinch.

Doesn't she hear it?

But then I notice the streaks of red in her hair by her ears and realize that perhaps she *can't*.

She's beyond this thing now, and it seems to realize it, too, for it sweeps one of its great, spindly limbs across the ground toward her, as one would slap away a gnat or fly.

Whatever wound she's sustained, it doesn't slow her down. The blade of the greatsword flashes in the silver-gold light. The steel cracks through the assaulting limb with a strange creaking moan that sets my teeth on edge, and the creature's wail cuts off in an abrupt and welcome peak.

In that momentary reprieve, Lyanndra recovers from the momentum of her swing, and it's as if everything stops.

And for the first time since entering this starsforsaken place, I see her clearly.

Moonlight cascades, impossible but undeniably real, through the perforated crust of the Caldera. It pours over her in a shining water-fall and lends her an eldritch glow that steals the very breath from my lungs.

Iridescent ichor drips from the blade of her greatsword. Her tarnished armor is splattered with a mix of the creature's blood—if that's even what it is—and her own. Golden hair, streaked with red, spills free around her shoulders, but it's her face most of all that grips my gaze in an iron vice.

The bloodied ridge of her nose and the smooth curve of her jaw are hewn from opal, the crimson anointing her right cheekbone like glistening ruby. And in this swirling mix of star and moonlight, her unvarnished eye shines like something from another world.

Something ancient.

Something forgotten.

Something beyond even the stars.

And when the Ushum's face swings back to hers, it no longer finds a Starless woman glaring back.

It turns to meet the Godslayer.

As if sensing the same shifting current that grips me now, the creature lets out a short, shrill howl. A challenge, perhaps, or a threat.

In response to the shriek, Lyanndra's face breaks out into a feral snarl. Cosmic light seeps across her skin. Her gauntlets tighten around the hilt of her greatsword as she shifts her stance. And then she, too, opens her mouth and lets out a roar so fey and primal that I think, *this is not a sound a person should make, but she is not like us.*

She is not of *us.*

For she stands, her chest heaving and eclipsed in dripping starlight, like a fell god of yore.

There is no celestial body that can move her, no deity that can stay her course. The tides yield to her. The night trembles when she speaks. She is a creature wrought by some distant and unknowable hand, stitched together from ash and moonlight, something not quite of this world.

She is not of us.

She is of the heavens.

She is the only star I need worship.

I love her.

And at that blinding singularity, the threads within me snap taut.

The golden bond that leads to Lyanndra sings with power so bright and gleaming that it sets my blood aflame. The other, lithe and dark, twists off into hot and quiet void, and with it comes the burning understanding of what this thing has been waiting for all this time.

Me.

Reaching deep into myself, I grasp that inky, midnight thread.

Hear me, I call. *I understand now. It's time.*

And then I pull.

The thing on the other side heeds my summons without hesitation.

It rushes out of the dark toward me, dry and ancient and very far away. The embers in my soul flare. Power coils deep within my chest, searing and alive. Black flame curls forth from my hands, my arms, and everywhere else, encompassing me completely until all that I can see is the blazing shape that forms around me and the unearthly glow of Lyanndra beyond.

The fire coalesces into a long, sinuous body, and I'm surprised to realize that this isn't the first time I've drawn upon this strange force.

Didn't it show itself when we faced the strix and again when we announced the death of the usurper after the Battle of Nexus?

The flame knits into the same flickering, ghostly creature now.

A great viper, with its mouth open, its fangs poised to strike.

Fangs.

They glisten in the silver-gold light of the Ushum and the impossible sky, as curved and wicked as any blade. And when that brittle thing shifts within me, I know.

I *know.*

The power I channel, the flame at the heart of myself—*this* is the Midnight Serpent.

This is the flint at the heart of my soul.

And when I glimpse Lyanndra, shining brightly through the haze of fire, I finally understand what this ancient force was trying to tell me.

A god for a god.

Power for power.

She is the Godslayer, and I will burn for her.

CHAPTER 41

Lyanndra

There's blood in my eyes.

The whole world is tinged red, and I can barely see through the scarlet haze. Pain sears relentlessly across the right side of my face. The hot wash of it cascades down my cheekbone to drip into the collar of my breastplate, where it creeps beneath my dragonhide leathers with sticky, copper fingers.

Below, lances of agony strike my ribcage. Something's broken. A rib, probably. The shattered bone rends with every motion, but I grit my teeth and force myself to draw in a ragged breath, and then another.

My heart thunders in my ears, sending a fresh surge of adrenaline rushing through my veins as I adjust my stance. I'm battered and bloodied, but not broken. Not yet. And though my field of vision is strangely narrow—*don't think about it*, I urge myself in an attempt not to drown in the seething panic the realization brings—I can still heft my greatsword. I can still damage this thing.

If I'm lucky, I can still kill it.

But even as I ready myself to strike the Ushum once more, the beast lets out a high, keening whine that sets my whole body on edge.

It's afraid.

Of me?

No.

Struggling against the crimson timbre of my vision, I squint up at the abomination's visage. Its features, so horribly tiny for such a large, lumbering thing, are crumpled in terror. As I watch, its neck swings to stare, not at me, but at something to the left of us both.

I turn my head, mimicking its motion.

Then I see it.

Fire.

Black fire.

The flames rear up in a menacing arc, and while the world is blurred, narrow, and smeared with red, I know what this lithe shape is because I've seen it before.

This is the same gaping maw that snatched the strix out of the sky the night Syran found me on the northern snowfields, the one that streaked through the air after he carried Kartas' body into the courtyard of the palace at Nexus.

It's a snake wrought of the Lord of the Midnight Flame's fury, and that echo of his rage flares up within me now as the great viper hisses and flickers at the edge of the chamber.

And cloaked within the swirling blaze is a familiar figure, his armor gleaming gold against the darkness like a single, brilliant star exploding forth from the void. Red hair flashes. Eyes, green as poison, find mine.

Syran.

Relief thrills through my aching body, followed closely by a hot rush of need. Syran is here.

He's *here.*

And as the serpent above him rears its flaming head in a graceful, deadly dance, I catch a flash of silvery flame where its fangs should be.

Fangs.

My eyes, or at least the one that isn't wracked with pain, widen.

Could it be?

No.

No.

It's not possible. How could the fang be sitting beneath our noses this entire time? The odds are so slim, so impossible that it's foolish to even consider, and yet….

Syran's gaze slides from mine to fix upon the Ushum.

The creature is already lumbering toward him, though it seems hesitant to get too close. I take the opportunity to lash out with my greatsword, cutting through the thin gristle of its limbs as it goes, and while it shrieks out at the losses, it makes no move in my direction. Instead, it's focused entirely on my crossed star and the shock of flame that rises above him.

I can't blame the beast.

Like this, Syran looks ethereal. Impossible. *Divine.* The stardust that runs through his veins ignites at his command. And in this moment, I understand why the Demigods were so quick to name themselves so. The power Syran's father wielded was brutal and frightening, but the shimmering behemoth my crossed star summons now is beyond that. It's awful in its intensity, as beautiful as it is deadly.

This power, this dark and raging serpent, is a whisper of something ancient, something forgotten.

And now it is unleashed.

Almost too quickly for my eye to follow, the midnight flame flashes in a scorching wave toward the Ushum. There's no time for it to move out of the way. The spectral body of the viper coils around the creature's limbs as the thing shrieks and wails against the onslaught. And where the fire touches, the spindly appendages blister and crumble like old ash.

Spurred by the sight, I toss myself back into the fray.

Limbs, like brittle trunks of saplings, crack beneath the crushing force of my greatsword. Black embers swirl through the air as the Ushum thrashes against the joint attack, but I do not relent, and neither does Syran. Even though I can't see him from this side of the creature's molten form, I can feel him.

He came for me, as he vowed.

Ressa's machinations didn't matter. Aaro's venomous tale didn't drive him from me.

He did as he promised.

He chased me to the ends of Alastria, to this baking prison beneath the Caldera where we face, together, the blasphemy of the gods.

At that realization, a burst of tenderness so bright and strong that I swear it must glow from beneath my armor, explodes within me. And from the way the black flames surge in intensity, I think he must know it as surely as I do.

I'm going to tell him, I resolve.

As soon as this battle is won, as soon as the Ushum falls, I'm going to speak the blazing truth that's been building inside of me for so long. I think of his arrogant outrage when he fought me for the first time and the desperation on his face when he thought he was going to lose me. And when I came upon him getting hopelessly accosted by the strix, he gazed upon me with such triumph and longing that it was as though I was a goddess come to answer his prayers.

But he's wrong.

It's always been the other way around.

There are no gods that I worship, no stars that hear my pleas. But when I raise my sword, Syran follows. When I crumble, he gathers the pieces I leave behind and holds them patiently in his arms until I'm ready to mortar them back into the approximate places where they belong. He does not make me whole, but he makes me stronger.

If I am the arm, he is my blade.

He is my crossed star, and he belongs to me.

And above all else, I love him.

The surety of it drives me into a frenzy. Using the momentum of my body, I crease my greatsword through the air in a wide, circular swing. I count six snaps as brittle limbs break against the cleaving edge of my blade. The Ushum shudders, and when I glance up at it, I realize that it has very few arms and legs left on which to stand. Shimmering, viscous ichor drips lazily from its many wounds, slopping on the dry ground and splattering against my armor. It sizzles where it hits, but it doesn't burn through the steel.

If we keep this up, we can render the creature lame. With no limbs, it won't be able to break free from the last remaining husk of the Caldera. But I'm not so cruel to consider leaving it like that, broken and alone down here in the dark.

Together, we'll kill the Ushum. Not out of hatred or fear, or even to protect the kingdom.

When I strike the final blow, it will be out of mercy.

As I drive my blade through yet another limb—an arm, given the terrible pink hand that clutches at me from the end of it—a foot attempts to kick my legs out from under me. Without pausing, I drive the heel of my boot into the thin appendage. It snaps beneath my sole with a wooden creak.

But it's not the thing's limbs that I'm interested in.

If I can get to the neck, which whips around to brush the crumbling crust of the Caldera, then I can end this. All it will take is one clean strike.

"Syran!" I call. I don't know if he can hear me. My voice is dull in my ears, muffled by the endless buzz of the Ushum and from the damage it did earlier when it screamed. But in spite of the volume and the way my face aches with each movement of my jaw, I shout, "The neck!"

To my immense relief, Syran seems to understand because the flaming black coils of the serpent roil upward to twist over the Ushum's body.

At the burning contact, the creature roars.

The sound vibrates through the chamber, clattering my bones in their sockets and wrenching ancient rock down from the heights of the ceiling in great, jagged bursts. Beneath it, the beast's hide steams and hisses where the midnight flame licks it. The membrane blackens until it bursts under the heated pressure, and molten ichor slides forth from the wounds in a putrid, burning waterfall.

I gag against the stench and stumble backward, away from the fiery torrent of viscera. Heat shimmers off the ooze. Rocks melt and twist at its caress, and I have no doubts that if I were to touch it, it would roast the skin right off my bones.

I manage to clamber to safety at the edge of the chamber. The temperature is a little more bearable here, and I'm able to suck in a few heavy breaths while I watch Syran work.

He stands on the other side of the Ushum. Though he's alight with midnight flame, he does not burn. He's as he always is, broad and unyielding, his neat, angular features rendered harsh in the eerie glow. And when his eyes catch mine once more, the heat that sparks within them has nothing to do with his fire that consumes him.

The intensity of his gaze should frighten me, but it doesn't.

Instead, I feel another rush of longing so powerful that I can't tell if it comes from him or from me.

And then, even as his eyes remain on mine, the flaming serpent moves once more.

It swirls around the Ushum's body in a tightening spiral. Limbs crack beneath the pressure. The thing's membrane bubbles and bursts, spraying more ichor across the floor of the chamber. Yet, the viper's head moves higher, sliding up the towering body until it reaches the thin base of the creature's neck. There, it rears back with its mouth open wide.

Fangs flash silver in the unnatural light.

A great hiss rends the air.

And then the Midnight Serpent strikes true.

Flaming jaws clamp around the curve of the Ushum's neck. The sound the creature lets out is high and grating, but the flames don't falter, and the sheer violence of the assault forces the appendage down toward the steaming ground.

It's close, so close.

Just a little more....

Now.

With a roar to match the Ushum's, I raise my greatsword and launch myself toward the creature's exposed neck. The pain radiating through my face doesn't matter. The splintering of my ribs fades to nothing. And through the red film of blood that coats my working eye, I see the black flames that crawl across the wicked edge of my blade.

Steel sinks into flesh, or something close to it.

The Ushum screams.

So do I.

My blade cleaves down into the gelatinous, steaming trunk of its neck. Unhindered by bone or cartilage, the weapon slams into the ground unexpectedly with the force of my thrust. Black flames cough up in its wake, along with a spray of ichor that I just barely manage to avoid by ducking low beneath it.

The buzzing hum of the creature cuts off without warning.

Beneath me, my legs buckle.

The ground surges up at me as I remember just how much everything hurts—my face, my ribs, my *eye*—and I just barely comprehend the thick, wet smack of the Ushum's severed head falling at my side.

Then I'm next to it, staring into that slack and terrible face as the midnight flames creep up to embrace it like the mother that would never come.

"I'm sorry," I mutter.

But the child of the stars can't hear me.

Not anymore.

CHAPTER 42

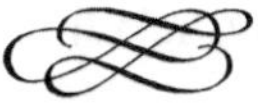

Syran

The Ushum is dead.

Its body shudders, and a second later, it collapses into a deflating bubble of ichor and ooze.

Black fire consumes the corpse in a greedy frenzy, rendering the mass of membrane and limbs into nothing but steaming ash. The face, too, is quickly swallowed up in flame, and it takes everything in me to keep my eyes from drifting toward it.

Instead, I seek out the Godslayer, who lies on her back close by the fallen god.

"Lyanndra!" I bellow.

She stirs, but only just.

Fear, hotter than any flame I could conjure, grips me tight in its searing fist. I sprint across the length of the chamber toward her, barely cognizant of the patches of ichor that sizzle through the soles of my boots or the midnight flames that curl around me.

All I see is her.

And as I run to my crossed star, she turns her head slowly. Too slowly. Pain flashes in her left eye, and in the other....

By the stars, there's so much blood. I can just barely make out five deep slashes beneath the crimson stain. They start at her hairline and crease down over the base of her nose, slicing through her right eyebrow, lid, and cheek before tapering off near her jaw. I can't tell how bad the damage to the socket is, not without washing the blood off and a healer's hands salvaging whatever's left, but it doesn't look good.

My heart shatters.

I fall to my knees beside her, not caring about the loud hiss as splatters of the Ushum's essence sizzle against my greaves, and wrap both hands around one of her small ones.

"Lyanndra," I murmur, as though her name could coax her back to me from wherever it is that she drifts.

"Syran." Her voice is soft and hoarse, but it seems to thunder through the vast space in the absence of the Ushum's hum. She meets my gaze with her uninjured eye and curls her fingers around mine. The weakness in her grip is alarming. "You came."

Blinking back the sting of tears, I nod. "I'm here," I assure her. "I have you."

She flashes me a pained smile. Blood coats her teeth.

"I vowed to you that I would chase you anywhere," I whisper to her as she raises her free hand up to trace the line of my jaw with the shaking fingertips of her gauntlet. Blood smears in their wake, hot and vital.

"I'm done running," she breathes. "Take me home."

And before I can reply, her hazel eye flutters closed.

"No!" I urge. "Lyanndra!" I draw one hand away from hers and reach beneath the collar of her armor to brush against the clammy skin of her neck. It takes me a moment to find her pulse.

It's weak, but steady.

She's alive.

Automatically, I open my mouth to call for Torran, but his name dies on my lips as quickly as it comes. He's not here. Neither is Kartas or anybody else who can help. It's just Lyanndra and me down here in the dark.

Nobody is coming for us.

I'll have to do this myself.

Resolute, I grab Lyanndra's greatsword from where it lies next to her. As always, the weight of it takes me by surprise. She makes the weapon seem featherlight when she swings it, but that only speaks to her skill in wielding such a monstrous hunk of steel. Even though golden ichor shimmers over the metal, I slide it into the sheath at her back. I know she'll chew me out later for returning the sword to its scabbard in such a condition, yet there's no other option.

She would, after all, be more furious if I were to leave it behind.

Then, with all the gentleness I can muster, I slide my arms beneath her unconscious form and lift her. A hiss of pain escapes her lips. The sound stabs at my soul, and I briefly consider putting her down again, but I fight the notion back. No good will come from lingering here. I need to get her out of the dark embrace of the mountain and into the care of a healer before she loses more blood, before she drifts too far from me.

I glance over at the opening of the tunnel that brought me here.

Now that the Ushum is dead, the only light comes from the flickering glow of my midnight flame, and from the pale wash of the moon that filters in through the damaged crust of the Caldera. The passage leading away from the chamber is a dark, gaping mouth in comparison.

Will I be able to find my way out again?

I'll have to, I resolve.

Getting lost down here is not an option.

My legs ache as I carry my crossed star into the yawning darkness. The wound at my ribs snarls with every step I take. Fear—of losing her, of watching her wake up only to realize what's been taken from her—pushes me forward in spite of my own injuries.

I cannot fail her.

Not again.

I don't know how long I trudge through the endless tunnels. It seems like a few moments, or maybe an eternity. The whole time, I'm vividly aware of the way Lyanndra's body melts against mine. Her face, the side not torn up by the Ushum, rests against the golden plate of my armor, and every so often, her hot breath fans against the exposed skin of my neck, reminding me that she's here and alive.

This is the woman who killed a god.

Not the echo of one like my father, but something unearthly.

Something truly divine.

And while my flame—the fang of the Midnight Serpent—may have subdued it, it was her blade that cleaved the head from its neck. It was she who stood before the Ushum and gazed, unwavering, at the terrible burden of its truth, when I couldn't bear to look upon it even in its death.

She is the Godslayer.

I'll carry her for as long as it takes.

And by the time light finally seeps into the ancient rock of this tomb, I think I might truly weep.

Up ahead, dry, warm daylight floods in through the mouth of the tunnel. I squint against it as disquiet turns in my chest.

Wasn't it night?

Weren't the moon and stars visible through the damaged ceiling back in the Ushum's chamber?

Or was that some trick of the senses, or perhaps even some strange magic wielded by the creature?

If Torran were here, he'd know the answer. He'd want to discuss it at length so that he could search in his books and scrolls until he found what he was looking for. But he's gone, and with the Godslayer fading in my arms, I find that I don't particularly care how or why the beast turned day to night.

All that matters now is Lyanndra.

As soon as I step toward the mouth of the cave, a cry rises from the other side. I barely process the words, though I recognize Orobos' face peering down at us once my eyes adjust to the welcome brightness.

"The Godslayer!" the soldier gasps. I'm surprised to see the fear that settles across his features beneath his upturned visor. "Is she...?"

"Alive," I say.

"And the Ushum, Your Highness?"

I want to tell him to *fuck* the Ushum, but I hold my tongue. Instead, I grit out, "Dead."

Orobos nods and then reaches down toward my crossed star. I don't want to relinquish her, not to him, not to anybody, but I can't climb out of here with her in my arms. Reluctantly, I shift her so that he can draw her still form up and out into the daylight.

"She needs a healer," I call after him. But as he disappears from the opening, he's already shouting for one, barking orders like a true general.

A second later, two more people take his place. One is a Celestial Knight, and the other is a Starless man about my age who shares the same dark eyes and black hair as Lyanndra's father. Is this one of her brothers, or a cousin, perhaps?

Either way, he and the soldier both extend their arms to me. Though it's rather undignified, I grab their hands and allow them to haul me from the depths of the tunnel, for it would be even worse to wriggle out of the ground like an errant worm, especially with the gift Aaro left upon my ribs.

And then finally, I'm out.

Dragging my feet from the mouth of the cave, I collapse back against the brown rock and blink up at the sky.

The air here is fresh and devoid of the stench of the Ushum. Sunlight beats down on my face and hands, but it's positively cool compared to the raging inferno we experienced beneath the Caldera.

Still, I don't pause to enjoy it.

"Where is she?" I demand of the knight who pulled me out.

"Your Highness, you're bleeding," the soldier counters as he attempts to guide me back down, but I push him away. It's the Starless man who points over to the side, where three healers, their cream-colored cloaks swirling in the thin breeze, hunch around a prone figure.

Lyanndra.

Biting back a hiss of pain, I drag myself to my feet and stagger over to where she lies.

The wounds to her face look worse in the stark light of day. Beneath the violent crimson stain of her blood, her skin is shockingly pale, and while it's hard to track her breathing beneath the tarnished plate of her armor, I catch her chest rising and falling at uneven intervals as the healers assess her injuries.

I don't want to get in their way, but I can't bear to part from her, either, so I lower myself down onto the rocky ground beside her and reach over until I can clasp her fingers against my palm. The metal of her gauntlet is cool against my skin and slick with blood.

Footsteps approach, and then a voice draws my gaze, though I don't let go of Lyanndra's hand.

"Demigod." I tilt my head up to look at my crossed star's father, who stares down at me with an unreadable expression. His eyes flicker first to Lyanndra, then our joined hands, and finally to the bloodied gold of my armor. "You're wounded."

At his words, one of the healers glances back at me and opens his mouth, but I shake my head. "The Godslayer first," I order.

"Yes, Your Highness." Though he looks uneasy, the Celestial Knight bows his head before returning to his task.

The Starless man frowns. "If she were awake, she'd tell you you're a starsdamned fool."

"Probably," I agree.

We stare at one another for a long moment, and just when I think he's going to curse me out further or tell me to get away from his daughter, he crouches down and nods to my golden armor. "Let me see," he says. It's not a demand, but it's not a polite request either. Rather, it's something in between.

A test.

"You're no healer," I argue, though there's little fight in my words. In truth, I'm too exhausted to do much else than hold Lyanndra's hand.

"Maybe not," he concedes, "but I was a soldier, back in the day. You wouldn't be the first man I've patched up after a fight."

I try to muster up a glare to ward him off, but instead, I find myself reaching up with my free hand to unclasp the straps of my breastplate. What harm will it do for him to take a look at my injury?

He waits patiently as I fumble for a moment before I finally manage to free the buckles. Then he does the rest, easing the armor from my chest as I draw in a sharp, pained breath at the motion. I wasn't wearing enough protective layers when Aaro sliced me. How could I have been so stupid as to let my guard down around that horrible little snake?

"You really are a fool." The Starless man shakes his head at the sight of my wound. "Did you cauterize this yourself?"

"I had no choice," I reply.

From the knowing gaze he levels upon me, I think he understands that it's the truth. There was no time to stop and dress it properly, not with Lyanndra heading down into the heart of the mountain. Even then, I was almost too late.

"We all do stupid things from time to time," he mutters. He draws a clean rag from his pocket and presses it against the wound, though not as roughly as I thought he would.

At my side, Lyanndra lets out a groan of pain. Her fingers tighten around mine, then slacken once more. But no sounds of alarm rise from the healers, who only murmur and continue their work. Even so, my panicked heart thunders in my chest.

In front of me, her father withdraws a skin from his belt and pours water on the rag before dabbing it back against my ribs. Concern is etched deep into his sun-worn features, and I wonder if perhaps he's helping me only to distract from his daughter's condition.

"Sir," I say, catching his attention.

One dark eyebrow arches in genuine shock at my civility.

"What is your name?"

For a moment, he's silent, but then he answers, "Morlas." Fixing his expectant gaze upon me, he asks, "And you?"

"Syran," I tell him, though I'm sure he must already know. And then, hoping that I'm doing it right, I stick out my free hand.

Morlas hesitates for only a moment before he claps his palm into mine.

"Well met," he says.

And I think, perhaps, he's right.

CHAPTER 43

Lyanndra

Pain.

It's the first thing that surfaces through the still, clear waters of my consciousness. The sensation starts as a deep ache that thrums through my skull, only to grow in intensity as awareness slinks back to me, bit by bit.

My face stings. No, that's not the right word. It *burns*.

There's something pressing against it, not tight exactly, but firm and strangely sticky against my screaming skin. I fight to open my eyes, to see what it is that's binding me, but I give up almost immediately when a bolt of agony flares through the right side of my head.

I hiss out a sharp breath through my teeth. All that does is jolt something to life in my chest—the familiar, rending tear of broken ribs.

Fuck.

I can't see. Everything hurts. Panic races through my veins as I struggle to move, to sit up, to do anything at all, to....

"It's all right, Lyanndra," a familiar voice murmurs from somewhere to my left. "You're safe. I have you." A large hand folds around one of mine, and another finds my shoulder, pressing me gently, but firmly, back down. Warmth seeps from his skin and into my bones, and I immediately settle.

"Syran?" I whisper.

Fabric shifts, and then lips brush the crease of my knuckles. "I'm here," he assures me.

And he is. This is no dream or illusion dredged up from my aching mind.

Syran is real.

Here.

Mine.

But are we still under the Caldera? The last thing I remember was watching the flames creep over the Ushum's face. By the stars, that *face.* Sorrow cuts almost as deep as the pain does. No matter how much devastation the creature caused, it wasn't evil. It wasn't even hungry.

It was *scared.*

A second press of Syran's mouth against my hand drags me back from the brink of my shame. I latch onto the gentle pressure in hopes that it will anchor me to the present.

It works, for my awareness comes creeping back to me.

This isn't the mountain. The stench of the Ushum is gone, replaced by the nostalgic perfume of fragrant spices—*somebody's cooking*, I realize dully. Gone is the hard rock beneath me. Instead, I'm lying on a mattress stuffed with sheep's wool, a material favored by the people of the Southern Caldera instead of the straw used in the north or the luxurious down of Nexus.

So when I ask, "Where are we?" I think that I already know the answer.

"Your family's homestead," Syran replies in a hushed tone. Or maybe he's speaking normally, because there's a hollow ringing in my ears that makes everything sound like it's coming to me from deep underwater.

I nod, or at least try to. Pain sears down the right side of my face as I tip my jaw, and I'm once again reminded of how battered I feel.

"Try to keep your head still," he advises. "The injury... it's bad."

"How bad?" I demand. My mind struggles to recall what happened. Did the Ushum strike me? Yes. Yes, it did. I remember its tiny nails digging deep into the skin of my face, catching on bone, on my *eye....*

When Syran speaks again, I can hear the carefulness in his tone. "Don't think on it now. You should rest."

"How *bad?*" I grit out again.

For a moment, I worry that he won't answer, but then he lets out a distressed sigh and squeezes my hand tightly against his palm.

"Your eye...." He shifts, this time bending over me so that his mouth presses against my knuckles once more. "It's gone."

I hear the words. I feel the shape of them on his lips against my skin. And maybe some part of me knew from the very moment the Ushum struck.

But it's one thing to hold awareness.

It's another to accept it.

"No," I insist. "That's... not right."

Syran's head shakes against my hand. "I'm sorry, Lyanndra," he whispers. "I'm so sorry."

"No!" I repeat, but there's no fight left in my voice, only grief that bubbles up in my throat like bile.

My eye.

Gone.

How will I fight? How can I be the Godslayer if I can't see?

As though he senses the despair that wells inside of me, Syran shifts so that his body presses gently against my left shoulder. "The other one is fine, just swollen shut," he says. "And you have two broken ribs, but the healers think you'll make a full recovery."

Except for my fucking *eye.*

How could this happen? It's not unheard of—I'm not so much of a fool as to think that. In fact, during my time as a soldier, I saw far too many facial wounds like this and even helped to treat some as best I could until a healer could intervene.

But I never thought it would be me.

How could this happen to *me*?

And it's with this question plaguing me that I once again drift off.

It's not sleep, exactly, but it's quiet and dark. I doze through sounds and mumbled voices, through the ghost of Syran's hands on mine and an unsettling, peeling sensation across my face.

And when I come back to myself again, I feel sharper than I did before. My broken ribs still grind, and the right side of my head still feels like Barra took a particularly large bite out of my skull, but the sharpness has given way to a dull, thunderous ache.

A small mercy, but one I welcome all the same.

And this time, when I try to open my eyes–*eye*, I correct spite-fully–my body actually obeys the command.

At first, the light is almost too much. Everything is hazy. Not red with blood, like it was when I killed the Ushum, but soft around the edges and slightly distorted.

The bed comes into focus first. There's a thick quilt, patched together from colorful old smocks and carefully embroidered with the shapes of lizards and running horses, draped over me. It's famil-iar, though I can't quite place it.

But before I can study my surroundings further, movement draws my eye. At my shoulder, a shape eases into view, and the way my breath catches in my chest has nothing to do with my shattered ribs.

Syran.

He sits at my bedside with his green gaze fixed unblinkingly on mine. In place of his golden armor, he wears a simple tunic and trousers, and his crown is nowhere to be seen. Instead, his long, fiery hair is braided back into several intricate sections. It takes me a moment to recognize the pattern as the one my father taught my brothers when they came of age.

I reach up to brush one of the plaits with my fingertips. My ribs protest at the movement, but not enough to keep me from touching the man I've yearned for over the last few months.

Without saying a word, he catches my hand in his and brings it to his lips. He kisses each knuckle with such reverence that I can hardly believe it's real.

That *he's* real.

"I missed you," I whisper.

He smiles, and when he speaks, his voice is tinged with relief. "And I, you."

Warmth settles in my chest. "How did you know to come for me?" I ask.

Syran's expression darkens, and I can feel the echo of his sudden rage through our bond as he utters, "Aaro."

The name hangs in the air between us.

A curse.

A blasphemy in its own right.

Ressa's words squirm through my memory at the mere mention of my former betrothed. She sent Aaro to him. Even now, even after the Ushum, does Syran still think that I would do such a dreadful thing as lie with Aaro?

I need to tell him. I need Syran to know that there is no world in which I would choose anybody but him.

"I didn't... I would never..." I stammer, trying to find the right words, but my brain is still locked in that strange, watery haze, and it's quickly becoming a struggle to speak at all. Finally, I settle on, "Ressa. She did this. She was behind all of it."

And to my surprise, Syran says, "I know."

I would have widened my eye in shock, if moving my face didn't hurt so fucking much. "You know?" I gasp.

He nods. "When that sneaky little bastard was spinning his tale, I realized that the bruise on his neck held the pattern of your armor." Fresh anger gleams in his eye as he asks, "Did he hurt you?"

"Not as much as I hurt him. But after what Ressa said, I should have killed him when I had the chance," I reply.

"I apologize for taking that opportunity from you," he says, though he doesn't sound the slightest bit repentant.

"Aaro's dead?"

"Yes."

A cold tide of satisfaction washes through me. I was willing to give him a chance that night in the field, but it seems that some people never change. The sense of justice I feel is quickly overpowered by the realization that if I had just told Syran about Aaro's transgressions from the start, then Ressa wouldn't have been able to play us for such fools.

Syran seems to notice my sudden shift in mood because his expression softens and he pleads, "Talk to me, Lyanndra."

I shift in the bed, as much as I'm able. "I... I should have said something about Aaro sooner. About all of it." I draw in a shuddering breath and add, "I'm sorry."

"How were you to know what he had planned?" Syran asks. He still holds my hand, and now he presses my palm flat against his chest. His heartbeat pulses beneath my fingers in a reassuring rhythm. "Neither of us suspected that Ressa was in Breem."

"It's not only that," I insist. "I thought you believed him. I thought you had forsaken me."

Anger and regret war for dominance over his angular features. "*Believed* him? Not for a fucking *second*," he growls, though I know him well enough to understand that his ire isn't directed at me. "And I would never–*never*–abandon you, Lyanndra. Surely you know that?"

"Then why?" I argue. "Why didn't you come to me in our dreams?"

"I was furious. I... wasn't thinking clearly. And we left for Breem that night, and I didn't want to risk Aaro overhearing me speaking in my sleep, not when our voices carry over from our encounters," he explains. "I thought... I thought I was helping, bringing Aaro back to you so he could stand at your mercy for what he tried to do. But I realize now that I should have come to you." Grief settles into the depths of his gaze as he utters, "I was a fool, and Torran paid the price for my mindlessness."

Torran?

What does Syran mean by that, *paid the price*?

And from the way my crossed star's expression folds, I have the terrible feeling that I know what the answer will be when I ask, "What happened?"

"He's dead."

The words seem to echo through the room with the ferocity of the Ushum's wail.

Disbelief strikes first.

I picture Torran and those shocking blue eyes, and think, *how is that possible*? He was undeniably old and had a certain frailness about him after Kartas ran him through with an arrow, but he was still brimming with life and that strange, knowing intensity he always held in his gaze.

"How?" is all I can muster.

"Aaro." Syran's voice is tinged with bitter hatred. "He stabbed Torran. I made sure he suffered for it. For everything."

"I'm sorry," I whisper.

For not forewarning him about Aaro.

For Torran.

For failing to kill Ressa, who manipulated us all so expertly, down in the tunnels.

Syran nods. His loss, deep and endless, pours through our bond as surely as it spills across his features. Instead of speaking, he sinks down off his chair to kneel next to the bed and then leans forward so that his head rests gently against my uninjured side.

I close my eye at the warmth of his touch.

I've waited so long for this moment, to see Syran again, but I never expected it to come like this. And while I wish I were well enough to take him in my arms properly, I settle for sifting my fingers through his braided hair and smoothing the unruly, escaped strands away from his forehead.

There's so much I want to ask, but now is not the time.

Did he feel the same raw power that coursed through me during the fight with the Ushum? It was like when we faced the strix all those months ago, but *more. Deeper.* It shuddered down to my bones, down to the very threads of my soul.

And what of the flaming serpent he summoned? I have no doubts that it was the fang of legend, but *how?*

And how is it that I–*we*–killed a god, and yet, I've never felt weaker?

Questions churn through my mind as I rest my hand against Syran's cheek. His skin is damp beneath my fingertips.

My heart aches.

We both lost something, I realize.

Will either of us ever be whole again?

CHAPTER 44

Syran

"You don't have to do this."

From where she stands before the barrel of water outside her family's homestead, Lyanndra tilts her head and skewers me with a glare that could have silenced the Ushum. Even with one eye, her message is clear.

She'll do whatever she damn well pleases.

It's only after I hold up my hands in surrender that she turns back to the barrel.

There are no mirrors or looking glasses out here in Breem. Given how common they are in Nexus, I never realized that they were considered a luxury elsewhere. For the last few days since I learned this, I've been assessing every corner of the homestead in an attempt to figure out what other mundane items the Starless go without on a daily basis.

But Lyanndra doesn't let the lack of a conventional mirror stop her. She wants to see herself now that her wounds have started to heal, and without a looking glass, still water is the next best thing.

With brutal certainty etched across her features, she spares me one last glance.

Then she leans over the barrel.

I hold my breath.

Her expression doesn't change, but I feel the echo of her emotions tumbling through me in a chaotic wave.

Shock. Horror. Disgust. Fear.

Despair.

Resignation.

I want to go to her. I want to wrap my arms around her and tell her that no matter what she sees in her reflection, she's still beautiful. The scratches, scabbed over now and beginning to scar where the skin has healed, are a mark of her strength and ferocity.

Just like her golden helm, these are trophies of war.

Of victory.

Yet, she doesn't view them this way. I feel it in the long silence that creeps between us and in the way the grief never quite makes it onto her face. It speaks, louder than any words, through the bond, so strong and insidious that it almost forces me to my knees.

But I refuse to yield to the weight of her anguish. I made a vow to her that I would carry her burdens when they become too much, and I will shoulder this one for as long as she needs me to. This will not crush her. This will not take away my moon's luster.

She will not fall to this.

Anger—at the Ushum, at the stars—broils in the pit of my stomach as I close the distance between us. Lyanndra doesn't move when I come up behind her. Mindful of her healing ribs, I wrap my arms around her and rest my chin on the top of her head.

"Tell me what you're thinking," I plead.

One hazel eye meets mine in our joint reflection. Seconds tick by. I know this is hard for her, but I will wait as long as is necessary.

And then finally, she mutters, "I barely even recognize myself."

I draw back just far enough to press a kiss to the top of her head. "You're different than you were before," I say. "You slayed a god."

"Don't patronize me, Syran. I lost an *eye*," she counters, though there's no real venom lurking behind the fangs of her words. *"Look at my fucking face."* She gestures sharply down to her reflection, which ripples when the tips of her fingers brush the water's surface. "Do you see the Godslayer there? A queen? Because I see neither. I don't even see *myself."*

Something hot flares within me. Deep in my chest, the Midnight Serpent hisses and twines.

"I see *you,*" I tell her firmly. "Lyanndra. The Godslayer. Queen of Alastria. My wife. There is no wound—no god—that will make you unworthy or less than you were before. And when you doubt that, even for a *second,* remember this: There is no power in the fucking stars that will ever stop me from loving you."

Surprise flashes through the bond, as quick and decisive as a blade. And then something else follows on its heels, fierce, burning, and drenched in moonlight.

Unyielding.

Before I can react, Lyanndra spins in my arms. She grips the front of my tunic with desperate hands and pulls me down so that my lips hover just above hers.

"What did you say?" she hisses.

If I knew her any less intimately, I would think she's angry—furious, even. But I recognize this passion. I crave it. And I tease it from her now by brushing my mouth over hers as I repeat, "I see you."

She rolls her eye. Her nails bite into my skin through the fabric of my tunic, and I grin as she snaps, "No. The *other* thing."

"Oh," I say in the lightest tone I can muster. *"That."* Then, I lean down further, dragging my lips over the crease of her mouth and the tempting skin of her cheek before I finally reach the shell of her ear. Only then do I whisper, "I love you."

Time stops.

I breathe in.

My heart beats.

And then Lyanndra releases her fingers from their death grip on my tunic, only to trace her hands up to cup my jaw. I allow her to guide me back just far enough so that her eye can meet mine.

"You love me?" she asks, as though she can't quite believe it.

"Until the stars fall."

It's the easiest vow I have ever made, and I'll swear it a thousand times over if that's what it takes to make her believe it. I will remind her every single day if I have to, every hour, until it's etched so deeply into her soul that she can never doubt it again.

"I love you," I repeat before pressing a gentle, scalding kiss to her lips.

Her mouth chases mine as I pull back, this time searching for answers of my own. I think I know them already, *feel* them already, but I need to hear her say it.

By the fucking stars, I need *her*.

Her eye sears into mine, her stare unwavering.

"What would you say," she murmurs, "if I told you that *I* love *you?*"

Fire sparks in my heart as a smirk creeps across my face. "I'd say that it's about fucking time."

She smiles.And then she says it.

"I love you."

One breath.

That's all that passes before I claim her mouth with mine. She drags me mercilessly down into her depths, and I let her. I drown for her, willingly and completely, because there is no other air to fill my lungs, no other blood to surge through my veins, no other embers to fan within me until I burn and burn and *burn*.

The kiss isn't gentle.

Though I do my best not to press upon her healing scars, I want her to know just how much I yearn for her. It's been so long since we last took pleasure in each other, and even the precious stolen moments we've enjoyed have been few and far between with Lyanndra's parents and her endless stream of siblings bustling about.

Every instinct screams at me to bend her over the barrel and take her right here, but I don't.

Her ribs are still mending, and the wound Aaro left me, while more or less healed, continues to pull uncomfortably whenever I move my arms around with too much enthusiasm.

So for now, I settle for tasting her in my second favorite way.

But like most of our moments of privacy here in the shadow of the mountain, this one is far too fleeting. Around the corner of the homestead, the door to the yard swings open, and somebody barks, "Syran!"

The voice is demanding and unmistakable.

Inwardly, I groan.

Lyanndra's mother.

Ever since I got here, she's been taking advantage of both my height and my devotion to her daughter. At her direction and without complaint, I patched the roof. I cleaned the hearth. I swept cobwebs from the rafters, chipped pieces off the block of charcoal they use for fuel, and even helped her father and brothers repair the loft in the barn. My injury seems of no consequence to her, not when I can make myself useful.

Knowing full well that I'm about to be assigned some menial task that will probably leave me covered in grime, Lyanndra breaks the kiss and flashes me a wicked grin.

I shake my head, silently pleading with her not to give me away.

Her smirk widens. She cocks her head and quirks her intact eyebrow, while the other makes a valiant effort to follow suit. And for a moment, I think she's going to call out to her mother and turn me in, but then she grabs my hand and pulls me around the back of the homestead just as the family matriarch shouts my name once more.

Even with her injuries, Lyanndra moves with quiet, predatory grace. I follow suit, doing my best not to burst out laughing until we make it to the safety of the barn.

As soon as we step inside the stable, Barra swings her huge head over the door of her stall and lets out a low whicker. Lyanndra offers her a scratch behind the ears before continuing toward the back of the space, while I simply nod to the beast in hopes that she understands. While I've touched the kelpie before, I'm still wary around her, especially when she opens the gaping crease of her jaw and snaps her teeth in my direction.

The first time the creature did that, Lyanndra informed me, "She likes you." I didn't have the heart to tell my crossed star that I think Barra does indeed like me in the same way that the strix did—for dinner, and not as a guest.

Now, I skirt uneasily around Barra's head. Her gleaming red eyes track me as I follow Lyanndra into the shadows at the back of the barn, where she's already climbing up the short ladder that leads to the hayloft. I don't even both averting my eyes first from her swaying ass and then, seconds later, from the tantalizing view that flashes beneath the skirt of her borrowed smock.

She glances down just in time to take in my appreciative stare and rolls her eye.

"Enjoying yourself?" she asks.

I grin. "Quite."

Then I haul myself up the ladder after her.

There's barely enough space for a single person up here amongst the clutter, let alone two of us, but we make it work. Lyanndra shuffles so that she's perched upon a hay bale, while I take up most of the floor. To anybody who wanders into the barn, we're effectively invisible like this.

For a long while, we sit in silence. The only sounds are the bleating of the goats and the gentle stamping of hooves in straw. The air is dusty, the smell of sweat and fur balanced by the sweetness of the hay, and the sun that streams in through the gaps in rafters is lazily warm against my skin.

I understand now why Lyanndra favors this place and why she spends so much time at the Celestial Court's stables. Perhaps I'll commission the royal builders to build her a loft there. I think she would like that.

Maybe she'd even reward me for it.

Different scenarios—my tongue buried deep inside her, her mouth closing around my aching cock, her moaning as I pound relentlessly into her—parade through my mind. They'll have to keep me sated until we return to Nexus, but then....

My mind continues its salacious wander for quite some time, and it's only when the daylight cures to gold that Lyanndra says, "Tomorrow."

The word snaps me back from my fantasies.

"Tomorrow?" I repeat blankly.

"We go home," she clarifies. "To Nexus. It's time, isn't it?"

Home.

I picture her spread out on the black silk sheets of our bed or bent over the railing of the balcony. I'm sure we can find some use for the desk, too, if we try hard enough.

So without bothering to disguise the eagerness in my voice, I agree, "If you feel well enough to ride, then I'll follow anywhere. But home sounds appealing."

In response, she offers me a soft smile that shines like starlight amidst the growing shadows of the afternoon. "Then it's decided. We depart for Nexus at dawn." But then her peaceful expression falls, and she says, "I think we should station a few Celestial Knights here and in the other villages before we leave."

Disquiet traces cold fingers down my spine. "Do you really think Ressa and that… that *shadow* will be back?" I ask.

"I don't know," she admits. "But I wouldn't put it past either of them to target my family."

"They'd be fools to do so. Surely, they know by now, as most of the kingdom does, that you felled a *god*. What hope would either of them have against you?"

Lyanndra sneers, as she's wont to do whenever my former betrothed is mentioned. "The shadow can only be wounded if it chooses to first become whole. And *my sister*," she spits out with particular vitriol, "is utterly mad."

"Ressa is *not* your sister," I state. This is not the first time we've had this conversation, and I fear it won't be the last.

But she just shakes her head in response. "Are you sure of that, Syran? My parents—we aren't blood. I could be *anybody's* sister, or daughter."

While I can't deny her point, still I insist, "It's impossible."

She narrows her eye at me. "As impossible as you embodying the Midnight Serpent?"

And I want to say that it's different, but I know deep down that it's not. Ever since my flame subdued the Ushum, I've been struggling to come to terms with the fact.

Something ancient burns inside of me.

Something forgotten.

Something arcane.

"The book Torran found spoke of a connection between the Moon Prophecy and the fang of the Midnight Serpent," she continues. "The shadow thinks that Ressa and I are the sisters from the prophecy. Do you really think this is mere coincidence?"

No.

I don't.

Dread claws forth to feast upon my candor. I know Lyanndra can feel it, and though her frown deepens, she says nothing more. For what can either of us intone that will change what Torran uncovered in his blasphemous texts?

The fang of the Midnight Serpent will usher in the Moonlit Age.

The end of the Demigods.

The end of Alastria.

The end of *us*.

Finally, if only to break the dreadful silence, I say, "It's not like you to take Demigod superstitions to heart."

Lyanndra's eye flashes as she rises to meet my challenge. "I don't," she replies. "But the shadow clearly does. Right or wrong, we need to learn more about the Moon Prophecy. It will do us no good to move forward in ignorance."

I nod. "Then we shall, as soon as we return to Nexus." *Without Torran*, I think with a pang of grief. How are we supposed to find out anything at all without him?

She must feel my sudden sorrow through the bond because she reaches over and laces her fingers through mine. As the warmth of her skin seeps into my palm, I'm gripped with the longing to leave this place. I want to sleep in my own bed with Lyanndra curled into my side. I want the familiar foods served fresh from the palace kitchens and the practiced greetings of the courtiers.

I want to go home.

Shifting slightly to face her, I ask, "Shall I speak with your parents this evening after dinner?" While she, too, desires to take her leave of Breem, I know that part of her must feel conflicted. I'll brave her mother's sharp eye and her father's judgment if it means making this easier for her.

But Lyanndra shakes her head.

And she doesn't have to explain herself. I understand.

She wants to do it properly this time.

She wants to say goodbye.

CHAPTER 45

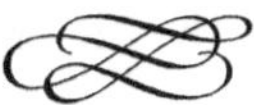

Lyanndra

We're going home.

The thought rises with me as I slip out from beneath the quilt of my old bed for what I hope is the last time. It's still dark, though the edges of dawn paint the room with a thin, watery glow.

Beyond the wax paper covering the windows, I can hear the bustle of the host's encampment, which is in the process of being torn down and stowed away into several wagons borrowed from nearby villages. Most of the Celestial Knights will accompany us back to Nexus. The few who remain will guard Breem, and by extension, my family.

A creak sounds upon the threshold.

I turn in time to watch Syran, who's probably been sitting awake half the night, creep through the shrouded doorway. He's already dressed in the gleaming gold shell of his armor. Against the backdrop of his cloak, he looks like a star personified, like something out of a vision.

Like a god.

His eyes catch mine, and he smiles.

Love, warm and brilliant, blooms through me. I can't tell if it's my own, his, or a mixture of both, but I welcome it all the same.

It amazes me how he can still gaze upon me with such reverence in spite of my injuries. What does he see that makes him choose me, again and again, in the face of all logic and wisdom?

For, I'm bare to him now.

I no longer need to wear the bandages. The wounds are shocking and gruesome, though I know they'll grow less livid as they continue to heal, but there's no practical reason to cover them. Still, it occurred to me after seeing my reflection yesterday that I could hide the damage away.

Yet, a few strips of cotton won't erase what was done to me.

My stomach churns as I realize that I'll have to confront the Ushum's mark every time I glimpse my reflection, whether it be in a mirror, a barrel of water, or the shockingly spotless surface of Syran's armor.

Resolution burns through me.

I will find a way to deal with my narrowed vision and this face I no longer recognize. I hid myself behind the Flaming God's golden helm for long enough. Let people see the proof that I put a god to my sword and survived to speak of it. Let them whisper of my victories. Let them understand the price I paid.

I am the Godslayer.

And if I have to live with this, so does everybody else.

Across the room, Syran's smile sharpens into something on the edge of lecherousness. "You look like you're plotting a murder," he whispers, keeping his voice low so that he doesn't alert my parents to his presence. "Who are we killing?"

"You, if you keep staring at me like that," I hiss, which only makes him grin wider.

"Like what?" he challenges as he stalks toward me.

"Like you love me."

That gets a rise out of him.

Literally, given the pink stain that washes over the high angles of his cheekbones and the way he reaches down to shift himself beneath his armor.

Now, it's my turn to smirk. "Are you well, Syran?" I ask sweetly.

"No," he growls. "But I can think of something that will help."

He lunges forward, quick as a flame, and wraps his arms around my waist. It's all I can do not to squeal when he presses the hot length of his body against my back. Then his lips are on my neck, his teeth grazing my skin while his hands skim over every part of me, save for my healing ribs.

"Once we're alone–be it in our chambers, a room at an inn, or on the fucking *ground*–I'm going to show you *exactly* how much I love you," he promises. His breath ghosts over my ear, and I tremble against him. "I'm going to burn for you, Lyanndra, down to my very soul."

By the *fucking* stars.

I want him.

I *need* him.

And just as I think I'm going to combust for the heat of him, he steps away.

Chilly morning air rushes in where he was standing, but when I shiver, it's not just from the cold.

I know he's teasing me. There's nothing we can do here, not unless we want the entire homestead to hear us. But he's not the only one who can use his body to his advantage.

Without sparing him a single glance, I reach up and pull at the tie that holds the bodice of my simple nightdress shut.

Laces unravel.

Fabric parts.

Behind me, Syran lets out a deep, wavering breath.

His eyes burn into my back as I shrug the garment off of my shoulders, allowing it to slide down over my skin until it pools around my bare feet. Underneath, I wear absolutely nothing.

And when I bend down to pick the nightdress up off the floor, Syran groans.

"That shadow was right," he mutters. "You really are a beastly little thing."

Even though he can't see me, I roll my eye. I never realized how much I would come to regret telling him about that particular part of my encounter with the figure. He hasn't stopped calling me that since.

I'll never admit to him that I actually like the way it sounds when he says it. In fact, an army couldn't torture that out of me.

So to punish him, I let the show continue. I take my time retrieving my smallclothes, leathers, and armor. Only when the sound of the host's horn cuts through the morning air, signaling sunrise, do I finally dress.

"So cruel," Syran murmurs as he kneels to strap on my greaves. I can do it myself, and he knows it, but there's something devastatingly intimate about the way he takes such care to adjust each buckle and clasp. He performs the ritual with the devotion of a saint. And when he's crouched before me like this, I can't help but imagine the other ways he worships me on his knees.

Heat pools between my legs at the thought.

Suddenly, I can't wait to get back to Nexus, where I'll hold him to his promise with ruthless efficiency.

It doesn't take long after that to don the rest of my armor. After sweeping Syran's velvet cloak over my shoulders, I tuck the golden helm under my arm. But before I can make it to the door, my crossed star catches my hand.

"Aren't you forgetting something?" he asks.

I shake my head.

Mischief sparks in his emerald gaze as he draws something tucked away beneath the curve of his breastplate. Gold flows like liquid across his bare palms. Delicate stitching, dark as midnight, swirls over the fabric in the shape of a great serpent. And though some of the edges are a little ragged and spattered with old, dry blood, I would know it anywhere.

Syran's token.

It shouldn't shock me. Didn't Ressa say that she had Aaro steal it and bring it to Syran in an attempt to frame me for treason? Of course the Lord of the Midnight Flame would hold onto it. Of course he would bring it back to me.

Yet, warm surprise filters through me like sunlight as he steps forward and draws the strip of cloth around my left arm, nearest to my heart. He stands close, far more than is necessary. His breath fans my cheek. Strands of crimson hair brush the column of my neck, and I sigh.

"There," he says once the token is tied just above my elbow, back where it belongs. "A favor for my champion."

Smiling, I stretch up onto my toes and turn my head to catch the corner of his mouth with my lips. "And a kiss for my maiden," I jest.

"I fear I received the short end of this bargain, if that's all the thanks I get," he growls. Then he swoops down, capturing me in a searing embrace that leaves me gasping for air. It's only when a loud thud—a footstep, I realize with a jolt—sounds from the doorway, followed by a decidedly indiscreet cough, that Syran pulls back.

I peek around his broad shoulder to catch a glimpse of our interloper and immediately cringe. Blood rises to my cheeks. Still, I have enough decorum left to nod to my father, who looks equally embarrassed to have witnessed such a spectacle.

Syran, on the other hand, seems to possess far less grace than I. "Morlas! We were... I was just... I was helping Lyanndra with her armor," he stammers in a manner that's decidedly unbecoming for the King of Alastria. "Putting it on, I mean. Not... not taking it off... or anything...."

My father's stony expression doesn't change. He waits until my crossed star's voice trails off into nothing before he suggests to him, "Why don't you go saddle up Barra? I'd do it myself, but I'm afraid I'd lose a hand if I tried."

The mighty Lord of the Midnight Flame, whose face is flushed a delightful shade of pink, nods once. He spares me an agonized glance before he skirts through the doorway, giving my father as wide a berth as he's able.

Once he's gone, I grit my teeth.

Any second now, my father is sure to unleash a diatribe against the Demigods and their king, and my decision to marry him.

But the silence only stretches on and on until finally I look up at my father to find not anger, but a strangely soft expression that I can't quite place.

"Do you truly choose him?" he asks when I meet his eye. "Not the throne he can give you, nor the power that comes with it. *Him.*"

I don't need to even think about my answer.

I nod.

Because if Syran were a Starless peasant without a gold piece to his name, I'd want him. If he abdicated his royal title and spent the rest of his life following me across Alastria as I helped our people, that would be enough. And if I weren't the Godslayer, it would still be him.

Always.

Until the stars fall.

"When he came riding into Breem, he was like a man possessed," my father continues in a tone so gentle that it's almost unnerving. "He was so desperate to get to you, to keep you from harm. And when he brought you out, and you were bleeding, he… he held your hand, Lyanndra. The whole time. Wouldn't even let the healers have their way with him until they treated you first. I had to fight with him just to let me look at his wound."

Something warm curls around my heart, and I admit, "He never told me."

"That's because he's a starsdamned fool," he replies, "and a proud little bastard, though I suppose that's to be expected from a king. But he's a good man, even if he is a Demigod, and more importantly, he *loves* you."

My eye widens in surprise.

How does my father know that? Did he overhear one of Syran's many admissions yesterday?

The panic must show on my face because he laughs.

"It's obvious, Lyanndra," he says. "He looks at you like you're the sun itself, like you're the sole light in his universe. And no man would sit by your bedside the way he did or put up with your mother's nonsense if he didn't care for you. You're lucky. And so is he, because you gaze at him the same way."

My cheeks burn, but I don't deny it.

Is it really that plain to see?

"Now enough of this," he says, finally shifting from his spot in the doorway. "Your mother is waiting to see you off."

Inwardly, I recoil.

This is the part I've been dreading.

My father is a soldier. He knows what it is to leave a place and not know if he'll ever see it again. But my mother lost me once, and I worry that she won't be so quick to give me up again, especially to Syran, who she seems to hate.

She's waiting for us in the kitchen. From the puffy, red skin around her eyes, I surmise that she's already been crying for the better part of the morning.

When I enter the room, she jumps to her feet and stares.

Having my eye ripped out by the Ushum had the unexpected benefit of warming her to me once more. Instead of shying away as she did after the skirmish with the marauders, she took every opportunity while I was healing to fuss and dote to a stifling degree. And, of course, she did her very best to ensure that Syran and I never got more than a few minutes alone with one another, lest anything scandalous occur.

Now, she almost seems surprised to see me in my armor, instead of one of my sisters' borrowed smocks.

"Lyanndra," she murmurs when I approach.

"Mother," I say back.

We regard one another for a long moment.

She's the first to break our uncomfortable stalemate. She strides forth and gathers me in her arms as she did when I first returned to the homestead. Her embrace is tight and warm, and she smells faintly of coriander and cumin, the spices of my childhood.

When she pulls away, she cups one hand on my unmarred cheek.

Her eyes snag upon my wounds and the empty socket left behind before meeting my gaze.

"I don't understand your spirit, Lyanndra. Maybe I never will. But you're my daughter regardless, and I want you to be happy," she says.

I nod.

She offers me a thin, tearful smile before pulling me back against her breast.

"You're going to make a beautiful queen," she whispers. And while part of me recoils and hisses, *not anymore*, the rest of me strives to believe her words.

By the time she releases me from her hold, I'm ready to go.

"I should check on Syran," I tell her, "to make sure that Barra hasn't decided to eat him after all."

My mother shakes her head. "I can't believe your father braided that man's hair. A *Demigod*. What was he thinking?"

"And I can't believe that you put Syran to work like a housemaid," I argue.

"He did a good job on the roof, I'll give him that," she huffs. It's her equivalent of a shining complement, and I'll accept it as such on my crossed star's behalf. "He'll have to do the other side the next time you visit." She narrows her eyes at me. "You will come back, won't you? You know you have a home here in Breem."

"And you're always welcome in Nexus," I reply, dodging her question entirely.

That seems to placate her, for she reaches out and grips my hands tightly in hers.

"I love you, Lyanndra, whatever path you choose," she says earnestly. "Don't forget that."

I nod.

I won't forget.

Breem has left its mark on me, and it runs deeper than I care to admit.

CHAPTER 46

SYRAN

Lyanndra is stunning.

Sunlight gleams off her tarnished armor. Beneath the golden halo of her hair, the fury of the Ushum streaks, red and vivid, across the right side of her face. Her stolen cloak swirls at her back, and I think it looks far better on her than it ever did on me.

It doesn't take her long to notice my stare. When she does, she tilts her head slightly in a silent question and quirks her uninjured brow.

I smirk at her.

She rolls her eye.

Heat rushes through me at the sight.

By the stars, I love this woman. From where she sits astride Barra, she looks every inch the ruthless, cunning warrior I know her to be. Even with her golden helm off and strapped to Barra's saddle, her new scars only add to her fierce countenance.

She fought the Ushum and lived.

How many soldiers can say that they slayed a god?

How many queens can claim that they served their kingdoms with such honor?

Fuck the Winter Solstice, I decide in that instant. I'm not going to wait a second longer than necessary to marry her. We don't need a ceremony or the endless ramblings of the clerics. The stars have already spoken. There is no ritual left that could bind us further, for we are already one in all the ways that matter.

Lyanndra will be my wife.

My queen.

My everything.

And I will be hers, her fire and her blade, wholly and without restraint.

A Celestial Knight approaches on horseback, drawing me from my thoughts.

Interestingly, he stops before Lyanndra and bows his head to her first before he offers me the same courtesy. Perhaps I should find the order of his actions insulting, but instead, it only wicks the flame of my pride higher.

When the host rode from Nexus under my crossed star's command, they didn't respect her, not entirely. Whether it was because she is Starless, a woman, or a combination of both, I do not know, but I was painfully aware of her stoic acceptance of their minor insubordinations.

But now, the soldiers ride at her command.

It's the Godslayer they turn to first. It's her they obey. They've seen her as I have, as a woman of honor and a brother in arms.

And in time, they will follow her anywhere.

"Godslayer," the Demigod says. From the voice alone, I surmise it's Orobos who hides behind the visor of the helm. "The host is ready."

She acknowledges him with a nod and then glances over her shoulder to where the Celestial Knights are amassed at our backs.

Aside from some charred earth where the cooking fires were and a few patches of trampled brown grass, there's little sign that there was ever a camp erected on this land. Beyond, the soldiers are already in their full armor. Many sit atop their horses, though several seem to have lost their mounts somewhere along the way. I imagine that they're as eager as we are to return to Nexus.

It's time.

Lyanndra turns back to her parents, who linger just out of reach of Barra's wicked teeth.

Like his daughter, Morlas is stoic and composed, though I don't miss the way his eyes glisten in the morning sun. He steps forward and reaches one hand out to her. She takes it and smiles. "May your journey be an honorable one," he says softly.

Lyanndra nods.

I expect him to step back after that, but he doesn't.

Instead, he turns to me.

His gaze flickers first to the braids in my hair, which he insisted on teaching me how to weave in the early days of Lyanndra's recovery, before he finally meets my eyes. And I may not know everything about the Starless and their regional customs, but I'm no fool.

I've noticed the same pattern plaited into his sons' hair.

So when he offers his hand, I take it willingly. "Thank you," I tell him. "I will not forget your hospitality."

"And I will not forget your integrity," he replies, "or the way you care so fiercely for my daughter. It's an honor to name you as my own."

Something twists in my gut. It's not painful, exactly, but it's heavy and unfamiliar, and I'm not sure what to think of it.

Though the words stick in my throat, I manage to choke out, "The honor is mine."

He nods. The gesture is eerily similar to Lyanndra's, and I'm reminded once more that sometimes family transcends blood entirely.

Only then does he return to his wife's side.

In stark contrast, Lyanndra's mother is a mess of tears and emotion. Even now, she fusses over her daughter, passing her neatly wrapped parcels that, judging by the tantalizing smell of them, contain the dried herbs and teas that the people of the Southern

Caldera favor in their cooking. They exchange quiet words, their voices too low for me to hear, before she finally withdraws.

I grit my teeth and hope that she won't approach me.

She doesn't.

After stowing the parcels away in her saddlebags, Lyanndra raises one hand in a silent goodbye. Her parents do the same.

And then it's done.

We're ready.

The Godslayer is the one to give her command. She stretches her left arm up higher in lieu of her greatsword. The token tied above her elbow flashes brilliantly in the clear morning sunlight.

Behind us, the host stills.

Then she brings her hand down in an arc, her fingers creasing through the air toward the road.

Toward Nexus.

Toward home.

The host does not need to be told twice.

Our short trip through Breem is a blur. I barely take stock of the villagers who gather to see us off or of the gifts they hand to soldiers as we go. All that matters is the woman who rides at my side and the way she nods and occasionally smiles at the people we pass.

Seeing her like this, I have no doubts that she was truly meant to rule.

And then we're out.

The low buildings of Breem grow smaller in the distance with every passing minute. At our backs, the shadow of the Southern Caldera clutches at us with stubborn fingers, but it loses its grip soon enough. And in spite of the arid beauty of this strange, brown land-scape, I can't say I'm loath to leave it behind.

Nexus calls to me.

It's been weeks, nearly a month, since I slept in my own bed. Lyan-ndra has waited longer still. The fortnight it will take to journey to the Celestial Court will, with any luck, pass quickly and without incident.

But there's something we have to take care of first.

Something I've been dreading.

Lyanndra must pick up on my sudden trepidation because she guides Barra closer and fixes me with a curious glance.

"I...."

How do I speak of the bitter truth I now face? Even though I held Torran in my arms, even though I scrubbed his blood from under my nails, saying it aloud means admitting it. Forcing the words out makes it real.

So I settle on telling her, "There is something I must do before nightfall."

She doesn't question it.

She only nods.

My grief builds as we venture closer to the place where Torran was killed. Guilt seethes through my veins.

I should have come back here sooner.

I should have sent soldiers to retrieve the fallen Demigod's body.

But my pride kept me from such reasonable actions, for I told myself I had to face this myself, and to delegate the task would be disrespectful. And I would not leave Lyanndra's side for anything, not even for my departed advisor's honor.

But now, when we reach the campsite about an hour before dusk, I realize that the real discourtesy was in leaving Torran's remains here to fester.

The area is a mess. It wasn't neat when I left it, but it's clear from the scattered debris that opportunists—predators and looters alike—took advantage of the situation.

With fresh regret rising in my throat, I slide off my mount. Beside me, Lyanndra does the same.

She studies the area with grim resolution, but I have no need for such observations.

I know what I'm looking for, and I find it without difficulty.

It's clear from a single glance that Torran's body, wrapped in the faded gold fabric of his tent and partially hidden behind a rocky outcropping, has been disturbed. The cloth is ripped—bitten, I think, not cut–and I don't want to see what's left behind, but I force myself to look.

Bones. Bits of rancid flesh still stuck to them.

Silver hair, long and somehow still braided.

Rich purple robes, torn and frayed.

I stumble backward. Vomit rises in my throat, and though I try to swallow it back down, I lose that particular battle with violent abandon all over the hard, brown rock of the ruined campsite.

The Celestial Knights, at least, have the decorum to turn and pretend not to notice as I retch.

But Lyanndra doesn't falter. She crouches beside me and rests her gauntleted hand on my shoulder. The pressure is grounding, and I focus on it as I struggle to catch my breath.

How could I have left Torran like this?

Logically, his body is just a vessel, long since empty and devoid of whatever magic made him the Demigod I knew. But my anguish leaves no room for reason.

"I should have put him to the pyre," I whisper once I've well and truly emptied the contents of my stomach out onto the stone. "I should have...."

Tears well in my eyes, and I know if I say anything more, they'll fall in earnest. And if I break down now, I'm not sure I'll be able to hold all of the pieces of myself. I'm not sure if I'll be able to stitch them back together.

The only allowance I grant myself is the quiet comfort of Lyanndra's touch. She says nothing at all as I lean into her, letting her hold me up. There's no judgment or scrutiny in the way she looks at me. She's simply there, a silent sentinel keeping watch over my grief.

We linger for a long time, until the shadows stretch their beckoning fingers toward evening. If we stay any later, we'll be forced to camp here for the night, and I can think of nothing worse than to spend one more sunrise in this starsforsaken place.

So when I finally find my voice again, I call, "Healer!"

One steps forward, his head lowered in deference.

"Prepare Torran's body," I order. "We will inter him in Nexus, as custom dictates."

The Demigod bows. "Yes, Your Highness."

While the healers are used to preserving fresher corpses, I have no doubt that this one will be able to ready my advisor's remains for the journey ahead. I should have sent one from the very beginning, but I made my choice, however misguided. Now, the soldier will have to do the best he can.

It's only after I direct several other Celestial Knights to comb through the rest of the campsite and salvage whatever they can that I remember there's another dead man here.

"Aaro," I say to Lyanndra.

She bristles at the name. "Where?" she asks through gritted teeth.

I point to the general direction where I left the Starless snake's body. Satisfaction, hot and sinuous, twines in my gut as I remember how the pain flickered across the traitor's handsome face, and how he begged for my mercy. It's a welcome reprieve from my grief, and I bask in without shame.

Aaro deserved to die.

He earned the end I wrought upon him.

Lyanndra wastes no time picking her way over to the spot I indicated. Desperate for any respite from the reality of Torran's condition, I follow, though I hold no real desire to look upon the wretch once more.

When I catch up to her, it's to find that, like the Demigod, Aaro's body is far from untouched.

Without the minimal protection of the golden fabric, the Starless man's corpse was even more vulnerable to scavengers. Pieces, some identifiable and others not, are scattered across the area. I can only hope that Lyanndra doesn't wish to bury or burn him, for if she does, it will take hours to gather up all the strewn bits of her former betrothed.

Still, I will suffer it, if that's what she wants. Whatever she asks of me, I am powerless to resist, so I inquire, "Are we to put him to rest?"

"Rest?" she scoffs. Her eye flashes with fury, though I know it's not directed upon me. "Tell me, Syran. Do you know why the Starless bury our dead?"

I shake my head.

"We believe that souls come from stars. But bodies—those are born of the earth," she explains. "When a person dies, their remains are given to the ground so that their soul can receive new flesh when they return to the world once more."

"What happens if the dead are not buried?" I ask. The concept of rebirth isn't too dissimilar from the Demigod canon, but the mechanism is very different.

"The souls cannot be reborn," she answers. "They're doomed to wander, unable to live again, unable to find peace." Her eye drifts down to Aaro's remains once more, and she sighs. "That's one of the reasons your father was so hated by the Starless. He would burn our people to nothing but ash. He made sure that there was nothing left for us to bury."

My stomach churns at this fresh horror. How was I so unaware of the depths of my father's depravity?

Sensing my disquiet, Lyanndra reaches over and takes my hand. I lace my fingers between hers and squeeze.

"Are we to bury Aaro?" I ask, my voice barely rising above a whisper.

She stands for a moment, her eye landing on each piece of the traitor's body in turn.

And then, just when I think she might not reply at all, she shakes her head.

"No," she says.

I nod.

Some men don't deserve peace. Some men deserve to suffer.

CHAPTER 47

Lyanndra

Torran is dead.

I should feel something, shouldn't I?

Though I never quite considered the ancient Demigod a friend, he certainly was a staunch ally. The sheer wealth of his wisdom was without competition, and he never treated me badly, even when I was no better than a glorified prisoner of the Celestial Court.

But my heart is still.

Shouldn't I grieve? Where is the sorrow, or the sadness? The tears?

Why do I feel nothing at all?

I'm just numb.

And as I sit on the cold, worn pew and wonder what's wrong with me, Syran's voice ebbs and flows through the cathedral, echoing between the rafters in a rising tide.

I don't understand the words. They're ancient, I think, and though they're little more than gibberish to my ears, the syllables make my skin crawl with a strange, uncanny sort of recognition, as though I've heard them before in another life. Or maybe it's just the hushed atmosphere of this cloistered place that makes me uneasy.

A few moments later, Syran's chanting stops abruptly, and I'm jarred to my feet as the Demigods in the cathedral rise as one.

At my right stands Carolissa. I can barely see her in my peripheral vision, not anymore, but I suspect from the way she lets out a shaking breath that she's just barely holding back tears. Orobos looms on my left, his golden armor gleaming eerily in the low light.

And though I'm between my comrades, I feel oddly out of place.

These funerary rites are foreign to me. Unlike the Starless, nobody here wears black. They're adorned in their usual finery. The only difference is that they each hold a small cloth square—purple, like the fabric of Torran's robes—in their hands.

I, too, carry one in my open palm.

The swatch, Syran explained to me when he burned one for Kartas after the Battle of Nexus, represents the connection woven between the dead and the living. According to Demigod custom, the act of setting the threads alight frees a spirit from any earthly ties, thus allowing the departed to find their way into the next life.

But it's not that easy to let go.

What stitches still bind our ghosts to us all so tightly? How can Syran ever hope to singe them away to ash?

There are so many. *Too many.*

His father. Ressa, in a way. Kartas.

Torran.

My heart clenches at the thought of how much he's lost.

From where he stands upon the dais, Syran's eyes find mine. Grief simmers in his gaze. And though his face is a pale, blank mask, I know that this is a porcelain expression, poised to crack under the slightest pressure.

I *feel* it.

Syran is aflame.

It should be Torran up there at the altar. He was the one who oversaw the tedious rites of the Celestial Court and chanted these eerie, unfathomable words that Syran now intones. No matter how many hours my crossed star spent with Carolissa and me in the library this afternoon attempting to pronounce the ancient language, he is no replacement for the old Demigod.

There is a gaping wound here in Nexus, and in Syran's heart.

But time heals all injuries. And while they sometimes ache and grumble, they always close eventually.

Yet, how can I help him reach that point when I, too, still bleed?

For Syran isn't the only one who's had something dear ripped away.

My eye.

My *fucking* eye.

The physical injury is more or less mended. The swelling is gone, and the shocking red of the scars that line the right side of my face has faded to a raw pink. But there is nothing that can distract from the hollow of my empty socket and the phantom sensation I still feel there every now and then.

The courtiers and guards stared upon our return to Nexus earlier this morning.

Horror was the predominant reaction, followed closely by disgust. But it was the way that Carolissa's face crumpled with pity that was the hardest to bear, and it took every ounce of my patience not to snap at her when she offered to find me a patch or cloth with which to cover the damage.

My eye is gone.

What's the use of hiding it?

A piece of me is missing, one so vital and integral to my very being that I didn't understand how valuable it was until it was so cruelly torn away.

Without it, I feel slow and off balance. How am I supposed to fight like this?

I will find a way, I tell myself grimly.

I always do.

Even when I was just an anonymous girl rattling around in my father's stolen armor, hoping to the stars that nobody would pull off my helm and discover the truth of me, I persevered.

The odds were against me then.

I survived.

Later, when I found myself unwittingly battling the Flaming God, it was I who walked away the victor. And didn't I endure after waking up from the rage of Syran's flaming blade?

So I will persist through this fresh horror all the same. This won't be the end of me. I will claw my way out of this, inch by fucking inch, because that is who I am, who I've always been.

I am the Godslayer.

I will not falter.

I will not fall.

And I certainly *will not* fucking give up and die.

That's the reason I refused to bandage the empty socket and the unsightly scratches that are carved, indelibly, into my skin. It's why I politely, but firmly, informed Carolissa that I would feed any eye patch she tried to bestow upon me to Barra.

Maybe I'll never feel normal again. I might never find my footing or face my enemies as formidably on the battlefield as I once did. The hollow where my eye used to be is a tear in the very fabric of myself. It will always be there, glaring and inescapable, no matter how I try to patch it.

But I'll learn to live with it, and, in time, it will become a part of me. And after spending so long concealing my truth behind the visor of a helm, I'm done hiding.

This is who I am now.

This is what I've lost.

People will see me as I am or not at all.

I am the Godslayer, and *nothing*, not even the very stars, will take that away from me.

So it's with this searing resolution boiling through my veins that I stand through the rest of the funerary rites.

And stand.

And stand.

And stand.

And as the minutes tick by, my resignation quickly sours to impatience.

How much longer can this possibly last?

My armor is heavy. Though they're mostly healed, my ribs still ache. The place where my eye used to be itches. I want nothing more than to trudge up the tower stairs to Syran's chambers, take a long, hot bath, and fall into the downy comfort of his black silk sheets–the comfort of *him*.

But he needs this, because he blames himself.

I can feel the guilt of it creeping through the bond, bitter and insidious. Questions and regret roil just below the surface of his blank exterior, and though his voice is steady as he works his way through the sacred texts, he can't hide his turmoil from me.

His grief is mine, and I'll bear it beside him even when he buckles under the weight of it.

The service continues.

I endure.

And then finally–*finally*–Syran utters one last, mysterious phrase and shuts the ancient tome that rests on the podium before him. He steps back, raises his hand, and calls to the flame.

Black fire furls to life in his palm. In the midnight glow of the shifting shadows, his face looks different somehow. Older.

Ancient.

"O stars, hear our plea," he booms out. Power shudders through his voice and across the bond, like an icy finger trailing down my spine. The others must feel it too, for they fall as still and silent as the corpse we lay to rest. "Accept now the blood of our brother, spilled in wrath and taken in fury. He is of you. May the heavens embrace his spirit. May death deliver him unto the gods."

"May death deliver him unto the gods," the Demigods answer as one.

A thread of silence, so taut that it feels like it might shatter with a single breath, grips the cathedral.

And then Syran lights the pyre.

Midnight flame blazes forth over the altar where Torran's remains wait beneath a woven purple shroud. The fabric ignites immediately, sending a curl of smoke twisting up toward the rafters. The scent hits me next–whatever herbs the healers used to preserve the body, the acrid stench of the cloth, and the unmistakable reek of burnt flesh.

That smell.

By the stars, that *smell.*

Nausea claws its way up my throat. Images of the battlefield–twisted, ashen bodies and the shape of the Flaming God looming forth from the haze–flicker through my mind even as I try to force them back. And though my golden helm rests on the pew behind me, my free hand automatically reaches up to tug at the strap beneath my chin because I need to breathe, I need to get it *off*, I need....

Then the panic passes as quickly as it came.

Still, my heart pounds against my ribs. I force my arm to drop back down at my side. In the other hand, I clutch the swatch of purple fabric so tightly that my knuckles blanch white and my blunt nails press into the calloused skin of my palms.

I glance around, hoping that nobody noticed my brief affair with madness.

Luckily, Carolissa seems none the wiser when I turn my head to catch a glimpse of her. She pays me no mind. Instead, her eyes are wide and fixed upon the flames, which cast flailing shadows across her avian features.

Orobos, too, is focused solely on the pyre. From the time we spent together in the host, I know that he, like Syran, was brought up with these customs. Maybe he's not the most devout of the Celestial Knights, but he is still a Demigod. For him, this is sacred.

When I return my gaze to the dais, it's to meet Syran's knowing stare.

He felt it, didn't he?

I wonder just how deep our bond really goes. Did he see the battlefield again, like when he stumbled into my nightmare, but through my eyes? Or could he only just sense the momentary, drowning fear that the memories dredged up?

Either way, I don't want him to worry, so I shake my head just slightly.

Later.

Almost imperceptibly, he nods.

Between us, the pyre burns.

It isn't until the flames start to die that Syran finishes the ritual. Wordlessly, he approaches the fire and stretches out one hand before turning it over to drop the contents of his open palm into the blaze.

Purple fabric swirls into midnight embers.

Across our tether, Syran's grief burns.

One by one, the Demigods step forward and offer their swatches to the fire. Some of them speak in low, hushed tones. Others say nothing at all. And once each has paid their respects, they exit down the aisle of the cathedral in a solemn procession in honor of the dead.

I wait, even as Carolissa and Orobos take their turns. The courtier offers me a teary nod before she leaves. Orobos lingers until Wayre and Noros join him, and then they, too, wander out into the night.

And then I'm the last one left.

Syran watches in silence as I step up to the pyre. And though I don't believe, not in the way he does, I still picture Torran as he was.

Ancient, but young in spirit. Those shocking blue eyes that seemed to stare right through me at times. The silver hair and distinguished robes.

He didn't deserve to die at Aaro's hand.

He didn't deserve to die at all.

Fuck the stars, I think.

Then I let the square of purple cloth slide through my fingers and down into the flames below.

Let these stitches burn.

CHAPTER 48

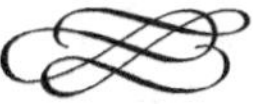

SYRAN

Torran is dead because of me.

It doesn't matter that he insisted on journeying with me to Breem or that he threatened me in the process. I'm the fucking *king*. I should have left him at the Celestial Court, even if I had to order the guards to hold him back.

I should have been wiser.

And the ancient Demigod isn't the first to lose his life in recompense to my foolishness.

How many people died in the Battle of Nexus because I did not recognize the treachery playing out right beneath my nose? And before that, if I was not so much of a coward, I could have acted as the Godslayer did that fateful day on the battlefield.

I could have put an end to the Flaming God.

Yet, even now, my stomach still churns at the thought of raising arms against my father. How is it that I am a grown man now, who sits upon the very throne of Alastria, but still I shrink back at the mere memory of the former king?

What is this hold that he has over me?

Will I ever be free of him?

"Syran."

Lyanndra's voice is the light of a single star cutting through the darkness of my thoughts. She's a siren, luring me in, and I will lose myself to her willingly, for there is nobody else I would rather cling to in this drowning sea of grief.

So when she reaches for me, I fold my hand into hers without hesitation. Her calloused skin is warm against mine. At my side, the shape of her is solid, unyielding.

Mine.

Her face is unreadable as she steps closer and raises her free hand to brush away the tears that streak down my cheeks.

Have I been crying this whole time?

Shame floods through me at the thought of the whole of the Celestial Court watching such an emotional display, and I turn my head away from her. I don't want to see the judgment written across her features. It's bad enough I'll have to feel it through our bond.

But that moment doesn't come.

Instead, I'm hit with a wave of anger so strong that it momentarily overwhelms my grief.

"Don't," Lyanndra commands. She trails her hand down to cup my chin, and then she gently, but firmly, forces me to look upon her once more. "Don't hide from me, Syran."

And at those words, that last thread of my decorum snaps.

Tears come now, hot and unwelcome, as I lean into her touch. And when I crumble before her, she draws me close with such ferocity that I wonder, not for the first time, why the stars chose to bless me so.

I bury my face into her hair and mutter, "If my father were here, he would tell me that it's a disgrace for a court to see their king display his emotions so openly."

Fury swirls from across our tether. "Your father is *dead*," she snarls. "The only disgrace he should have concerned himself with was the war he waged."

And with a burning pang, I realize that she's right.

Why should I hold myself to the Flaming God's standard? His rule was not strong. His word was not mighty. He wielded his crown with fear and fire, but not respect.

Never respect.

I think of Lyanndra and how she rode this morning through the gates of Nexus with her face bare and her head held high. When anybody stopped to stare at her condition, she met their gazes with unwavering intensity.

I killed a god, her all-knowing eye seemed to say. *You cannot touch me.*

The people whispered, too. The tale of the Ushum was passed around in place of silver, scalding through the city like flames across the battlefield.

"Knight-Queen," they murmured in the streets, their voices colored with awe. "Godslayer."

And when she rode by, resplendent in black and gold and reeking of power high on the back of her kelpie, the people of Nexus knelt in her honor.

For the Godslayer.

For their Knight-Queen.

For my crossed star.

Unlike me, who was born into the royal line, she earned her crown. She paid for it in blood and ash, with her eye and her heart, with every piece of herself.

It is *her* rule that I should follow now.

It is *her* wisdom, not my father's, that should whisper to the darkest parts of myself.

Now, I clutch her tighter where we stand before the altar. The pyre has burned down to embers. Tomorrow at dawn, I will return to this place to collect what's left of my beloved advisor so that I may put his ashes to rest.

But for now, there's only Lyanndra.

She presses into me, the hard curves of her armor digging into mine. When she nestles her face into the crook of my neck, I'm surprised to feel wetness against my skin.

Does she weep for Torran?

Or does she mourn for her eye?

Perhaps it's both.

I want to take her pain away. Whatever the stars ask of me, I would do, if only to keep her from this agony.

But how else can I possibly help her?

I already told her that I still think she's beautiful, with or without both eyes, and she must know that it's the truth, for she would feel any deceit through the bond we share. Whatever scars she reaps in battle, I will love her all the same. And if she were anybody else, I would present her a scarf to cover the wound, as Lady Carolissa did to a sound rejection.

But Lyanndra is *not* anybody else.

She is fierce. Honorable. Kind. A warrior, through and through.

Lady Carolissa offered her the wrong thing.

For Lyanndra doesn't hide.

The Godslayer has no scars on her back.

She does not turn away from her enemies.

And with that realization, I think I know what I can do for her. All I need is a moment alone, and the help of a certain studious Demigod.

With my mind made up, I focus on the woman I hold in my arms. My skin burns where her breath fans against my exposed neck. Tendrils of her golden hair escape from her braid to brush my nose and lashes. I press my lips to the top of her head, and she sighs.

"What happened earlier?" I murmur as she melts into me further.

She shakes her head against my shoulder. "It was just a flash of the battlefield, that's all."

Ah.

Another ghost, then.

Will these hauntings ever stop?

I glance at what little remains of Torran.

No, I think bleakly. *Some shades never leave us, no matter how much of them we burn.*

Picking up on my melancholy through the bond, Lyanndra drags her lips over the skin of my neck. The distraction is effective, if only for a moment.

"Lyanndra."

I breathe out her name like an invocation. If this wasn't the cathedral–if we weren't standing before a funeral pyre–then I know what I would do. There would be no question, no hesitation.

But this is not the place.

There are spirits here, and I would have my crossed star alone tonight.

Yet the promise of it–of *her*–sears through my veins. I want to throw her over my shoulder and whisk her away up to our chambers, where I'll demonstrate to her exactly how I worship my gods.

On my knees.

At her mercy.

And if I linger here any longer in her starlight, I know there will be no escape for either of us, so with great reluctance, I pull away. As I do, I brand a kiss to the corner of her mouth and whisper, "Meet me on the training grounds in one hour."

She shudders at my heated touch. "And why should I do that?"

In spite of everything, I smirk. I dip my head just low enough so that my nose barely brushes hers. "Because I want your blade against my throat," I growl, "and my heart in your hand."

Then, before I succumb to my most base desire, I turn and stride from the dais, leaving Lyanndra, her cheeks stained pink and her mouth half-open, behind.

By the stars, she's *stunning*.

Desire snaps at my heels as I force myself not to run back and take her right there before the altar. *Soon*, I promise myself.

But first, there's somebody I need to speak with.

I find Lady Carolissa exactly where I think I will: the library. She sits alone on the top balcony, at the same table she occupied when we first approached her regarding the Ushum. She scrambles to her feet when she catches sight of me and curtsies.

"Your Highness."

"Lady Carolissa," I return evenly. "I would like to give the Godslayer a gift, and I need your help enchanting it."

Her eyes widen as I explain my plan to her.

When I'm done, she replies, "My powers are weak at best, Your Highness. I do not know if I can do what you ask of me, but I will try." Though her tone betrays her lack of confidence in her abilities, if there is one thing I've learned about the young courtier over the past few months, it's that she is capable of far more than she believes. I have a feeling she'll surprise herself tonight, but first, we must sneak down into the reliquary to actualize the next step of my scheme.

I worry that Lyanndra will still be in the cathedral when we arrive there, but we find the sanctuary blissfully empty. Only Torran's ashes remain, still smoldering atop the pyre.

Lady Carolissa pauses before the altar.

"I never thought…" she starts before her voice trails off into nothing. Her eyes, still red from weeping, shine with fresh tears. "He seemed like he would live forever."

Grief slices at me anew. I fear that if I try to speak, I will simply shatter, so instead, I only nod.

We continue on to the reliquary in silence. I summon my flame to light our way as we creep down into the dark and then to set the sconces ablaze when we reach the antechamber.

The cloistered space is much the same as when we last left it, aside from the charred remains of the arachnae that have since been removed. Power curls through the air, and this time, I welcome it.

There is no need to fear the Midnight Serpent that flexes now deep within me.

We are one, this ancient beast and I, and we want the same thing.

Burn for her, it whispers in the dark flint of my soul.

Yes, I promise.

I will set myself ablaze.

This time, I don't need a map to find what I'm looking for. Hesitating only long enough for Lady Carolissa to catch up to me, I start down the right-most passage branching off from the antechamber and turn into the first room we come across.

The item I seek is precisely where we left it so many weeks ago. Lady Carolissa eyes it warily.

"Is it dangerous?" I ask.

She reaches out and passes a hand over it. Her avian nose scrunches as she concentrates, focusing her powers on the object before her. Then, after several long seconds, her face relaxes and she answers, "No, Your Highness. Whatever this is, it holds no harmful energy."

I breathe out a sigh of relief. "Can you enchant it?"

"Yes, Your Highness." Above the relic, her fingers twitch. Her gaze seems to drift, untethered and unfocused, toward the middle distance, toward something I cannot see. "It's strange," she murmurs. "It's as if… it *wants* me to."

Disquiet ripples across my skin.

Is this right? I ask the Midnight Serpent that sleeps within my chest.

Give her the moon, it whispers back. *Let her see starlight.*

And because I would give the Godslayer anything–any constellation, every ember I possess–I say, "Let it have what it wants."

Lady Carolissa nods.

She summons her gift.

The effects of her powers are not visible, but I feel them all the same. Life, or something akin to it, hums through the air. My grief lifts, if only slightly. My thoughts slow. Even my flame feels brighter, somehow, more vibrant.

But it's over in seconds, and then everything fades once more.

"Is it done?" I inquire.

She steps back and nods. "Yes, Your Highness."

I pause for only a moment before I reach out and pluck the object from where it sits within its black velvet box. The surface of it is warm to the touch. Not hot with lifeblood, not even close, but not dead either. Not completely.

Once again, Lady Carolissa has undervalued her worth.

After thanking her profusely and escorting her back up to the cathedral, I take my leave, for the minutes pass strangely down in the reliquary, and I suspect that my hour has almost run out. I have just enough time to rush up to our chambers and use my flame to put the finishing touches on the object before the midnight bell tolls. Then, I'm off once more, tearing through the palace until I finally reach the training grounds just as the final peal echoes through Nexus.

She's waiting for me there.

Lyanndra.

She stands in the center of the cleared space, a silhouette in the dark. Her tarnished armor blends in with the night, and though her golden helm is nowhere to be seen, my token flashes like molten starlight at her arm.

"Godslayer," I say.

My voice rumbles through the silence. At the sound of it, she turns her head just slightly. From this angle, I can make out the edges of the scars that creep across her features. My eyes linger first on the curve of her jaw before wandering upward to where I long to taste.

Those same lips once announced the death of a king.

That mouth snarled into the maw of a fallen god.

And when she speaks my title now, she sets my blood aflame.

"Midnight Serpent."

She regards me carefully, as she would any opponent.

Moonlight catches her single eye.

Her greatsword is gone, swapped for the familiar dulled longsword she uses when she spars against the Celestial Knights. She shifts it now into her armored left hand and lifts the other to her mouth. As she did the first time we met, she snags the metal in her teeth and pulls the glove free.

Then she tosses the gauntlet down onto the ground between us.

The message is clear.

Fight me.

Fuck me.

Just remind me I'm alive.

CHAPTER 49

Lyanndra

The Midnight Serpent strikes.

Black fire swirls in his wake, but the flames don't touch me–*can't* touch me.

Too fast for Syran to follow, I pivot beneath our clashing blades, forcing him off balance. And when he stumbles, I slap the flat of my longsword against the broad meat of his shoulder.

His features twist in a grimace.

I offer him a feral grin in response.

Adrenaline pulses through me with every throbbing beat of my heart. Sweat creases down the back of my neck. My chest is tight where my ribs are still tender, but I relish the pull of it with every breath I draw.

I'm alive, the pain reminds me. *Against all odds, I remain.*

And to prove it, I surge forward.

Syran is ready for me this time. Bracing his stance, he presses out in a flawless parry.

The only problem is that my sword is not where he expects it to be.

Instead of meeting him head-on, I duck low at the very last moment so that I finish the last few feet of my approach in a precarious slide. The risk pays off, for he doesn't see it coming, and I'm able to smack him soundly on the shins with my blunt sword before he even realizes what's happening.

"Fuck!" he hisses.

"Do you yield?" I demand in the most imperious tone I can muster.

He narrows his eyes at me. "Make me," he challenges with a snarl, "you *beastly little thing.*"

I bare my teeth at him.

Syran smirks.

And I'm so caught up in his smug little grin that I almost don't notice his next attack until it's too late.

His blade sings through the air in a flaming arc, glittering in my peripheral vision like a constellation. But it's on my left side, not my right, where my missing eye would not have caught it.

Anger sparks.

That absolute *bastard* swapped his sword hand so that I'd be able to see his strike.

Fury ignites in my chest as I spin out of range of his weapon, only to dart back in while Syran recovers. With great satisfaction, I whack the flat of my blade against his armored torso, wincing only slightly as the sound of the impact tolls across the otherwise deserted training grounds.

"Don't you *dare,*" I spit out at him as he staggers back. "Don't you *fucking dare!*" He at least has the decency to look contrite as I glare and snap, "Fight me like you love me, or not at all."

"You want me to prove my love to you?" he growls, his voice simmering with something that's definitely *not* rage. "You want me to show you how I *burn* for you?"

"Yes," I say defiantly.

Something bright and feral flashes in his eyes.

We both know he's powerless to refuse.

He's on me then, a beast unleashed, wreathed in fire and midnight fury. The sheer power should be overwhelming. It should terrify me into submission, into surrender.

But it doesn't.

He doesn't.

As our blades clash once more, I stare into the soul of him, of this man who is more than he thinks he is, who struck my heart full of venom the moment I first threw my gauntlet at his feet.

Something within me rises to meet him now.

Using my size to my advantage, I slice my longsword low, aiming to take him out at the knees. But at the last second, he slides free of the blade's trajectory, and my weapon whistles only through air.

I know you, a voice within me seems to whisper. *I waited for you.*

A tongue of flame rushes past my head, inches from the spot where the Ushum took my eye, and I fling myself to the side before it can singe my hair.

I see you.

And I do see him then, clearly and without obstruction.

He raises his sword to strike–no, to *feint*, I realize just before he employs his trickery.

I'm ready.

He charges.

So do I.

We meet in a mighty clash of armor. He's so much bigger than I am, but my center of gravity is lower. I have the advantage here.

I use it.

I jam my shoulder directly into his diaphragm. His surprised shout cuts off abruptly as the air whooshes from his lungs.

Then he's down, and I'm on top of him with my hand over his heart and the dull edge of my sword pressed against his jugular.

"Do you yield?" I grit out.

Green eyes flash up at me, but there's no anger there.

No.

It's pride that glows across our bond, followed quickly by a blast of fierce longing.

And I know what's coming before it happens. Syran spins us so quickly that the whole world seems to tilt, but I let him pin me under his solid weight, because more than anything in this starsforsaken kingdom, I want *him*.

His fiery hair curtains my face. My heart races in time to the pulse that rages against the angle of my blade, still pressed into the delicate flesh of his neck. And those eyes never once leave mine.

"For you?" he whispers. "I will always yield."

Then his lips are on mine, branding me with his fire, claiming me as his own.

"Syran."

His name spills out, a plea and a prayer, and I feel exactly what it does to him when he drives his hips against mine.

I don't have to ask for what I want.

He already knows.

Before I can even react, he snatches the longsword from my grasp and tosses it off to the side. I barely notice when it thuds against the dirt nearby. I'm too busy gasping as he sweeps me up over his shoulder like I weigh nothing at all.

It's undignified.

I should demand he put me down.

I should *make* him.

But there's something powerful in the knowledge that I can strip Syran down to such raw and unbridled need. So I don't resist. I simply allow him to carry me across the training grounds and into the empty corridors of the Celestial Court.

It's a small mercy that the hallways are deserted at this late hour. If we ran into Orobos or Lady Carolissa like this, I would perhaps have to remove my other eye so that I could never behold the mortification I'd surely find upon their features.

Syran, for his part, seems entirely unashamed. He stalks through the halls with the confidence only a king could adopt. He even has the audacity to rest one hand on the curve of my ass as he hefts me up the stairs to his chambers.

By the time we reach the door at the top of the tower, I'm squirming with need. Could he possibly take any longer to summon the fiery key? But then I hear the click of the lock, and within seconds, he's got me over the threshold and onto the smooth black silk of his sheets.

If I were any less preoccupied, I would likely take a moment to bask in the warm familiarity of the room.

The homecoming can wait, however, for there is a large and rather impressive distraction standing before me.

"Lyanndra," he breathes.

He stares down at me with his fathomless green gaze, and I shiver in spite of the heat of it. What does he see when he looks upon me? Will my differences strike him now that he can place me beside his memories?

But there's no change in his reverence or in the swirling desire that grips us both in its velvet clutches.

He wants me.

As I was.

As I am.

As anything I will be.

And in this moment, my eye doesn't matter. All that does is the way he swoops down to cover my body with his, the hard press of his golden armor against mine, and the bonfire taste of him as he claims my lips with his.

"Do you have any idea how much I've yearned for this moment?" he whispers as he abandons the kiss, only to trace his mouth along the line of my jaw. "How I've longed to taste you once more?"

I do.

By the fucking stars, I do.

Because I've been plagued by the same searing need from the moment I left Nexus. Dreams weren't enough. The stolen kisses and brief touches we exchanged since reuniting in Breem only drove me closer to the madness that overtakes me now.

The reality of this situation, of *him*, is so overwhelming that I can't form any coherent answer to his questions. All I can do is focus on the hot fan of his breath across my cheek and the way his teeth graze the shell of my ear, and the only sound I can muster in response is a moan so lewd that I feel myself blushing beneath Syran's appreciative gaze.

"I pictured this moment a thousand times over," Syran murmurs as he guides his fingers toward the nearest fastenings of my armor.

I arch into his touch.

"I imagined taking you right here, in this very bed," he continues in a low purr. "And I spent myself into my hand thinking of you writhing beneath me."

He pulls the first tarnished plate from my body and tosses it aside.

"Then I wondered what you'd look like in the bath, with your hair wet and your mouth wrapped around my cock."

A groan slides from my lips before I can stop it.

Syran pauses only long enough in his mission of divesting me of my armor to flash me a wicked grin. Then he's stripping off my greaves and the dragonhide leathers underneath so that I'm almost entirely bare before him.

"But I think," he growls as he sits up to remove my smallclothes, "that I would have you on my face."

There's no time to argue, even if I wanted to. Like he did on the training grounds earlier, he turns us with fluid ease, dragging me up his body as we go so that, as promised, I end up kneeling above him.

With anybody else, I'd be ashamed to be seen this way.

But when Syran pulls me down onto his mouth, I am powerless to resist. I'm immediately lost in the way his tongue slides between my legs, in how he drinks from me like I am all he wants, all he needs.

Pleasure sears through me. My breaths come in short, panting gasps as I rock my hips against his face. He holds me in an iron grip, his fingers digging into the muscles of my thighs while he tastes every inch of me.

I cling to his arms, the sheets, anything I can reach.

"Syran," I moan.

In response, he delves his tongue deeper into me.

By.

The.

Stars.

I'm going to unravel. I'm going to come undone riding his face in this debauched position.

And he's going to make me.

My whole body shudders as I peak, and through the haze of my pleasure, I swear I can feel Syran grin against me.

And when I collapse onto the bed beside him, my suspicion is confirmed. He smirks, entirely unbothered by the way my essence coats his chin, and asks, "Was that better than the dreams?"

Knowing how much it will infuriate him, I shrug.

The challenge flashes in his eyes.

Syran is stubborn, and he can be a right ass when he wants to be. But two can play at that game, and between the pair of us, I'm willing to bet that the odds are in my favor.

So I take my chances.

I sit up and will my legs not to tremble as I stand. Then, without a single glance back, I turn and start to walk away.

A growl rips through the air.

He's taken the bait.

Still, I yelp when Syran's arms close around me. The warm metal of his armor digs into my back, a delicious contrast to the pleasure that still ebbs through my veins.

"Where do you think you're going, Godslayer?" he hisses in my ear.

"To clean myself up," I snap, "because *somebody* made a mess."

He trails one hand low over my stomach until his fingers just barely brush my core. "You call that a mess?"

I nod.

"No," he snarls into the exposed skin of my neck. "But I swear it, Lyanndra," he vows, "I will make a mess of you yet."

And he does.

After shedding his armor with shocking speed, he settles against me once more. The heat of his bare skin steals my breath away. He splays one hand over my ribs and ghosts the other over my breast, drawing out another moan from deep within my throat. I can feel the evidence of his desire pressing into the small of my back, and I can't stop myself from grinding my hips back into him in search of the friction I so desperately crave.

He lets out a low laugh at the way I squirm, but the sound quickly unravels into a groan.

The truth is that he needs me as much as I want him.

Maybe more, if the way he sinks his teeth into the crook of my neck is anything to go by.

So when he guides my back toward the bed, I'm done fighting. I'm done running. I melt into him willingly as he lays me down and settles his weight on top of me.

Only then does his blazing intensity soften into something so tender that my heart clenches at the sight of him. "I love you, Lyan-ndra," he says earnestly. "I love you with all that I am, every spark of me. Whether you slay the gods or become one. Until the stars fall."

I press my forehead against his. "Even in the darkness," I promise, "I will love you."

If his flame were to consume the very heavens, I would stand beside him with my blade drawn. He is mine, beyond the call of any celestial divinity, and I mean to claim him.

Nothing—no gods, no constellation—will ever come between us.

I swear this silently as he pushes into me. I moan it into the night with every thrust of his hips and touch upon my body.

He is my heart.

My fire.

Mine.

He trails a burning pathway of kisses down my neck and along my collarbone. Further down, he snakes one hand between us to rub that sensitive spot just above where he drives his cock into me.

"Syran," I murmur.

"Lyanndra," he breathes in reply. "Godslayer. *Knight-Queen.*"

Every name.

Every part of me.

They all belong to him.

And he claims me now, even as his hips stutter, with my name on his lips and my hands tangled in his hair.

My own ruin arrives on the cusp of his.

Without thinking, I sink my teeth into the hard muscle of his shoulder, gripping him with every ounce of my strength as he spills himself into my slick heat. I don't let go until he collapses on top of me, thoroughly spent.

I could stay like this forever—our bodies tangled, breaths mingling as we struggle to descend from the heights of our joint pleasure.

But it's Syran who moves first.

He rolls off me, and I think he's going to linger at my side, but instead, he rises fluidly from the bed and crosses over to the desk.

I watch him as he goes, half out of curiosity and half in appreciation as he bends to retrieve something from one of the drawers. It's only when he turns back to face me that I realize the object he holds is a small velvet box, black as his flame.

"What is that?" I ask.

"A gift."

He settles back down onto the bed beside me. Though my body is deliciously sore, I make the effort to sit up. When I'm comfortable, he presses the box into my hands as though what lies within is the most precious thing in all of Alastria.

I'm baffled.

What could this possibly be?

"Open it," he urges after a few long seconds of nervous silence.

Feeling oddly shy under the vibrant intensity of his gaze, I do as he asks and flip the lid of the box open.

Inside, nestled amid a swathe of velvet, sits a single orb.

It shimmers, iridescent, between silver and gold in the dark glow of Syran's flame, never quite landing on one or the other. Is it metal? Stone? I can't tell. *Maybe it's neither*, something within me whispers. And there's a shape etched into it, a swirl that looks rather like a circle at first glance. But when I raise it to my face to inspect it further, I realize that it's a snake, coiled and ready to strike, burned into the otherwise unblemished surface.

This can't be what I think it is.

Shining like starlight.

Etched in flame.

Unmistakable.

An eye.

Syran has brought me an eye.

"How?" I gasp.

"The reliquary," he explains in a hushed tone. "I saw it while looking for the fang. Lady Carolissa enchanted it. She wasn't strong enough to make it see, but it should move with your other eye." Then he glances down at the box and adds, "If you want to wear it, I mean. I will not be offended if you choose–"

I don't let him finish that sentence.

Instead, I stand and pad over to the washroom, where the tall mirror looms over the basin. Syran trails after me. His anxiety creeps across the bond we share, but I ignore it for now.

I'm too busy lifting the orb from its cushion.

Will it fit in the empty socket? How do I even do this?

The only way to find out is to try.

So with a trembling hand, I press the sphere into the hollow where my eye used to be.

To my surprise, it slides in painlessly, as though it was meant to fit there all along.

I blink. The feeling of my scarred lid sliding over the eye is strange, but not bad. I could get used to it, I think. This could, in time, become a part of me.

And when I turn to face myself in the mirror, I realize that maybe it already is.

For the woman who stares back at me is the shape of the Godslayer, fierce and unyielding. As Syran promised, the eye moves in time with my own, as though it belongs. It's a star in the face of darkness, a moon in an unending night.

In my reflection, Syran steps up behind me.

"What do you think?" he asks.

I meet his gaze in the mirror.

I think I look like some ancient warrior, like the Starless kings of yore.

But when I finally speak, I settle upon, "I look like a queen."

He grazes his hands down the sides of my naked body until they come to rest at my hips. In the mirror, his eyes are aflame.

"No," the Midnight Serpent whispers, his velvet voice curling in my ear. "You look like a god."

EPILOGUE

Ressa

I have been deceived.

I am not too proud to admit it.

First Syran, then Kartas, and now the shadow—they all betrayed me. Used me. *Lied* to me.

I hiss out into the darkness.

The sound reverberates through the cavern, sending those horrible white lizards scurrying from where they linger on the walls. I hate them. How dare they have no eyes, when I am forced to see the treachery that paints my life in bloody smears?

In a quick, practiced motion, I dart my hand out toward the nearest one. My fingers close around the slick, mucous skin of its body. It squirms, but I do not release it.

I'm far too hungry.

I've become quite adept at catching the creatures, I muse as I feast upon my supper. Who would have thought that a courtier so refined as I would be able to survive in such harsh conditions?

Yet, I am far more resourceful than even I believed.

After my flight from Nexus, it was relatively easy to steal what I needed from the wretched Starless hovels nearest the Midlands. The fools seemed none the wiser. The Celestial Knights, too, never quite picked up my trail, and it was with relative ease that I made my way to Breem as the shadow directed.

And what a horrible place I found!

Hot and dry during the day and strangely cold at night. Brown. Dusty. Uniform. Always in shadow from the hulking mountain that looms overhead.

How is it that Syran would favor a daughter of this dreadful region?

How could he favor *anybody* over me?

I grit my teeth and immediately regret it.

Pain shoots down my jaw as my muscle tenses. I wince. I don't need a healer to tell me that the bone is broken, not that one would ever help me now. It's just one more reminder of the Godslayer's brutishness, of what she's taken from me.

My *sister*.

A growl rips from my throat at the mere notion.

It's preposterous. Slander. An insult of the highest order.

And yet....

"No!" I shriek.

Because the tail end of the lizard is all that I hold, I throw it now with all the force I can muster, imagining that it's her, that it's the Godslayer, consumed by the Ushum and left to rot down here in the dark.

But it does nothing to quell my anger.

She was *right there*.

She was so close that I could have closed my fingers around her wretched throat. I could have sealed her into the tunnel, or bashed her head in with a rock.

But I took the shadow at his word.

I *trusted* him.

And his betrayal cost me everything.

I could have killed the Godslayer.

I could have killed her!

When I howl again, I have nothing left to hurl across the chamber, so I resort to kicking up a great cloud of ash instead. It's far less satisfying, but it will have to do.

This dust is all that's left of the Ushum. While I wasn't there to witness it, it doesn't take a scholar to surmise that Syran burned it to death with his flame. There can be no truth to the rumors that filter down from above, those whispers that claim the Godslayer was the one to vanquish the fell creature.

And it certainly can't be right that she lost an eye.

Syran would never stay with one so disfigured. Besides, the Godslayer was no great beauty to begin with, and I imagine that any further degradation of her appearance would only serve to drive him away.

This hearsay must only be gossip. It cannot be true.

I shall not entertain it further.

But nothing will change the fact that Syran was not as fooled by Aaro's theatrics as I was led to believe, nor that he rode back to Nexus with the Godslayer by his side, seemingly intent on keeping her as his queen.

It will not change the fact that the Godslayer still lives at all.

Summoning my powers, I filter all of my rage into my hands and then unleash it, without hesitation, into the heart of the cavern.

The cave shudders, but it's nothing–*nothing*–compared to the strength of the Ushum.

The strength of a god.

Still, the way the stalactites crash down from the ceiling is quite satisfying. Each impact sends up a plume of ash, and it's one of those clouds that an outline forms.

The outline of a man.

Of a shadow.

"You," I snarl as the shape shimmers just out of range of my clenched fists.

Deceiver.

Liar.

I expect him to address me with his previous courtesy, but it seems we are beyond such decorum now, for he whines, "You ran, Ressa. Why did you run?"

"You betrayed me!" I shriek back. My voice echoes through the heart of the Caldera like the great roar of the Ushum.

The shadow surges forward.

I stumble back, expecting him to strike out at me, but he doesn't. He simply hovers inches from my face, staring me down with those blank, colorless eyes.

"I set you free," he murmurs. "Without me, you would still be rotting away beneath the palace."

And even though I know he's probably right, I howl, "You misled me! You never meant for me to kill the Godslayer!"

The thing doesn't argue. He doesn't deny it or tell me I'm mistaken. Instead, he utters, "I needed to speak to both of you, together, before you took your revenge. Would you ever have agreed if I told you that?"

Doubt, sour and creeping, pushes its cold fingertips against the base of my neck.

As though sensing how my defiance crumbles, he continues, "I revealed the prophecy to you, did I not? If I desired to lie to you, dear lady, why would I show you the truth? Why would I not continue to deceive you?"

"But...."

The shadow *lied* to me. He was supposed to be my friend, my ally, but he, too, tricked me. Just like Syran. Just like Kartas.

So why did he release me from the dungeons?

Why did he guide me here, to the land of the Godslayer's pitiful beginnings?

Is it possible that this machination was necessary to open my eyes to something greater? Is the lie just a pathway to a larger truth?

"Do you believe the prophecy?" the figure asks. His voice is gentle now, coaxing.

"Yes," I reply.

Because I *am* a daughter of the moon, aren't I?

I was practically born a queen, elegant and regal. And I was promised to a king, was I not? I am beautiful, like the women foretold in the legend, and as devout as any Demigod, and so I am as sure as I am of anything that I *must* be one of the sisters.

And I need not fight an Ushum to know which of the two I am.

"I am the savior of the Demigods," I tell the shadow with all the authority of my station.

"Are you sure of that, my lady?" Before me, the shadow shifts and writhes, darker than Syran's flame, blacker than eternity. "For it was not you who killed the Ushum that threatened to rise and destroy all of Alastria. So I ask again: *Are you sure?*"

Am I?

I think of the great molten creature that slumbered in this very chamber. When he first brought me to it, I screamed. For two days, I spoke not, ate not. My mind would not let me because I saw something beyond myself.

A celestial beast, burning in its glory, a brutal confirmation of the stars that watch over us.

I saw a god.

It matters not to me that it was cast out from the heavens as an abomination. It was still divine.

And the Godslayer destroyed it.

Whether it was Syran's flame or her blade that consummated the dark deed, her hand was the one on the hilt. It was her past that led her here. It was she who was responsible for killing the Ushum.

Naturally, she must have enchanted Syran to follow her in such a blasphemous endeavor. He would never defy the stars without her influence.

He would never stand against a god.

So it is the logical conclusion to reach that the Godslayer, if she even *is* one of the sisters of the prophecy, will only bring ruin to the Demigods. She felled the former king and has bewitched the current one. She murdered the Ushum, a relic of the divine.

And if she would destroy my people, then it is I who must save them.

"Well?" the shadow prompts, jolting me from my thoughts. "Are you sure?"

"I am." I stand proudly before him, every inch the noblewoman I was bred to be. "I will bring glory to the Demigods."

For a moment, my companion says nothing, and in the silence, apprehension slinks in once more.

What if I'm wrong?

What if this is another lie this creature weaves?

But then he speaks again.

"Prove it."

My dignity bristles at his challenge. Does he truly doubt me?

I bare my teeth at him. I will complete whatever task is necessary to show him that I *am* the one he seeks, and that the Godslayer is worthy only of death.

"What would you have me do?" I grit out through my broken jaw.

Instead of answering, the shadow reaches for me with one amorphous hand. From the strange hue of his wrist, I surmise that this is where the Godslayer injured him all those weeks ago. The sudden urge to close my teeth around that spot, to feel if it's as solid as it looks, burns through me, but it's gone as quickly as it came, though the memory of the temptation still lingers.

"You poor thing," he murmurs. Fingers, barely there, caress the bruise, and I wince. Before I can admonish him, a strange warmth tingles through the spot where the bone is split.

My eyes widen.

Is the shadow a Demigod?

A healer, perhaps?

For this is magic I recognize, of that I am sure. Is this somebody I know, swathed in a disguise of darkness?

Unease licks its wicked tongue down my spine as I force myself to remain still under my companion's ministrations. He is not hurting me, after all. Even now, I can feel the strange prickling discomfort of the bone knitting beneath my skin, a sure sign that he means to help.

By the time he is done, my jaw feels much more tolerable. The bruise will likely linger, but the worst of the pain is gone.

"Thank you," I say when he finally pulls his hand away.

"You are most welcome, Lady Ressa," he replies. "Consider this a sign of good faith, for what I will ask of you is an undertaking of proportions most divine."

It is a fair exchange, so I nod, signaling him to continue.

"Prove that you are the sister you claim to be," he commands. "Convince me of your piousness."

And he tells me the truth of it then, and reveals exactly what I must do.

I must retake the Celestial Court and my rightful place as queen.

I must end the Moonlit Age before it begins.

Only then can I pursue my ultimate goal.

Only then can I feel her blood between my fingers.

Only then can I finally kill the Godslayer.

ACKNOWLEDGMENTS

First and foremost, I continue to be endlessly grateful to Amy for putting up with my nonsense, and to Lianne for letting me continue to borrow her name. Thank you to Devin, who is extremely tired of hearing about Syran but listens patiently anyway, and to my mom for calling me after reading *The Godslayer* to ask if that amount of spice was normal for romantasy. I also want to give a special shout-out to the Indie Author Collab crew (you know who you are!) and to my amazing Street Team (you also know who you are!) – thank you all so much for the amazing support, for the Hate Kingdoms, for #team-Barra, and for coming on this weird and wild journey with me!

Want to be part of the chaos? Come say hi to me on Instagram: @alina_kramer_author

ALSO BY ALINA KRAMER

Star Crossed Crown Series

The Godslayer

The Midnight Serpent

www.ingramcontent.com/pod-product-compliance
Lightning Source LLC
Chambersburg PA
CBHW070305310726
48976CB00005B/1581